MANDRAKE ROOT

Norma T. Harari

Order this book online at www.trafford.com
or email orders@trafford.com

Most Trafford titles are also available at major online book retailers.

Norma T Harari
5 Givat Downes
Haifa 34 345
Israel
Tel: 972-778252834
E-mail: normah@netvision.net.il

This is a work of fiction. All of the characters, names, incidents, organizations, and dialogue in this novel are either the products of the author's imagination or are used fictitiously.

Printed in the United States of America.

ISBN: 978-1-4269-5058-2 (sc)
ISBN: 978-1-4269-5241-8 (e)

Trafford rev. 12/21/2010

 www.trafford.com

North America & International
toll-free: 1 888 232 4444 (USA & Canada)
phone: 250 383 6864 ✦ fax: 812 355 4082

MANDRAKE ROOT

Here are the Lord's words to me saying:
Go, shout in the ears of Jerusalem
Saying so said the Lord
I was indebted to the bounty of your youth
The love of your marriage vow
Your trust in following me into the desert
This land yet bereft of seed

Israel was holy to the Lord
The first fruits of the harvest…
Jeremiah: 11

Translated from the Hebrew by Neil McCrudder

CHAPTER 1

"Josephina," David said, "you had a letter from your ex."

"He's not my ex," I answered, fearing he had read my mail. I needed my privacy, which is not an ignoble desire I assured myself carefully, watching David smile to himself as he poured gin and tonic into the tumbler he'd taken from the copper washbasin he used as a bar. I was apprehensive. If something was wrong with McCrudder, I'd be on a plane for New York saddened at leaving David and Jerusalem. The thought of leaving the place intermingled with the poignancy of leaving the man. Though why either should had taken such a hold on me is beyond my comprehension. If I reshuffled the deck and deal McCrudder and Jerusalem it would be a losing hand. Yet, by all the gods in heaven, I do love McCrudder more than I love David—more than I love my sons in fact, and even more than I love Jerusalem.

I worked the glossy card out of its girdle. Couldn't McCrudder had found a reasonably large envelope? The postcard was a picture of a maroon and gold-embossed thin oriental man pushing an azure-eyed crab along tan sand with two crossed gilded sticks. "A Jewish groom, Kurdistan, wearing the traditional cap," said the information that was neatly printed on the side margin of the picture. McCrudder had remembered my birthday, but had got the signs of the zodiac mixed up; mine is Capricorn the goat, not Cancer the crab, and anyway who ever saw a crab with azure eyes? Leave it to McCrudder to make subtle mistakes! He had written, "Overlook the sign of the zodiac; sent card because it is beautiful," and inside was the hand-printed inscription:

I am indebted to the bounty of your youth
The love of your marriage vow
(The Prophet Jeremiah)

He was tinkering with the Bible again. Why couldn't he make do with the King James Version like everyone else? He had signed his given name. I never call him Neil. I don't know why, I just don't. I was truly upset. McCrudder, my husband and lover, knows how to make his presence felt and knows how to make this welling need for him, this feeling of my betrayal infringe itself upon me.

"Open the rest of your mail," David said, putting his cold hand on my shoulder, trying to divert my mind with a dose of McCrudder's rankling equanimity. "She married several times," was her epitaph, and each time it was to the same man; the thought hit me as I opened the envelope addressed to me by my older son.

"Dear Mom," Jeremy wrote, "I'll be at Rosh Hanikra between 10:00am and 12 noon with my unit, Sunday through Thursday, January 9 through 15. Expecting you in the cafeteria on the cliff. Hope you can make it. I'll be waiting, Jeremiah McCrudder."

He had signed his name in full in case I thought he was not my son but some other kid named Jeremiah. Now he tells me. At least I can depend on his brother Ovadia to be nice and normal, a chip off the old block—my father's block, McCrudder's father's block—some old block; though with our luck he'll probably turn out World Surfing Ambassador to Djakarta, Singapore, or worse yet—Jerusalem. It's all McCrudder's fault. I was hardly around long enough to do the damage.

I plugged in the typewriter and began typing. I had plugged up emotion by typing out words more than once. David was now sitting on his brown leather easy chair sipping his drink, staring at me. Love, I typed, was wholly given or not given at all; evil had degrees—hate a little, hate much—but love just is. I exxed out this line and began again. My name was Josephina McCrudder, I was Jewish, middle aged and a second-rate writer. I exxed this out as well, enjoying the sound of exxes redecorating the line out of existence. No use being too hard on myself. McCrudder, my second husband, was David B. West's best friend; that is, they were good friends until McCrudder found me in David's bed and I wasn't only taking a rest—nice sentence, and not far from the truth.

David was putting a magazine together in Jerusalem with a format similar to that of the world's most popular newsweekly for which we both worked: he as Jerusalem correspondent and me as a freelance writer. "Good ole' dependable" they call me, always ready at the drop of a contract to travel far and wide in the name of human interest.

Don't let the name get you; McCrudder was Jewish. He wasn't born one, but being an intellectual with deep feelings for The Book, he converted during the Second World War—you remember—"the bigger one" and then he married me. He was meant for the priesthood, any priesthood, even the ecological one he now espouses. The wind was McCrudder's novel invention. It churns out energy, turning turbines with none of the cancerous side effects of coal, the resuscitated devil of the 19th century. Hail to the wind, the soon-to-be-conquered spirit of the future. David, on the other hand, was born a Jew, but had spent a lifetime pretending he wasn't, though why he chose to buy an apartment in Jerusalem and set up business here was beyond me. I mean, a country with four million inhabitants speaking Hebrew and Arabic does not seem the ideal place for an English language journal called *Middle East Aspect*, the name with which he had launched his venture, vinegary champagne and all the trimmings, tra la. I could feel my mind drifting but I won't let that stop me; on with the typing!

David had asked me to go to the Lebanon and interview Hadad. I did as I was told, though he made it sound as if he were sending me to hell. He was not far off, to be honest. I asked Major Hadad, the self appointed leader of the free Christian forces in Southern Lebanon, several pointed questions and got quizzical looks from him and set answers from his interpreter. He knew both English and French quite well, and was just using the interpreter as a front to hide his disdain, a world-weary lack of understanding of man's ignorance. And no wonder—just a few kilometers down shore in the Israeli township of Nahariya, the international sporting community, Christians most of them, were competing for first prize in the world's newest skill, wind surfing! Green, red and orange plastic sails moved by man and wind power; intimations of McCrudder. I understood all this as I openly flirted with the taciturn bone-weary man before me whose relatives and friends lay bleeding on verdant hills defending the singed cedars of Lebanon from the marauding P.L.O. Turn all Lebanon Moslems and communists and surely love will reign supreme. "The Organization's" will had liberated Lebanon from itself, chucked out every opinion other than its own, and white will be all of a shade. I put my pencil and pad away, and smiling brightly thanked Major Hadad.

I made my way to the Israel side of the border thinking that this tightly sprung man, carefully choosing Arabic words, which his interpreter turned into clear English sounds, was meant to rule a small fief. He was not, after all, planning to conquer the resplendent USS of R, the US of A, or the Philippines. Why shouldn't he be allowed to do so? I walked past two young men in the United Nations' blue sitting in a white truck and found myself at the Friendly Gate in the Good Will Fence. Poor United Nations, I ruminated, the realization of man's better dreams, the precursor of the sane world community, so wrapped up in red tape it could hardly make a moral decision. I mean whose morality are you going to uphold?

"Miss," a young woman whispered, donninga flowered lamé gown, a gossamer red kerchief over her tightly braided hair, discreetly keeping me from crossing over the line. "Miss, I want to go to college in America." She held my hand to my hip with hers in a gesture of desperate supplication. She was a shepherdess. Her betrothed had been killed while they were out grazing goats. The goats were all a bloody mess and so was the boy. She wanted to understand things better, she told me, caressing my hand. Turning towards Beaufort castle—the crusader's fort up on the hill where the strafing artillery fire had come from—she said, "Palestinian freedom fighters."

"Whose freedom are they fighting for?" I asked.

"I do not know," she answered, "that was why college in America is a good idea. I will find the answer."

"Never trust a Druse," a sophisticated Maronite student tells me in perfect English, "they'll say anything, and pretend to be anything to save their skin. I had to believe that God was a Christian and was on my side," she adds when I question her further.

Oh God! Who are the good guys in the resplendent factionalism of Lebanon ruled over by warlords of clans founded on blood feuds up in the Chouf—escape route for murderers and horse thieves of all shades allowed by tacit understanding to avoid justice in the wilderness of these mountains, the sea the final boundary? Regarding these blond, blue-eyed children, possible descendants of Normans, Gauls, Romans, second sons escaping murder in the Royal houses of England, Ireland and France, wild eyed Kurds, warriors with hearts of steel and brains working in devious ways, now being asked by the Western democracies to be good kids, and make peace. But the blood of generations flows not gently in their veins, so they hack each other to bits every several years giving vent to the pent up curse still powerful, "With blood and spirit, we will sacrifice to you, O Walid!" in the name of Allah who was a Shi'ite, an Isma'ili, a Latin Church Christian, a Greek Orthodox—in the name of Christ, peace. How are you going to translate this into words my clients will serve up for tea and afternoon coffee, regurgitated hash for the martini crowd?

Well, you'd think this was enough human interest for the day. But no, when I called David to tell him about my abortive interview with Hadad, he asked me to go to the Hospital in Zfat to inspect the bodies of four Palestinian terrorists or freedom fighters (pick your prejudice), who, according to the Dutch UN contingent had been defiled by the Israelis; you know penises in the mouth and other gory details. When the bodies were rolled out of their refrigerated compartments in the morgue, we saw four boys, faces blasted off, limbs attached as an afterthought—teenagers dressed in dungarees and T-shirts lying obediently in their bullet riddled sleep. How I wished they'd cover up those faces. It was indecent to be staring, much less photographing these dead children who were no older than my own sons. Sweet thunder! What was I doing here apart from trying to make a living?

Less than an hour after this instructive experience with Hadad, the shepherdess, and the four dead youngsters, I was back in Nahariya having bummed a ride from an Irish UN official. I had always had a soft spot for the Irish. We drank midmorning coffee near the sea watching boys and girls from Norway, Spain, and Venezuela sailing just narrow metric space from the havoc on the other side of the line and I must admit those ten kilometers—as wide as the world in mind—got me thinking, something I earnestly try not to make a habit of doing. I mean living with McCrudder for 20 odd years had worn me out on that account. There's a lot of thinking to be done in Ireland and about Ireland—McCrudder's special sphere of interest—and lots of gamy words such as peace, honesty, and the ways of man to God. Anyway, I was too emotionally drained to go back to dear old David. Perhaps there was a difference after all between men and women reporters. I decided to stay the night in Nahariya and be fresh and sparkling for my interview with Conforti of Tutti-Frutti. I could use the time to put my notes in order. David, my employer, deserved the best I could give. I was not a shirker.

"Get him to talk about groundwater contamination," David had said, "carcinogens, doubts about chlorination as a safe disinfectant technique, chlorinated alkenes, alkenes, alkylomense, arsenicals, chromium, radio active substances, chlorinated hydrocarbon pesticides, enteric viruses, the national water company channeling raw sewage into the only fresh water reservoir in this country, Sea of Galilee, Jordan River, Dead Sea, the ecological problem, the political problem. Ask him why the Cement Works was planning to hack an additional 270 dunams, such a huge acreage, out of the 50,000 Carmel National Park. That sort of thing."

"David, darling," I'd interrupted him, giving him full advantage of my sexy languid smile as he once described it, "overwork is detrimental to the elasticity of your arteries, worse than an overdose of sodium chloride; anger more destructive to the liver than alcohol."

"What interests me," he said, completely ignoring my remark, "is the lack of any standard by which to judge and penalize industry. Conforti was the chairman of the Haifa Planning Council for Energy Conservation, a member of the board of both the Cement Works and the Tutti Frutti Conglomerate, a bit of your conflict of interests, but there's where the drama is, the ying and the yang, free enterprise and the necessity for government restrictions. He should come up with the answers. Here we are in a place without an underpinning of checks and balances, a free for all, the Wild West—not that establishing standards necessarily diminishes pollution, makes more work for the law courts, that's for sure, but Israel was small enough and compact enough to serve as a laboratory for the larger nations. Show your legs if you must!

Actually, my decision to stay overnight in Naharia was chosen because this charming Irish lad had entreated me to spend the night in his apartment—me, middle aged Momma that I was sharing a pad with a tall, muscular, curly-haired father of three. "The children," this splendid example of manhood politely told me, "are away with my wife and her family in Scotland for the holidays."

I'd let him take me to Mont Fort, Crusader Castle, east of Naharia on a steep incline and below like a petit point tapestry, plush dark green trees awash in serene light. Standing there amidst the ruins, I could hear the knight's broad breasted steed make its way up the precipice. Feeling mellow, I agreed to see the apartment.

He was right. It was worth a look— under a skylight, gold jonquils, cinnamon brown chrysanthemums, a variety of shrubs in marble pots arranged around a sunken pool in the middle of which a banana plant unfolded its raggedy leaves. The whitewashed walls sported bright, rectangular patches where paintings had once hung, endowing the place with a haunted unreality.

He led me past a brick and laminated oak kitchen into a small bedroom he called the guest room. "You have a private bath right here," he said as he opened an inconspicuous door into a noticeable area: a tan sunken bath, a window in the ceiling diffusing light on the violet rug, red plastic faucets of a peculiar modern design camouflaging utility, and a creeping Jenny hanging in a basket, weeping pink petals on the brown-veined marble counter top.

"Must keep the roots moist!" he said giving a wanton wink with his left eye, and reaching up to pour a glass of tap water into the pot. "Usually the moneywort was yellow—hence the name."

No, no thanks. I can't bear the thought of moist roots giving life to flowers trailing long into the night. In New Hampshire, it's late afternoon, the day was very hot and close. The fields were blooming. The smell intoxicates my senses. "Milkweed," McCrudder said snapping the stem in two, "put one drop here, one there," he kisses my breasts with his ice lips.

"Thank you so much for your kind invitation" I say aloud, "but I wouldn't dream of inconveniencing you." I lower my lashes meaning to placate him with my dazzling smile. I always appease officials. They make entrances and exits so much easier. I walk over to the picture window overwhelmed by the view: an expanse of sky, TV antennas, and the snow-tipped mauve hills of Syria.

"Please take your shoes off," he stage-whispered across the room.

I beg your pardon? I'm tempted to say but settle for a nice, direct, "What?"

"Take your shoes off if you're going to walk over there. The rugs at the cleaners and the downstairs neighbor may just barge here in his long johns whooping his Brooklyn war cry, 'Shaaraap!!!' He's a retired taxi driver. 'Cheap to live out here on Social Security,' he told me a few days ago, but me, I am one hundred percent American. Last Halloween my wife was away with the children. We had a little party here, causing a slight disturbance of the peace. He walked in, red as a pumpkin, threatening to call in the troopers. The one thing I wanted to avoid was confrontation with the local gendarmerie. Fortunately he doesn't have a telephone, but since the irrigation water regularly seeps through that crack in the floor and fills up the electric fixture in his bathroom, I had to tread lightly. We had a number of retired Americans back home. I know the type."

"Do you own this place?"

"No, the owner has gone to America for an indefinite period of time. Seems everyone, not withstanding the taxi driver downstairs, was packing up and making for the new world."

"Yes, America will soon sink to the bottom of the sea under the impact of the world's accumulated population."

He laughed. I was tempted to capitulate and stay the night, but in time, as I was putting on my heels in fact, leaning on his arm for support, it dawned on me that he was being debonair to a lady reporter because he too thought it the best part of valor to keep on the favorable side of a representative of the media. For a moment there, I wished it were me he was courting. There was something so terribly sexy about the sky blue UN uniforms of these princes of the common dream of the truly supra, super government, riding their pure white chariots made in Sweden.

Tuesday, January 9: David sent me down to Eilat to interview the UN personnel taking the sun on the banks of the Red Sea, members of the Dutch and Ghanaian contingent who had filed the complaint on the ravished bodies of the PLO terrorists lying in the morgue. David thinks there's a story behind the allegation. This was all supposition on his part. However, this was David's hunch and I, I kept reminding myself, was in his employ. I went by bus feeling reverent, aware of myself as a member of a tribe whose dealings are in metaphysics, ready to meet the UN soldiers, White and Black boys in adventure land taking a little vacation from the rigors of Southern Lebanon.

I read my notes jotted down without thought, whatever filtered through my mind, through my fingers, graphite on paper—flat fins of fish time, inland lake carved out by atomic detonation during King Snefru's reign, c. 2,000 years before the Christian era and who can prove otherwise; radioactivity was found in strange places, man building and destroying, learning to use the power of split particles visible only to his imagination—un-be himself. The knowledge lies dormant for thousands of years, and then man rediscovers toys, reworks the mechanism and destroys himself once again. Cyclical beauty; poetic perfection in a drop of water.

I read phrases without my usual shyness, in spite of my usual shyness, because this was not McCrudder who demanded sense, who challenged me to put everything into paragraphs, beginning, middle and end: "Try starting at the beginning, Josephina, put mind in motion before opening mouth," he would say, letting me make a fool of myself and then measuring purple patches with a slide rule, faulting me on an embarrass de richesses, softening the blow in a foreign language. How can I live with his duplicity?

David looked at me indulgently, with index fingers gently rubbing his nose, relaxing in his chair, the one he takes with him wherever he goes: one typewriter, three prints, one easy chair following him from apartment to apartment, one country to another as if to prove McCrudder's theory; modern communication had done this much for us, given us the means to indulge in self, the self we cannot help but take along with us. And McCrudder feels we are shaped by our structures, and should in effect build the structures which house us, buy the clothes which cover us, the food which nourishes us all with considerable thought for we are what we eat, what we wear, where we live. Everything had to be a rationalized choice—even having babies.

This, David and I had in common: we trade in words, currency for current ideas and even sex had a price; he'll have me on the explicitly stated condition that I give myself to him entirely, accept him as leader and follow him. "Someone had to lead," he says. "I don't believe in marriage by consensus." What did he mean? A part of me wants to go along with his stipulation; it's less complicated than the matrix of life offered me by my husband and friend, the companion of my youth to whom I was indebted beyond my ability to render the debt quit. Oh dear David, I had not yet thoroughly committed myself to you.

We look forward to destruction, I read on, in hopes of change and so we descend the bullet-gray crushed boulder-strewn hill which was Jerusalem, the walled city, and down to Jericho, the oasis whose walls were destroyed by a tribe of determined desert dwellers—ever down to the oil slick sea where North European swimmers take the cure in its chemical buoyancy. Soon the face of things will be changed by a canal dug from the Mediterranean Sea into this, the lowest point of the world—the desert will bloom in wheat, barley, cucumber, and aster to glorify an Empire as it did then.

The UN personnel I interviewed were indistinguishably boring: boys with beautiful manners and few enough words to intimate mystery. Who can withstand unraveling a mystery?

They were young, prone to sleep with the girls from Nahariya, and the villages up North—exotic girls whose families come from Boukhara, Afghanistan, Morocco, Kurdistan who were taken to live in strangely quiet, clean European villages snowbound, under populated, stretching under a sun which shone indifferently and mothers-in-law who fill long days with unworded distaste and Christian smiles of love. You can go back to your Jewish homeland, but the child stays here in the sugar-spun village where your warm reds and shadowed purples are vulgar patches in the spring onion green and sedate yellow of early thaw. But here, out in the Negev desert, the UN boys can give in to their biological needs mostly with camels or unwary tourists; the Bedouin girls are too clever for them. They understand the Biblical injunction,

"Thou shalt not let thy cattle gender with a diverse kind; thou shalt not sow thy field with mingled seed."

They consider the liabilities and the tents of their fathers are sweet and the goats not a burden for they are born to love grandly, not easily fooled into compromising situations by polite young men smiling engagingly.

They were extremely correct, sat at attention waiting til I finished my sentences to the very last syllable and then used evasive words to hide whatever was to be hidden.

No, they hadn't actually seen Israeli soldiers hacking dead terrorists' reproductive apparatus, but they had been told things like that happen. I realized I could sit at that hotel table in Eilat facing the clumps of newly planted palm trees, drinking beer till I burst, and I would get no more information from these kids than what they were willing to let me believe. Though carefully uncorroborated, some sort of threat had been made, that was clear enough. What I finally surmised, but couldn't swear to, was that news of Israeli army brutality had been made public in return for assurances from the terrorists that neither they, nor any member of their families, or their friends living in Nahariya, Southern Lebanon, or any other point on earth—the arm of the PLO was long and deadly—would be hurt. I left them with little regret. They were happy to see me go. Though they got up in a body as I got up, their good manners only served to intensify the feeling that something was wrong. I had to admit I had not made much progress.

And the girl from Marseilles riding this bus, a bubble in the timeless desert, caresses the dark downed leg of the boy too frail to be noticed in a crowd. Were it not for their love, they would be shadows. His eyelids close in gratitude. She leans back between his bent knees and ask to be taken. He melts into her for comfort keeping his passion discreet for he knows there are social rules to be upheld even on a bus moving serenely down the vaginal track of the earth.

A Scandinavian knight sitting triumphantly tall in a reserved seat like mine, his arm round the shoulders of a dark girl wearing a Jewish star on her scrawny chest, proof, if proof be needed, that she too was a member of the tribe though watered down by the chill air of the top of the world, raises his head to a singing commercial on the radio, "Drink Schweppes" in Tel Aviv, in Porto Rico, Madrid, and Oslo. "Schweppes Orange was OK." He smiles beatifically at the familiar name, the well-known tune; he was home.

I follow his gaze up to two brawny Israeli soldiers holding on to a bus strap, independent as any ferocious Norseman riding the sun across the Irish Sea on to the edge of the world setting monks to flight, as any Swede sailing the Black Sea, down the Dnieper, the Volga to the Caspian to trade with Baghdad. Constantinople: conquering the principalities of the white Russians, the Prince of Lithuania himself. My modern knight lowers his gaze to another member of the Jewish army, a thin dark boy whose appearance better fits the preconceptions of what a Jew should be. I catch the Scandinavian's pleasure in a diminutive solder's discomfort, a back bending exhaustion, sitting on the floor of the bus with a rifle hinged and folded down to essentials; no engravings, insignias, flowers, carved woodwork, or marks of ownership—simply a compact implement of destruction to erase life, gripped pincer tight between inner thighs. His superiority reaffirmed, the knight holds the girl with whom he was willing to mix his blood protectively closer. They sleep like children and I can't keep my eyes away from the couple from Marseilles sitting on the floor behind the soldiers, the girl's hand gliding over the boy's leg; the whole scene like liquid marshmallow seething over a campfire.

I try to paint the atmosphere, the state of being; life in words, curdled milk dribbling down the corner of baby's puckered lips. Oh Lord, I was becoming introspective, retrospective, a finalized story even damn psychic for suddenly looking at David tenting his nose with the tips of the fingers, I see us dancers on the periphery of fame—the letters of thanks, "for your kind words," from the private secretaries of the Kennedy's, De Gaulle, and Sinatra decorating the wall in gilded frames interspersed with photographs of Kissinger, Bugsey Segal, and Mao; hasty signatures in the corner dedicated to "What's your name again?

CHAPTER 2

It was unbearably hot in Eilat.A dry heat, unfriendly, beseeching me to choose shade, a breeze, movement to make me feel alive, to make me want to stay alive. I tripped over the bodies of kids in sleeping bags and hit the water. It was cool, pebbly, and slimy like a lake in the Catskills, but the water tasted bitter, saltier than the Atlantic; a completely defeating taste. I felt poisoned. Then, I did something really weird. I forced an oyster, no bigger than a dime, loose with my fingertips from a rock under my feet and sipped the innards. My mouth filled with the brash taste of petrol. No matter how much I retched, the smell and taste would not leave me.

I picked my way ashore, fingers scraped, feet torn by crustaceans and broken coke bottles turning the violet-blue sea blood, red as its name just to hound me and preoccupy my mind with definition.

I recalled Eilat less than two decades ago so startlingly pristine, untouched by man for thousands of years, now a quagmire of rubbery death—prickly azure-eyed sea urchins—purple and white coral doomed to oblivion by oil from the bowels of tankers burping and farting their satisfaction, unloading themselves all the way to the Persian Gulf. Thankfully the oil would soon run out; alternative methods will be found to keep the wheels of industry turning, McCrudder's wind driven turbines—the genetic tinkering of Florence's husband, dear old Ray. I suddenly felt an overwhelming sorrow for all God's creatures, these crabs and oysters, the seaweed and coral. This heightened susceptibility to the atmosphere was frightening.

On shore, a child was filling a plastic container with a black-quilled sea animal, its pinpoint eyes pierced into my conscience. I overturned the pail with my toe. The child kicks me hard in the shins, and ran crying to his mother who, rolling her fat carcass over on the sand, waddles up to me, "Why don't you teach your child some respect for life?" Attack was the best defense. The woman pushed the boy down on the wet, shaded evening sand and rants in Hebrew, "Ze beseder motek, tamshich lesacheck," and turning back to me tells me in English to mind my own damn business. The child was on vacation and wants to gather specimens for his fish tank at home. "When he's through, she reassures me unpleasantly, "he'll return everything to its place."

I wade in to the ink black sea up to my waist, my skirt heavy around me, keeping the canvas bag I'd bought in such a hurry in a Jerusalem supermarket—BOTTLE printed across the outer oblong pocket in neat white letters and along the horizontal compartment the word, DIAPERS—raised high above my head. Miraculously my notebook, my clothes and the key Gloria had sent me when I informed her of my pending trip to Eilat were dry.

"Use my flat," she'd said on the telephone, "Why spend money on hotels? Stay as long as you like, enjoy! We won't be using it this year, why shouldn't you?" She'd sent me the key wrapped in a little note, "I haven't given up hope of seeing you. Drop in whenever you can. Always here for you, G."

I'd been putting off visiting her ever since my arrival, was it less than a week? She would probably hold it against me, for each time she called and offered to come up to Jerusalem; I'd had a ready excuse, excuses only bordering on truth. A part of me didn't want to face her and by facing her, face myself. Well, my face looked all right, but what had happened to hers in the interim? I saw her shrouded in rented sackcloth, hair mud hard, skin wrinkled ridges flowing salt tears as she squatted on the cold, tiled floor mourning her mother-in-law. I played with the idea of calling on Florence and Ray who lived in Eilat.

"Oh cor blimey," she'd shouted across the years on the phone, "a voice from the past! Sure, sure Luv, anytime, whenever you're in Eilat. Ray," she throws in gratis, without connection, "spends part of the week in the Weizmann Institute in Rehovot." I'm always wary of unsolicited information, filling up the spaces, expletives spat out like little curses.

I first met Florence in Marseilles in 1958, she and Tom, with whom I fell in love—bang—like in the movies, in soft porn novels at the turn of the century read under hand stitched eyelet quilt covers; me and the upstairs maid in a brothel in Chelsea making do with our wares, two huge flower-tipped breasts and a tightwad vagina. Florence wrote to me religiously every September on the Jewish New Year, guilt ridden I suspect of that night in '63 when she'd put me up in her bedroom and then had a grand to-do with her husband Ray, while I lay there on a mat at the foot of their bed trying to turn off the sound of their lovemaking. I guess I shouldn't have walked in unannounced or maybe Ray shouldn't have returned from the army sooner than expected. I watched from under the bedclothes as she took off his boots, his sweaty socks, kissed each of his toes. The rotund little man stared down at me with a look that said, "you see how she is, what can I do?" And all this after she'd told me what a drab and uninteresting sex life they had.

"On Saturday when the babies are asleep, we shut the door and he gets what he deserves."

I'd come across Ray's name on short articles in technical magazines put out with the aid of USA grants, funds showered on Professor Ray Berg, modifier of the nucleic structure of microorganisms producing barrels of artificial oil numerous enough to checkmate the real thing spurting out of stabbed veins under the Saudi desert, hush hush. Oh grand DNA! And the information he could have imparted to me just down my alley. Strange how things tend to form patterns. Ray Berg Ph.D., studiously sitting on a deck chair juggling the data in his mind, a sleek and self satisfied fold of blubber over the minimal triangle covering his crotch, "We've heard that before haven't we Florence? Professor X at lunch last Thursday." His comments annihilating my comments. I gave up on that one; Gloria was enough of the past.

I walked barefoot along the border of sea foam lapping coarse sand, delivering White Sea anemones—life and death, everything so stark, naked as the truth. The dream quality of Bedouin working throughout the night, and in the morning, having found that someone had entertained himself by uplifting a precisely set stone, creating decrepitude awash in corsages of oil-soaked seaweed and flagrant grass, cast off Levis, South Sea shirts, jackets fit for a New York singles bar, and with lithe brown bodies and finely boned hands sporting an elegantly curved pinky with a fingernail grown long to pick a nose or scratch a bottom, reset hexagon-shaped rocks into cement, reworking boardwalk into a facsimile of Rio de Janeiro—the architect must had been a Jewish immigrant from Bahia and the Indian was in him. Down among the sands, crabs in seedtime giving life to meaning, but it's only words. I was thrown free of time and space, watch mud pile mountains black as ebony turn crimson and the houses in Aqaba across the bay light up in electric light, an impregnated belly, a boom town metropolis of a million stars, energy enthralling the mind with grandeur, and Eilat in its Coney Island patina, a cheesy, dazed neon heaviness in the primeval lava. Down among the sands, thoughts, an atmosphere which had become a part of me, an inability to differentiate time past and time present, as if today were yesterday in Queen Sheba's court and I was bringing the wonders of my spices and perfumes in trade for King Solomon's discernment, his analytical mind.

"You want to buy a Seiko, cheap, no tax, Abu Dhabi," a tall slender Bedouin, a proud desert chieftain doing a little bit of business on the side, asks. I shake my head in refusal, walk on quickly towards the tiny commercial center where over-stuffed men and women feed on falafel, ice-cream, and pizza, trip over a newly dead Doberman pinscher, a silver riveted leather collar around its well brushed thick neck, lying there between the wheels of an automobile so large only an oil rich sheik from round the bay can keep its engines satisfied. Had the dog been a child, would the driver have been more caring? I'm turning sentimental; age was creeping up on me, I'll soon find myself nipping little children's cheeks in the streets.

The taxi that slowed down to the wave of my hand took me to the address written on the tag attached to Gloria's key. I followed the driver's finger down some steps, through an alley, frantic with fear for reasons unknown. The silence, utter and complete, fell heavily around my ears. I walked into a graffiti-smeared hall in the three storey building—little girl hugging a teddy bear, black ringlets over huge brown eyes, white ribbed cotton underwear, curled on a mat before a door opposite the one with Gloria's name. I greeted the child. She rubbed her fists over her runny nose, turned her body away from me. I open the door. I was not alone. I switched the lights on, dull yellow, bulb and saw in white parchment typed and tacked to the back of the door, "To Whom it may Concern. Number one: desert cooler." I switched it on as per instructions, not forgetting to turn on the water tap. There was a sudden a loud noise, the revving up of a motor filled with sand, my ears tingled, and I was surrounded by sudden humidity in the sullen air. A little field mouse ran across the floor to its hiding place under the kitchen sink, which was overflowing with muck. The stench was unbearable. I pulled back the curtain, the remainder of someone's wedding dress, sleeves and all over a cord on a window frame; a limp talisman of evil—rather than a harbinger of good fortune—blowing in a painted breeze. Outside between two water pipes rooted to parched earth, which must once have been a garden, two clotheslines span someone's hope of matrimonial bliss. Clotheslines for nooses! In moments of desperation the entrepreneur in this Jewish body comes to the fore, nothing was ever lost. The bedroom had a new bed, with ironed sheets in the closet as per instruction number three. Tired as I am, I can't see myself lying down on that mattress, using that cracked, unflushed toilet in the windowless cubbyhole in the corner; the flue, a dank air tunnel behind the shower, which was meant to take body odors away, brought snakes, centipedes, and a thin line of self-contained ants making their way steadily to me.

Through the bedroom window, a long narrow aperture covered in bilge green mosquito netting, were the curious hills of Eilat, mud caked hillocks shaped by an errant infant, throwing shadows on the pitted wall where an animal hungry for lime must have sharpened its claws. The desert cooler stopped its racket.

I was growing more frightened by the minute. Something was wrong. I had to get help or possibly even use someone's toilet, so I ran out the door. There was an end to self-containment. I couldn't impose myself on the next-door neighbor as the little girl guarding the entrance was in a fitful sleep. I ran up the litter-strewn stairs to the second floor landing where two apartments face each other—both equally outraged—window sachets were torn from casings, doors ripped from frames, and floor tiles unearthed. Faucets, toilet, sinks—everything was extracted. The sickle moon had turned itself off and the grime could be felt rather than seen. In the utter darkness that came upon me with unexpected suddenness, I screamed.

A form came towards me and I let myself be helped up the stairs. A door was opened to wonderland: a clean room painted clay yellow, with burnt orange pillows on the straw rug and the soothing low tones of Billie Holiday from a shiny hi-fi. A young woman asked if she could help me. She was wearing Levis and a white sweatshirt with a red and black seal stamped on the waistband. A little boy was watching television. The colors seemed to blend with the humming desert cooler, possibly making the same noise as the one downstairs, but toned to a level of acceptance by the general tranquility of the room. I was more perturbed than ever.

"The owners of most of these apartments have abandoned them," she explained. "They can't be sold—no buyers; jobs are scarce, the price of copper has fallen in the international markets, and King Solomon's mines in Timna had closed down. And now with the proposed evacuation of Sinai, there just aren't enough jobs. When there is no money, marriages break up," she said very seriously. She tells me proudly that she's a guide in the underwater observatory and her husband owns his own semi-trailer, which, with 18 wheels and weighing 40 tons, can carry containers empty or full. They've bought a small private house up the street, which has a closed patio where the child can play. They would even show it to me if I wished to see it. I refused, and refused the husband's offer to fix the sink and the toilet in Gloria's apartment.

"Something got stuck," he said, "always happens."

"No, no, thanks I'm all right now," I said and then I must had fainted dead away. I was stranded in Nabatia, a city abandoned when the Romans rerouted trade to their own advantage.

I ran around the bone dry lime white system of sophisticated underground cisterns built to trap rainwater, shouting as loud as I can, "there are tons and tons of water under the Negev sands, enough to irrigate acres and acres of vegetables for hundreds and hundreds of years. But what will happen them—to the world, collapsing water beds turn earth to baseball smashed to smithereens by Haley's comet or another comet not his, brighter than a thousand suns?" I opened my eyes; my face was covered in tears. Water was being forced down my throat. The three of them were looking down at me.

I'm Gloria's friend, I explain. I'm meant to sleep in her apartment, but now, all I wanted was a hotel. They exchanged glances, words; I'm offered a lift. Then I changed my mind, I wasn't going to give in to fear. I walked down to the apartment and used the toilet. Disgusted, I sat on the bed embalming pious words. I can't help myself, force of habit. I try to shut out the sound of feet shuffling in and out of the flat opposite, presuming knowledge of the occupant's profession. At five o'clock in the morning I switch off water and gas taps as per instructions, six, seven, switch off desert cooler, eight, use the toilet again, add to the stench and don't give a damn— bid bye-bye to wee mousie and family, and open the door to escape.

I see a short emaciated girl dressed in knee high white boots; white T-shirt and black leather mini skirt gather the sleeping child into her arms. There was so much gentleness in the act, vulnerability like fine china broken to shards on the gray tile floor. I look away from the violet eye shadow, pancake makeup, bronze bangs over brown eyes—this Momma had earned her daily bread, every bit of silver to cross her palm honestly gained. I walked down to the bus terminal, the only person on the street, and pass a garden locked and barred. Within, dogs set up a cacophony like the tribes of Israel chanting to Baal. The multitude of sound nips at my heels, blends with my footfalls, chastising me for my ignorance, I run faster. The sun makes its way stodgily up from the horizon. The unspectacular dawn gives form to day, inconsequential, and ordinary.

At the bus station, I fit myself into the only available seat on a bench next to a short, flabby-hipped man wearing a navy blue beret. He was waiting for the ticket booth to open for business, and for the bus to take him to Sinai where he works for the army, he told me in French accented English. There was a bitter look on his cherubic face, a sparkle of disappointment in his dark eyes. "Yes," I answer his direct questions, "I am an American. Yes, I am on my way to Santa Katerina."

"I was born in Tunis," he said as if he was telling me that he's just by chance landed here on magic carpet number nine straight from the perfumed court of the Spanish Emir. "Do you know where Tunis is, or anything about the history of Tunis?"

"Sure thing," I'm about to say, trying to move away from him without showing my contempt for his thigh sticking to mine, Menahem Begin's voice coming through the hotel window in Haifa, moving the masses with his song; Nasser, different square, different circle, same barrage of syllables to the solar plexus, don't relate to what I'm saying, who knows what I mean, just follow the static, follow the mood, script of the time. Original scenario: Adolph Hitler, b. 1889 (?) died 1945 (?). Let the evil seep in, checkmate the good, neutrality doesn't hurt, no action, no reaction, voodoo cheers to the leader, the deity of the python, great mover, demonic de-god, any leader. The importance of a leader to lead the band. Hurrah! I mean in times like these who can find the kernel for the chaff?

"I was in Algeria in 1963 and in Cairo. I worked in the copper mines in Timna till they closed the mines down."

"Oh yes?"

"During the war, the Germans brought inmates from the concentration camps; the Nazis meant to conquer all of Africa, all the world, very cruel they were and proud you see. I brought bread in my cart to the hungry prisoners in a wheelbarrow under cabbages I grew for the German army. I was a silversmith, and only pretended to be a farmer, and grew cabbages to help the prisoners." He smiled, a wry smile full of soul, the kind of smile that might have softened the hearts of the Nazis if they'd had a heart. "A member of the Knesset was then one of the prisoners, printed my name in a book, sent me the book with his signature, printed my name in the book, eh!'

"Yes of course," I answered so tired I can hardly speak, repelled by the softness of his flesh pressing ever closer against mine. Who was this man anyway, simply a pawn in the greater game? The German was willing to let him smuggle in a few loaves of bread, keep hope alive in the devastated bodies building barracks for the next wave of prisoners soon to join strata upon strata of decomposing hope turned to bone, turned sand.

"It was not easy," he said, "for a man my age to rise with the sun and not earn enough to feed the family." He got up and walked away from me. I found myself swimming on that bench and my crushed body fell to pieces. I pasted my mind together and run after him. He's waiting in line in front of the ticket window. I try to catch his eye, but can't get through to him for the crowd.

"It was a great pleasure talking to you," I shout. And looking steadily into his eyes, add, "I'm a reporter."

"Yes I know. A bientot!" He dismisses me, his attention fully given to the shadowed experience behind the ticket cage.

No longer sure whether I want to go to Santa Katerina where my editor, all smiles, tough as nails, wants me to go, I ask about transportation to Jerusalem. There was standing room only on the direct bus, but there would be another one at noon via Beersheba to Tel Aviv. I must reserve my seat now.

"Look into Santa Katerina!" Lillian Ciegal orders. "Do a little research into the ecological imbalances in the new old world—give it the woman's angle you're so recognized for. Hell! In positions of authority, women can be quite as ruthless as men. Mme de Beauvoir, Ms. Kate forgives me mine transgressions. And falling into the old trap too. Take note, never work for husband or lover, never mix business and sex—clause AI in the independence manual. Woe to she who heeds not!"

I walked out to buy a sandwich and noticed that they've just opened the public toilet near the sea, and there's a group of young Bedouin sitting under a clump of newly planted date trees smuggled in from an oasis across the Jordanian border, eating pita and goat's cheese, under a shatteringly white keffiah meant to protect a head from moon or early morning sun.

The general department store was ready for business. I walked through the open glass doors, a solitary customer peering at goods; international junk displayed in internationally programmed efficiency. I bought a Japanese painting, a serene mountain covered in staid snow, a straw hut of pasted split stalk lacquered gold made in Hong Kong. I took a taxi back to the flat—the same driver I had before, who has a curious look in his questioning eye. I was smart enough not to part with information. I asked him to wait, glanced at the orphaned mat, opened Gloria's door, propped the picture against the wall behind the kitchen table with several nice words of thanks for the use of the accommodation, locked the door and tested the lock. I know whoever was using the flat will find the way in despite precautions, but hopefully an anonymous intruder will be good enough to wipe the accumulated rat feces off my present. I'm becoming so polite—must be the holy atmosphere in this holy land. Christ!

Back at the bus stop, I once again stand in line at the ticket window not sure where I want to go. Before I can regret my dawdling uncertainty, Yair, the owner of the heavenly apartment above Gloria's, comes looking for me. He was going to Jerusalem, and would I like a lift? His truck was parked just outside.

Happy to have my mind made up for me, I bounded down the road after him. He opened the door of the sleek pewter colored van decorated in cerise thunderbolts, helped me up, drove a short distance, parked opposite a bank. I watched him take out a card, look secretively at it, punch out numbers on keys that slid out at the push of a button to meet his fingertips. Slowly the box regurgitates newly minted bills.

"Got the cash?" I ask playing the moll.

"This was a special magnetic card," he shows me, "you press the number, place it in the slot and your money comes out. The computer tells you how much money you have left in the account, if any."

"This is progress," I blurt out, not knowing what I'm expected to say.

"It's quick," he answers near another bank and encore, once again for the homefolks. Third time round, I was absolutely stunned. This time he turned away from me, emptied his bladder in the bushes and rubbing his hands together in a gesture of satisfaction, climbed back into the driver's seat looking at me out the corner of his eye almost shyly and again he slowed down. Was he about to go to yet another bank, take another pee? No, the couple from Marseilles—the lovers sitting at my feet on the floor of the bus the day before—are waving us to a stop. They asked where the supermarket was. Yair pointed out the direction. They are effusively grateful; the last human beings on this planet suddenly finding a kit with compass and instructions on how to get the hell out of here and join the rest of mankind on solar star X200.

Modern supermarkets, automated teller machines, projected international hotel complexes in the Sinai desert by the purple sea, billboards advertising the best diving in the Middle East—perhaps the world. Come one, come all, last chance to see the remnants of a sea population dying out in the oil clogged morass, largest oil slick of all times, last chance to see the world as King Solomon lived it while dilly dallying with the Queen of Sheba in his winter palace yet unearthed. And Sharm e-Sheikh, Yamit, Sinai given back to the Egyptians, to the wind, the sun, the Bedouin for safe keeping; coca cola bottles on pristine sand, archaeological proof of Western civilization in this desert where once again only a rare and hardy ascetic who was sure that he had found the ladder to the understanding of the Godhead, will dare tread his way to Santa Katerina. But for now, among the skull bones of those who came before him, the monk deals in the tourist trade, selling soda pop to sightseers from Tel Aviv—tourist package deals, with Cairo and the Sphinx thrown in. And I had culled information from the media rather than feel it with my bones.

Here I was in the cabin of an air-conditioned truck dressed in a Dacron skirt striped pink and mauve, only slightly damaged by my later afternoon dip in the Red Sea, an off white synthetic silk blouse caressing my sun hurt skin, a pink flowered Indian scarf over my medium-brown colored hair; all the rage in Rome.

"Brunettes are in, gray heads out," Emile the hairdresser at the King David Hotel in Jerusalem tells me. I've tied the scarf in Second World War factory-worker style with a knot atop my head. Don't get your golden locks caught in the wheels of industry—now it's fashion, yesterday's necessity, and tomorrow's mockery. I can feel myself getting old, walking into myself round the other end, the girls we once were, never forgotten, never repeatable. I stretched my legs, and admired my high-heeled sandals—hardly a practical choice nor a very fashionable one, but my legs are my redeeming feature. Here I don't compromise, my tosie wosies lacquered red; the shade of Yair's tribute to the wind on the sides of his truck, pow! A bolt from the dark pushing us forth.

This kid was turning me on, a kid not much over twenty-five. What do I know of ages? I'm a forty-ish woman, menopausal, my muscles turning to fat round my bones, and yet these young kids keep giving me the come on. What do they want from me? McCrudder said I'm a flirt and simply provoke men and that's why I get my backside pinched; a damn sight more honest than innuendo, less painful than McCrudder's lack of subtlety, which he thinks was subtlety itself, camouflaging disinterest with the pretense of caring. What was I supposed to do to prove my innocence? But then, of course, with McCrudder, I'm always in the wrong.

"Don't imagine I'm just an ordinary guy," Yair announces as my silence gets to him, "I've studied at the Hebrew University."

"What did you study?"

"The Middle East."

"What was the Middle East—I mean what did you study?"

"Arabic and the cultures of the people of this area."

"Oh yes, how very interesting." I feel his black, insolent eyes watching me, waiting for reaction, a diversion from the concentrated drive up a lustrous tar road drafted straight on drawing board by the hand that rules! McCrudder pushing graphite in a long thin line on white paper—a monotonous idea, carried to fruition by bureaucrats and tar mixers without question, the morning sun breaks into glass splinters.

"I quit in my third year, couldn't make a living out of it. My Akkadian was very fine. Care for private lessons? Nobody cares for private lessons in Akkadian."

"Well, do you make such a good living driving a truck?"

"Not too bad! Lots of activity now we're giving everything up for a chance at peace with the Egyptians."

"Are you against a peace agreement?"

"I'm not for; I'm not against. It's one more move. They make a move, we make a move. Everyone wants to win and peace was the big prize; meanwhile we make war on and off."

"Tell me, was it true the Bedouin near Santa Katerina are Romanians?"

"If Romanians are Romanians, then maybe. According to legend, angels carried the body of Santa Katerina to the Jebel, the mountain, where Moses was supposed to have received the Ten Commandments. I, myself, like her best. She was the patron saint of wheelwrights and mechanics. Out here in the desert it doesn't hurt to have a patron saint. There was such a beautiful wooden panel of St. Peter at the monastery, 1400 years of history there. You had seen it, no?"

"No."

"The monastery was an outpost of Byzantium. We Jews understand Christianity, it was a way of understanding ourselves; same pack of cards, another game."

"I had never had the urge to understand Christianity. But I had seen Byzantine Art."

"Ravenna?" he asked.

"No, Istanbul. I've never been to Ravenna."

"Pity," he said flashing an astounding smile, strong teeth, blood red lips, black mustache, piercing eyes reminding me of another smile, another time. Thomas, whom I haven't ever forgotten, whom I shall never forget. How indelible are memories, how beyond rational control.

Yair must have thought I was a butterfly out to catch his honey; actually I was only trying to look good. What more could I do now but opt for an attempt at beauty? I had lost all else: my innocence, my hope, my belief; not a bad line, I tell myself looking over at Yair. He had now established his identity and was perfectly relaxed. I played up to him, my body rather pleased, my mind less so, splitting body and mind a la McCrudder; he would not had approved. What had I turned into? Damn philosophical problems on a long and tiresome ride watching the desert fall away on either side of me.

Looking back I see the architect had created a gentle curve observed only in retrospect, a gentle curve to entertain the mind. I'm feeling guilty. I haven't pulled my weight, had let the team down; haven't gone to Santa Katerina, the monument dedicated to the intelligent, beautiful, and courageous Egyptian Queen who refused to marry Emperor Maxentius preferring the martyr's death on the spiked wheel, which burst afire shooting wood splinters into crowded flesh come to watch her death throes. Oh virginal Katherine and oh Lillian Ciegal, childless editor of Geography Today; always come out fighting, never admit to error, someone else was always to blame, "no one was going to put one over on me!"

We were now driving round the edge of great canyons, strata of pale mauve, yellow veins of red iron ore. I can almost hear the subdued tones of the cadres of civil servants at the international border, pencil in hand, implementing rules, regulations, orders, and policy while I sign forms in triplicate with a plastic pen manufactured in the plants of a senile millionaire scattered world wide, who hires and fires a sailing crew in an attempt to win the Americas cup in the Newport Regatta and damn the cost. We are all economically integrated in the bubble we live in. Why didn't I go to Santa Katerina, today when the going was still easy—no need for a visa, affidavit, recent pictures signed recommendations, no police escort attaché case in hand or undercover agent for the CIA, KGB, IRA, Egypt, Israel, Iran, Iraq, Libyan secret service demanding raison d'étre. Who are you really? I'm just a journalist picking up debris. Oh hell I've done enough research to write a learned account without having to be there in person, I rationalize the issue. Why do I do these things to myself?

"I will deliver you to your door," Yair says, "but first you will come with me to Motza. This was the gateway to Jerusalem, what you call an affluent suburb. I was moving a family from Eilat back to Jerusalem. They've lived in Sharm El Sheikh and Yamit. Now they do not want their children to go through the traumatic experience of seeing their house demolished once again."

"They're going to get a lot of money, I understand, those people from Yamit."

"Betah, of course, they build a future, invest years of their lives reclaiming the desert; bleed for this land, grow cucumbers so beautiful it was a pity to eat them— half of Europe was eating cucumbers grown in the Sinai desert and now it's all going back. The Egyptian leader was tough, all or nothing—compromise was weakness. Money, money you say. What was money?"

I watched him talk, not really listening to him.

"You do have the smile of a mamzer," I said, using the Hebrew word for bastard with its affectionate connotation of wise guy.

"That's how I got my woman," he answered, "charmed her with my smile."

We get to Motza at noon. I stand there beside him watching the cavernous innards of the semi-trailer being emptied of refrigerator, washing machine, dryer, upholstered pillows, brooms, pails, bookshelves, bed railings. The owner was a slender sun burnt woman, her arm around a ten-year-old kid, who looked dolefully on. What does she have to be so woebegone about? She's moving into a copy of a Frank Lloyd Wright house I'd fallen in love with in Madison, Wisconsin, projecting eaves gracefully curved over glazed glass windows reflecting trees and clouds.

The burly porter, Atlas in a shock absorber, a rubber hump on his back and neck to keep the world from rolling away, reappeared at the edge of the platform. He reeled and almost dropped what I had come to realize was an Israeli's most treasured possession, the color TV set he held tight on outstretched arms as a gray rat runs between his feet. The woman, palm over mouth to stifle that one terrible high pitched scream held her son's head closer to her heart with both her hands as if he too were an object that might be carried off, tripped up, broken into a mass of splinters by a denationalized rat furtively seeking shelter in a spacious rose garden he seemed to had no trouble calling home.

"Arab nationalists murdered most of the Jewish population of Motza in the thirties," Yair whispers sharing a secret that should explain all.

"Look, Yair, I'll take a taxi into Jerusalem," I said, too exhausted by the woman's undamned emotion to stand around while his truck was being freed of her household goods, especially when it was clear he'd been engaging me in easy conversation in order not to fall asleep on the long ride up to Jerusalem. Well, glory be, I still do serve some purpose.

"No! No!" he shouts insulted by my bad manners, "please! I will take you home."

It was two o'clock when he dropped me off at "Six Day Street" where David lives; where I live. I was tired and sad, a sadness quite unlike me. All I wanted was a hot bath and a warm bed; a sweater over a sleazy shirt just wasn't enough to keep a clammy cold Jerusalem afternoon out of my bones. I dipped into the ridiculous bag I'd bought, fingering pages of notes made on the Lebanese border; all these quotes from Haddad via the interpreter that I want to keep for reference, and of course I couldn't find the key.

CHAPTER 3

It was Monday, January 18, at 10am and Conforti's secretary asked if I could return at noon. Professor Conforti had been delayed, but might be back by then. I chose not to wait in his office as she suggested, and decided not to call up Gloria as I should had done, but contacted Mailla Van Eyke instead on a studied impulse. "When you're in Haifa," my editor had written, not *if* mind you, *when*, "get in touch with my cousin, Tel: 04227727!"

A naturally shy child, a beautifully rose cheeked nymph under a cascade of raven curls, her toe in her mouth, one of her eyelids drooping over her dark brown eye, well trained voice turning to distempered lisp, No, Niet, Veto.

"It's no secret you're shacking up with David West." What she meant was that she knew David was kingpin on the staff of Horizon Productions, multimedia sponsors as they billed themselves, they give the public all the crap it can handle. In the race for middling imperfection, his baby came in a profitable first— and was nice company for my friend and lover, who was all I had now, and possibly all I deserve. I couldn't afford to cross an employer, so I called up the little Aussie cousin as stipulated.

"No," Mailla Van Eyke said, "come now, not later, now! I'll put the kettle on. Follow the path!" I walked down a flight of flagstone steps to a catwalk leading to a house so still it seemed to be taking a little nap in the mid morning rain. Creepers swirled lazily round iron bars, gripped concrete, hoisting them to the roof where they hung suspended, ejaculating seed to earth in desperation. It was the wrong house number. Within clipped borders, blue zinnias lolled heavily on tender stalks begging to be picked. A black schnauzer, saliva shining on its bristles, tells me to take heed. I could feel canine teeth in my flesh so I made a quick getaway down another flight of stairs leading to yet another landing. A dark haired man holding a rubber hose from which magic liquid flowed into the abyss below, pointed down more steps in answer to my question, the condescending angle of his head making him look more like the maître d' at the entrance to the Plaza dining room, a lackey to man and money, than an acolyte in the sanctuary of a goddess of fertility as first suspected.

I followed the directions and find Mailla dripping wet, taking lingerie off the clothesline.

"Can you believe it? He is splashing that bloody water all over the wash and me after I've told him more than once."

"Maybe he thinks he's doing you a favor watering the zinnias."

"Pus and gangrene—he's just plain ornery, mean down to his fuckin' balls."

"Pardon me?" I'm tempted to say at the risk of sounding like a Victorian lady of means.

"Oh come on in." I followed her to a room empty room except for a white chair and a narrow bed. "I could have a clothes closet built there, a kitchen cabinet here. I could have classy cupboards, but for now this will do. Look…" She shows me her swollen hands, parched dry skin, an oozing rash between her index and middle fingers, "Male intrigue, big boss man in a multinational octopus enterprise. All they care about was profit. Sure those bloody detergents wash out the dirt, but look what they've done to me." I'm about to suggest she buy rubber gloves. She laughs dryly, drops her wet clothes on the floor and stands stark naked before me. I burst out in a nervous giggle. Was I supposed to admire her small, well-shaped breasts and narrow hips? She reprimands me with a schoolmarmish look. My face muscles ache with conflicting signals.

"I've had to scrub this place clean. It was caked with dirt, layers of dirt when I moved in and now after I've painted it, made it livable, the owners want it back." She walks over to the door, closes it, and puts on a pair of slacks and a sweater hanging on the knob.

"Didn't you sign a lease?" I opt for the obvious.

"No, they are my friends; were my friends. Come into the living room, the humidity is killing me. I have shooting pains to the tips of my fingertips." Her eyes are startled buttons; the wrinkles above her lips purple furrows. I make a mental note for future reference: unattached ladies in their mid fifties have no sense of humor. She had no sense of humor. I feel better.

"Have you written anything lately?" I ask, following her out of the room, trying to get her to talk about herself—what else matters?

"How do you know I write?"

"You look like a writer," I answered, dampening the urge to say, oh, it was just a wild guess. You look strange and strange people dabble in the arts. If it isn't diaries, it's landscape painting, amateur acting, and dance a la Graham, crossword puzzles, or the banjo.

"Shit, I write textbooks," she said and picked up a book from a pile on the radiator, cold as a corpse. She turned the pages one after the other revealing beautiful illustrations, glossy paper, exquisite print lines from Gibran, Shakespeare, Nehru, Toffler, Herzl and Fromm over pictures of moon detectives, murder victims, haggard lovers in the charcoal hulls of wrecked ships, a pointillist pop picture of obese husband and chubby wife staring at each other across the shiny aluminum toaster on the breakfast table, "LOVE" ballooning out of puckered cherry lips.

"Provocative material; compare Shakespeare to Khalil Gibran—was love a constant star we measure perfection by, or was it sharing a bed and still keeping part of yourself free? I once met someone in Greenwich Village who knew someone who used to be Khalil's lover, an old woman in ruffled lace with a brittle smile, and dusky memories in the cobwebs."

"Did you pick out the graphics?"

"No, the publishing house put the thing together, I chose the lit. The moment this thing came out the policy was changed, my class could no longer dance among the eucalyptus for English credits—not your Israeli eucalyptus mind, dried leaves on peeling trunks, real Australian eucalyptus growing thick in the wood, sweet smelling, long, thin leaves, heady, pungent—they didn't want to encourage creativity anymore. I was given the boot for taking the kids out to smell the eucalyptus, and dance in the woods. The three Rs, back to basics was the new rage. What was more basic than smelling the good earth, feeling it with your bare toes? That's why the book was scrapped, Big Brother act—teach them to write not think. Those birdbrains want kids to grow up totin' the flag."

"What do you mean?" Her intense seriousness frightened me; I looked towards the front door. If she went wild, could I escape?

"What do you mean, 'what do you mean?' Fodder for their guns, ballots for their boxes. Keep the proletarian hordes faithful to the party machine, that's what they want, that's what they mean."

"What party?"

"The party with the power."

I sink deeper into the bed she calls "her settee," protecting myself from brazen anger, shooting tongues of flame into my chest. Put yourself together Josephina. And all this for Lillian Ciegal.

"Coffee or tea?"

I realize just in the nick of time that coffee was the brew of the oppressed plantation workers in Brazil and West Africa and quickly say, "Tea." To each his victim of exploitation.

"I'll let it steep, can't stand tea bags." She turns away from me to concoct her brew in discreet privacy. Her buttocks are tight knots; her hair close-cropped curls emphasizing a slightly pointed skull equally stressed. Mary Martin in South Pacific—"gonna wash that man right out of my hair"—third row left, stage makeup and judicious lighting to no avail, she was an old lady playing feisty nurse young enough to get her man. She hands me a green mug bordered in red hearts, her body in the tight fitting sweater and pelvis hugging pants seems to be offering itself to me.

"I had a friend in Greece; you don't want sugar do you? Poison, poison…" The mad twinkle in her brown eyes as she bent close with the sugar bowl, corroborates my instincts of Italian, married a Greek restaurateur, a widower who studied History with us in night school, a nice comfortable man, a goy like her. "They rented a house in Crete. 'Come any time,' she wrote. On my way back home, I'll visit them. They're my friends. My apartment back home is still there, nothing fancy mind, just livable. Out of my window I could see an old Jew sitting on a bench. I wondered what he was doing there, so ragged, so used."

"You feel sorry for solitary Jews on benches," I said for the sake of saying something, but she, measuring out milk with a steady flow of language, carried on.

"In Australia I'm a Zionist; here I'm not sure, people buying and selling, their noses in the air, proud, living on the Carmel, large apartments, fancy goods. Back home it can get viciously cold, all that shale, all that coal, all that gas all the uranium you can bargain for in the veins of the earth and I die of the cold."

The viperous envy in her voice makes me feel uncomfortable. I move my ass nervously on her "settee." She places her cup full of liquid on the radiator ledge in front of the large window, throws her head back to tan herself in a non-existent sun, and exercises her neck muscles.

"My auntie lives in Tiberius, old lady, old house. I could do something with it. I asked her to will the place to me when she passes on. She got angry and said, 'over my dead body.' When? I asked, so now she doesn't talk to me. What does she need a whole house for? She'll only leave the place to the government. You'd think a lifetime of paying taxes would satisfy a government, but no, governments are insatiable vultures, hovering about waiting to eat all they can."

She leans her head further back, her palms taking the full brunt of her bony weight. What does she hope to find out there in the street behind? A fancy house high on the Carmel range, a chauffeured limousine and the lips of Valentino to kiss her on cue, How dare an old woman hang on to life when her freedom and independence depend on her demise? Life was truly unfair. What was I doing here, wasting my time with this woman, placating her by drinking her grayish liquid pretending not to see little brown spots of fat floating on the surface, demarcating every swallow I took. Foul play! I'll probably die of lead poisoning or whatever it was in the earth used to make this clay vessel.

"When I was a child," she smiled coquettishly in the direction of the road behind her, "we lived in a house with garden half again as big as this street," and suddenly it hit me. Here was Patrick White's Jew, ugly, plain, with no background, but a possible connection with Hitler's furnaces, a Jew in name only who had inherited some facial characteristics and the wanderer's soul, a human being whose Jewishness was an interpretation of what others consider a Jew, a woman who had no pride in her heritage because she had no knowledge, just an indefinable mass of anecdote and superstition swallowed with ritual food and wine at feasts in her deteriorating house which alone keep her from being what she really would had liked to be, Irish Catholic Australian, descendant of the 18th century thieves, murderers, and rapists who are truly Aussie. What compromises people make for the sake of a bona fide "in" background. I felt better for my mental harangue. The sufferer of a disease becomes an expert on symptoms.

"When I was sick after my book was turned down by the educational bigwigs in their vast and complex bureaucratic machine," she said basking in the gloom behind her, what a ludicrous position for a heart to heart, "I died within myself—died, went mad, heard myself talking to the psychiatrist in front of the panel of cretins who were to decide whether I was nuts, my fate depended on their decision. One moment I was just an ordinary woman on a bench and then I was above this woman, beside her in back of her, in front of her waving my hands wildly like someone stopping traffic. Hoooollllddiiit, you bunch of Jew-baiters, the woman that was me shouting at the man in the black robes. You don't like my nose, look at my nose you dirty Italian, Indian, brown Irish-French-Italian-Greek-Australian aborigine, I can't hide my nose. You want me to reshape it for your convenience? If it weren't for my nose you wouldn't know I was Jewish, you'd like that; that would please you eh? Not for all the jobs in the Australian Board of Education. You all had something to hide, stick it up yours, you crumbs, she shouted ever louder to the consternation of the sober citizens in the sober room, saying the things that had to be said so I could get my early pension. I watched the judge turn pale with indignation. I was fascinated by this woman who was me, who wouldn't sit down quietly on the bench with me; who wouldn't listen and just kept shouting. They took me away, calmed me down with pills, and stuck plastic noodles up my veins. See?" she showed me the extended blue blood vessels on the livid flesh in the crease of her inner elbow, fishes for a cigarette from a pack near the mug of tea she hasn't touched, her pent up sexual energy jumped forth, and drove deep into me.

"Van Eyke," she said taking the unlit cigarette out of her mouth, spitting out some slivers of tobacco, "Van Eyke fell in love with a diamond lode, oil rigs in the Indian Ocean, veins of gold, coal, iron, nickel, and left me in my pink satin dress and silver heeled sandals sitting on a gilded chair in a ballroom waiting for him while he swilled beer with the guys, cheering on the Australian Rules, a little biking along the river, a picnic here and there. I excused him, I forgave him. The truth of the matter was he ran off with an aborigine girl whom he'd met on the road to Canberra. She was herding cattle while her father appealed to the United Nations to keep the government from drilling oil and disturbing the great lizard god, the Great Goanna.

I stood on the beach of the vast Australian Island inhabited by the aboriginal gods—diluted with Christian devils and angels, the mores of good and evil, foreign incantations rattling along the unlimited coast rankling the spirits of the flower, the tree, the animal in the totem, rationalizing them out of their cyclical grooves and looked towards Arabia far out in the shimmering horizon. I planned to cross the Red Sea to Jerusalem to pray to my forefathers. I too had my patriarchs. So tell me," she said lighting the cigarette, "I need to prove myself with all this sustained writing effort, money in the bank for whom, for what? Now I've written one novel I'll never write another. Aussie writers are a selfish bunch of individualists; don't give a woman a break. Still I'm not dumb, not me, spend my lunch breaks trading tips on penny mining stock. Let Van Eyke dig, I'll buy."

The smoke from Mailla's cigarette got to me. I walked over to the front door, and opened it for some air, hoping she'd get the hint. I may not be into health food and zinc tablets;

I may not have The Judges and Prophets on my side like McCrudder, but I draw the line on smoking. I'm determined to live at least as long as he.

Mailla picked up the mug and twisted the cigarette on the marble sink counter as if she meant to put a probe through the center of the earth, cauterize the veins of minerals Van Eyke works to scarred nothingness.

"Propaganda," she shouts at me, "filthy propaganda, and industrial propaganda. Those jerks are trying to destroy the tobacco farms, close down the tobacco factories; thousands of people out of jobs, industrial disquiet and boom! Bring forth the atomic bombs from the arsenals, the atomic wastes into the oceans and then a quiet sleep. Don't stop smoking tobacco; wear titanium bracelets to ward off cancer instead. It's all a Commie plan to create political unrest in the industrialized West. Don't trust them, don't trust any of them. Get the unions and the bosses together and who wins, the gorged tax gulping Central Government. What about the little feller, what about me? I feel my life tumbling down about my ears."

I can't quite believe her, the words sound like a well-rehearsed script she picked up somewhere.

"Come on, I'll walk you to the bus stop," she said. I had served my purpose. She had alleviated herself of words. I had this effect on people, leading them to reveal their hidden self, the self they want to verbalize but didn't dare, and then becoming the object of their hate for being the cause of their unmasked image.

"You need some tampons?"

"What?"

"Need some tampons?"

"No,"

"Just thought I'd let you know I still had it." She takes my arm and rushes me up the stairs.

She'd been married thrice she tells me in rhythmic breaths as I try to keep up with her pace; once in her youth, once in her thirties to Van Eyke and six years ago to a Dutch undercover agent she met in Bali. She never wanted any children, was glad she had had four abortions, the exact number of live births Van Eyke and his woman had achieved in so many years. She never wanted another man in bed. It was too easy to get him there and then after all the laundering, the washing up, the bath and toilet scrubbing, the fitting herself into his desires, he throws in the towel and was off, leaving you with your cavernous loneliness.

"People like you," she goes on, taking the stairs two at a time, "who had never read the Kabala, the Zohar, commentaries, couldn't possibly understand someone like me. Know which book makes the best seller list year after year after Gone With The Wind? Have you ever thought why? Halevi's *Adam and the Kabalistic Tree*. Have you read it?"

I may not be in the habit of reading Kabala lady, I'm tempted to shout up to her, but I've been known to dip into the Bible from time to time.

I've argued the fine points of character as fate on long, lazy afternoons with McCrudder, sipping mint tea, looking out at a storm laden New York skyline. Samson again: I never could understand how much a strong man could have allowed himself to be enslaved by that Delilah woman.

"Brutality and cunning," McCrudder intones, "are the characteristics of the leader in times of turmoil. Samson was straightforward. His goodness bordering on stupidity shines through the brute strength."

What was he trying to tell me? I get bits of thought and I seem to be getting hold of it but I can't unravel the subtle tissue of the idea to its very end. If character was fate, form was fate, body was fate, and sex was fate.

"Oh Samson, honey, you told me a lie again and again. Now tell me the truth. If you really loved me, you wouldn't be leading me on this way."

Philistine Government Ministers: "Give this harlot, this vestal virgin consecrated to the god Dagon, this lady who had a passionate get together with any wayfarer under any tree grafted to assure juicy fruit, give her the money, she'll deliver the Jewish God child, tethered and tied."

TV science film: The key to pain and pleasure in the brain are both connected to the reproduction of the race. God, how does all this make my life any easier, my survival more sure, I who was not a consecrated child?

McCrudder puts the Bible I've been reading, while trying to keep up with his changing vision, on the night table and, overwhelmed by his own passion, kisses me full lipped on the brow, a gift of such extravagance, I slip further down under the quilt and cry myself to sleep. Oh bugger McCrudder!

I puff my way up to Mailla just as the bus slides to a stand still. Mailla had timed our arrival just right.

"Here," she said, handing me the packet of paper she's been warming under her armpit, "take my manuscript. Keep it. I had enough copies. Read it! When you finish, just throw it away. I'd appreciate an honest answer though, not shit. I've written the stuff for my nephew back in Perth. 'Auntie,' he said when I called him up and told him I was making aliya, coming to settle in the holy land, 'don't come back.' He's ashamed of his aunt, business people, money in the bank, shit!"

I grabbed the bundle and panted my way to a seat. Looking back at her receding figure, I see her all angles barely touching. Meanness lies like a film over her fragmented form, a red aura of molten liquid frozen silver in the sudden downpour. I had studied her carefully, every rut and runnel of her time-beaten face. I felt I knew her well, well enough to model an exposé on the deep-seated anxiety of frigid, multi-divorced cousins of pushy editors to whom life had dealt a bad hand and who pays back the world in kind. Title: Lonely Woman Wronged by Life; to be handed personally to Lillian Ciegal whom neither Mailla nor I had mentioned.

CHAPTER 4

I stood next to David's door, knees together, bladder stretched to pain, like an incontinent child seriously thinking of letting go right there watching my hot urine freeze to pingling ice splinters in the lobby, six floors below. David walked out of the elevator and found me crouched and shivering in the hall. He didn't seem at all surprised.

"There's an extra one right here," he said opening a closet to the right of the front door, where the silver cylinder turned, which lazily measured kilowatt hours. An inconsequential little key lies respectfully on top of the black box. "You are one scatterbrained female."

I know it isn't my brain or lack of it he was contemplating. He wants his due and he'll get it. I'm pretty good at pretending desire, but not just now.

"Darling, I'm too tired."

"Darling," he says, "the more my wife 'darlinged' me, the less she cared. Are you ok?"

"Yes! Fine." Just fine, David, dear David I repeat to myself lunging for my typewriter, typing out the notes I've made in Eilat, reading them over quickly before I force myself to crush them into a ball, squeeze the life out of them and regretfully throw the bunk into the garbage feeling noble at having rid the world of so many more words; words written on the Lebanese border, the Jordanian border, the soon to be Egyptian border. I had fenced myself in words. There are words and there are words, I try to solace my soul with rationalizations, hoping David had read Mailla's manuscript, which I'd managed to place in his hands before plunging down to Eilat.

I watched him go over to his makeshift bar and add ice cubes to his drink.

"When did you set up that interview with the Chairman of the Haifa Planning Council for Energy Conservation, Director General of Tutti Fruitti, your Conforti to be exact?" I said enunciating every syllable of the man's title in a tone meant to underline my displeasure with the whole enterprise. "Can you imagine a more cynical name for a petrochemical plant, the worst polluter in the Haifa bay area, which releases enough barium into the sea to poison every Jew, Moslem, Christian, Druse, and Bahai, and every fish-eating soul in the area for miles around and is potential industrial bait?"

"They used to be a food processing enterprise," he said as if by excuse, "established with government funds. When they changed over to petrochemicals they left the name; some loophole in the tax law."

"Well that makes everything all right I guess, doesn't it?"

"Tomorrow, 10am; his office. Be a good girl, get that material this time."

"Mailla?" I remind him.

"Ah: yes, Mailla." He grimaced as he settled down in his easy chair. "Does your friend douse her daisy wheel with perfume?" He sniffs the manuscript he picked up from the side table, rippling the pages in a nervous, pressed-for-time way.

"When I got to Haifa the last time to get, 'the material' you're so anxious about, Conforti wasn't there, not at the appointed hour, nor when I returned as per arrangement with his secretary, at five. 'Force Majeure,' she said. I waited all afternoon playing around with the idea of visiting my old friend Gloria. She's in mourning for her mother-in-law, but I'm a coward about opening up old wounds. You want to know where he was? Don't get up. Listen to this. He was in Manila. What makes you so sure he'll honor his commitment this time?"

"Trust me," he said as he got up and took both my hands in his, knelt down, Valentino, the Sheik of Araby—one of David's endearing characteristics, he thinks sincerity itself, life with no qualms, happy end, Silver Screen.

And me, wide eyed innocent, I always fall for his routine, comforting myself with the thought, true or partially so, that he left Ernestine, his wife and his four daughters for any other reason than me, jealous as I was of his fatherly ways with these young women all married now who call up at strange times whispering, "Daddy?" No, David isn't home or if he was I answer with my skin turning to goose bumps. Little me caught robbing the blind man's tin cup.

McCrudder and I walk hand in hand in the soft rain of a Paris May. My nose is red—the color of apple he's picked off a cart, setting pyramids of fruit cascading, cracking skin to odor of apple blossom. I let go of his hand, so warm, and bought a book from a secondhand stall, Roan Stallion by Robinson Jeffers. On the frontispiece,

August 1939
To Gladys,
Here's to more happy days.
Bud

"Robinson Jeffers," I address myself to David, my employer who doesn't serve my tenderness, doesn't really want it, "describes an Indian woman driving a horse and wagon across a turbulent river, a perfect photograph of a scene, but no more. Since I can't seem to find a deeper level of meaning, the poem doesn't move me. I mean brute strength was brute strength was brute strength kind of thing."

What I was trying to tell David was that he should read Mailla's book with some compassion rather than scan paragraphs, tuck down corner of page after page so the author will had the dubious satisfaction of seeing someone's hand had touched her work. I know the method well. I make a scene of taking the sheet of paper out of the typewriter.

"What happened to you in Eilat?" David asks knowing Neil McCrudder's letter had upset me more than I mean to let on.

"Nothing," I say, "nothing really. It was more a feeling. If I tried to put it into words it's just verbiage, garbage, garbiology; roll it up and throw it in the wastepaper basket stuff."

"Come on, it's me you're talking to, remember?"

"Yes I remember; it was you who sent me there."

"Yeah, me and the Geography Today." He was referring to my other journalistic commitments, Lillian Ciegal to whom I owe my (allegiance) fealty. I was not yet exclusively his.

"I went by bus."

"By bus? Why didn't you get in touch with the Government Press Office? They had a limousine service for visiting correspondents."

"You know I like my independence. But since you asked, I did get in touch with them. The girl in charge seemed to be on one long continuous visit to Egypt. I was apologetically told by one of the office workers that the Prime Minister's office pays traveling expenses so she justifiably prefers touring to doing her job. When I finally did get through to her, she was a complete loss. She barely spoke English, knew enough to inform me, though, that one limousine was being serviced and the other being used by the office staff. Don't get me wrong; I'm glad I used public transportation. I saw a tired boy and girl caressing each other for comfort. They had decided to take this last bus of the day to Eilat, standing room only, because they couldn't afford the price of a hotel room, or so I suppose. I mean you had to have a pretty good reason for traveling on the hard floor of an air-conditioned bubble floating down towards the bottom of the world. They sat in the aisle between me and the pneumatic door while I considered ice floes, the tips of icebergs in the endlessly long Dead Sea, which I'd imagined, was a small inland lake, having seen it only on maps; ice floes that turned out to be islands of salt. That evening in Eilat, I found them asleep in each other's arms on the beach. It was touching. I wished I were so freely loved."

David and I had met on a plane to Algeria. The year was 1963. He told me he was a foreign correspondent and I told him I was freelancing, a nice nondescript word covering many possibilities, I almost said evils. He believed me. Actually I was an errand girl, really not much more, substantiating facts in tomes in the library was my forte, tracking down useless facts to keep readers from writing letters debunking items of information blossoming forth week after week on glossy paper. Give me a fact, any fact, in no time flat, I'd corroborate or point out the fallacy. No reader, no court of law dared contend my fancy footwork. So good an underling was I, so absolutely grateful to be back working for the magazine, too harried at home, at work to really learn to play the power game, no one suspected my unspoken desire for a promotion.

It was McCrudder who thought a change would do me good.

"Berlin," he suggested, "a divided city."

"Jerusalem," I said, "one divided city was like any other." I remembering feeling good about that wall going up between the two Germanies, divided they fall, united they may well turn to destruction once again.

My sympathies were with the Russians, with each nascent state seeking independence from the imperialistic forces that had enslaved it—the Congo, Cuba, Vietnam. Though I had some reservations about Red China, Mao Tse Tung was cute. I never liked Chiang Kai-Shek's wife.

It was early fall, Algiers was still smoldering. Clothes, toys, collapsed buildings in mounds of rubble, children sleeping on valises or in them, families torn apart leaving for France on every available ship and plane, scars so deep it seemed they would never heal. Ben Bella freed from his French prison elected President. Dream of a socialist, equitable society, it all begins with dreams. Rev. Luther King: "I had a dream," and Barbara Streisand singing, "Happy Days are Here Again," with such a plaintive voice one wonders if she didn't had some presentiment about the days to come.

I was frightened and David helped me out by bedding me down, comforting me, introducing me to the right people. When we got back to New York, Lillian Ciegal of Geography Today bought my article and pictures. Suddenly, guys with whom I'd been riding up and down elevators for months with evasive stares up to the ceiling, began to smile broadly, and called me by name. I was asked to lunch. Things were looking up at home too. McCrudder was glad he had sent me; had encouraged me to go. I mean I was on that plane on my own volition, but it was McCrudder who'd made me feel confident enough to buy the ticket. He no doubt regretted the generosity of his gesture for as soon as that article appeared I was no longer merely the research assistant, I was a gadfly, here, there, and everywhere.

"Honey, why do you want to have this crap printed?"

"It isn't crap," I answered sweetly, "it's a woman's life as she's lived and felt it on the background of history."

"It's a loser's life."

"It's a STORY, an ongoing STORY, to quote Miss Piggy."

"This is business; who's going to buy an ongoing STORY of a silly woman?"

"Other silly women."

"J.M., Get her a copy of "how to," he said, "direct her efforts to the needs of the market, violence, the sentimentality you can bank." He was angry now, he only calls me J.M. when he was good and angry; male ego frustrated by a silly woman. Fie!"

"You mean the get in and get out variety, no conscience, no poetry, no mind, buy it in Canarsie, throw it out on 42nd Street," I shout, giving in to a gender of hysteria I can easily fall into, "reading time 17 minutes, 2 seconds, thought time optimum vacancy between the eyes, how to become a whore to her agent and as few adjectives as possible eh?" I say mimicking David's constant advice.

"Sure thing baby, the citizen of the world has seen it all on TV, and has become word weary and picture tired. Ennui and déjà vu, the diseases of the dissipate gentry, are now the carriers of the multitude. Rape, murder, the most absurd kind of transgression was surveyed by an eye covered in boredom fluid. We are born old, unaffected by life, uncertain of love filters for electronic muck, and you want to sell me pithy statements meant to move me. I am solid as a rock. Why should I or anyone else listen?"

"Isn't there enough mayhem in the stuff I've brought out of the Lebanon?" I'm tempted to ask. Changing tactic, I went over to him.

"Let's not talk about it right now." I pecked that spot on top of his head that's just starting to go bald. He reached back, placed his cold glass to my cheek, I kept my lips to his shiny pate. "Just read it, ok?"

He nodded, not shaking on the bargain man-to-man, just sitting there waiting for me to decide my next move. That's David—doesn't take much of what I say at face value, but lets me talk myself down layer by layer to the point where I express basic wishes. Possibly he considers me flesh just as McCrudder considers me equal and perhaps David West was right.

"I might have missed Conforti, but I did get to see Ben Bella on TV. The secretary put the news on, trying to keep me from going into a rage, and there he was looking as he had a quarter of a century ago. He'd just been freed from house arrest after all these years. The press hadn't forgotten him. He was filmed walking down a brightly lit street outside the wall enclosing the white stucco house that had been his prison, looking like a petulant child who'd been persuaded against his will to come out from under the bed. He squinted in the sudden light, refusing to answer questions put to him by the reporters flocking round him, but otherwise he looked just the same, as if time hadn't passed.

David snuggled deeper in his chair, and rubbed the side of his nose with his index finger as he sipped his drink; complete concentration, "you haven't changed that much since then either; haven't changed much at all."

"Neither have you," I lied, wondering how to take his remark. "Josi," he says, his voice husky with emotion, had you ever seen an adult female cat after copulation when the tom dismounts and runs off for a bit of a rest? She twists and turns on the asphalt baring her belly to the sun, desultorily licking her vagina, cleaning herself for the return bout, so full of sweet tension, she can't help but announce her happiness, wags her tail, meows for tomcat to return and do his trick."

I burst out laughing. His hands were cold, they tickled, and what's more it seemed such a well-known routine. I allowed him to undress me and then I was in his power; I knew it would happen. He could slap my bottom as if I was animal, he could caress my breasts as if I was mother earth and I was grateful—grateful for being wanted. I was the necessary means to his satisfaction, an object without which at this point in time, he would be shattered. And when he was through and I was through, we rose to ourselves and I kept my eyes averted like a virgin. I could not look at him now that I had given my bodily self so entirely. I made some coffee, fed his stomach. We went to the movies, saw Tess of the D'Urbevilles. I loved Polanski's direction. David called him a pervert. I sat close to him with the back of my hand on his leg, showing possession. He took my hand in his, and held on tight. During the intermission he bought me ice cream. I thought of the train puffing out the 19th century, with steam clouds rising in the unmolested air of the Dakotas, staining a pearl blue sky above a solitary Indian on a white steed, evaporating into nothingness in the vastness of it all. Anna Karenina finding the solution to an unwieldy Czarist society under the chug-chugging wheels in a train station, and Tess, for whom the train meant salvation, reprieve in Brazil. But her husband had been there and knew in his Christian soul that there was no heaven on this small planet, no easy place of escape—just a constant readjustment to changing frames, changing boundaries, heavy blobs of time; electric telegraph time, Kierkegaard time like Druid time—gone forever. McCrudder was right, he was always right.

We who had lived through the Second World War, who had witnessed the systematic annihilation of man by man in the name of necessity, must learn to accept responsibility for action, taken or not taken. We must learn to live in harmony with our world and to understand that our world was the building up and breaking down of states of mind. We must force our senses to keenness so we can accept the change within us but only that change which will not spoil the rhythm of the unchangeable, the world itself. No ideologies, or frames of reference that had proved false Messiahs, will do. We must learn to use technology to better the environment of man and the place to start was in our very living rooms. The aim must be to preserve life. The most altruistic was finally the most self-serving.

And that was what I was afraid of, rooms—walls, chairs, frames, office suites within office suits, flights of stairs behind doors within floors reaching the sky in multistoried office buildings, the eye of the camera in surveillance, whispers over wireless telephones, symbols known to a select few—dying of heart attack, slow death on the desk as the communication channels of the world blink Manchester numbers, crackled silence magnified to sound while the secretaries in the outer inner sanctum polish toenails and dream of escape into trains, tubes rolling out of concrete tunnels—and the TV announcer, who had become your only companion, your daily kick to fill the yawing, needy space within the freed lover, husband, who was more intimate than a friend, talking on in deliberate smiles as you cough up your last breath.

I had to make a decision: go back to NY, to McCrudder, to the greatest, the largest, most efficient weekly newsmagazine of the century, to Lillian Ciegal—tend my own garden, McCrudder's late mother's garden, his sister's garden in New Hampshire, walk the line of curving surf narrowing my boundary to the space between sand and sea or stay here with David whom I was unsure of; share his flat, which was not mine, work for him, let him pimp my literary talents. I don't even own a closet and had to apologize for borrowing a clothes hanger for my dress. I could buy some I guess, but I had a closet full of shocking pink quilted clothes hangers back in NY with last year's clothes on them. I doubt I'll ever wear them again. McCrudder had probably packed them into my stork decorated plastic bags and given the whole caboodle to charity. He wouldn't dare give my clothes away to the Salvation Army; get rid of my clothes, get rid of me. I'm not dead yet.

McCrudder, I had hardened my heart against you and here you are big as life in this darkened movie house. I take David's hand in mine, and press my breasts against his arm trying to feel more than bone. He puts his arm around my shoulders; the pressure of his fingers reassures me. Yet, I know I had to make that decision. McCrudder was ever there, spurting inanities that I can't escape.

David and I walk against the whipping wind embracing each other.

"Be a good girl', he said as soon as we're back in his apartment, which was blessedly warm, "get that interview with Conforti."

It was important and bringing the now familiar file labeled "Background material—Josephina" close to my eyes, he kissed the back of my neck so tenderly, where I was most susceptible; I completely lost my senses.

CHAPTER 5

Thursday, January 11, 10:00am, and I'm sitting at a large elliptical light oak table. The room was comfortably dull. There are no windows so I can only feel the rain. The secretary had invited me in. There was a strange glitter in her bashful eye.

"Mizz McCrudder, I was asked to give you this." A note on heavy paper in beautiful cursive script I could barely decipher, looked as if it were written with a quill.

It read: "Dear Ms. McCrudder, may I call you Josephina? I had had the unfortunate news of a friend's demise. Will you be kind enough to meet me at my home tomorrow at 4:00pm? I know this is highly irregular, but so was death on short notice.

> Thou must be mild to us, Mary,
> Out of thy blood we blow;
> And what a pain was yearning
> Thou alone canst know.
> Rainer Maria Rilke

> Your humble servant,
> Walter Conforti"

It was now 11 o'clock in the morning and I've made it up the mountain to Gloria's apartment. I wouldn't drive in this country if you paid me, use public transport and get to know the homefolk, determined was my middle name. I sat on a straight backed Italian cane chair dressed in my red ruffle-necked blouse and black Ralph Lauren suit, wearing high heels meant to impress Conforti while she, in black silk mandarin pajamas, places little trays of

Armenian design filled with dried figs, apricots, kumquats, dates, raisins, almonds, pecans on a square side table, Italian glass and chrome, "Tu B'Shvat," she said the birthday of the trees. "And this," she shows me three small oval plastic frames, having dashed into an inner room and out again in no time, "this one," she hands me the violet frame, "was Guy. You remember him; and this," she continued, handing me the pink one, "was Abigail."

"Nice," I answered quietly, "if I had had a daughter I'd have named her Abigail."

"Read your mind, Josephina, and this," she shows me the blue frame, "is Yaron. He's 14 years old." I make a show of admiration.

It's raining oblique lines of fine drops cleaning up the grime a dry wind had blown in from the desert, if Gloria was to be believed. The wind, wherever it comes from, turns to hurricane strength, howls and grunts. The aluminum frames rattle in contest with the elements.

"Don't worry," she says, "when the house was built the bolts were shot right through the concrete, the windows won't fall out. You'll see, tonight the sun will be a golden bowl of cherries in the salmon pink sky."

"Pretty tasty," I answered, noticing that her glassed-in terrace was of similar proportions to McCrudder's back home in New York—another frame, another smell, and another mind. She must be heating her apartment with solar energy, otherwise how can she afford to keep this large room so nice and warm. Either that or she's been systematically chopping down the trees in the wood below.

McCrudder complains about the price of fuel, keeping the thermostat down to frozen bone level while I begged self-consciously for a little more warmth, he wasn't going to give in to Arab blackmail, not if he could help it. I could better understand Mailla's attitude; the rich are enviable. Here was Gloria so self contained, so sure she had made the best of her life and I, I'd rather not template the muddle I'm in.

"You haven't changed at all," she said gliding a gold locket, swish-swoosh, back and forth over the chain, setting my teeth on edge. She feels my gaze, puts her hand protectively over the locket engraved in a star of Bethlehem, blood red ruby in its center.

"Don't you miss the U.S.?"

"The mandrake was in bloom."

"The mandrake? You mean, 'go and fetch a falling star, get with child a mandrake root,' mandrake?"

"Yes, now, up here on the Carmel," Gloria points to a tongue of hill a venomous green projection of earth, "the mandrake blooms in January."

Fabulous! What was she suggesting, we go out there in the rain to gather mandrake?

"Josephina, the mandrake root taken in unmeasured doses, the exact amount being the sacred knowledge of witches—and you know what men had done to witches—makes a person vain. Male scientists have broken down the mandrake to its chemical components and reconstructed it in the laboratory thinking that by changing its shape they are changing its meaning and sweetie pie they have become as vain in their desire to recreate themselves as Narcissus and you know what happened to him."

"You tell me," I answered, tired, bored, and just a bit sexually excited by her enthusiasm.

"He pined for the love of the unattainable; the love of his own image, and jumped into the pond where it was reflected and died."

"Exciting," I said, as my stomach churned with fear as we screech around one more corner.

"Oh! Josephina, I do love you, don't you see what I'm leading up to?"

"Truthfully, no."

"It's the men, you notice, who are dying to love themselves, as a sex, are being destroyed. Aphrodite and Venus, the mothers who hold men enthralled with secret potions of love had been rationalized out of being. In our world, Josephina, it was the men with our helpful applause, our desire to be like them, masters of the laboratory and the conveyer belt, who had synthesized us and recreated the essence within. Male geneticists are doing away with the womb."

"Damn clever way to get rid of an Electra Complex."

"My mother-in-law gave it to me. When they told her she was dying, she gave it to me."

"The Mandrake?"

"No, no; the locket." She opened it to reveal an accordion string of little hearts. "She meant each of one these for one of her grandchildren. There are more hearts than children," she rises and turns her satin-pajama leg slowly to the left. "South" she intones, and then turning her other leg with as much majesty whispers, "North.

"Yoga?" I ask watching her move her legs alternately, in slow motion, to the right to the left.

"No, Tai Chi."

"When we first moved up here Abigail was only a baby. We followed the sun for a year, the kids and I. Here's where the sun enters the balcony in May, June, July, she points to faint lines on the iron railing outside the window. If you draw the lines regularly, you find yourself having recorded the trajectory of the sun from one end of the balcony to the other. Then we painted the lines vermilion because it was a royal color. But it looked tacky to the neighbors. They complained so we covered the railing over with gray paint. If you look closely you can still see the notches. It's important to find your bearings in nature don't you think? To get in tune with the earth; feel it?"

"Not much."

"I walked around naked, surrounded only by the sky in this, my private mountain retreat, we couldn't make out the sea for the trees," she said twirling about like a clockwork doll. "One Saturday morning we were eating breakfast, Abigail suddenly got up, ran across the street—there used to be a hill on the other side, not houses—came back with a handful of delicate white flowers she called snow."

"Garlic," Guy said, "smell!"

"Snow, snow," she insisted. It took some time for her father to calm her down. She was so sure the wild garlic strewn hill was covered in snow. If our economic situation had allowed, I think I would have dedicated my life to my children. Don't you sometimes think you might have been a better mother?"

"No," I answered curtly.

She breathes deeply, stares out the window at the line of froth touching the now pacified sky. "Look down there," she points to the fir wood surrounded by a wall on which beer bottles had been cemented and then broken. The sun shining through a cloud agreeably bounced off the jagged edges. "Seems a crude way to keep out the unwanted. What happens if a child should climb over?"

"Don't remind me. That's what happened to Guy. The neighbor called to tell me Guy was caught but I shouldn't worry. I picked him off the barbed wire. He just escaped being castrated by the little steel knives enmeshed in it."

"Children are a bother."

"Oh no, how can you say that?" Her look of contempt sent my eye scurrying to the pockmarked stone ball in the corner of the veranda. Was she planning to catapult the Roman missile of war across the road, destroy the wall that had caused her son injury or was it me she meant to obliterate?

"Josephina, don't envy me," she's read my thoughts. "Next time you come up here, I'll no longer have a view. They're building right opposite us. Instead of pine and sea and a hidden garden children willingly sacrifice a limb to enter, they'll have high-rise apartments throwing shadows on my windowpanes. I'll see the neighbors dressing for bed, brushing their teeth, flinging pieces of mascara smeared cotton and used condoms into the white oleander bush below and though I'll try to rearrange the blinds artfully, I won't be able to keep their bedding airing over the window sills, their clotheslines full of underclothes, towels, sheets, and diapers from my line of vision. I went to see the plans in City Hall. They look all right, but the builders always manage to add a few meters to the height. They're calling the building complex Pueblo Espanol—Castles in Spain—Roman pleasure domes reinstated, and instead of square windows, you get one arched one to go with the name. I'm so mad I could die."

"Move out," I callously advise. "Don't die, it isn't worth it. Why don't you sue?"

"Sue? By the time the case gets to court, the law had been conveniently changed. The city of Haifa had a history of being a worker's town, the poor don't get richer, they certainly can't afford to buy property up here on any terms, but the rich get squalor, why should we see the Mediterranean when a hundred families can share our loss?

The Worker's Union building conglomerate was not set up to build a house here, a house there, give them an air terminal, an army camp, a 22-floor commercial complex in

Teheran, Ghana or the Bronx and they'll shine. Josephina, they're scooping the mandrake out of existence with their pile drivers, their jackhammers, their pumpkin toothed shovels, leveling the mountain to rubble in milliseconds. Elijah will have no parking space for his chariot of fire."

She took up her "lotus position" on several large jade and pale yellow silk throw pillows, "the feet turned towards Heaven, meaning Buddha was meditating."

I thought I knew Gloria well, she to whom I'd been regularly sending pictures, postcards, terse notes from here and there, congratulations on births, bar mitzvahs, condolences—but I remember her in less affluent circumstances, pregnant, a small child curling his hand round her middle finger, drawing the washed out shadow of the woman before me towards the grocery store and me feeling so alone in this world, not wanting to admit how much I needed McCrudder, how much I missed my children, ashamed in a way of having slept with David who was in Jerusalem gathering information for articles on the Eichmann affair.

Her eyes were sad. The little boy, garrulous and cranky slid down her hip and ran across the street. Gloria, distraught, ran after him. An elderly man, whom she introduces as Uncle Moshe, brings the boy back.

"Good morning, Gloria, how are you today? Here's your boy."

"Yes," she said forcing a smile.

"I'm glad Piki was back Dod Moshe," Gloria said to the elderly man.

"Oh yes, she's back. The police found her up in the Galilee. It seems someone goes about stealing city dogs. He thinks he was doing a good deed bringing them into the hills. You see he was also in the concentration camps, and thinks dogs need freedom. Yes, Piki was all right, though a little skinny," he picked up the bright-eyed little dog who was overfed and content, and hugged the creature who looked as if it had been unjustly insulted, "but she'll soon be back to normal, you can depend on Mother and me. I am sorry," the elderly man offers me his free hand, "I am Moshe," he said letting go my hand. "Please bring your guest to our house to taste Momma's baking."

Gloria said, "Thank you," as if she meant "no."

The child was absent-mindedly stroking the Pekingese. The dog smiled, sagely moving its tail in an attempt at being frisky.

"You have a beautiful boy there," the old man said, pinching the child's cheek. "You will have much happiness from him."

Gloria shrugged off the blessing. "Josephina, it's such a miracle you knocking at the door. I'm so much in need of intelligent conversation. I can't read, I can't think, I can't make contact, I'm lost. I feel like a creature from outer space; my words seem to come from long distances and just hang there. I've tried so hard to make friends with the mothers my age. The harder I try, the more I am rejected. Now I don't care."

Her Aunt Frouma from Brooklyn had just sent her a Westinghouse refrigerator, the first frost-free model on the market, and a fully automatic washing machine, which were undreamed of luxuries to those around her. She couldn't fight envy, but yes; she'd come with me to Uncle Moshe's this once.

She was very reflective as she ordered her groceries, one bottle of milk, one loaf of bread, and one box of washing powder. "They don't have any good soap powder and this stuff ruins the machine, not to mention your hands," she tells me turning back to the woman behind the counter whom she calls Pnina. The woman, Pnina, looks like my aunt back in New Jersey. I mean if her hair were dyed platinum and she were wearing pedal pushers, she'd look like my aunt, but it's hard to imagine this peaked, tired, heavy breasted woman wearing pedal pushers.

"On account?" Pnina asks opening a thick dog-eared ledger."

"No, I'll pay." I watch her unroll bills from her purse, count out coins. I offer to help carry the groceries. "No it's all right." She puts her hands protectively to her stomach, so low you can make out the shape of baby swimming in the womb. She asks Pnina if she can put the bag behind the counter.

We walk out. I admire her silky, tan and brown pied-de-poul dress tailored with such finicky care, bust darts, inner pleat from the breastbone down, inserted sleeves, running stitch seams.

"My neighbor made it; she used to be a well-known dressmaker in Budapest before the war. Her sister was dying of heart disease, she had a botched up operation on the valve—the interns had to practice on someone. Her dog was growing old, gum trouble, and her third husband was a nuisance asking only to be cared for like a baby and she was such a perfectionist. I paid her what she asked for, but I know if it covered the hours she spent over this dress; it really was too beautiful. My mother-in-law brought the material back from Cyprus on her way to visit relatives in France. Aunt Frouma sent me a woolen aquamarine robe with silver ribbon edging, bought on special sale in Loehmann's, really fine wool but I've just misused it. I sent it to the cleaner's and the shopkeeper wanted to buy it at any price. It came in the same package with an ice blue chiffon nightdress and a pair of high-heeled velvet house slippers. It would be fine if I lived in a wall to wall carpeted Manhattan apartment but here it just seems incongruous," she said as she looked down at her feet, her ankles so swollen she could hardly walk in those outsized zori sandals, many sizes too big. "Oh my darling' Clementine, sardine boxes no. 9;" the rubber thong had rubbed the skin between her toes raw.

I remember feeling so sorry for Gloria as she flip-flopped along laboring up the street, thinking, "you won't get me caught up in a situation where poverty was my middle name," but, had I married Tom and lived in Israel, not divorced Joseph and lived in Israel, would my life had been different from Gloria's? Her husband was away on a month's army reserve duty, living so near the sea and unable to take advantage of it, no money, so bowed down with history and bad economics stifling her initiative; she didn't even have the price of a car or a swimming suit.

Why in heaven's name had she left the States? She was such a bright girl, could have gone on to do her Doctorate, become a college teacher, president of a ladies' U, live in a pigeon hole in mid Manhattan paying half her salary for a tight squeeze into a kitchenette in an apartment house filled with hollow people playing canasta in a silent universe. I'd resigned my job, not without regret, shortly after my marriage to McCrudder. Actually I'd been eased out—pregnant women were a liability to the good name of the firm—what had they been doing after work hours to get themselves in that condition? Ovadia was born and there I was back again on the job after a brief try at the advertising game. They hadn't forgotten what a whiz I'd been gathering information on the Pharaohs, and now I was kept busy piecing together facts on the winds of change in Cuba, Russian influence in the Caribbean next door. Everywhere was next door. Only your neighbor seemed far away.

"But you are a college graduate?" I announced grandly. "You should be able to get a job more satisfying, better paying than child rearing and house cleaning. Why don't you go and live in a kibbutz? It seems the only organization capable of dealing with the return of the Jew to this desert in a logical way."

I throw out the advice though in my heart I felt it was sheer inertia rather than conviction that kept people in the kibbutz; or in Israel for that matter, arguing splintered abstracts from the holy Marxist tree. What would the master have done under these circumstances or the other? Me, I was into a vague but no less idealistic equality for all nations, for all peoples, for all individuals; a democratic, liberal socialism. But the most benign titles seemed to have such evil connotations.

"The finance minister," she said, "is new at the job. In fact," she added, "everyone was a novice at making policy. It's mostly a matter of trial and error. And the people are passive. They just submit except for those who pack up and leave. I find myself looking out of the kitchen window and hoping the weather will clear up so that a tourist will have a good time and come back to bolster up the economy with hard cash."

"You are crazy."

"It's been less than 13 years, Josephina, since the state was given independence. My mother-in-law keeps reminding me how hard it is to find flour and water to make bread. Had we lost the battle of Haifa, most of us would have become second-class citizens with nowhere to go, the byways of Europe were still heaving with our unburied dead.

"Listen, don't be gruesome."

"Why not? It was gruesome" she smiled, a little reticent upturn of the lips.

And all I could think of was Neil McCrudder, who was suddenly very close to me at this moment.

"That day you came to see me," she says, her voice breaking through the plink of rain against glass, "what were the three of you talking about, all huddled together, giggling like schoolgirls?"

"Well honey, I hadn't spent my life researching other people's material for nothing, according to records signed by Eichmann—the central office for the emigration of Jews was established in 1939 under his jurisdiction—there were 48,000 Bulgarian Jews signed and accounted for. Only 7,000 of them were exterminated by 43 as per statistics in Yad Vashem in Jerusalem. Compare the number to the 2,850,000 Polish Jews executed and you can see the true extent of the annihilation in reproductive probability alone. Each one saved was a story. Did you ever stop to consider the engineering ingenuity that went into doing away with over six million human beings?"

"There was a Dutch woman in a public taxi in Tel Aviv: short frightfully thin child, who never grew to her full height, practical camouflage, dark brown sweetness asking for connection, 20 years after still surprised to feel sun on her skin."

"Our families paid so we could come to Palestine just before the invasion of the Germans. We had the money for certificates, the British wanted toll money before we passed the gates. There were those who had no money. They are dead. We saved ourselves and sent signed certificates back, save a few. But how many could we save? I was 23. When I go to Europe, I never speak to men of a certain age. Whatever they say, you can never be sure of them."

Her mother-in-law, Hannah, was a slender woman with broad shoulders white hair brushed to sheen in a bun at the back of her neck; eyes blue with white willowy streaks across the iris, blue-gray cotton dress, white organdie collar, ruby and emerald ring on her finger, gold watch on a chain round her neck, long slender legs, Marlene Dietrich top hat, and a walking stick. She was a combination of intelligence and kittenish sensuality. But even then, she had this acrid smell of death about her.

Place of Birth: Bulgaria. She showed me photographs; poses of love of self, young sylph on rock, look at my waist, my eyes flashing in narcissistic poses. The uninhibited Rabbi's granddaughter—photographs snapped before she left Bulgaria forever dancing with young gentlemen with waxed mustaches and slicked down hair, perfume and hashish was wafting through gas-lit halls into nostrils vaguely aware of unrest in the vermiculated society of Silesia. Rosa Luxembourg writing tracts, criticisms of Lenin to whom she did not intellectually bow down, never to know that the rebellion she had precipitated would lead not to love but war—not one war but two world conflicts, perhaps a third all powerful one where words, even gibberish, will no longer influence. But she isn't red enough for some and finds herself cross-eyed and coldly contemplating the bullet that terminated her life. Tut, such a nasty sight, brain bespattered, bloodstained female Jewess body on a German bridge on a Sunday morning.

Gloria was busy correcting school papers in the room next door. We had just had a meal of okra and tomatoes stuffed with rice. Gloria was poor, but not eating badly. We settled down in a room on a garish red brocade couch, with a ruby Turkey rug, and yellow rose embossed sateen wall paper. Red Rosa might had sat in a room like this one dreaming of turning every Prussian into a Socialist and then Justice would reign among the workers, among the non-exploited proletariat taking turns at giving orders round the Ford conveyer belt, nut bolt twist. Uniformity. PEACE.

Hannah got up abruptly, she was, she said, on the board of directors of the Ilan handicapped children's organization. There was no telephone in the house. She would be back immediately. She introduced me to Esther Sofer, Nissim's mother—almond shaped long lashed black eyes, a tiny nose, smooth fair skin, slightly bowed legs, too short for her regal carriage . I did what I do best.

Biography: Female, born on The Feast of Lights 1898 in Adrianople in Thrace. Esther was part of a generation, at least a milieu that was beginning to lose interest in its Judaism. Judaism was becoming a hindrance—a society of superstitious people and their customs of which she had tried to rid herself.

Esther's father had been a fine tailor who frequently traveled to Vienna leaving his daughter alone with her piano and her potted palm looking out at the street below through hand crocheted curtains. Her brother sold her piano while she was out flirting with the Bulgarian Consul's handsome son who admired her. What did she and he have in common after all? She would not marry him, not for love, not for money, not for prestige. Loyalty to her people was more important. Then she was left to wait out the influenza epidemic while her brother escaped to France to seek his fortune where, decades later, he was rounded up by some Nazi compatriots and sent up to Poland to be cremated. She visited Romania as a young woman after an unfortunate love affair, but remembers little of it. It's none of my business. Esther Sofer: 80-year-old woman, who is willing to let me tape her story. Food she can share, love was private.

Transcription of tape: Esther Sofer speaking in Judeo-Espanola for a course I took at NYU on Jewish languages.

Note: I had transcribed the tape as best I can, taking into consideration the fact that I was not thoroughly versed in the Jewish Spanish tongue, Spanish, Hebrew, Aramaic, Turkish (?). Ask McCrudder! Spelling as it comes.

Question: What kind of food did you like best as a child?

Esther: Juelos con carne, beans and meat.

Question: Isn't that fattening?

Esther: It was very tasty with rice. We didn't waste much time worrying about diets. At that time men wanted fat women. What do you want to hear about?

Question: Ashkenazi Jews believe that if an unmarried girl eats the egg of the korban, the symbol of the ritually sacrificial bird or beast, during the Passover feast she will remain an old maid.

Esther: That's all a big lie. The egg of the korban was put on a plate together with the patcha, the pied, thigh of a lamb and the haroses, nuts and apple chopped to resemble clay the

Jews used to make bricks for the pharaoh, and the apio, celery, vinaigre, are the tears... Why should I break my head? You're driving me crazy. Who wants to know all these things?

Question: Are there any Jews left in Andrianople.

Esther: A handful of Jews. After the war the poor ones were sent to Israel by the congregation. There they became rich, had money enough to buy Raki, but the rich they stayed in Istanbul. Now they buy shops, boutikas, and apartments in Tel Aviv in case they'll want to come.

Question: Tell me about Shavuoth. "The Feast of Tabernacle."

Esther: Demandale a mi Papoo. Ask my grandfather, do I remember him? How should I know, it was so long ago. We were dressed all in white, went for long walks. We didn't dine at home, went out in a horse and buggy, paseo-aser, a picnic. We ate dairy. Prihito was rice with milk and sugar, borekas, aphahes de paghas, yaprakes de parra, yalanji dolmas, rice mint and dill vine leaves, rolled like this—cooked in olive oil and lemon with a pinch of sugar. You always add sugar when you cook with lemon.

Question: Was that all you ate?

Esther: Si, bravo, se vida. On Yom Kippur, the Day of Atonement, there was nothing to eat. Rosh Hashanah, the New Year's Eve, was beautiful with the children, girls, the sisters-in-law, and the great aunts who came from afar to be together. You could feel the holiday in the air. We waited for these feast days. We were all dressed in white, new shoes, new dresses. When I was small we had a pair of shoes and a new dress for Pesach and for Rosh Hashanah, and many other dresses too. My father was well turned out in white spats and a walking stick, and went to the synagogue. At home the maids prepared the table. We said the bracha, the blessing. We ate "Yihirasonas." It was a Hebrew word meaning "God's will be done." We ate red pumpkin and honey and apples, kalavasa, prasa, instead of eating other things, we ate this. In the morning we dressed in white and the maids prepared a table of desayunos, "God was one." Yo estoy dismayada. Those who labor for their stomachs may their labors bring them to an understanding of God's glory. Davka, we lived well. Before there was no anti-Semitism. Quando vien el huerko, the devil de Hitler, Yimach Shmo—may his name be erased from memory—everything changed.

Question: When were you last in Adrianople?

Esther: Me? When I was in Edirne, Adrianople, era un bardak. I went to Aser Ziara... visit my mother's grave and my father who are buried there. We went to see el kever, the tombstone was all right. Then one of my cousins took me to my father's house. I was deskayada, unquiet; everything was a bardak, upside down, small, changed. Are you really so interested in all these things? Esta es la cosa que vas escrever? I don't mind telling you but what interest was it to you?

Question: Did you go to the Synagogue?

Esther: El kal, the synagogue, meant nothing to me. My mother stayed home with the children. My father was away in Vienna. I don't know what you're trying to get out of me but you'll never get much of that from me. I had some friends in Montevideo who used to be religious in Edirne; perhaps you will come to see them.

Question: Did you sing special songs on holidays?

Esther: You better ask someone else who was religious. As I said, we did those things when I was as old as that child sitting there, may evil not touch him. After the conflagration of 1905, we didn't bother anymore, fire broke out, war broke out; everything was spoiled. On the Shabbat the children kissed the hands of Maman and Papa to show love and respect. We ate huevos encaminadas, hard-boiled eggs, desayuno, breakfast after father returned from the synagogue. Not everyone baked bread at home in the oven, white bread beautifully shiny with egg and sesame. We ate fish, carp, in order to set off the day of rest from an ordinary weekday. Shabbat was beautiful. First course was fish, well done. We ate pastel de carne, frita de prasa y de espinaca, leak and spinach patties, despues se komen un ermoso composto de prunas frescas, es bien por el stomaco.

Question: Did you light candles?

Esther: Father blessed the wine; we were all washed and received the blessing.

Question: How did it feel being a Jew in Adrianople?

Esther: The Jews felt they were Jews and not Turks, but at the same time the minorities lived well in Turkey; the Greeks, the Armenians had much freedom. Istanbul was something else, the countryside was far away. We had to take a train, take a steamship. It was something else. Edirne was divided in two, there was the country and the city. After the great fire they built a new city, beautiful and rich. The poor, poor things went to the riverside. They suffered. There were committees that helped them.

Question: Did the Ashkenazi community have a separate synagogue?

Esther: In Istanbul, there was a synagogue for Ashkenazi Jews. In Edirne there wasn't. There were several Russian Jewish families in town but there was no difference between them and us. The same thing. There were 13 congregations before the fire ate everything up, after the fire there were two beautiful large synagogues, extremely well built.

Question: How did you feel in Turkey with the Ottoman Empire falling round you?

Esther: We never mentioned Palestine. It was defendu. During the First World War, I was a young woman. We lived well. Father read the newspaper. He was busy cutting frock coats. During the Second World War we came to Haifa. We had a legal Certificate from the British Mandate in Palestine. I was a widow for the second time. Nissim's father paid Turkish taxes and we came. Now, I will make coffee.

Gloria was standing at the door in some kind of culture shock. "What's up?" she implies with a steady look in her eye.

"Like Rosa Luxembourg, you had become a victim of your ideals."

"Why, because I was not a liberated female like you running around the world? I'm not a feminist, I don't believe in an international women's movement or in an international worker's movement. I believe in the right of the Jews to had defendable borders, language, laws, struggle for identify as a nation. We are the offspring of a murdered generation and we're paying for all our father's sins, those who did the murdering and those who had no time to pray for they didn't understand that they were scapegoats to their times. Do you think the evil in men's hearts had been dispersed? It was here hanging about. We are water-changing shape. We had pigeonholed our memories and are now ready for the new, the yet unperceived.

If I'm going to be aggressive, destroy to create a social order, it might as well be the struggle for a Jewish homeland, that's where I differ from Rosa and from you. Rosa considered herself a citizen of the world, as deeply affected by the suffering in India, Africa as by the homeless Jew wandering the face of the globe. I bet all she could think about when she was shot between the eyes were the children she'd aborted—no, sacrificed for an abstract ideal."

"But isn't Zionism an abstract ideal?" I was about to ask, thinking perhaps Rosa should have played the game as Gloria would had liked, put her energies into Zionism, assure the Jew a state. But Gloria no less than Rosa was so firmly sewn in the structures, she'd tear herself to pieces if she budged.

Why in heaven's name was she crying? She was jealous, no doubt, of me flying free as a bird, unrestricted by mere monetary considerations. I had more luck than brains meeting McCrudder with whom I swam in the Piscataqua River, kissing him underwater—Esther Williams and Gary Grant. Grant's lungs are stronger than mine. I find myself within the waves of sound expanding round my water-clogged ears, a cracked bell clonked out my life. I felt McCrudder breathe on my blue lips reviving me with outdated smiles.

"You are a free citizen," I blurt out, "why don't you get the hell out of here? If you're so unhappy, divorce! You don't have to suffer a lifetime for a momentary mistake."

"Marriage," she said, was a contract made before God and Society."

"What are you talking about?"

"You sign your name to a contract before witnesses and the Rabbi; it's both a civil and spiritual obligation."

"And the caterer makes the profit! Gloria, two people need no witnesses to their love."

"Aren't children the product of love and don't they need the protection of society?"

"Society is only another abstraction."

"And what is love?" she asked.

"Love was eternal," I answered, tongue in cheek.

"If love was so eternal, why did your marriage to Joseph break up?"

I refused to be insulted by her. I could afford magnanimity. I, who not only had Neil McCrudder, my husband, on my side, but the spirit of Camelot as well. Though I must admit it was Yuri Gagarin, the Russian, I was cheering both on earth and in outer space. Yuri Gagarin was my hero. But who could have believed that President Kennedy, waving the banner of King Arthur's court on high, presuming peace and good will to men an achievable goal in our lifetime, would hit the dust and the obituary column so soon. He was so alive, so sure of right over might, so sure his might was right. Che Guevarra, Fidel Castro, Khrushchev dead, even Gagarin falling out of the sky maybe, but not Kennedy, the architect of a new order of things, arbitration rather than confrontation; confrontation rather than loss of honor—the new politics, sexual or otherwise.

"I can't explain," I finally said, "but my marriage to McCrudder hasn't."

CHAPTER 6

No matter how long she sat in her lotus position, and contemplated the shimmering curtain of rain, deflating herself of anger, she'd never escape the Bronx, an ineradicable stamp on the soul. That we had in common. There's something about the Bronx, the intense forest of red brick blocks seething with pent-up frustrations of frozen snow piled high against outer walls within a box—heat coming up through pipes clattering and banging. What had the super put in the furnace? What had he brought down the dumbwaiter? The elevated train took you out of the borough you compressed your childhood into, shortening it as much as possible, dreaming of adulthood, a dime on a subway out! Anywhere was an improvement on the Bronx, like any other forest, like the Black Forest where witchy bitchy goo eats baked little Jew, defoliating now, computerized sorcerers headless geodesic—the answer was not applicable—the best had repercussions, hiccups, headaches. Try again! Factual information bent to truth, like truth, sapphire brilliance to diamond brilliance. Hitler was a clay god writing with a stylo on beeswax. USA army chemical defoliants in Vietnam, salt used to harden snow backing up into Spring flood—strip the bark of trees, forests to desert where secrets are less apparent, began low. There was little place to hide from God in the desert. What a dark mysterious forest are the blind tenement houses of the Bronx, blacked out eyes, guillotines under keystone, passing frames on the El taking us back home.

"What's your connection with Rosa?" I finally asked, thinking that for someone who claimed she couldn't read, she'd certainly read up on Rosa Luxembourg. I'd been gathering a few relevant facts on the Socialist movement in old Prussia and Rosa's name kept popping up due to my predilections no doubt. I was more than a little involved in the women's lib craze of the day. That is, I rallied round the flag, and joined the chorus, "Zum kamf, Zum kamf, Zum kamf, Oh War! Oh War! to you we are born, to you we had lost our Rosa!" But she seemed to had enough information for a definitive biography

"Listen," she said, running into an inner room and out again with a packet of blue air letters and white onion skin paper which she unfolds and reads a line here, a line there agitatedly.

"Aunt Frouma kept writing me letters, with tears that blotched the ink: 'Your uncle only wants to have a good time like a baby, forget about your uncle coming to Israel. He doesn't want to spend the price of a stamp on you. Your uncle is not interested in children; never wanted to take care of children. He was a man without feelings. He's afraid to spend a cent. He only wants money in the bank. I want everything to be in order for you. Your uncle had agreed to come to Israel for a month; I want your uncle to come with me. I want company. I don't want to go by myself and with little money. He had the money. Fix a good lock on your door; very important. We bought you a refrigerator, we bought you a TV set, and we bought you a percolator. You must take care of yourself; you're a mother of little children. You must take care. I want to see your smile, money in the bank never smiled at anyone.'

'We aren't coming. He said you are stupid. Why don't you come back to a land of liberty, a land of buying and selling, a land of prosperity?'

'My dear child, the moment you get the one hundred dollars, write to me. Please write; I love to get letters from you. Don't write about the money; tell me you've bought a red dress. Your uncle was interested only in having a good time and goes bowling three times a week. Send the children to the summer camp. Please write and tell me what you want. I've sent you half a dozen towels I bought in the white sales—ruby and chartreuse, clubs, spades, and diamonds on royal blue.'

"When my uncle died and shortly after Aunt Frouma, their house was sold for a good price, enough to buy all this," she raised her hand to the open sky before us.

"Lucky, she left it to you."

"By leaving it to me, she was leaving it to Israel, clearing her conscience. She died believing I had settled in Zfat. The North of Israel was all of a sameness to her, a place where she had lived for two years with my uncle, poverty stricken, in an abyss of ignorance filled with mystical belief in numbers, circles, triangles, among Kabalistic bone pickers, as she called them, chanting to powers they alone understood, to paraphrase her. She didn't want me to suffer as she had and yet she felt she had betrayed a trust, not lived up to an obligation. She had brought her husband over to her side of thinking and he had outdistanced her in every way.

"My uncle Will Zeituni, Aunt Frouma's husband, fought in Spain against Franco before he became a member of the American Republican Party. Aunt Frouma was my father's elder sister. She met her husband of this strange name on a tennis court in South Africa where they both had relatives. I know now "zeit," means olive in Hebrew, that Uncle Will was probably born in Zfat where she lived with him for a number of years, had in fact promised as a marriage vow to live there forever.

When I was a little girl, I used to stay with them in Brooklyn during the Christmas holidays. She'd get up very early, go down to the cellar and bring up a bottle of wine—wine she made herself, served in tiny glasses I used to call rosebuds, rosebuds of fairy nectar. My aunt was a fat, happy woman; motherly. She had no children of her own so she doted on the children of the neighborhood, indiscriminately donated her several types of wine, her fine cakes to the Church Bazaar and the Jewish League of Women. The Italian neighbors, with whom she got on famously, included her house in the neighborhood protection pool. Those five or six streets were an oasis of gardens and well kept homes in the chaotic earthquake fantasy of the shattered residential area. I still had the wine recipe. Take later summer grapes, mix with sugar. After ten days, when it was fermenting, force the liquid out through a straw. I never tried it—too lazy. What I do remember was her enthusiasm and the warmth of her fat breasts. We slender mothers had less body to offer children."

"Well, maybe, but fat isn't equal to security, is it?" I tried interrupting but no go. The name Aunt Frouma had pressed the button of her frustration. I was engulfed in words.

"But even when the inheritance was official, getting the money was not easy because of the completely differing mentalities, American and Israeli. The lawyers just wrapped me tighter in red tape. I was struggling with different conceptions of mind. The American grid had to protect their client's estate and the American way of life; the Israeli grids had to fight bureaucracy and attempt to explain its cockeyed workings to American grid that winked unbelievingly, taking steps not to be taken in by the obvious lie that was the truth. Do you understand? Look at these:

'Please be advised,'" she reads in a loud voice edged with anger, "'that Mr. Menahem Zeituni was admitted by the government of Palestine pursuant to a traveling document issued to him by the British Consulate at Buenos Aires No. 81472 and arrived in Jaffa, Palestine October 19, 1925 (Visa No. 7251/E/ C 41063); his name at the time was William Olivier. He resided in Palestine as a pioneer, departed from Palestine on May 12, 1927 on a Russian passport for Madrid Spain, had been a USA citizen since May 1945. Will you kindly let us have your check for...

Item: Building contractors are a difficult people, and yours appears to be an outstanding example of his class. Kindly enclose check for services rendered.

Item: I had to attend at the flat also at the Haifa Municipal Building Engineer's Department in connection with the deviation from the building license and the contract and regarding the transfers of foreign currency since the land registry requirements are very strict in matters of this kind when foreign residents buy immobile property ...Enclosed please find my bill for services rendered in the amount...'"

"I was so dumb believing in people and in the lawyers, one mercenary as the other, on either side of the oceans. The money came just in time, otherwise we would have had to go on sharing a flat with Hannah, Nissim, Sabta Esther. There was little building going on and a large influx of Jews from Europe and the Arab countries so whoever took over an apartment belonging to a fleeing Arab could live in it indefinitely for a minimal rent, a sort of squatter's right called 'key money' which really meant the property belonged to whoever lived there. When Rafcho and I got married, we were ineligible for any form of government aid mostly because we were not immigrants from Morocco with ten children but legally, so to speak, because my husband was a native. The refusal was a technicality easily overlooked depending on the mood of the officiating clerk. I wanted to go to a kibbutz but Rafcho wouldn't hear of it. My in-laws put up a glass partition and we had a room of our own."

"Unpredictably, the original owners took them to court. We all stood to be kicked out, but she won the case. As the judge pointed out, she had security of tenure as a protected tenant and the owners, five children or not, just had to grin and bear it.

"During the night I could feel rather than see her slide back the glass doors, peer at me plastered to her son's back, imagine her envy of us partaking of a pleasure no longer hers, while we watched Guy grow under the ganglionic plaster, which threatened to fall over his crib whenever the old woman upstairs got into a panic and remembered Auschwitz, spread her legs out and let go hot urine on the tar roof for all to see and her son-in-law decided his wife was to blame and beat them both up.

"And above the cot where our baby sleeps, was the home of the woman fighting it out with the moon," Gloria stretched her fingertips up to heaven, "the faster you run after it, the faster it escapes your outstretched arms—and her daughter, running, shouting begging Momma not to jump over the ledge. Husband and wife throwing meager belongings at each other on the roof as I watched cracks in the ceiling, along the wall grow longer and deeper, ever more intricate, the dented water pipe shaken from its casing by the furor dripping rivulets to streams as she howls at the moon, over the castle in Transylvania—ghouls trampling werewolf territory, the forests of Europe are turning brown with distemper."

The husband had a motorcycle with a sidecar like the ones the Wehrmacht used—the brr, brr, brr of the motor revving up in early morning sent a shiver of fear through me as though I were peeking out the side of a black window shade at two SS men, riding a wet moon-fed alleyway in a town, holding the world in thrall. The old someone who had once been a skeleton in Auschwitz and the fat had piled up in two illogical wings on either side of her dainty pelvis, hair sallow strips of bacon, fingernails mud caked appendages with which she raised tan cotton stockings falling in folds over her swollen ankles, and yet there was something not quite bovine about her, a spark in her puffy liquid brown eyes that spoke of childhood and care and even love vaguely remembered.

How could she be contt? They had no bathroom, no toilet up there, only a water tap in an inner corner of the roof they called a kitchenette; the grandchild, a five–year-old beauty, an absolute flower in the dung heap. There was police, blood, divorce and then the man lived alone with a lady friend and then another. And yet he was always respectful when we met on the wooden spiral steps leading to the roof, sort of a quiet, 'don't enter my space I won't enter yours.' And here was where I was to bring up my child! Each house was another tragedy, people drunk, women beaten up, abandoned, screaming, cards and gambling, whisky—anything to forget the concentration camps, the devils which seemed to fade out into dull blue respectful poses in the early morning till the 4 o'clock siesta.

"The smell of war was all around us. Rafcho was stationed in the Galilee under direct fire from the Syrian army, people were being killed on the borders and whole families massacred by home-made bombs put into shopping bags and gouged out loaves of bread placed on supermarket shelves, under greening hedges, round homes and schools, young men turning to a frizzle on electrically wired fence and the price of bread and clothes going up and I spent my days in court. Here, there was no objective criteria, no precedents; everyone was master in his own home, he'd fought the battle, won the war, made the rules. Everyone knew each other, understood each other, and made leeway for each other's weaknesses. They'd all been fighters in the same brigade.

"The judge, vexed and moody cried, 'you are all alike!' meaning that all Spanish Jews, my name gave me away and walked out. I rose in deference to her honor. My lawyer told me to sit down and apologized to the entire room, accusing me in a dreadful whisper of having lost his case. It was my fault. I hadn't followed instructions. I mean I didn't realize the court procedures were so different from American TV thrillers. I expected to put my hand on the Bible and swear to 'tell the truth and nothing but the truth' and my Hebrew was still not so good.

"A few weeks later, the Judge was featured in all the papers. She had managed to talk to a parrot and thereby prove to which of the two men contesting ownership, the parrot truly belonged. Her hair, peppered in silver strands, springs up and down in rhythm with her thoughts, those hazel eyes I remember, slightly cross-eyed, wide open like a star of the 1940s fighting off wrinkles, Bette Davis, palsied and arthritic, handing out an Oscar for "best actress;" a made-up cadaver trying to recapture days when one acid stare from her silver screen eyes and the boys out there on the ground on the sea and in the air, fighting the axis round the globe, knew what they were dying for. Marilyn Monroe, Kennedy's favorite gal will never grow into a ga-ga hag on TV. Cut. What a reason to die young.

"Do you remember that day you knocked at the door? That day you came to see me," she said, her voice breaking through the plink plink of the rain against glass.

"Sure, I remember."

Come fathers and mothers throughout the land and don't criticize what you can't understand. Your sons and your daughters are beyond your command. Your old road was rapidly ageing. -Bob Dylan, 1963.

David was in Jerusalem doing a follow-up on The Eichman Affairs. No, I wasn't interested in going along. What did a man in a glass box mean to me?

You must hand it to Eichman and gang, the one idea those inspired German brains refused to give up to the very last moment before the tides of war changed was their metaphysical justification for murder, their holy mission to make all Europe Judenrein. Two years after the trial, Eichman was still news.

Eichman: A poor-looking creature exhibited to the crowd, a lopsided, nervous tick flashing on and off like a pasted grin, the well oiled cog in the political wheel, mild mannered, servile, performing well in the name of Fatherland after all these years. What a pitiable sight the devil was when caught and served under glass. Such a ridiculous specimen whose signature on a piece of paper, whose voice over a telephone wire set wheels in motion, brains creating means for concluding a life and all in the name of government policy, typed in triplicate, filed away in the capsule of time.

"What were the three of you laughing about huddled together like schoolgirls on Hannah's new red couch? You and Sabta Esther like two bugs in a rug."

"Well honey, talking to people was my job. According to records signed by Eichmann—the central office for the emigration of Jews was established in 1939 under his jurisdiction—there were 48,000 Bulgarian Jews signed and accounted for. Only 7,000 of them were exterminated by 1943 as per statistics in Yad Vashem in Jerusalem, Compare the number to the 2,850,000 Polish Jews executed and you can see the true extent of the annihilation in reproductive probability alone. Each one saved was a story. There was a lot to talk about. Sabta Esther talked to me about cooking. She was a lovely woman. Did you ever stop to consider the engineering ingenuity that went into doing away with over six million human beings?"

On the way to visit Gloria, a Dutch woman in a public taxi in Tel Aviv: Short frightfully thin child, never grew to her full height, practical camouflage, dark brown sweetness asking for connection. Forty years after still surprised to feel sun on skin. "Our families paid so we could come to Palestine just before the invasion of the Germans. We had the money for certificates, the British wanted toll money before we passed the gates. There were those who had no money. They are dead. We saved ourselves and sent signed certificates back, saved a few. But how many could we save? I was twenty-three. When I go to Europe, I never speak to men of a certain age. Whatever they say, you can never be sure of them."

I knock on Gloria's door without warning. "Hello, hello, the American journalist?" Nissim Calderon in his khaki army knee-length shorts stretched to bursting over a protruding belly asked introducing his companion with whom he was playing Shesh Besh, a short, hairy-legged man, a stevedore like himself. The man gets up and shyly mutters his name in introduction holding out a pudgy, sweaty hand, which I shake and then he speedily takes his place on the stool opposite the open backgammon box inlaid in a mother of pearl geometric glitter.

"Raki?" Nissim Calderon asks, carefully pouring water into the aniseed, which by magic turns opal white. "La bienvenue, le haim!" He clears an armchair of bundles of Selection, the French Reader's Digest and placing the magazines carefully on the floor, asked me to sit down. On the small side table, a bowl of pistachios, and on a flowery plate, cubes of yellow marmalade covered in powdered sugar. "Loqum," he says. It sticks to the top of my mouth.

Gloria's mother-in-law, Hannah, opens rock candy glass doors separating the bedroom from the long narrow space called "the Salon."

She hugs me. "You will sleep here! We always have room for a guest," she points to the featherbeds stacked and folded on top of the other, covered with a yellow pique sheet. "The apartment was big enough for a family of ten, more. It expands for guests like the land of Israel for the ingathering of the tribes of Israel. We can always add water to the soup and make the 'tehina,' the ground sesame paste a little thinner. There is always enough."

"I'm staying at the hotel," I answered sitting down on the red brocade couch. I hear sounds of lovemaking coming through that rock-candy partition, which was just like my honeymoon alcove in Joseph's mother's apartment in Wadi Nisnas. We spent two nights there but if time represents more than hours in sequence, it was a lifetime, like forever. I feel sick; real physical pain. White lime flakes off into my hand. The sun jumps from one tiered chalk dais to another—foundations of houses no longer there. One green minaret had been left intact. A chorus of fat aunts, draped in all-encompassing black crepe weeds blowing gently in the desert breeze, intone "One good one and one bad one never fight" and twirl pink tongues round and round in their mouths, "Blahlahlahlahwoowolooloo" over and over. On the flood-lit scaffolding encompassing the Romanesque church, bricks painted chocolate brown, a man's choir in talitot and skullcaps sings a Gregorian chant, gravelly voiced, in Greek or was it Aramaic? It reaches me from afar: "This was a legal and binding marriage contract," with monotoned repetition, again and again. The congregation of voices rises above the Carmel Mountain, rolls down the vastness of the desert up to Mt. Sinai and God himself! What had I done? A bulldozer, with a great earth defying drill carried haughtily before it, closes in on me. I turn to flee. I was caught between the curtain of rainbow fed rain and the pine-bedecked mountain. I run up a flight of stairs. Joseph's mother opens the door. Her hands are covered in flour. She's baking semolina cakes for our wedding.

"May I use your bathroom, please?" I ask embarrassed by my bodily needs. She leads me to a white cubicle. As I run down steps, three flights at a time, I hear her pouring lye on my urine; the acid disintegrates the stiff bristled brush with which she tries to rub me away. The toilet drips tallow, and dissolves into the sky.

I run right. I run left.

I'm a paper doll of outsized proportions under the electric bulb, stuck like a plant in the blind alley, shouting hysterically at the birds to keep their beaks to themselves.

A plumber in black silk overall and frock coat was painting broad zebra stripes on the highway. He bows.

"Bravo! La tuya esta pregnada!"

Hannah or was it Esther Sofer, reaches out to me from the shadow. "Go get Gloria," she ordered, bringing a hanky doused in astringent lemony toilet water to my forehead. " Sh! Shhhh! don't talk now." The perfume had a blood red label gilded copper, 80 TURSTIK PE RE JA LIMON CECEGI KOLONYASI, Londra, Asfalti, Istanbul. The smell of Aunt Khoursey's cologne; Aunt Khoursey whom I loved. The letters floated before my eyes. "Go get Gloria."

Gloria's father-in-law cracked jokes, told anecdotes, and sprinkled the room with information culled from Selection. His air of congeniality brought me back to myself. Hannah, Gloria's mother-in-law sits close to me, warms me within the intimate circle of her reminiscences.

"Last week," Gloria said, as she absent-mindedly smoothed the legs of her silk mandarin pajamas over her knees, "there was a memorial service for my mother-in-law in the old apartment. Rafcho's sister's eldest son lives there now with his wife and two children. I hated it so much. It was the 'me' I never wanted to be.

"Like a child, I ran out into the street and sat on the fender of a car, a huge, slick relic of the sixties, a Plymouth I think, and watched the mourners come out, small men and women a little frayed for wear smiling satisfied smiles, the people who had judged me; gray old people, warming their lives between their hands, keeping out the stranger in their midst who might put them to shame. They were like birds of a feather jousting for the middle ground, keeping their territory free from competition. I worked so hard playing down my education. They turned arrogant, played me for a fool, the threat from outside, the educated one who might set them questioning their basic premises. They were so protective of the lives they had rescued from the flames of war, the earthquakes of change, furrowing for breathing space here at the edge of the desert.

"Before I understood that their white lies, their little intrigues, were limited to a small circle, inconsequential politics in a closed circle, it was my world that was being undermined."

"Do you realize Gloria," I said looking at the great expanse of sky, with dark racks of clouds passing majestically, purposely by threatening gale, "Eichmann, could have been your father or mine? In age, that is," I added, making amends for something—though I'm not quite sure what it was.

"Oh Josephina, you're nothing but an observer, a dilettante. All reporters," her eyes sparkle with pent up anger, "are voyeurs, keyhole peepers, empty people with synthetic wit, procurers, producers, distributors of the unfeelies. What are you going to write about in your precious magazine about the Lebanese crisis, right?" She didn't give me a chance to answer.

"When you began typing up your formula piece, keeping the wide and varied audience of your famed magazine in mind, how far back are you going to go in search of a cause? How many facts are you going to overlook because of your selective boorishness, how many conclusions are you going to draw on little knowledge for the sake of your journalistic style?

"During the Yom Kippur War, I ran around from bookshop, to kiosk, to newsstand, trying to find a copy of your magazine but every copy had been sold out. Here, there was a blackout on news and we all wanted to know what was going on. The BBC didn't supply anything but damn Arab propaganda and then downtown, near the Ritz coffeehouse on a side street, I found a copy. I was so happy, you'd think I was reading a peace agreement between Egypt and Israel when in fact, I was reading you; your knowledgeable, esteemed opinion. I could feel your style, your gleaning pen, even without a byline and you hadn't even been here for years.

"Oh how I envied you, traipsing around from one country to another," she said as she got up, no hands. "The trouble with you," she shouted from the kitchen, "was you ride too many first class airplanes, isolate yourself from the people. Hopping from one plane to another, one continent to another, running so fast you stay where you've always been."

She might be right, traipsing around from one country to another—it simply becomes a way of life, nothing enviable in that. The camera and the typewriter are sterile instruments, pictures and words outline our fleeting selves in hard lines, forms less true than the imagination.

If you use a strobe light to catch the frog, frame after frame, in the intimacy of his sexual position above or under his mate, within the nocturnal intimacy of the pond, force partners apart with your hands, not even afraid of getting warts, all had been scientifically pre-controlled, measured, then put male back on female, a number blazoned round their bellies, what had you learned about the mystery of the pond—that a big male frog croaks in a given timbre of voice to frighten away the smaller courtier and yet all frogs find a mate, or most do, and the frog hasn't become a giant through selective copulation?

If you light a votive candle within the cavernous dusk of the manmade cathedral, and pray for a mate, what had you learned about love? Thank God celluloid does not last. Pictures disappear, voices on tape fade, and old magazines are thrown into the garbage. There was nothing as dead as last year's news.

There was little you could do but record angles of vision, which in retrospect, as nostalgia, dictate our reality. If you tried to put the emotion, the dynamic of life into an article, film it, and record it, there would be no end of pages, no end of frames.

Why do I take this crap? All teachers are underdeveloped adults trying to hold on to their childhood by staying on in the classroom. I'm about to shout back, ready to walk out, rain or no rain. Before I can give action to thought, she comes out of the kitchen holding a plate of apple strudel, sugar coated, with a heavenly aroma.

"Gloria, I'm sorry I disappointed you; here I go apologizing for living, whatever we say, however we say it, the nature of words, the nature of so called facts, was as ephemeral as the changing nature of the clouds."

"Josephina, I hate to contradict you, but being hungry was much less ephemeral than the words which describe the state."

"OK, have it your own way." Who was I to argue about hunger with that buttery aroma of her strudel attacking my senses?

"Anti-Semitism in the world, the expulsion of the Jews, the burning of synagogues was a symptom of the economic ineptitude, moral degeneration, and attrition of the vessels of understanding."

"You're talking like a poet."

"Yes, I've become incapable of speaking English. I've been here so long, I find myself translating from the Hebrew."

"Sounds posh."

"You are a scoundrel Josephina Koenigsburger Kadosh McCrudder."

"Alas poor Yorik!"

"Yes, Josephina, be sarcastic, but I tell you terminal societies hate Jews as they hate anything they cannot understand, lack of humanity in any form was a morbid lesion, it festers, it spreads and the body dies They fear the spirit, the finality of matter, try to dissipate fear in hate and destruction just to feel alive. To love was by far the harder thing."

This woman was raving mad. What was she selling me, my Chinese Yoga-oriented friend, the lamb and the lion, heaven and hell, good versus bad?

"Why don't you try keeping your own population at home? It's really impossible to feel Israel was so important to Jews when you had so many of your citizens waiting to go to America, buying stores on Lexington Avenue, driving taxis, thankful for the opportunity of working like galley slaves for money in the bank. Yes, though as you say Israel exists as a state, a means of identity, the Jews aren't exactly banging down the doors of this earthly kingdom. Rather, like rats they warily sound out their old haunts, thrown out today, seep back tomorrow. How do you resolve the paradox?"

"Paradox was a matter of perspective."

I look at her in disbelief, what had happened to her in the years between my hasty marriage to Joseph and my present jive with a second divorce? I didn't want to get divorced yet I knew it would happen.

"Ridiculous Gloria, a paradox was a paradox, was a paradox. You can rationalize it out of existence but it was still there.

"The weak of purpose leave but the strong stay," she said, shaking her head almost in tears. "Was Yisroel hai v'kayam, the people of Israel live and are; we must prove to ourselves we are not moles in the garden, termites in the woodwork, but a living body of people and life means adjustment and change."

"Sounds good, but any way you put it the Jews were making a mess of it. Politically, Gloria, this place was a morass of contradictory ideas and as far as the environment goes, not to mention the economy." I'm thinking of those myriad notes I've read for my coming interview with Conforti. "You've blown it. And what's more the Israeli Jew mixes up simplicity with stupidity. There seems to be a need to escape excellence as if it were naughty to fit the mold of his Middle European Counterpart who did excel, as if it were a patriotic duty to be mediocre. It's about time the Jewish State outgrew adolescence. That was my considered opinion," I tell her, now irritated, overtired, and just plain hungry.

"You're right," she says, surprising me half out of my wits, "it came to me as a revelation when I was really down and out that the people in authority, shorn of this authority, are the most mundane of the species. How do they get such power? Who gives it to them? The answer was they are the heroes of our compromises, the bane of our lack of ethical, moral education. But you can't get away from the fact," she said, getting up and turning clockwise, seconds two, three, four, "that the Russian Jews had the idea of state when they came to Palestine. They had an idealistic, political entity in mind. After all, many of them were influenced by and influenced the Russian revolutionary ideal of material equality for all men while the Jews living in Africa and the orient, as a group, worked and prayed to keep the status quo. The Jews from Yemen, the Atlas Mountains, Afghanistan, India came here with a Jewishness that was not intellectualized. They were the poor—the rich found a way of not coming to Israel—but I agree no amount of heart, which was and was their greatness, without mind, will create a state." She turned counterclockwise concentrating on every minute movement of her body.

"Israel was a body without a heart, a state without a soul and now the two parts are integrating, a heart and spirit, without the moral obligations f Judaism, without the Bible as a guide, had little reason for existence." She turned ever so slowly in place.

"The Jews are a symbol that mankind was not merely a transient phenomenon on the face of this earth due for extinction. The monuments of the Egyptians and the Greeks are empty, forgotten prophesies, but our very existence still creates fear, sends a shiver down the back and like little children faced with something they don't understand. By killing the source of your fear, you murder death itself and you live forever in the yellowing pages of yesterday's tabloid or in the ruddy sandstone of Petra, and all this was a shortcut to standing free, three-dimensional surrounded by the elements that nourish our lives. To conquer fear by cutting up the business of living with your fellow man into edible portions was what the Jewish religion was about in a way."

"Like Momma giving baby a hot plate of chicken soup."

"Believe me plates of chicken soup are love, the sign of caring, and if you had cared for and loved your child, he or she may know how to transfer this love to the next generation. Plates of chicken soup are not fossilized columns."

"Goody, goody, don't you just hate yourself for talking so piously. We are all using the same words to make the same statements. If only words could heal."

"My nephew Nir," she stopped her dance and contemplated the clouds drifting swiftly across the window pane, "was kept alive by a miracle during the Yom Kippur War, '73 you remember—a remote control bullet parted his hair leaving an antenna wire hanging like a Chinaman's braid from the back of his head. I really don't know the details but it was some kind of electronic-sounding instrument that searches out human flesh. It did its job. It exploded in the head of the soldier in the tank behind Nir's. The dead officer was Nir's best friend, Avi.

"They had been on a trip to Europe together, picked up two Scandinavian girls on the road and were on their way to Switzerland to visit Avi's relatives. Before they left for Europe, they'd come over to wish Rafcho, the kids and me goodbye. Avi asked for some cocoa. He thought he was in Switzerland and would get the hot chocolate and whipped cream his aunt used to prepare for him when he was a child. All they got from me was local cocoa powder. Anyway when the news of the invasion of the Sinai came over the radio, they dumped the girls and tried to get home. They finally made it through London—so many other boys trying to get home, into uniform, into tanks, behind guns. Avi and Nir made it to the desert without bothering to inform their families of their arrival.

"Dressed in their ultra fashionable European jeans and sports shirts, thanking God for the good fortune that had brought them back home before the others, they ran right into death— at least Avi did. I mean who the hell would have believed the Egyptian capable of breaking through the impregnable Bar Lev line and on the Day of Atonement no less, the holiest day of the year. I watched my dentist scurry down the street, out to fight, as if he were going down the road to play a game of squash. We'd been unprepared in order to make it possible for the Egyptian to attack and win. In this way only, the argument went quoting supposed discussions simmering in Prime Minister Golda Meir's so called kitchen cabinet, could the Egyptian allow himself the luxury of making peace with the enemy."

"Funny about impregnable lines. Wasn't there a Maginot line and a Siegfried line? Beautifully illusory lines," I say trying to break through her emotion, coveting that cake of hers but she, so involved with her own musings, never saw my mouth drooling.

"The carcasses identified by Rabbis and Kadis, mother's sons all, were no illusion. When I heard that Avi had been killed I began to cry, not for him you see but for myself; for my inability to make the kind of cocoa he had had in mind. There was a life and there was none.

"The reason I tell you all this," she continued, unaware of my hankering for that strudel, "is a letter my nephew Nir wrote me from the Egyptian side of the Suez Canal. 'I cannot forgive myself this need to kill another human being. I was too young to kill, too young to remember the eyes of a man my age writhing in the sands. Aunt Gloria, I wish I could hug my enemy instead of killing him. As for my future, I think I'll follow your advice and go back to school.'"

"Did he make it?"

"Oh yes, he's married now, owns a filling station near Sharm El Sheikh. Last time I saw him he told me he'd given up Psychology and was into Philosophy. He's a simple boy really, but he had lived through so much, so much."

"La Vida Es Sue o."

"You are lost, Josephina, because you are lost as a Jew."

Gee whiz—now I'd had enough. "What was a Jew?" I ask in self defense, "my label, my tag? What about American, what about journalist, mother, potential divorcee, girlfriend, wife, sister-cook?"

"Yes," she goes on undauntedly, "unless you can free yourself from the cultural hold the acquisitive society had on you and come back to your people, your roots, you're lost. Unless you admit your Jewishness to yourself and become consciously aware of your place as a Jew in history, rite, and law, you are lost as a human being."

"That's a bit of circumlocution."

"Try to understand, Josephina," she said as if instructing a debilitated dodo bird, "when someone like you whose job was your identity who had had little religion, had been regimented through the school system, been given a certificate of merit for playing the game, for preserving the momentary myth of the day that Science was all, proof equal to truth, spirit rejected, the door shut in its face, the consumable all important, it was not surprising that belief was simply an unworthy byproduct of reality."

Film clip: glass and brick blocks of apartments with triple locked doors, privacy attained by the pretense that your neighbor was a shadow on a painted wall. McCrudder, the voice over the telephone, designing airports in Ghana and Ceylon, "take it easy, I'll soon be home;" my stomach a tight drum in which a creature moves at will independent of mine, and the nights I coughed and coughed looking up at the stars the tenants before us had painted on the ceiling of the bedroom overlooking the river, a paradise of solitude where I might die all alone. I might have told her, but she wouldn't had heard me anyway.

"Very clean floor you have!" I said. A direct tactic used to restrain her voice from rising to a higher pitch of excitement. If it becomes any shriller, it'll fragment the glass keeping the rain out of the balcony. I might enjoy her discomfort, but I don't relish the thought of flying glass ruining my makeup.

"Oh that. I don't bother much; the maid comes in once a week."

The little hypocrite, dancing about in a solar heated room big enough to fit in McCrudder's living area and indoor garden with place left over for her tea trolley displaying bottles of Campara, Vermouth, Pina Colada, Scotch Whisky, Napoleon Brandy, propping up the economies of foreign Governments—not to mention her apartment in Eilat, be it as it may talking acquisition to me who owns no Japanese color TV, Danish tuner, who owns no more than a transistor radio and manual typewriter and there she was a martyr to ideals expecting me to sympathize with her observations on the acquisitive society. She'll probably be the first gal on the block to enjoy the sexy backside of Zubin Mehta conducting the Israel Symphony on videotape in the intimacy of her own bedroom.

"Granted, I say evenly, the Jew had always had a spiritual identity with Jerusalem but we live only once for however short a period of time on earth and earth was matter, success was matter and matter was important, success was important. But of course you, who are part of a great humanitarian ideal, a stepping-stone in the realization of the communal dream of homeland, willingly give up the struggle for personal glory."

"It isn't always easy," she says, "but worth the effort to those who understand: 'We may select the battleground, we cannot avoid the battle.' Book of Chuag Tsu, classic of Taoist Literature!"

Tell it to the marines, we've had this argument before, and throwing discretion to the wind, I reached up for a piece of strudel, and bit into that yummy sugar glazed flaky dough and let the crumbs fall on her spotless floor, as they may.

CHAPTER 7

Gloria placed the cake tray on the Italian glass side table and from a shiny, insulated stainless steel jug, poured forth liquid into a gleaming glass tumbler, a concoction of orange, mango, banana and God knows what else she's breezed off on her brand new food processor—swish and there you are.

"Fruit juice?"

"No, but a wee bit of cocoa would do nicely thanks," I'm tempted to say just to be mean just to see her squirm.

I sipped the brash drink, take another bite of the warm sweet dough—when does she have time to do all this baking—look at the rain-laden clouds passing our frame, and not really listening to her. I never realized there were so many shades of gray.

"Remember your affair with David?" she asks and cross-legged sits down on the pillows, which set off her auburn hair and black costume to advantage.

What was she leading up to? Of course I remember David; that flight to Algeria, looking at myself in Gloria's mother-in-law's hall mirror, surprised at my heightened color, the brightness of my eyes. Even my hair had brilliance, not characteristic; I guess I was a walking neon sign, "sexually satisfied in Algeria," on—off, on—off.

I'd picked Algeria not because of my bias for the Middle East but because I felt the need to see Joseph Kadosh, my first husband and kick him in the balls. He'd gotten away with too much: a trip to America on my father's account, a camera and all the dollars he could make selling off my paraphernalia. I had to see what I was capable of, not yet 20 and stupid. I'd had an education all right, which proved my literacy, but it had failed to add to my wisdom. In my need to staff the greatest newsweekly of the age, my ability to discern one action from another was atrophied.

"I'll never forget your condescending remark to me, Josephina,'

"What remark?"

"As if you were the only woman in the world who had ever been loved."

"Were you shocked?"

"Yes!'

"You shouldn't have been, I was not promiscuous. I was not a virgin when I met McCrudder, but damn innocent enough to have been. And he was the most knowledgeable man in the world. He knew everything, understood everything. I couldn't believe a mature, handsome man would see anything in me. I wasn't much to look at."

"You were sensitive, Josephina, and funny. You walked into my strange life and I loved you, even envied you, because you were so sure of yourself, not afraid to send food back when it was not exactly as you thought it should be."

What was she reaching back to find?

"Guy had just had a nasty accident. He'd jumped into the gutter after a ball and the driver, you know how Israeli drivers are, didn't even noticed the child. His wife, who was sitting next to him and happened to be Guy's nursery school teacher, told me that if she hadn't put her foot down hard on the brake, the child would have been dead.

"You're very lucky," the woman repeated, and thereafter made a point of pretending I didn't exist in case I decided to take them to court. My mother-in-law, who should had been with Guy, was busy explaining to Amadeus the butcher, who was always so meticulous about cleanliness, that the reason his business had fallen off lately was because one of the mothers in the nursery school insisted her child had caught lice in his shop. There was an epidemic of lice in the neighborhood at the time.

"Rafcho came home and found the torn sandal on the sidewalk. He knew something was wrong. I didn't find out til much later. I was busy listening to a lecture on Semantics while Guy lay in the hospital.

"There were three women in the ward and a Russian immigrant, a child who had just been circumcised; there was no room in the children's ward. I felt so sorry for the kid whimpering while his mother hugged him, probably hurting him more."

"How old was the child?"

"Twelve."

"Well, McCrudder was thirty-five. He'd been in the army; he could take it."

"Aren't you being a little hard on him?"

"Hard, hell! It was McCrudder who decided two children were enough for any family. McCrudder took all the precautions. Do you know what it meant for a Jewish girl from the Bronx to marry a Catholic?"

"Marrying a Catholic couldn't have been any worse than marrying a waiter and you told me you were married in a synagogue; your husband had converted."

"Yes, McCrudder was willing to follow the rites, even circumcision. I owe him that much."

"What much?"

"His foreskin much."

"You are funny," she said.

"Glad to be of service."

I'm funny; I've traded in an Architect for a Journalist with a simpler head, that's all I wanted, a simple head next to me in bed. Who was I kidding? When I married McCrudder he became more important to me than my mother, my father, my God, my religion, my honor, my life.

"Josephina, come, I'll show you something. She jumps up eagerly. I allow myself to be pulled along like three-year-old Guy following Mamma unwillingly to the grocery, a sad, pouting defiance in his wide-open eyes.

She raises the plastic shutters and the slats roll up with an ear-shattering bang, out of control. "Look" she points to a thin, copper tree, shimmering under a crown of white petals and tightly shut pink buds suggesting hope of beauty yet to come, " the almond tree is in bloom." I fail to react as expected. She drops the shutters with a clatter, motions me back to the Italian cane chair on the veranda. "Whatever made you come back to Israel, Josephina?"

"Well Gloria, you once said, let's always be friends. I know how to pick 'em you said."

"Yes, I loved you then because you knew what you wanted and I was willing to be your friend forever on that simple assumption."

"Ok kid, but we haven't been friends. We have hardly corresponded. I remember writing you from the office when I landed that advertising job, the one I was thrown out of after two weeks because I refused the boss the king's prerogative; I wanted the job badly enough to sleep with him, but I'd just had a miscarriage and my body felt bloated, my spirit empty. It was an emptiness I can't explain, more profound than the imminent death of a parent always hanging over you, one more year and that much closer to being cut off. I gave McCrudder my youth, my belief, my innocence, he and myself gave me a bag full of aphorisms to live by. I so wanted a little girl, I would have swallowed his sex to fertilize my womb and I did, decision for me. I see a little girl growing up before my eyes licking his testicles like a bitch. And I resent his making that and she was only the stuff of dreams.

"He led me on for years, for *years*. I don't mind his inability to satisfy me, I do mind the fact that he pretended he was giving me what I wanted. I found myself not understanding and he, the owner of the knowledge, played with my feelings. I grew colder and colder as the realization of his physical infirmity grew clearer and clearer and he hated my knowledge, it spoiled his power over me. It isn't that I don't love him; it isn't that I expected him to be an A1 lover. I'd had a better lover before him; the trouble was that he didn't want me and I don't have the energy to encourage a reticent male into action. Love and sex don't always go together."

McCrudder touched my arm. The warmth of his palm warms my heart rendered lonely by the pretense of loving New Hampshire in Autumn. The gold and russet leaves fell on my hand as we walked towards the house. We were visiting Neil's sister and his mother whom I like. It's Thanksgiving. My flat crepe shoes screamed danger. If I walked too fast, I would slip on decaying leaves, fall, be paralyzed, sit forever on the porch painted white each Spring and stare at the sky peering helplessly out to find myself-more of myself than the shaded portion of my history loved by master who had created shade. I wanted my freedom because he was too smart, too knowledgeable of me—a me I cannot change in his presence. And anyway it was he who was the Jew, he who had read the Bible, who reads history, who discusses the bad hand the Jews were dealt in Christian Europe. His reasoning would put Gloria's meandering thoughts on the subject to shame. It was he who had become whole within himself, finally understanding what I, the indigenous member of the tribe, cannot offer him.

"Modern woman," she looks at me meaningfully. What was she leading up to? "was attuned to utter self-destruction beyond vanity. No longer aware of her role, which was the basis of her power; she sleeps as if she had taken an overdose of mandrake root. In the book of Genesis, Reuben, Leah's son having found a mandrake in the field at harvest time and gives it to his mother; her sister, Rachel, asks for it, as well as for her turn to sleep with Jacob, their mutual husband, that night. It was a minor request since Leah had borne him five sons while Rachel, for whose hand he'd worked 14 years, was barren. You know, of course, what he said to Rachel when she complained of her barren state? You see, it's the woman who controls birth, not man who doesn't accept the responsibility, the life-giving element of nature was controlled by woman.

"The mandrake," she looks out in space, "was purple like the violet, but its root was deep, very deep. You can't pull it out of the earth with your hands. You attach the root to a dog's tail at full moon and it comes out of the earth screeching in protest, it does not want to be detached. You are not to touch it if you value your life. But, if all the rules are followed, the mandrake root will make a woman fertile. Though, because it looks like the male reproductive organ, man in his vanity had always thought its magical powers of birth and death were his for the taking, increasing his virility, which meant aggression.

"Vanity, thy name was man, was more correct you see. Actually the mandrake root had the narcotic quality of making man less violent, and woman more giving. But the point was that man was dependent on woman to arouse his virility, make the necessary conquest not an aggressive act of violence but a garden of birth. We are mandrake roots," she stage whispers across to me, "we attach to the earth with fervor and man will not displace us no matter how he tries."

"I couldn't rape McCrudder or force him to give me another girl baby; the Mandrake doesn't grow in Central Park you know. 'And if it turns out to be a boy,' he asked, 'what will you do, drown it, put it out on the mountains to die?'"

I excuse myself to go to the toilet. It was sparkling clean, but I line the seat with paper, pick a tiny piece of fluff from the hand towel, and can't be too careful! What a jackass I make of myself, when I opt for honesty. How objective was truth anyway and we are ever dealing in truths. McCrudder deals in truths. He designs a bridge, if it stays up, he's created a truth if it falls down, and he's created an untruth. If he builds a glass house, 100 stories high, it was called beautiful as truth when all it was grandiose, pretentious nonsense, an edifice to accumulated wealth and power. The higher you go, the more you feel your power. But McCrudder was not satisfied with mere power and glory, fame and Frouma; no, he had to plant tomatoes and dwarf fruit trees on a terrace 22 floors above the ground, earthy and celestial truth.

"The painter," Gloria said as I sat down, "who whitewashed our walls was a defrocked priest." Spicy gossip. "He had that mincing, soft-spoken holiness about him like a fool or a saint—a quality both sexy and holy. He told Yaron and me, as he sipped the coffee I'd prepared for him during the breakfast break he insisted on taking—I'm an expert in Turkish coffee, Rafcho's mother—which he'd become disillusioned with the church and longed to return to his village. He finally did, married a young girl and adopted his brother's child. A passion so long pent up, he told us, unwrapping the sandwich he'd brought along, was not easily set free. He was still celibate, too deeply indoctrinated to change, his body too used to the white alb stitched and embroidered by pious women who believed in his purity. His wife was young; she would learn to live without that which she had never known. He was no longer a Catholic. He now believed only in the words of the Bible without embellishment, without pageantry. He sat under a tree in the village and taught the children, those who wanted to be taught. I could feel the devils that had forced him out of the church. I was afraid of him and glad Yaron had not left the house.

"He went over to the bookcase, found the Bible and began chanting lines from Exodus and explaining them to Yaron. Yaron argued with him. They were both reading the same text but their interpretations were so different. I was so proud of Yaron's familiarity with The Book, but then our children learn the Bible from infanthood in the public schools. Josephina, no matter what you tell me about your marriage, your husband did bring up your boys for you while you were gallivanting round the world reporting facts based on little information. Did you ever ask yourself if your husband enjoyed playing mother? I think he just felt greater responsibility for your boys than you did."

"You may be right. McCrudder was a good father. He did worry about baths and washing behind the ears. He was into loving fatherhood long before it became chic, so sure of his maleness, he didn't had to play up to the social norm of what a male was supposed to be, but Gloria, he doesn't love me. We've grown tired of each other. He's stopped needing me. I've seen him in the light of day. Sex in the light of day. Explicit pleasure, a kick in the pants."

"Pants?" She glares at me suddenly angry again. What had I done now? "That's the trouble with you, love me, love me." You're USA, Western Hemisphere Capitalist selfish. Josephina, you are not a loving person. Even your woes sound like hashed over movie scripts."

"That's your interpretation isn't it? You're welcome to it." And all this because I hadn't gone ecstatic over a blooming almond tree or was it the mandagora root. "No matter how marvelous a father McCrudder was," I tell her what she wants to hear, "I did feel guilty about the kids, slightly guilty. I bought them too many gifts trying to make up for it: ski jackets zippered on the diagonal, designed by Pierre Cardin straight from Cannes, black leather shorts from the Austrian Alps, too many clothes that they refused to wear. They were in the T-shirt, dungaree stage, and wouldn't be seen dead in the fancy duds."

"My kids wore hand-me-downs and I was desperate," she said and she brought a tray of dried fruit up to my nose. "Oh Josephina, I do love you, I always fall for your stories."

That's me, Ms. Comedy herself, always leave 'em laughing. I don't want to argue, so I bit into a date. "He named the boys Jeremiah and Ovadia! Had you ever heard such stupid names for babies?"

"Babies grow."

"But still how many American kids do you know who answer to the name Ovadia or Jeremiah? But that was McCrudder all over again."

We brought them up with such care, such enthusiasm. When Jeremiah was born my cup truly flowed over. He was a beautiful child. Neil was thrilled by the miracle; those toes, those hands were once a part of us and we were one. Neil recorded the baby's voice, measured him daily. I kept a diary and we both agreed to keep our respective parents far away from him lest they soil this paragon of beauty with their old world ideas, old world curses, which I suspected had come over in the pockets of grandparents, under the planks of ships from the ports of Dublin and Dubrovnik, except on babysitting days, which our parents at first took in turn.

Neil's mother lulled the boys to sleep with Irish lullabies, little endearments and Neil's father, on hands and knees, followed the kids around telling them stories of the Little People in hazel wood, Celtic knights whipping the rain with a broadsword, killing the dragon, saving the Princess.

"By the way, Gloria, do you realize that the Jews of Dalmatia, where my mother's family originally comes from, were sent by the Romans to trade in slaves; that's Slavs. The Jews there speak a unique Yiddish, a combination of Hebrew, Latin, and Serb, I believe. Not too many were left after the great Gestapo conflagration."

"Are you making that up, Josephina?"

"No, there was some truth in it. Anyway, we couldn't allow our parents to instill stories of rebellion into our sons. There was rebellion enough on both sides of the family. Neil's grandfather had been a blacksmith who dreamt of being a free Irish and paid with his life for his ideas and my grandfather, on my mother's side had been a blacksmith who dreamt of a free unfettered community of men in a red-bannered world and ended up in Hitler's crematorium. That's what brought us together in Central Park, a comprehension of ourselves as the descendants of rebels, blacksmiths and seaport dwellers, lovers of fish and the oceans.

Men were still dying for Ulster and Communism and I didn't want our sons to be part of the bloody mess the old world had turned into. Neil did not press the point. When Jeremiah was 13 years old, he begged, he sulked, he threatened to do away with himself if we didn't send him to a Catholic parochial school and then he did a complete about face, went out to Texas to study Agricultural Engineering where he was seduced by an Israeli woman, an official of the kibbutz movement who represented Israel at the State Farmers' Industrial Fair. She was bowled over by Jeremiah's computerized farming acumen, his easy acquaintance with automated, integrated, component sprinkling systems which were his own brainchild. She attacked him with a barrage of brochures. He got his degree extra quick, borrowed money from Neil's father and off he went to the Arava desert. I don't doubt my sojourns in this country influenced him in some way, but it was McCrudder who was really to blame. I was hardly around enough to do much damage. It was he who fed the boys stories from the Bible before they could read, it was he who spoke Hebrew to them on whimsical expeditions into Bronx Park where they 'dug up' ancient Phoenician and Philistine strongholds. When Jeremiah arrived in Ashdod Port with the gadgetry he'd procured, the official's daughter came to meet him. It was love at first sight. Mother knew what she was doing. Now I'm supposed to adore Eudora. Jeremiah wants me to love her, as if love grows on apple trees.

'Mother, I hope you get along with Eudora. I want you to like her, it's important you know. She's part Irish.' That's the first thing he told me in the kibbutz dining room before the wedding. He wanted me to love his bride, because she was part Irish like his father. I should have been touched. He may be phased out with amour, head over heels and all that but hay should I love her? I have, in fact, almost decided to hate her.

"Ovadia goes to school in Massachusettes, had his heart set on studying International Law, or so he told me, though he may be in Carmel teaching surfing to underprivileged kids during term break. From Law, to Politics, to human relations—setting the world right. I sort of desperately hope he's in Boston.

Why couldn't my sons have turned out nice middle class boys dealing in nice middle class profession, designing software in Southern California, gliding just for fun over the surf in Monterey Bay where we spent our summers with Mother and Janos all tidy and *comme il faut*. Actually I haven't heard from him for quite a while now."

"Do you know who Ovadia was?"

The nerve! Asking such a question of the wife of a firm believer. "Not really, you tell me," pretending ignorance for her sake.

"First of all he lived at the same time as the Prophet Jeremiah. If we work at it, we may discover what your husband had in mind when he gave them those names. Ovadia, one of the theories goes, was the son of an Edomite who had become a Jew. This was only theory of course. Just a minute, I'll show you something." I watch slim, attractive Gloria rise from her pillows, an island of bliss, open her mouth and shout. "Yaron, where's the Tnach? The Tnach! I want to show Josephina that picture of Petra in the Tnach!"

"Don't get hysterical Ma," Yaron shouts back opening his door letting out the rhythmical base drumming stereophonic sound, volume meant to tear the music of the spheres to fragmented remembrances. Pink Floyd, "The Wall."

"Y've just got ta hear the lyrics Ma", "What d'ya think?" Ovadia reading the words aloud to me with intensity, as if true revelation was secretly coded within them. "Cheap philosophy for the masses," I say in response. He smiles that crooked shy smile, "Oh man!" he said in desperation at my ignorance, three summers ago when I was still a mother and he still a child.

The boy comes into the room holding a heavy volume in his arms, an electric guitar hanging round his neck.

"Say hello to Josephina."

"Hello Josephina."

"Hello Yaron. If you hand me my bag there, I have something for you." I take out a chess game I'd been given, courtesy of Singapore Airlines, and hand it to him remembering other little presents I'd taken out of other bags. Yaron seemed pleased with my inconsequential gift, tousle headed child, 14 years or more, short for his age, soft down on suntanned skin, a body yet unformed, part female, a clay pipe in his supple-wristed hand, a wreath of pink and blue roses on his head, boy in blue, adolescence forever Picasso. I look deeply into the boy's eyes and I know he isn't as naïve as he looks.

"Here," he shows me a picture, "this was what Mother was talking about."

"Yaron, please shut the door. That noise was killing me." I watch him bound into the sound, already lost within the waves.

"Look closely Josephina, this was an Edomite dwelling. What was fascinating was that this Greek-like temple was sculptured out of sandstone. If you look closely, it's a false front like a movie set. The natives were cave dwellers, lived in the hollowed out rock in the back."

"Putting up a social front eh Gloria?" My attempt at humor falls flat on its face. "What does all this have to do with Ovadia?"

"The Greek temples were open to the elements, set to a mathematical perfection, the gold rectangle, the symphony of life and art, calculated, unafraid to stand free because they were based in mind. The Pythagorean mysteries. These columns had their hearts in the rock, their center in the rock, fearful the structure will fall if freed. Ovadia understood that man must stand free surrounded by the elements, question their essence, unafraid of the answer even if it threatens to splinter a way of life."

"We all fall apart sooner or later."

"What lasts longer, the search for truth or this bastion of rock?"

"Well Petra, judging by what you're showing me, was still standing and so are the Pharaohic mausoleums."

"I love Jeremiah, it's such a lovely name, say it, you had to open your mouth wide and let the sound reach out. Jeremiah! The music, the rhythm, his sincerity. He's a prophet of love.

He never wavers. Even when he was thrown into a deep chasm to die of hunger, he was not cowed. He felt his message was God's message; the people must free themselves from bonds of matter, the sacrificial implements, which served as a substitute for, thought. Jeremiah! The sound embraces you and you know you are close to God, close to perfection, which is beauty and the knowledge of God—simple, unattainable always tantalizingly near when you make the effort. Perhaps some people reach that aesthetic state of perfection through pure mathematics but I couldn't, I didn't.

"Are you happy Gloria?

"Yes."

"Would you have changed anything in your life?"

"I would have changed the evil in man's heart, the screaming of people dying in war, in furnaces, the ridiculous throwing of bombs. I would have stopped destruction. Oh how I wish I had a Japanese garden, a garden with gravel and waterways and trees and rocks, a shadowed paradise full of mystery. You know when Buddha was asked to define the Ultimate reality, he pointed to a flower.

"The lotus," she rises turning round like a clockwork Chinese doll, clockwise counting 'one, two, three.' The five petals of the lotus, each one a phase of life, Birth, Initiation, Marriage, Rest from labor, Death, eleven, twelve." She turns counterclockwise, studied turn, slow count.

"Do you make up your own mythology as you go along?" I ask dizzy watching her move around the clock.

"Oh Josephina, I believe each individual has the right—no, the obligation, to find in himself the essence of himself. Only then can he successfully give of himself."

"You are an idealist."

"No, a Taoist, spiritual and physical self discipline does lead to an awareness of the essential oneness of the universe, the single path."

"It may also lead you to a stoicism where you don't act at all. How's that going to get you a state for the Jew?"

"Each of us in our own imagined circle but part of the group of dancers following the master, concentrating on the rhythm of the earth as we each concentrate on our own rhythm, a clockwork independent within its shell but aware that it's a part of other independent clockworks. My Tai Chi teacher was more dancer than philosopher and so we dance in rhythm with the world, old people and young, women of beauty and less beautiful specimens of the human race."

"Gloria this was the twentieth century not the tenth century rectangular grid of the T'ang capital."

"You're right, that's why I can only speak for Israel and not the world. Our rivers and are not yellow and our earth not red, but we must understand that our garden, our world garden was simultaneously physical and spiritual. When we get our heart and head together, we'll get our ethics, our mores together."

"And then Israel will be the ideal religio-political entity, a perfect little Vatican imbroglio."

"You haven't heard a word I've said Josephina. If we are going to survive as a state, it will be because we are smarter and better than anyone else. At least those should be our goals to use our heads to maneuver ourselves around the political entities surrounding us, and our hearts to check ourselves against the moral code of Moses."

Gee whiz now I've had enough. I realize the girl's sick in the head, pirouetting round in union with the cosmic waste and void, presuming, though, she hasn't left the general area of her home for over two decades, she had been party to the one great event of the century, the foundation of the Jewish state, which given full rein of the imagination, was almost her own doing.

Intimations of McCrudder, driving towards the orphaned terraces of Jerusalem, files of information in his head; which of Solomon's wives built which raised dais to which god on which of the pebbly strata, giving names to plants that might had grown in Solomon's gardens, the hanging gardens of Babylon, figuring out dates for destruction of Solomon's temple, the exact date of the Exodus, true identification of Hyksos—not Asiatics, not Trojans from Hissarlik in NW Turkey—but Arabs, nomads from ancient Mecca, the Amalek. Chronological tables, comparing written documents, chards of pottery, assessing variable levels of probability, signs, interconnections and the upheavals of draught, meteors, floods and other disasters; low dates, medium, late dates. What a strange idea, because words sound alike, they are alike. A rose was rose was a rose just isn't so; a rose was the rose in our mind, the rose in our heart, the rose in the garden. McCrudder, you and your metaphysical meanderings on well traveled routes between the physical and the metaphysical. I break up a twenty year old marriage over the name in the rose in an ancient tomb, which McCrudder calls lotus, let him call a sink a honeysuckle vine, what difference does it make, but the absurd thing was that it does matter.

I can forgive him the nights when moved to tenderness, I stick my index finger up my vagina, feel the soft tissue, cry at my dissatisfying self love while he, secure as a kitten, lies folded and content on his side sleeping soundly. I can forgive him making the children a copy of himself, but I cannot stand his knowing more than I. He knows everything. He can fix a leaking roof, trace the source of damp in the wall, probably bring down the rains if need be. He reads the Bible in Hebrew and Cicero in Latin. He speaks Modern Greek with the peasants in Cyprus and God, Turkish with the Turks exchanging words with a crow woman standing against a white stucco wall so that she laughs a full gummed, coral laughter. And yet everyone loves him. He plays the pipe and the Oud and sings like a tenor in a vaudeville show and I was his ladylove. I can fault him only on fussiness. He demands clean rooms, well-ironed shirts stacked one atop the other in a closet reeking of verbena, and food in pretty color combinations on sparkling plates. He was in fact everything I wish I were. Thinking of him dead, such a convenient end to a relationship, the merry widow more appealing reality than the gay divorcee.

I was a liar. The sex might not always have been good and there were those several times my soul, bond slave to my body, shattered. But there were times I was loved generously and well, with my skin alive, my being softened and I thanked God Neil McCrudder had been given me as husband and lover.

I suddenly think of Mailla, and hope David was reading her manuscript, carefully this time because I asked him to. He'd do anything for me. It might turn out to be the masterpiece of the age, reveal the times as they are, an interim period between debatable theories which strip the earth of coal, dig into its heart for oil, put solar ships into space—never let the fields go fallow. If you do not learn by experience, turbulence will teach you nature's lesson and we'll go whirling round and round the overheated, discarded plant looking for homeport. Why can't I love David as he loves me?

"Ima," Yaron shouts from his room, "I'm taking my bike."

"Have you eaten your lunch?" she shouts back.

"I've got no time, Mom please. I've got a football game with he kids from the Military Academy."

"Come over here, Yaron." The boy came into the room.

"Sit down and eat your lunch. It's on the table."

"Ok."

"Wash your hands."

"I did. Oh Ima, not fish again," his voice comes to us from the kitchen, "I'm not eating the fish."

"You'd better eat it," Gloria shouts back, "we're having the stuffed eggplant." She turns to me. "I've cooked some stuffed eggplant for lunch. My mother-in-law's recipe. Actually I make it better."

"I'm going," Yaron announced

"Be back by five, Yaron, please sweetheart. Be here when the groceries are delivered. Take care. Say goodbye to Josephina."

"Goodbye Josephina." He bangs the front door shut. The large apartment was suddenly very still.

CHAPTER 8

It's raining again, heavy, splashing rain weeping feldspar brilliance while blocking out the view.

My mother-in-law never let me look at her photograph albums. She hid her youth from me like a miser. It was only when we were sitting "Shiva," the seven days of ritual mourning for the dead, I found their hiding place near her bed. Do you know what it feels like to be free to walk through a person's life when she was no longer there, handle a lifetime of secrets, watch them turn to dust, uninteresting memorabilia she guarded with a jealous mind I resent even now.

Gloria sighed and wriggling round, forced her heels deeper into her crotch, knees flatter on the lovely colored pillows. "A little over a year ago, Rafcho and I went to a family wedding with my mother-in-law dressed in flowing orange organza. 'Don't you dare!' I shouted at her across the Cornish hen. I mean going to a wedding with a corpse while my husband dances with the bride he had fished out of the swimming pool, the hotel guests in tiers above like a wedding cake applauding, was bad enough, but having to jump into a pool after her, her false teeth, large tombstones in a skull of paper thin skin sporting a platinum blonde wig , mouth to mouth resuscitation to a cadaver, was too much. She came very close to me. 'Call the waitress!' She ordered in an imperceptible whisper. The tired waitress read her desires correctly, thankfully placed our uneaten birds into the plastic bag my mother-in-law held open for her under the table, daintily between the fingertips of both her hands. Do you understand what I'm trying to say Josephina?"

"No, not exactly."

"When she felt the end was near, she made it to the hospital on her own by bus. Before going off, she phoned to say she'd been watching "Dallas" on TV and she suddenly felt all her organs breaking up inside of her.

'Ima, can I help you?' I asked. 'No,' she answered, 'I'll be all right.' I should have gone with her.

"That evening I stood at the foot of her bed, her eyes were colorless liquid splits in transparent skin, her fingers curved like the claws of a bird, nails manicured and polished silvery coral, her favorite color. It looked indecent that polish sparkling with dewy life. I had this urge to get some acetone and clean her nails, but I held back. I'd bought her two coral gladioli. I handed them to the nurse who put them in a vase close to her. 'Thank you,' she whispered under her shallow breath. Her knees were folded so high above her chest I could hardly see her lips. Then very slowly she lowered her legs, her lips twitched, her whole body begging me to hold her frenzied fingers. Josephina, I couldn't go round to her, put my ear down close to her mouth, hear the last moment revelation she was fighting to impart to me. I couldn't fulfill her wish, instead I ran over to the nurse. The plastic bag with the important-looking directions had collapsed

'All right,' the nurse said dryly with a shrug of the shoulder, and I running back shouted, 'What a beautiful view' and stared past her, out the picture window where three palm trees, great amber sacs of fruit below joyous leaves, clustered. She saw through me, let out a wisp of air in resignation, her upper body shuddered and then everything was still. I walked out on her in her moment of need playing my game to the last and that's what bothers me. She had quelled my feeling for her with her terrible independence. She needed nobody, nothing. That night she pinned herself together and died, leaving no vibrations to haunt, to harm, no pulse of being, as if she had never been."

Gloria settled further down on her pillowed throne, upturned palms gently on her knees. "Once, when my mother-in-law was recuperating from an overdose of a cancer healing drug which burnt the skin on her breast to raw flesh, I bought her a book of 19th century landscape paintings. 'Look at it,' I told her, 'look at beautiful things, think beautiful!' She rebuffed me, wanted to fight away death with a studied routine she never varied from food, a walk, her volunteer work, the Pink Ladies in the hospital. I wanted her to die according to my principles, looking passively at beautiful reproductions. She wanted to fight death with all the energy at her disposal. Josephina, believe me; I kept trying to make her friend, pretending to be the person she would had wanted her son to marry. I was always a step below her standard. And in the niche above the bathroom, rotting in straw cases, the naphthalene drenched dresses of a dowry, hand embroidered in Varna. If my Aunt Frouma hadn't remembered me in her will, I'd still be living there

Staring out at the curtain of rain, I can just see her mother-in-law jumping into the pool, Kennedy era elegance transported across the oceans decades after the act, she who had consoled me for hours one Saturday after in 1963 on my way back from Algeria—sentimental journey through Wadi Nisnas where I'd lived with my first husband for two nights in 1958. There were garlic wreaths drying on the balcony, tin cans labeled "5 kg pickles" planted in sweet smelling herbs, weeds, carnations—alleyways hanging direction East to West, becoming other, becoming chalk.

Photograph: Fair-haired four-year-old Hannah, her mother had just died and her father, the rabbi, had married her younger sister, as was the custom among the religious. Stepmother. Shy, tallow-haired, braided innocence in a room obviously not hers, looking at her sister's clothes on the double bed.

Photograph: Mother, tall dark young woman, her waist pinched in the Victorian style of her time, her husband older than she, a head of black hair to match his shining eyes, stands proud beside his wife.

Photograph: stepmother, very young, wounded resentment in her eyes. She had lost her right to a fiancé of her own who would court her with boxes of bonbons wrapped in cellophane and large satin bows, and instead had been forced to fit herself into her dead sister's life. It must have been terrible finding your sister's possessions in the closet and her child on the floor. She would have died, her only escape, if her husband, who had married her as a social necessity and could never divorce the sister nor bring back the wife, hadn't died first.

Photograph: Hannah's nubile beauty smiling proudly as she recites a poem by Bialik in the Spanish-Jewish tongue, which she had translated from the Hebrew.

"Senor Papoo," she told her grandfather on her twelfth birthday," I've made up my mind, I'm going to Palestine." She'd been a good runner, had almost made the Maccabee Sporting team at 14, which was going to Palestine to compete with clubs from other countries When the girl was 18, she got herself engaged by proxy to a third cousin living in Haifa.

Photograph: school picture, cousin, lover to whom she had promised her troth, found her married and pregnant in Haifa.

"Ah!" Gloria's mother-in-law said, "I was sure I'd look my fiancé in the eye and say no my love and move on. I would never had believed I'd become a rare animal in a cage."

It was a marriage of convenience so she could get an entry visa into Palestine from the British Mandate Government. She'd wanted to become a physical education teacher. When Nissim Calderon, the "fiancé," saw her, he refused to let her go, married her that very week. She showed me her wedding gift, dull white sapphires in a badly wrought gold ring, as little gold as possible, just enough to hold the stone in place—the times were hard, and so they lived unhappily every after.

I never knew whether I was comforting Gloria's mother-in-law or being comforted by her that day so long ago, but I remember that I left that evening with a feeling of buoyancy, a feeling that my youth must not be squandered and I blessed her.

I went back to the hotel, the same hotel room Joseph and I had shared several years back on our wedding night. Not much had changed. The long line of noise came up through the storm windows meant to cushion sound as before. The smell of busted pipes seething excrement into concrete walls was still pungent.

This time I didn't even bother with the possibility of crossing international borders North into Lebanon, go South to Cairo instead during one of the hysteria inspiring get-togethers of the multitudinous crowd clambering for a sight of Nasser, the conquering disciple—one more demigod come with promises of a chicken in each pot, a steed in each stable. Being part of the tidal wave of men shouting to a prescribed script in rhythm was the most frightening experience of my life. I found myself taken up in the general frenzy for war in the name of Allah and would had run barefoot into the desert sands, climbed a tank turret, rushed in against the "Zionist pig" with no thought for my life, in the knowledge that as food for flies, vultures, snakes and curious centipedes, I had fulfilled my earthly self.

I had never felt such relief to get out of a place, as I felt then. Religious ecstasy in the name of whatever principle, crowds of people losing their ability to think as individuals, transferring themselves into pure emotion for an abstract cause, was abominable. Yet, such heights of ecstasy are not everyday occurrences. How many of us reach ecstasy of any kind?

The tenants downstairs, a religious couple with two daughters, immigrants from Poland with a secret they jealously guarded, treading lightly on the balls of their feet in felt house slippers lest they share a sound with the enemy outside. Everyone was potential danger. Shah! I walk through a buffer zone of silence at their front door which, if trespassed, would destroy a world shuttered in by sun split slats, bumpy remains of yellow paint hinting at another way of life, clasped tightly to the window by iron cast knobs of Minerva's head.

Then Amadeus, the butcher, moved away. but I couldn't help seeing those hunks of meat, dismembered carcasses on hooks, brisket, steak, a rack of ribs, shoulder clods, dripping blood around him as I slept with my child in my arms in the suspended silence of later afternoon Amadeus was ambitious, worked hard to satisfy the customer, but the place was a maze of political wheeler dealing. He knew nothing of the complexity of religious meat affairs.

The Torah decrees that one may not taste meat before one had separated a portion for the priest, who was totally landless, and a tithe for the Levite, the choicest pieces of liver, kidney, sweetbreads and brain. Amadeus moved away, opened a non-kosher store in the German enclave on the Carmel and was doing well. But then it was a great unknown world for him and a little tragedy for me, his moving came as it did so soon after Pnina, the grocer's wife, died It was she who convinced me fainting spells were labor pains, sent me off to hospital with good words to have my baby. My obstetrician, a severe lady, said she was going to Romania on vacation. I walked to the window without my shirt on in her colleague's office. He looked at me with disapproval as if I were a woman walking naked in a public garden, and I, alone, screaming Mother! Mother! The doctor peered disinterestedly down at me, drinking coffee. The next morning the midwife comes in, "you were wonderful" she said to one woman after the other, and just walks by my bed. I had cried to the heavens for help, no stoic expression of pain as was the custom; and the other mothers in the ward complaining, "the American used too many diapers." Mother showed up a few days later for a weekend in Haifa. "Although the doctors in New York," she wrote, "were not able to find out what caused my pain in Israel, I was feeling no pain now. Once I regain my strength and when my leg loosens up and ceases to be stiff, I will put out of my mind the unfortunate experience I had in Israel with my health."

She couldn't decide how to sign her letter, so she just left a gaping space. Pnina's husband sold the grocery and then there were no smiles left at all. Then Rafcho's brother was killed in Sinai, went up in smoke in a tank in Abu Agila on the way to Suez. It was a beautifully cool day in June, my mother-in-law dried eyed and stoic served coffee to those who had seen the death notice on the door and came up. They cried. I cried. The boy's girlfriend was in shock. She couldn't believe life had been denied her lover.

And then Miklos, the boarder left. He was a strong, tall man with a lovely gray mustache and soft gray eyes. He'd ridden a horse in his youth, brought up as a peasant on a farm. And then he took his trombone, the accordion with which he doused us with Balkan dance music and ran off with a base fiddler. We once went to hear her play, lots of oomph, a woman who never grew out of being a child prodigy, never adjusted to her mediocrity, inviting applause with a bravado crescendo and a raise of the bow. We clapped like crazy, more for her style than the sound of her music. I believe it was love. She was a recent immigrant from Budapest and under the law of return, as the ingathering of the tribes of Israel was called, was entitled to an import tax-free refrigerator, a meaningful bounty, as you are aware, in this country.

For me, his leaving meant no more Saturday afternoons smoking cigarettes, sipping slivovitz, watching him take the pocketknife he carried with him on the death march in Hungary from his baggy gray trousers, carefully fold back several blades, inspect their honed edges on his fingernail, flip one back, wipe it scrupulously clean on a white handkerchief, slice the spicy pork sausage, stab it on the point of the chosen blade, offering me a slice, which he knew I would refuse, as I dreamt of white poppies and yellow butterflies in my very own apartment, an impossible opium illusion and then it happened. Aunt Frouma died; that was her death was not fortunate, but you know what I mean.

It was then I got entangled in red-tape, minor officials, little people who had been trampled upon by the German in Europe, the British in Palestine, suddenly with the power and authority at their fingertips, masters all. Your future depended on their signature, an indecipherable squiggle. They didn't even have to identify themselves with a readable given name, a family name; they were responsible to none but themselves.

eReticent anger, which only generations of time could temper or so I thought, but I was wrong. Some probably inherited the physical and spiritual disability of the recipient of German experimentation, but that child upstairs, as if by miracle, turned into a medical doctor and another child down the street grew to womanhood and had a family with all the habits of the bourgeois grandparents, piano and ballet lessons for the children."

"My mother-in-law," Gloria said contemplating the brilliant line of sea foam below—if you look at it too long, you're apt to go berserk. "was a believer in the 'scientific,' which she called modern meaning better, and considered herself free, having disposed of every incantation, magic potion, household ghost stamped upon her childhood memory. As for God, let him be, he doesn't bother you, you don't bother him.

"Near her grave, a man was kneeling, blackening faded letters on a tombstone with a fine brush dipped rhythmically into a small square bottle labeled 'Oregano.'

"I watched the ball of chemicals like a malign sun set over the bay each night, so menacing and still, disintegrate my mother-in-law's newly laid memorial stone, erase her name from the face of the earth as it had erased her body. It was then I felt my own inadequacy, my own short span on life. Even now she makes me feel guilty to be sitting here with you in the afternoon, not peeling potatoes or darning socks."

"I have this feeling Gloria,"—I can be brutally honest, this too was an aspect of truth, "that her greatest regret in departing this world was that she didn't get to see the next installment of 'Dallas' on T.V.; never found out who shot J.R. It seems to me that she lived a whole life in the shadow of her ideal of self regretting her inability to live life at the peak of that one last dance in the gas-lit ballroom in Varna."

Gloria, there on her pillow, looks down at her hands shedding tears. I could feel the rising welt hot on my cheek as if she had physically slapped me.

"Please, please," she said getting up, coming over to me and hugged me tightly, "please never say anything like that again, even if it's true."

CHAPTER 9

"Find a newsworthy context, we'll see about it." HEADLINE STOPPER: Tarararam! Lillian Ciegal

Photographs: nameless faces, a moment of life, creations torn out of context, out of association pick up a random black and white photograph whirling in the sand grit breeze in Tel Aviv. Someone bothered to photograph the man painting the whore in the doorway—business as usual as the bombs recreate the topography of a town erased from the face of the earth, proof of life—no longer relevant.

How can I explain to my editor that tens of thousands of fathers and mothers and undernourished babies in Ethiopia, victims of natural disaster and possibly bad politics, was not the same as concentration camps in Europe during the Second World War? No one cares enough to be convinced.

"There's something that's always bothered me, Josephina," Gloria repeated my name to get my attention. "Rafcho and I came to your hotel, that sleazy hotel you'd insisted on staying in on purpose to show us up, or were you trying to repent for your sins by suffering? I asked you to come with us to a restaurant, the Bulgarian one down near the port. It was dark, there were not enough streetlights; the place looked deserted. I never liked to walk in the Arab quarter of town at night. I hung on to Rafcho, but he didn't offer enough protection. You walked into that restaurant and demanded shashlick. When it came you said the meat was not lamb. You refused to believe the waiter when he said it was. You didn't believe Rafcho either when he told you the waiter was an Arab. You were so influenced by your own copy, you couldn't accept the fact that Arabs lived in Haifa, worked and studied quite calmly alongside the Jewish community. 'He's a Christian,' Rafcho explained to you, 'not a terrorist.' You were so antagonistic. 'He may not be a terrorist,' you said, 'but neither was this lamb.' You'd been around and you knew the difference. This was turkey, you said. The poor waiter, being loyal to his employer, kept insisting that the dry flesh cut up into cubes too perfect was anything but the best lamb available in the market. You refused to eat it and told Rafcho not to pay for your portion, which he never meant to in the first place, he couldn't afford it. He was broke and I was mortified.

"Whenever I remember that feeling of being so economically dependent on a man, so thoroughly immobilized by poverty and a sense of duty as wife, mother, daughter-in-law, it was awful. Rafcho's salary as a clerk in the Cement Works was low, and I just couldn't bring myself to ask for money from someone who was almost a stranger if the truth be known, I feel a flash of shame that just eats me up. I mean Israel completely blotted out my personality. I had to start life over again, newly married to a Bulgarian-Israeli not as a middle class college educated American woman, but as a lower middle class drudge. I began having babies and no matter how hard Rafcho worked, he never earned enough.

"I remember the three of us looking at each other. You understood the situation and got up to pay the bill telling the waiter, as we walked out, that there would be no tip for his services. He looked sorry to have treated a guest badly, but his boss came first. I envied your lifestyle that was so different from mine. I felt so downtrodden, so rotten; it's haunted me since."

"Water under the bridge, Man," that's what my son Ovadia recently told me when I tried to apologize for having been away from home to often when he and his brother were growing up. Gloria, forget it!"

Guilty? Maybe I should had stayed put at work, forever, and candle melting to a heap of wax under a buzzing fluorescent replica of daylight. Obituary: She, who had known her place, humble, as it may have been, unlauded during 30 years of selfless service, never giving up the spark of hope for a better deal, had now left us. She was a poet of her kind.

"When I met Rafcho," she's back at true confessions, "I fell in love with his directness, his honesty. I thought we simply used different words for the same conceptions. And even though he wasn't a great lover like George, my boyfriend, I found his world more satisfying. You Josephina wouldn't understand because you had never given yourself to anyone, you're too busy describing you out of identity, covering events with a jaundiced eye. Rafcho gave me back my self respect."

"That's a pretty suit you had on." She'd changed her Chinese pajamas for street clothes while I admired clouds. She looked sophisticated in the well cut brown tweed, buttercup shirt, pale yellow silk ascot, gold gypsy earrings, pierced ears, primitive svelte but inside she was a quagmire of the crap she had inculcated into her during these last two decades.

"Rafcho," she said testily not even acknowledging my compliment with a nod or a smile," may not be perfect but then neither was I." She struggled to put on a tawny boot bending way back on her pillows for leverage. "You never did like Rafcho, did you?"

"He felt intimidated by me. I do that to men who are not sure of themselves." I give her one of my standard answers with the realization that maybe she doesn't like Rafcho as much as she pretends. "Why did you marry Rafcho, simple Rafcho without a High School diploma to his name? I'd never have married a man without a University degree," I say in an attempt at humor, after all I'd married Joseph and he was no college Professor.

"First of all, Josephina," she struggles on with her other boot, "simple was an adjective and though I might have begun teaching English without knowing what an adjective was, you world-weary wordmonger should know that adjectives are given to interpretation. Rafcho's simplicity, as you call it was seed, the word that opens Aladdin's treasure cave, sesame seed the source of oil and sauces and cakes, the flavor, the inner strength. You can depend on sesame for life. Have you ever tried feeding hunger with diamonds from sacks, bangles served on mortarboards, the kind you hang tassels from? Rafcho's simplicity was his strength; I need a man with inner strength, a person I can depend on. 'As an unintelligent man seeks for the abode of music in the body of the lute so does he look for the soul within the mind-body material?' Yung-Chia Ta-shih-Mahayaha Buddhist, closely related to Taosim.'"

"Lilies grow when the root was nurtured," I had this urge to say in a last ditch attempt to keep her from reliving more old memories. There must be some meaning to all this.

"George, my first boyfriend," she went on, the place so still I can see each one of her syllables stand free in mid air, "was a Ph.D. from MIT and they don't come cheap. We met at a dance at my college. I was in my sophomore year and fed up with studies. I suddenly came face to face with my limitations, with the limitations of Math. I knew I would never look at another mathematical formula with the same fervor I used to, never again had that thrill of solving a problem. I was into questioning axioms, first causes and that could only lead to trouble.

George must have felt my insecurity. He fell for me, or rather, fell all over me. I'm sure you won't believe me, but sex and love were the same to me then, are the same to me now, I couldn't imagine the one without the other. There weren't many women interested in mathematics in the sixties; it kept the boys away but not George. I moved in with him and bolstered his ego when he was down, gave him some of his best insights, researched his paper, typed up his footnotes and bibliographies til I saw double. George taught me to be free, unhindered by social precepts of right and wrong. He said he wanted to take my mother out of me, the Jew out of me and all this to Brahms in the background. It took me some time to realize that George was a Golem, he performed according to script. I was so afraid of losing him I became a zombie, desensitized to feeling. Giving in to every physiological urge broke me down and Josephina, I allowed him to strip me clean of my clothes, my identity, my self-respect. And I died. I died, and ended up on the psych's couch holding on to my father's last letter to me, D-Day.

"My father was killed on June 5, 1944, chinning his way up a rope on a cliff in Normandy. A German cut the rope. I had two pieces of memory, a grappling hook and a yellowing card he'd sent me from England. 'Cycling down a road in England/Fine and dandy/ cotton candy/ a bicycle fit for two,' and yellow balloons. He'd been a commercial artist."

"Forgive me, I didn't know, I didn't mean to hurt your feelings, Gloria."

Mea culpa, mea culpa, why the hell do I always keep apologizing? With a name like Koenigsburger, my ancestors too came from somewhere, were murdered somewhere, burnt at the stake in Toledo, in the gas ovens of Auschwitz. I also had a background, roots in the ash so to speak.

"I transferred to NYU. That's where I met Rafcho's sister, this really pushy cripple who sat next to me at a psychology lecture. She knew all the answers. She was studying physical therapy 'helping myself by helping my fellow man,' she told me. She lived in a rented room in a cold-water flat on Second Avenue. I just couldn't ask her home. Mother had this peach wall to wall carpeting in the sunken living room and a breakfront heavy with silver and cut glass brandy glasses and this woman didn't even had hot running water and in her condition, wobbling about on a pair of crutches. I invited her to a Cambodian restaurant in the village. She thought she was in the kibbutz dining room or something, and ate so quickly, and her hair a stringy, mousy brown robin's nest, the skin of her face and hands scaly and chapped. It must have been the food she ate or the lack of it. No gloves, no coat in the cold. I was embarrassed more for me than for her.

"When I won the scholarship from the Rockefeller Foundation with a letter praising my academic abilities, Irving, my stepfather, took Mother and me out to dinner. We went to Radio City to see the Rockettes.

'It's not so much the quality of study you'll get,' mother said, 'but the connections you make, they are for life.'"

"They must have been very proud of you."

"They would have been more proud if I had shown some inclination for the law. Irving needed someone to take over the business, he's semi retired working as a judge for the UN employment service, something like that.

'The world was instantly ours when our daughter became a college student, I don't want to push you into Law School, but Irving would be so pleased. Do you know what it would mean to him, to us to see you a member of the Bar?'

"They were both disappointed when I failed to get my prestigious degree from my prestigious school I mean mother was a tough act to follow. Hunter College, an active member of the Alumnus society, cajoling funds from friends and acquaintances far and wide. She began her career as an elementary school teacher and worked herself up to principal. I mean I had something to live up to.

"My mother—did she think her ongoing soliloquy would remain unchallenged—is a rather glamorous, blond haired socialite attired in a classic suit and white blouse open at the neck in a generous V to show her bony chest off to advantage. Sorbonne you know, class and dignity, and father was a retired Colonel in the air force—lights, camera, action!

"Actually my Mom used to work in a jewelry shop on the Grand Concourse. Dad was always worried she'd get mugged, but nothing much happened."

"What about your crippled sister-in-law?"

"Oh her; she's working for Helena Rubinstein. She began going there and turned into an unwrinkled beauty, rosy skin and auburn hair. She decided she could help mankind better in New York, to quote her, took several courses in chemistry and was now working for the firm, and had never been back not even for her mother's funeral."

"You're kidding!'

"I'm not."

"Maybe your mother-in-law felt guilty about her daughter and took it out on you."

"Sure! I've often given it the old Freudian routine, crippled daughter, guilt etcetera, but Rafcho's sister couldn't stand her mother. In fact the only time I ever got a civil reply to a letter from her, rather than a note or a harried phone call, was when my mother-in-law decided she'd like to go to New York to visit her. She sent this desperate, long letter asking me to convince Rafcho to keep Hannah home.

"I tried to fit into the prestigious women's college atmosphere don't imagine I didn't. I dyed my hair blond, wore it in a pageboy brushed to sheen, a straight bang over my eyes. I got skinny and turned pale white. My golden freckles just disappeared. I almost faded into the snow bank. But no matter how artfully I buttoned the mother of pearl buttons on my cashmere cardigan, arranged seed pearl necklaces round my Peter Pan collar, the wheat gleaner of the steppes somewhere in my peasant background—there must have been some intermarriage with the converted Khazars—kept coming to the fore. The family lived in Russia for over 400 years. Scratch a Rabbi's granddaughter from Kiev, find the blood relative of a Khazar warlord from the steppes of Russia. I should know.

"I sat on the campus lawn which gently sloped into a lion's lair which I could distinctly see, engulfed in the general niceness about me which made me uncomfortable. I was afraid of the chapel, its serenity, its appealing music, the thunderous rises and lows of the organ courted me with ominous undertones of tenderness. I forced myself back into the snow bank, a crocus fighting for life in a wintered spring. No one could decipher the graphic pattern of my grief cutting into my brain. 'I'm from the Bronx, not Hyannis Port you know,' I sang in my icicle soprano until I broke into splintered laughter at my own pretense."

She got up, great plastic shutters on ball bearings floated across the view erasing the wavy line of silver spume delineating sea from sky

"Come on," she leads me brusquely to the dining corner, which, unlike her veranda, was Middle East, above the entrance to the alcove, a red horseshoe and copper chamsa charms, palms up against the evil eye, Armenian pottery, carnelian, dark blue sapphire, loam yellow, topaz, Bedouin camel saddle bag, brilliant red and black, plastic maroon table mats embossed in golden Arabic calligraphy. The plates are square white porcelain, cherry blossom sprig on the side, Japanese cutlery square cut and practical; black lacquer bowls. Different stage sets for different moods—Gloria was definitely between acts.

I delved into the stuffed eggplant fighting this need I had to wipe the cutlery, clean; some of yesterday's supper may still be clinging to the tongs—too many restaurants had brought me to this. Bitter! Scoop out the eggplant seeds my dear. We of the generation of mother's mothers, who were gassed down to rancid oil in the crematoriums of Germany, had to learn everything from scratch.

Eating stuffed eggplant in a T.A. restaurant: Slight man, nearsighted and undernourished sits down opposite me, unasked.

"Red army Jews with Slavic sounding names, turned up noses Stalingraad, chevron-shaped front, spread the German army out as thin as possible. The kraut fell into the Russian net—prisoners-of-war, men and boys. I saw mountains of rifles and guns pair of beautiful revolvers with shell work on the handles. I thought of taking one but there was no ammunition," he tells me, putting his lower dentures in between two lone silver capped teeth demurely behind his hand. Men killing each other for reasons forgotten—the classic fear of the ancient Roman, Russian Bolshevik hordes through the vortex, through the well cared for dachas of the Prussians; the orderly detachment which allowed for scientific murder. And in truth these straight-shouldered little men, row of medals on chest, doctorate from Krakow University, are not beautiful. These men courageous enough to had escaped the ghettos, the box cars, the concentration camps, the prisoner-of-war camps weeping like little children for love, little love, a little piece of bread, life. They smell of muddy trenches and flowing blood and the fear of death and yet they beg for love within the hard ego line of Me. I. Will to live. Lenin versus Rosa. Rosa, a train, the proletariat was like a train on the railway line, can't move without the engine and the engine was the intelligentsia. Lenin was right, the engine can move the train even against its will, but if there was no coordination, then the cars bump into each other, turn over, are derailed. Lenin was right: one shouldn't discriminate between the engine and the boxcars. Not individual terror like the peasant revolts of 1905."

"But what kind of terror?" I asked him.

"Rosa, Salon communist. Do you know who Dora Kaplan was?"

"No," I replied.

"She killed Lenin. Politics," he said.

And someone in her featherbed and perfumed pillows asks, why live? What was I to tell her?

"Where is the toilet," I ask the sullen waiter. Leave oily, icky gooey eggplant, follow painted hand, pointed index finger on the wall up the staircase into a man zipping up his trousers. There was only one toilet. Well if you're going to opt for equality, the toilet was the place to start.

"Let's go," she said just as I bring a fork full of juicy vegetable to my mouth.

"You don't mind following me around a little bit do you?"

I fit myself into the small Volks, an invalid of better times. "In Japan," I said, throwing caution to the wind, "mothers-in-law are known to kill off their pregnant brides to insure their position in the household. The same can be said of certain African tribes for different reasons of course. But you, you seem to have loved your mother-in-law mourning her as you do."

"Far Eastern saying," she said as my head ricochets from the windscreen. I turn to her holding my temple, with tears welling up in my eyes.

"Are you ok?"

Does she hate me enough to drive this way on purpose? She swerves the car in on an incline wedged between a white UN station wagon and a dark blue Porsche.

"Only be a moment!" she shouts taking the ignition keys with her. I look at the handbrake and it shudders like a hound's phallus in ecstasy. If I touch it to test its credibility, it'll stick out a crimson gland penis, quiver and shake, crash clear through the supermarket shop window. I hear the mandrake itself with a terrible crack sending tremors through the earth. I get out, break the electronic signal at the entrance, and wait for the door to slide open in my wake, and walk into the supermarket.

Gloria was holding a bunch of muddy spring onions, shouting at the top of her voice at a slight man in a nicely pressed shirt. She forces the onions to his chest. He looked down at the streak of dirt, his mouth wide open, his eyes rolling round in their sockets in utter confusion. The customers are taking the man's side, the butcher and tones of the Muzak from the intercom system counterpoint the commotion. Gloria walks over to the meat counter, tall and snooty. I run after her.

"What happened?"

"Nothing much," she said then ordered a kilo of steak for Rafcho. "He only eats ground steak. Want to hear the script?"

Me: Can I wash these spring onions?

The Manager: No, no, it's against the rules.

Me: Why should I have to pay for wet earth? There's more earth here than the weight of the vegetables.

The Manager: If you don't like it don't buy it. So I handed him the bouquet of onions that's all. Listen Josephina, I've learnt to fight back. This guy, at home, lords it over his woman like the oriental he is. He knows it's wrong to sell mud-caked spring onions in a filthy box under the counter without a price tag—bet he's doing some moonlighting on the side. After this entire supermarket was part of the Workers Union, practically a monopoly. If I don't fight back he'll put the money in his own pocket and I'm not living like a pauper to support him with my taxes. They're so full of their own self esteem these guys. When they get a little power, they forget it's the customer they're serving and not the other way around." The butcher hands her the meat and thanks her profusely.

"I've complained more than once to the authorities. I'm a member of the Better Business Bureau. I won't let them shit all over me. I've had my day as acceptor of the norm. The supermarket complaint clerk wrote back to tell me that even if the manager was wrong, they expected civil behavior from the customer. I was rapped on the knuckles for being a naughty girl but I got the satisfaction of having this so-called manager reappraise his behavior."

"It doesn't seem to have helped much."

"Every bit helps. Apathy was the handmaiden of bureaucracy," she replied putting the groceries into the shopping cart with a gesture of accomplishment.

"McCrudder does most of the shopping, except for special occasions. I'll wait for you outside."

I stood in a fine haze, a patch of sun valiantly trying to glow though, thinking she may be right. Maybe it was more civilized to let your anger out at the manager rather than telling your troubles to an electronic scanner silently decoding magnetic lines, flashing, "Thank you" "Come again." No hands, no voices, no sweat.

"Why do you shop here if you get such bad service?" I ask when we are once more seated in her car.

"They have the freshest eggplants, squash, peppers, potatoes, parsley, and onions in the neighborhood—everything I need for the trouloo. My mother-in-law used to call it Gvetch and I, Kvetch because that's what the vegetable stew looks like, now she's dead. Anyway, they deliver and I'm a working girl." She hands me the safety belt, which I buckle—on a wing and a prayer. "It's time we stop whirling ourselves nonsensically into ever tinier, more lethal, electronic components," she says backing out. Zoom. "This male oriented world was playing a game of blackjack with rationalized, computerized stratagems against the house, we're the house the world we live in was the house. Do you know Daniel Bell? He said it, 'maximum payoffs at minimum risks, minimal payoffs at maximum risks and a payoff which was provided with a criterion, a smidgeon of regret.' I hope I'm quoting him correctly. Imagine a criterion of regret; that measure of regret."

My life's at stake, sip the belladonna amaryllis from your ring, a dram, ten drops, just enough to dilate your irises and let the sun seer your brain, and ever afterwards you can lie there supine on the beach and let the world dance on while you breathe in rhythm to the music of the stars and become a black hole projected to the space beyond. Tic a licka boom!

"I wish I understood you, reporting great events when the when the real story was in the minds of an ordinary guy who, when asked directions, puts a bullet through the brain of the inquiring stranger just like that—his life was worth the momentary thrill of pressing the trigger to see what happens. What do you expect me to do, let the damn supermarket manager sell me spring onions caked in mud?"

"Ok, calm down!"

"Because they can feed strategy charts into a computer memory bank, they think they've got the competitive edge on the house. They've got the iron will to play till they win, but what they don't take into account is that the house changes the rules at will and there aren't enough strategy charts to cover all the possibilities. Look at the blunders the Germans made on D-Day, Rommel speeding along the roads of Europe to his wife's birthday, the Luftwaffe recalled from the front and Hitler's aides refusing to wake him before 9:30am. Poor guy needed his rest. And my Pop got it in the head. Ridiculous coincidence staged in your magazine article as reason. Self destruction may be why we're on earth, but I don't think so because like Tantalus we are being given the means of self destruction, which we thought was exclusively ours, but it was constantly being pushed away just that far by better technology and we had to use all our ingenuity to play the game over. Playing the game was the aim. Destruction and reproduction, reproduction and destruction."

"Sounds good—like a samba. Yeah boom, boom, yeah!

"Seriously, Josephina, technology may or may not be a social system depending on how you view it, but if it is, then it was a system of values, but how can you build a house on values that change as computers become smaller and smaller, more and more lethal, changing the biology of man, the definition of man and all this in the hands of guys transient and powerless before the monster they had created; changing values, changing ethics, more diabolical and incomprehensible than the elements. I mean when there is an earthquake, you know it's happening because man has sinned and you feel guilty, pray to the gods of the seas, of the plants, the God of moral value. We had transgressed, we appease, try to find the path to righteousness, but now you have to appease not an angry God, but an ever shrinking technology, in size that is." Her voice was cracking with emotion.

"Are you saying technology is a myth?"

"Yes, but like all myths it works as truth. Technological information was real, so real that young men fall in love with electronic pulses on a cathode ray and are willing to kill the President, the dragon, the most powerful symbol of the day to win their lady-love who too, only exists as an image on the screen."

"God, you're right," I say to divert her and put her mind back on her driving. "The earthquake seems too imminent a probability. Have you ever loved any human being as wholly as you loved Clark Gable and William Holden? Have you seen pictures of Holden lately with a full set of porcelain dentures held to his skull by screws and a dainty silver band? John Wayne and Gary Cooper, the invincible, dead cold in the ground do make you consider the transient nature of myths. And the worst blow of all, Rock Hudson with whom we dreamt of sharing pillow talk: a homo."

"Josephina, war was a homosexual game. They've got us up there with them multirolling the clouds. Fuck it all. And you Josephina are the stupidest party to it because by reporting wars you think you are above being enslaved by the system."

"Thanks," I said, putting all the sarcasm I could muster into that one word.

"Do you realize, Josephina, the amount of money invested in the educational system to spit out little male wonders that will design, fly, and service one of those F16s and to what end? It's shocking to see how insignificant in size these lethal weapons are. So much disaster in such a small body designed to sexually attack a similar body; horseflies in heat on a sun ray on the kitchen window. Whoever gets on top first blasts off the underdog."

"Horseflies in heat?" Underfly, no underdog, I feel like correcting her, I hate messy similes, or moronic oxymoron's. What is an oxymoron?

"You who are imprisoned in a man's world, think you're free. Your man took over your household chores and threw you out into the world to mount great birds in the sky, fly from continent to continent. If the women of the world had lost their function, are no longer mistresses of the womb, the home, or our intrigues, it's because they had stopped feeding men and therefore had freed them of their dependency on us."

"Create dependency, that's a fine political game."

"We women had become servants to manmade machine printed plan, welding little wires into perforated holes. It all comes down to the war of the sexes. There was little we can do except to be women and even that prerogative was becoming questionable. The homosexual promiscuity of the times was a male oriented plan to wipe us out altogether. A male dressed in lace and feathers bends over, offers his ass, and was given pleasure. The vagina's lost its exclusivity and women are helping the situation along, sticking bottles up, pretending glass can fertilize a diseased womb."

"No, that would be self-defeating, and would cause inflammation of the vagina, and sure death from viruses of such potency. Men of medicine, to follow your logic, would have good reason not to find a cure. Homosexuals had impaired genes, that's why they are homosexuals in the first place, prevented by nature from reproducing, hence the rise of homosexual-linked diseases not seen since the Middle Ages." I say rationally, having of late been bombarded by a barrage of articles on the rise of venereal disease and the genetic question of natural selection. Next step, the plague and the decimation of the over populous earth, sets you thinking along McCrudder's line: what part free will, what part the will of the gods?

"Man," Gloria goes on in all seriousness, "no longer had to rape the white goddess by the light of the moon in order to pacify wheat gods, the gods of the wind, and the sea. Man, fully dressed in polished shoes and mandarin collar was the sole master of the button The button was pushed in and whoopee, instant power—power was what man was about."

"Are you saying the push button and the female are analogous?"

"Any way you put it, we are being destroyed by male fantasy rifle barrels, submarine periscopes, high rise buildings."

"Women," I say commenting on the obvious, "should then be designing trenches, cushiony trenches."

"Men dig trenches," she said triumphantly, changing gear "to protect themselves from shooting phalluses."

"You mean they dig trenches because they want to die in the birth canal."

"Look at it this way: the moment woman gave up her role as earth mother, the harvester of the seed, the poultice applier, the pus and infection nurse, the source of solace, she could no longer use food politics, children politics, bed politics, not even inheritance politics to keep him in line. Man, now completely independent of her, was free to create factories, shackle us to the machine as he had forced our bodies into corsets to find a legit reason for prancing about murdering the whale, and to give himself reason for his life.

Liberated from the role of provider, he became dissatisfied with his sexuality. In the older days, overtaxed with work, he took what he needed, turned around and went to sleep. He had no need for a manual. The animals taught him what to do and women accepted dutifully as payment for providence. We, and we alone, had swept out our household gods, our little Astartes. Man's imagination can run rampant now we no longer enclose their natures. They are free to destroy civilization, us."

"Josephina, don't be sarcastic with me. They had solved the mystery of life and birth. I hate men, their armies, their organizations, which are meaningless for anything other than aggression. We are being trampled down so we know who is boss."

"Sure, Daphne and Aphrodite—cool reason and sexual charm leading to passion, destruction, procreation, destruction, cherchez la femme. Tralala boom de yeh! We are out of tune with our men; the whale was to blame."

"If I didn't know you better," she leaves the car to steer itself, death row! "I'd say you were a fool."

"Don't let that stop you, I know my limitations. Gloria, what's the matter?"

"Rafcho is in the reserves and I can't get through to him. My daughter is in the army, West Bank, checking credentials of Arab builders of Israel military installations, she's becoming so independent. And Guy, you remember Guy, finishes his military service next month and was going to go to England to study textile design. He may take a liking to the place and never return."

"Is that all?"

"No, that's not all, damn it. My neighbor's son committed suicide in the army last week, a bright boy and a few months ago another one died by accident. He forgot to unload his rifle and while cleaning it a bullet hit him in the heart. I'm worried about Guy and about Abigail. This fucking male-oriented world is killing me and mine."

She backed up into a parking space, slams on the brakes so violently that I feel the pain shoot up my spine to my neck. What would years of this kind of impact have on a body?

CHAPTER 10

I stand there, stunned by Gloria's mad driving, looking at small canvases of flowers in impressive wooden frames—les fleurs du mal—in shades of yellow. Large canvases of Massachusetts Bay—red white and blue picture postcard recreations of a cleansed New England, transplants of what the artist's eye had seen and her mind had refused comment—propped up against a stucco wall under concrete eaves of the municipal arts center called "The House of the Rothschilds" on one side of the courtyard a small farmhouse, which might last forever, on the other, a grand, newly constructed theater popping tiny Japanese tiles in graded shades of gray a windowless building begging to be socked in the eye, punched in the solar plexus, given some vent for sunlight.

Gloria introduces me to the artist, a woman in her mid-fifties wearing a plum-colored body stocking, plum-colored woolen leg warmers striped in the colors of autumn leaves and a cambric shirt, white on white openwork, hanging loosely about her down to her knees like a wash worn alb, which might once have belonged to an extra large priest.

"This is Josephina McCrudder, Karen. Keep my friend company! I'll be back within the hour."

The short woman, with silver gray hair cut in a feathery bang over one dark brown eye, offers me a slender hand, fingertips sticking out of a brown mitt, brown to match her Dutch clogs clack-clacking as I follow her across the courtyard.

"Come sit here with me. I don't like to leave my paintings alone for too long!"

I sit on the concrete edge of a flower bed, fine pin drop rain biting into my nostrils, contemplating the fortitude of a blind building popping tiles, exposing sack cloth underpinnings expanding like a pee stain on a child's bed sheet.

"You see that gook over there? The one slumped over to get a better look at my pictures?" She points across the yard to a tall, emaciated man in a long raincoat, cap in hand, thinning strands of long black hair brushed carefully over his scalp.

"You mean the gook under the waterspout, getting his bottom wet?"

"I was driving Norm, two weeks ago, piled high with these picture frames. At the traffic light near the gas station this creep, I swear it was him, opens the door and tries to get in. "Just let me talk to you" he insists. I don't answer, put my foot on the gas and was off. Almost ran over a little girl coming home from school. I went to the police. They gave me photo albums to look through. I couldn't find the creep's face anywhere. But, girl, there must be a helluva lot of rape going on in this here village judging by the number of mug shots they had on file. Look at that hound dog sniffing at my pictures like they're juicy steak."

"Who's Norm?"

"Norm, the car. Just a minute, a customer."

"Listen Karen, I'm going in where it's warm, ok?" I mean how long was I to sit there leaning against a prickly bush of roses inside a rain cloud?

"Sure. If you want me, you know where to find me. I'll be in and out so don't feel abandoned or something. Keep smiling."

The cafeteria was warm. I was inhaling that particular odor of grayish fatty soaped institutional dishwater, watching people outside turn up collars to keep the drizzle out, admiring my feet in the high heeled pumps, which I had chosen to wear to impress Conforti, perhaps because he had stood me up, forced this second trip to Haifa on me where Gloria had brought back memories I had carefully kept hidden—not that they matter much. My life was a film strip of no particular interest yet, the memories which lie in the spaces between the words in my mind, slow motion frames, stills, screen themselves in restaurants, in the airplanes I enjoy climbing in and out of as if flying above the clouds I'm being led ever nearer some awesome truth.

Gloria was right. Everyone seems to be right.

My first marriage, which lasted six weeks, two days, and two hours took place in 1958 here in Haifa, ten days after I arrived in the country on the Eve of Yom Kippur, the Day of Atonement, and found myself walking along a beach of fine white sand in Askelon with nothing to atone for. I had caused no one any harm; no one had caused me much. I had just been accepted, tentatively, as a researcher for a great newsmagazine, tentatively because the elderly lady behind the temporary glass partition forming a cubbyhole, which served as an office, had told me to see the world. She'd hired me because she liked my name, Josephina Koenigsburger. It sounded like a name that had traveled. I sold the war bonds my parents had bought for me during the spiritual siege and took off for frozen Paris, pinch-bottom happy Napoli, Istanbul, and Jerusalem—what could be more traveled than that? I was the envy of all my friends teaching elementary school back home in the Bronx and Harlem.

On the quay in gay Marseilles I met a chubby Manchester lass and this meeting, as often happens in literature and life, was to affect the drift of my affairs. If fate had brought me face to face with this girl dressed in an orange sou'wester, I guess fate knew what it was about. Florence had just been robbed. Her knapsack with her passport, her money, her clothes, was gone. I must have looked like the protective mother type, the kind that the disoriented and lonely latch on to. Some guy, "a dark fellow" thought she was a whore and had propositioned her. She'd walloped him one with the full force of her knapsack and he began to bleed from the inner corners of his eyes down either side of his nose.

"It was a god-awful sight to behold, luv, but he deserved it. I went to the police. Excusez moi, I said and they burst out laughing."

She sat at the edge of the quay nervously swinging her high-heeled pumps—navy blue suede vamps, punched out daisies—back and forth. She looked like a tarty whale hunter.

"I'm on my way to Istanbul and Jerusalem," I said, matter of factly, trying to calm her down with inanities.

"That's where I'm going," she wept like a stormy North Sea wiping her runny nose on the back of her hand. Tom, the group leader would come to her rescue, she was sure, and would find a way to get her to Israel despite the loss of her passport. "He never disappoints. Her peachy complexion was splotched wine red when she mentioned the hallowed name. And sure enough Florence was saved by Tom: tall, dark, imposingly authoritarian, leader of men holding Florence's royal blue passport, embossed golden lions like those on the velvet curtain protecting the holy scrolls. These British—incorporating the pithy symbols of the world's civilizations, making them their own.

"One of them was a unicorn you numskull," she said when I pointed out my revelation. This was Tom. Thomas Spencer, meet Josephina.

I had the immediate side effects of the love disease. My skin goose bumped, and I turned pale. I could feel the blood draining from my arms, my legs, setting my head reeling so fast I almost lost consciousness. I wanted nothing more than to keep my skin close to his, feel myself in him. No human obstacle would ever separate this man from me. With knees wobbling, I looked into the burning embers of his soul—eyes filmed with diffident reserve meant to awaken thoughts of subterfuge in the musky desires of my heart—man clever enough to subjugate woman by making her feel equal, perhaps even superior. He held on to my hand for a long moment, letting me force my fingers clear of his grip.

"We're with Habonim," he said and taking a hat from his backpack, placed it on my head explaining the subtle differences between various Zionist organizations.

Florence broke in: "Josephina, we're all mad about him," she laughed pulling him away from me.

I walked around the Topkapi Museum, no longer myself so inundated by this love, which I could not believe was not exclusively mine, past fanciful scrolls of knights in armor, the hidden face of Mohammed, pink mountains, scabbards and pearls and felt myself alone in this atmosphere which bespoke of the comfort of the senses drowning out thought in pleasure. The respectful silence, the shadow and light aroused contemplations of veiled ladies in harems reclining on tasseled silk mattresses at the edge of a pool where smirking pink and white water lilies float face up, their roots enclosed in slatted wooden boxes at the bottom of the gold and midnight blue mosaic floor. I had seen all this on television, genies in bottles. And there before me, "Portrait of Sultan Mohammed II, Conqueror of Constantinople," the final death blow to the gold and turquoise Byzantium—a big fat guy holding a dishtowel in one hand and a delicate phallic flower up to his nose, luxuriating in the future use of young lads from Serbia, Greece, and Albania, his slaves all.

I walked out of the museum not unaware of the beauty around me; the sky and the sea, determined not to admire the cats of Constantinople, fine healthy toms and felines satiated on pesticide-free rats, secret explorers in the dirt, the utilities which didn't work, the capricious mystery under the surface—a girdled anger. I, who might have sacrificed true love for a handful of art brochures in Istanbul, was afraid for my life.

"Taxi!" I shouted at a moving vehicle. The car rolled to a stop in front of me. I remembered seeing it parked across the street when I walked into the Museum; the driver's gaze following me, burning into the small of my back.

"Can I help you miss?" he asked.

"Yes, will you take me to the Pera Palace Hotel?"

"I would be delighted," he said stretching across the front seat to keep the door gallantly open for me. God this isn't a taxi! The heck, anything was better than walking around alone in a foreign city and he does have superb blue eyes; a man with blue eyes can only be true!

"You are a tourist?" the young man asked politely, "American?"

"Yes," I answer, "what else?"

"You want a smoke?"

"I want a smoke?" God, this man will lead me into an opium joint, pump me full of hash. My loving Ma and Pa back home on Creston Avenue will see me no more. I, who alone amongst all my pals was practically handed a job with the best, the most widely read news magazine in the Northern Hemisphere, not to mention the world, will forever lie naked under the Sultan's bed, doped, brain washed, undernourished, beyond hope, ready at beck and call to hand him his potty, white flesh dragged off and bartered for a consignment of small-pox vaccine "ingrafted" by the old ladies of Andrianople; proved preventative for the deadly contagion—I'd just read Lady Mary Wortley Montagu's letters sent from Turkey in the 1700s, probably taught Pasteur a thing or two.

"You would like to see Istanbul?"

"No. Yes." My adrenalin was flowing untapped into my blood, I should have taken up judo.

"You would perhaps like a drink?"

I move my head in a sign of negation, but deep in my heart, I was ready for adventure. The editors will hack my story to bits. They are not being paid to be sympathetic but two, three lines of my own personal experiences will be printed. I will go to hell and back for the chance.

"I see you are Jewish."

"How do you know?"

"You are wearing a 'Cova Tembel.'" It was an Israeli hat. "Tembel" means idiot and "Habonim" was printed on it in English and in Hebrew. It was very conspicuous. I am, myself, a member of Habonim.

"You are then on the way to Israel or back?"

"On the way."

"Good, I will request you a favor. You do not know me. Allow me to introduce myself. I am Robert Chiprut. Will you do me and my family the goodness of delivering a letter to my cousin in Haifa?"

"Will you take me to my hotel?"

"Yes, of course. We are there, see!"

I jump out of the car and into the lobby of my hostelry, respectful sleaziness of a movie brothel in Old New Orleans. Hours pass. I do not want to go up to my room though lured by the promise of a breathtaking view of the Bosphorus from its window. The telephone buzzes. I hear a fine tinkling of the bell on the receptionist's desk, a brass nipple pressed into a rotund bosom.

"Miss Koenigsburger," a soft voice pages me—the Madame's valet asking me to go up to room 222 where Ataturk himself is in full regalia, his sickle sword hanging from his hip. He removes a revolver from an inner breast pocket, fez from his blond hair and bowing asks me to undress him—I feel his breath on my neck as I bend down to take off his silken slipper.

"Telephone, Mademoiselle," the clerk bows politely. I walk over to the phone.

"You will not change your mind?" Robert Chiprut whispers.

"Aren't there any mailboxes in Istanbul?"

"Shalom," he bangs down the phone. I rub my ear and thank the receptionist. "Peki," I say using the word I've been hearing repeated over and over. It sounds like a woodpecker pecking away at a hard nut tree, "Peki, peki!" The clerk looks at me strangely. I go back to the red plush chair, a faded grandeur—aristocratic presumptuousness, like sitting on a corpse's unrealized dreams and watch the dull interior turn dark as the day faded. I had not come unprepared. I had read a biography of Ataturk. Fikriye, the girl who loved him, who committed suicide when he married Latife, whose spirit he broke, and this was the man who with wit and will pasted together a nation from a fallen empire. It's unfair being merely a shadow in a man's history. I will be nothing but a Cleopatra to my Anthony or a Theodora in all her autocratic splendor, never a Fikriye or a Latife.

"Tell me, when are you planning to go back to Israel?" The taut, wiry body of Robert Chiprut was leaning over me.

"Not going back, going to."

"Well, yes, when?"

"I'd like to leave tomorrow. I can't afford two nights in a hotel" I lied.

"I can arrange for you to fly El Al, first class, tonight. I'll take care of the ticket. You may even get some money back. There is kosher food at no extra cost. If you like, I will put you on the plane at twelve."

"That's very nice, but I've already made my arrangements; the price of my ticket includes this stopover in Istanbul."

"May I invite you for a drink?"

"I'm very sorry. I only drink Coca Cola."

"We drink water."

He raises a carafe from the inlaid mother of pearl side table, raises a glass up to the light to inspect its faultless cleanliness, pours out the liquid and like David Niven, sophisticated, and knowledgeable, hands it to me. I, playing the glamorous woman of means, Bette Davies, wait for him to drink the clear water first just in case it's poisoned. He drinks. Only then do I sip it, being careful to keep my lips dry.

"What's in it for you?"

"Don't be so unreasonable, you are a beautiful girl. I would like to help you have a good flight." I might have looked dumb but I had had four years of college. I wait.

"I would like to give you this book as a present," he raised his voice in question.

"Oh!"

"Yes, *Kerouac Big Sur*."

I was beginning to like Robert. He was charming without being overbearingly male. He had an air of dignity mixed with a hard edge of control, which fascinated me. I felt ill at ease, blushing, divulging my embarrassment. The book had made a big impression on me mainly for its vivid scenes of defecation. It should have been called "Big Shit."

"Will you accept it?"

"What do you mean?"

"Put it into your handbag when you board the plane?"

"I've read it."

"Read it again!" he smiles reservedly. My heart begins to beat a little quicker. I feel the sexual excitement melt me free of all restraint. I remember Tom just in time. I never did get to see the Bosphorus from my hotel window. Robert dined and wined me, drove me to the airport and had me on the plane to Tel Aviv by midnight sharp, seated next to a girl who looked not a day over 16. She was holding a cherubic baby to her breast. The mother, for so I believed her to be, faultless complexioned milk-white skin, thick black lashed large deep blue eyes, was enormously fat. Here was the Sultan's nubile wife, dressed in gauzy aquamarine pantaloons and pearl encrusted vest, newly acquired symbol of purity to be defiled at leisure in a garden of flaming hibiscus and white geranium while the peacocks languidly fanned iridescent green, gold and purple tail feathers.

"Madame, will you be so kind as to pick up the baby's titin? It fell, poor baby."

"Sure," I bent down to the rubbery thing. This Maman—in ballet shoes, keeping her shapely ankles together like a good girl at school, smiles sweetly accepting the lost article.

"My name is Josephina. Are you Israeli?"

"No, Mademoiselle, I am Turkish. My name is Jalle; her thick pink lips open round perfectly shaped tough, pearly white little teeth. She comes closer to me. I smell musky perfume. I can't be more than a few years older than her, but she feels like my mother. I guess being a member of a Harem, gorged on ass's milk forced down your gullet from a porcelain spouted gourd, sprinkled with rosewater from a cobalt and gold phial I'd seen in the Museum, does things to you, not to mention dallying in the company of a squadron of healthy-looking, half naked eunuchs.

"You are kind," she whispers politely, exchanging the dirty pacifier for a new one, tearing the cellophane open with those even baby teeth. "This is not my baby. I had bought a bicycle for losing weight. It comes from London I bought it with this coat, pretty, no?"

No, it isn't pretty. The snob, dressed in esthetically inferior coal compounds thrown round her shoulders with a nonchalant elegance as if she were wearing baby seal pounded on the head with clubs off the shores of Newfoundland to grace the skin of the pampered ladies of Hamburg in midwinter. When she moved, the label on the lining clearly states, "as close to fur as you ought to come." No, this was no harem bunny. I can just see her let down her hair and began to rock, "Rock, rock round the clock."

"My bicycle comes with a book of instructions. I know English well but the instructions are difficult. I studied English till the age of 15, but my teacher was very jealous. She was almost 30 and not yet engaged, no "dot" you see. My dowry was so nice, packets of sheets and pillowcases tied with pink ribbons smelling of fresh lavender and my name and his embroidered in tiny stitches my aunts learned from the nuns. I too went to a convent school and then to the International School. You see I was full of figure and I had a boyfriend. Maman and Papa feared for my virginity and gave me in marriage to my cousin. He was older than I, but so handsome. When Papa asked if I was willing, I said yes, wouldn't you? My baby was three months old; not this one," she caressed the sleeping child. "My very own tout petit enfant."

I thought it bad business to ask what she was doing with a "tout petit enfant" not her own. I shouldn't have feared, she told me anyway.

"The father does not want to leave the kibbutz, you see, and the mother does not want to leave Istanbul. She loves Turkey. We all love Turkey. The father's parents gave me the child to take back as my own at the last minute at the airport. I cannot refuse. I cannot leave the airport. I cannot leave the baby on the ground.

"What about the Greeks, do they love Turkey?" I'd read all about the massacre of the Greek community in Thrace. I wasn't as ignorant as I looked.

"The Greeks?"

"The Greeks were massacred by the Turks."

"Oh yes," she sighs, "Grandmama tells stories. She remembers coming to school one day to find half of her class missing. The nuns didn't tell her why her friends were gone, but she knew. The nun she liked best was crying. She stole money from her mother's purse and brought the nun an umbrella. The maid was accused of stealing the money and was dismissed. When Grandmama married, she couldn't have children. So she went to a Chacham, a wise man who took her down into a cellar under the house. He knew she couldn't have children because of the maid. He gave her a special drink, frog's head and lizards, and she drank it and she became pregnant with my mother. I had no trouble—first night and it took. I was with child. But I think, Josephina, Grandmama spoke of Armenians, not Greeks. Are you then Christian?"

"No, I am Jewish."

"Yes, we too are Jewish. My family was from the Bulgarian Turkish border, Iderne, Adrianolple. There are no longer Jews living there. Grandmama speaks German. She studied with German nuns."

We landed at dawn. I had not slept much, the baby had slept soundly; the girl had not stopped talking. I found solace and silence in the bathroom from time to time. Lod airport was in torpor of sleep. The steel bird regurgitated its cargo, there was a momentary rustle of action and the airship like a sleepy dove, put its head under its wing and dozed off like the others. I was alone. The Turkish delight and baby had been scooped up by a baby blue de Soto, which slid by and disappeared. I was irritated by the calm, reached into my maroon gold striped woven wool horse-feed bag—that's what Joseph, when we were married, told me it looked like—I loved it, took out a tissue and discovered my copy of Big Sur gone.

Fortunately, my traveler's checks hadn't been touched. At the tourist information desk, a well-scrubbed girl who had just come to work agreed to make a call for me. She disinterestedly handed me a name on a scrap of paper. "Yes I have a room for you in Tel Aviv." When I thanked her she turned away angrily, "This is my job."

A porter took my bag to a taxi. I tipped the disgruntled man and climbed in behind the driver.

"Got any dollars?"

"No."

"Nylon pants? Give you a good price."

"No, only the ones on me."

CHAPTER 11

Bette Davis, star of the 1940s, now palsied and arthritic, handing out an Oscar "best actress"—a made up cadaver trying to recapture days when one acid stare from her silver screen eyes and the boys out there on the ground on the sea and in the air, fighting the axis round the globe, knew what they were dying for. Marilyn Monroe, Kennedy's favorite gal will never grow into a ga-ga hag on TV. Cut. What a reason to die young. Waitress, resentment so intense, it snaps like the resilient gray rag she used to wipe up the slops. Snap! A monster look; a hex, between the eyeballs.

Karen strode in, "Just made a sale," she announced triumphantly. "Painted these canvases last night. The paint was still wet. Flowers seem to be what the Israeli will buy. I lived in Rochester when I was a kid and there was a funeral parlor on the corner. I grew up with the smell of decaying flowers and embalming fluid coming out at me as I tried to escape on my bicycle. Got the frames half price, bought two hundred at one go. Maybe I'll make a buck. Got to keep Norm fed. He's costing me an arm and a leg in garage bills."

"Sit down. I'll get you a cup of coffee," I said. I got her a cup of coffee and myself a bottle of Evian mineral water, doing a balancing act with the glass over the bottle, the milk jug on the saucer and wondering if this graying streetwise filly could be trusted.

I've been working hard at ridding myself of my New York deviousness having decided to go straight, think straight, say what I mean, mean what I say.

The gawky waitress in her little apron and funny cap peers at me through very thick lenses, with a resentment so intense it snaps like the resilient gray rag she used to wipe up the slops. Snap! A monster look; a hex. Why was I always being intimidated by waiters? What does she want, blood? I've been sitting here less than 15 minutes. I place the coffee in front of Karen and pour myself some water hoping the natural bubbly springs of France had escaped contamination by particles of matter we can't deal with. I've been reading too much material for Conforti's interview—getting ready to hit him with pithy questions about polluted water, possible collusion in high places of government. It was the same the world over, but David was sure this was news. After all the Sea of Galilee, the Jordan River and the Dead Sea had theological connotations of world import; they are not your everyday backyard river and lake. Like Karen, he's only out to make a buck, turn a perfectly straightforward bit of non-potable water into a four hour TV feature. Headline News: Enteric viruses or was it bacilli, due to untreated excrement from the township of Kiryat Shemona, allegedly found in Ye Sacrosanct River Jordan.

"I've just finished reading a book," Karen said, sipping coffee with obvious satisfaction, "where the main character, down with syphilis, gets a young girl into his hospital bed and dies in coitus with this underage thing locked in his desperate embrace. It took surgery to pry them apart, would you believe it?"

"In a society," I say sounding saintly and wise, a lot like McCrudder, "where death was a lark and sex was so dispassionate, the pleasure principle badly interpreted prevails. There seems to be little hope for the future."

"I don't know about the future, but it sure opens up the market up for some easy nirvana. Here, I'll tell you a story! This summer I went to New York on one of my annual migrations. My friend Stan from the rag trade invited me to dinner. Why should I deny him my company? We had this magnificent dinner, seafood, white wine. Me, I could hardly get anything down, I was so busy pricing the silk shirt on Stan's back; hand-woven, hand-dyed purple polka dots on white—must've cost a fortune. After dinner, we went down to the main floor. Get this," she stabs the air with quick little motions giving form to her thoughts, "a huge space, I mean big, the walls covered wall to wall in foam rubber backed antelope skin, softer than the real thing, maybe it was real, a seamless herd of antelope skins. As my eyes got used to the dark, I see this tall jock walking toward me with a huge erection. I mean huge, a real boom. I looked away. Me? I mean where does a girl look faced with purple hairy balls dingle-dangling on either side of this blood-stiff lance? Truth," she peers at me across the table to see if she's shocked me, "was truth."

Gee whiz, you don't have to apologize to me! We educated, economical independent ladies know all there was to know, more than any whore in Amsterdam who used her pet dog's tongue to massage her clitoris—ask any vet of your acquaintance. I once interviewed one or anyone in Amsterdam. The whore may be forgiven—after all she's in business. We modern ladies of social repute think being crass was being honest, being free. Shades of McCrudder. I hit the roof.

"My heart," she leaned back against the chair really having a ball, "was beating real fast, I was turning hot all over but he, cool as a cucumber, lay down in the central arena took on one girl, rolled over and on to the next, a real sex machine. And those girls, only euphemistically girls, 6 to 60; all right, 8 to 80 dry founts athirsting, if you'll excuse the expression. It's a package deal, dinner, booz and all the sex you can handle, a real bargain and me, I shouldn't take advantage of a bargain. They write on the box, 12 for the price of 11 and I buy five dozen. But this I couldn't take. I just walked out. I had had a few drinks, a snuff of coke for the road and there's my heart. 'Stan,' I said, Stan was an old admirer of mine; lousy dresser but great admirer. 'Stan,' I said, 'I'm going to have a heart attack!' He knows my symptoms, called a cab and sent me back home to Mother. She said, 'my poor daughter all alone.' God I'd just come back from more company than I'd bargained for and she was feeling sorry for my solitude. 'When I was a child,' she told me, trying to lead me back to the ways of the Lord with stories of the old country, 'six or seven at most, father sent me to buy kerosene for his reading lamp. Mother had died in childbirth and baby brother, swollen from lack of love, died against my bony chest. He died from water on the brain. His lips were pursed in desperate hope of milk and life against her child breast. The nipples were just beginning to swell, spongy soft lung from a quartered chicken'—her words. 'Your grandfather,' she tells me for the hundredth time, 'sent me kopek in hand to the kerosene man. He filled the bottle, put it on the counter. "What more you want brat?" but there was something more I wanted, something he wouldn't give, a kind word. I though the kerosene man would be kind, but he sent me back broken hearted through the snow. I forget what I did yesterday, but the kerosene man, that hurt was so real. My father, the smart socialist, married one, two, three; like your Harry, a nice widow 15 years younger. My daughter, forget Harry and his new woman, find yourself a man. A woman needs security.' There was a poet in my mother. She was an illiterate bard, but no art critic that I'll tell you."

I stared into the yellow rounds of her eyes, the running sore on her upper lip, which she had taped over with a piece of transparent sticky paper, which takes on qa whole new meaning.

"Oh this" she puts her hand to her lip, occupational hazard, the free wheeling sixties, love for the asking, no talk, no laughter, no regrets."

"No tears?"

"Oh, there are tears all right. No, not what you're thinking at all—a viral disorder of another kind, my tongue feels like sandpaper, too swollen for my mouth, couldn't complain out loud just feel miserable. My poor mother must have mistaken the symptoms when she came around to save me."

Here I was pretending acquaintance with venereal disease when it's McCrudder growing weeds in his indoor garden that knows the secret poultices of yore. Will they eradicate the next plague, not a flea on the back of a rat, but some unfathomed mutation. Each century and its plague.

I didn't really want her to go on and reveal more of her intimate life because it was getting sickeningly clear to me that we are performing roles, the roles of the times. We had no more free will in this accord than our grandmothers in their humiliating Amazon posturings. Oh for those pre-Freudian days when judiciously dosed cups of tea was the norm for woman scorned and that kiss stolen by hubby from the parlor maid under the stairway leading to the conjugal bedroom was put forever right.

"Do you know the difference between Herpes and love?"

"Herpes is forever," Karen said rushing out to attend to a customer. The gook slumped out of sight behind the pillar holding up the edifice of civil pride. The customer, a tall raw boned woman, with tufts of greasy hair sticking out of a woolen cap pulled down well over her head, looks at the pictures. A good-looking man follows her gaze, picks up three pictures, three bunches of flowers. The woman, holding the paintings tight against her breast with her hands, raises herself on tip toes, flat brown shoes with blond crepe soles, kisses the man. There was such transference of affection between them, that I felt a shock of loneliness, a feeling of desperate envy. I got up at noon, terribly mixed up. My hotel room was small, with cold iron bed railings, thin, lumpy cotton filled mattress, a small clothes closet, table and a chair painted in thick baby blue oil paint. The morning sun filtered through paint worn wooden slats; the shutters kept closed with brown raffia that painfully creaks in the sea breeze. The chintzy curtains fluttered heavily. And everywhere the smell of salt, streaks of salt on the blue and white ceramic floor—the master plan forgotten in mid tiling so that the lines form mad, irritating angles. I dressed quickly keeping my eyes averted from the floor and walked into the hall.

"Top o' the morning to ya, Rosie," the clerk greets me. He had obviously mixed me up with the former guest. I call up Florence in Habonim, having first been obliged to grease the clerk's palm for the use of the telephone. Good thing I brought my purse along.

"Oh luv, so nice to hear from you."

"Where is Tom?"

"Tom is in Escalon visiting family from South Africa. He'll be back. Come and visit. You can share my room. Do come!"

"I'll see," I answer without committing myself one way or the other, having made up my mind right then and there to go to Escalon. I took a taxi—three quarters of an hour passed like minutes—everything was going to work out, I assured myself. I, Josephina—Astarte, goddess of fertility, and Tom—Dagon, fertility fish god of Crete, inseminator of fish eggs and Josephina happy forever after in Escalon "The Bride of Israel," thriving city of the Pharaohs, the Greeks and the Arabs, captured by Richard The Lion Heart in the 12th century, destroyed by Saladin. Empires built and destroyed, but our love would last forever. Had I, Josephina Koenigsburger, not taken a course in Bible Literature, done my term paper on Samson: Predestination VS. Free Will. Professor O'Connor back from Italy in her pert and pink and white checkered low bodied, wasp waited dress, petticoats and crinoline ballet slippers—smiling like Vivien Leigh, Scarlet O'Hara the morning after, so different from the ascetic nun image she had projected all winter long. She'd made no bones about the fact that my being Jewish was to my detriment, but she fascinated. I gave her my best, had even taken to reading the Bible on the elevated, swaying round on the worn leather loop, much to the consternation of sharp nosed ladies who tut-tutted as I fell over on their laps.

I walked along the shore dressed in my teensy weensy yellow polka dot bikini holding my shirt and jeans in one hand, the straps of my sandals in the other. Tom came towards me. It didn't seem strange at all, predestined in fact. The ways of love are wondrous and rare.

Dumbfounded by those dark eyes, painted Pharaoh eyes, hypnotizing me, mesmerized by his flashing smile, his white teeth, his narrow lips pulsating blood, the fine black mustache, drop everything hold my arms open to him.

"The girl from Marseilles, the savior of our Florence."

"Josephina Koenigsburger," I blurt out.

"Josephina, of course so glad to see you again. Shall I give Florence your regards?"

"No, no, it's all right. I've been invited over, I'll see her there."

"Tra," he raised his thumb up to the sky in what seemed to me a singularly vulgar sign. I follow his eyes up the hill to a gargantuan female dismounting a Vespa.

"Your girlfriend?" I ask as she comes prancing towards us.

"A friend," he said catching the dame round her waist, "just a friend. She's a hairdresser from Norwich."

"Norwich? Are there Jews in Norwich," I asked standing very close to them trying to beguile him with my charms.

"This was Josephina Koenigsburger. We met in Marseilles under trying circumstances."

"Well over the fast," the hairdresser says.

Arm in arm they stroll away. I wave goodbye, pick up my things, turn, run on along the beach. Oh if I had known about Gloria's mandrake root then, I would have challenged death and taken the potion. I was dying to have a baby and Tom would be the father. I would never abort, but courageously carry the child, growing bigger and bigger, possibly dying in childbirth on the beach of Escalon while Tom was in the arms of the siren hairdresser. What distress. She was a witch; a witch from Norwich conspiring to keep Tom from me.

The witch; the witch of Norwich I incant running into a deserted palm bedecked park, along beds of blond brush flowered cacti, into a flock of crow-like men coming forth from a house of prayer. Embarrassed, I run back to the beach, find a hidden cove, put my clothes on and take a taxi back to the hotel so exhausted I sleep around the clock.

I'd meant to ask where the shower was, but I couldn't face talking to anyone. I returned to consciousness at 1 o'clock, hungry for food, with a nagging pain in my head. From the other side of the wood partition separating my room from hers, scratching, giggling, crying sounds of a woman in pain. A male voice saying, "Ok baby I've got it in, stop thrashing about, it'll come out," and sighs and cries. This woman was suffering, really suffering; teary hiccups of pain coming clearly through the wall. What was the brute of a man doing to this poor female?

I slip on my dungarees, my checkered cotton shirt that makes me look like a lumberjack, and went out into the hall to complain to the management. The man behind the desk was very short. His nose just rose above the wooden plank on which the guest register lay open. I can see my name, Josephina Koenigsburger; I must have signed it, but when?

"Yes?" he asked, eyes expressionless behind thick granny glasses. "Yes?"

I was about to shout, "Police! Murder!" when out of the door adjoining mine, a sweet, barefoot, blond girl wrapped in a striped hand towel, pupils dilated like two camera lenses glazed over with some basic knowledge, privy to secrets not in the realm of mere plebs like me. She came close to the clerk and inquired softly, "Where is the bathroom please?"

"To your right, Miss!" the man said pointing in the direction of a door. She runs towards it, little hops and skips on the balls of her feet. In no time flat she's back, bumps into a tall dark kid, coming out of their room.

"Oops, sorry," she says.

He jumped back to let her pass through and in a gesture of ownership, shut the door behind her, and strides confidently into the bathroom. The man behind the desk was very short. His nose just rises above the wooden plank on which the guest register lies open. I can see my name, Josephina Koenigsburger. I must have signed it, but when?

"Yes" he asks, his nearsighted eyes expressionless behind thick granny glasses, "Yes, Miss; can I help you?" I'm glad he hasn't called me Rosie this time.

"Is there nothing I might be doin' for ya, Miss?"

"No, no I'll be OK. I'd like to buy some food. I haven't eaten since breakfast yesterday."

"Rather tricky on Yom Kippur." He disappears from view. I bent over the desk to see what he was doing. He's squatting on a floor sliding sheets of paper into envelopes.

"Vote Mapai!" he smiles up at me. "Have one," he hands me a circular, "weigh the alternative. Just slip this little chit into your voting box and you've got the most long-lived, unrivaled, stagnant political party in the whole Middle East. Nothing like a rising democracy, Miss. Are you sure there was nothing I can do for you?" Did I spy an Irish policeman in that voice?

"Are you a policeman?"

"No Miss," he swooshes his tongue over an envelope flap, hammers it shut with a bang of his fist—Momma tenderizing the meat back home in the Bronx.

"Are you Irish then?" I ask putting on my brogue. It comes easy. After all I had marched with Angelica Edwards and her Dad in three St. Patrick's Day parades and I loved Angelica like a sister, not to mention the fact that I'd been brought up on Hollywood actors playing leprechauns.

"Yes, how did you guess? I'm from Dublin," he said between licks.

"What are you doing here then?"

"I live here."

"Are there Catholic Jews?" Boy was I getting information. My future reading public would eat it up, slurp.

"I'm a Jew. My family lives in Dublin."

"You're leading me on. Yes, you are."

"Would I do a thing like that, Dearie? You just get yourself to a library and take O'Connor's Annals of Innisfallen from the shelf, you'll read, and there's no denyin' the truth of it lass, that in 1079 five Jews came over the sea bringing gifts to Faidelbach, that was Hua Brian."

"What happened?"

"They were sent right back, gifts and all. I'm not sure about the gifts, but they got the boot all right. There may be a restaurant open, hereon Ben Yehuda Street in the center of town, though I doubt it. If you're going for a walk anyway, would you mind delivering this?" He handed me a packet of envelopes, the Hebrew letter "M" printed black on cheesy yellowish paper. "Second floor above the Tnuva Dairy, The Histadrut Worker's Union Caf. Here's the address. I didn't think you'd mind."

"No, not if I'm going there anyway."

I lock my room and place the key gently on the counter so not to disturb the preoccupied clerk and go out in search of food. I follow directions, walk to the center of town. The streets are deserted. The houses, a reconstruction of Romantic dreams c.1920, turrets and oval verandas, the peeling plaster revealing great patches of raw concrete, Bauhaus gone to pot here far from the Weimar Republic where it was conceived. There was nothing more depressing than deteriorating houses, their drooping wooden shutters hanging low over sightless eyes reminding me of Uncle Hymie who held his eyelid open with a bar of silver soldered to the inner frame of his gold plated glasses.

I got to the restaurant. In the window, a papier-mâché collage, gray eggplant salad on a dirt ingrained blue plastic plate, glob of mud brown coffee in a white cup, two yellow rolls on a satiny paper napkin, a pat of margarine on a tiny stainless steel tin all arranged on a blue plastic tray. I was so starved, I would have settled for that, but the place was shuttered and barred with two great padlocks hanging despondently from their staples.

The scent of coffee wafts by my nostrils; I follow it through a dull narrow hall smelling desperately of cleanliness, the sign over the elevator, a large Hebrew letter "M," identical to that on the envelopes I'm carrying — same on the door on the second floor from which the heavenly smell of coffee spills forth. Home base. Behind the glass door, a shadow moves. I knocked. A middle-aged man with a humpback and a gleaming smile of welcome opens the door invitingly.

"Shalom, Tali."

"I'm a tourist," I blurted out in self-defense.

"She didn't mention that. Let's get to work. I had to get a few sentences straight. I've tried improving my enunciation, the words come out clear enough, but the rhythm was still foreign." He leads me into a room, a mattress covered in a grass green hand-woven spread a little frayed for wear, offers itself to me. Below, the slumbering silence of Tel Aviv rises to enwrap me in thoughts of oblivion.

"Don't worry, Avi, you'll be all right," a tall, slender, strikingly handsome guy, wiping his hands on a dishtowel enters the room.

"This was Tali," I'm introduced to the paragon of manliness, Mr. Universe himself.

I smile wanly. "Shalom," I whispered under my breath.

"First, I must tell you," the humpback says, "I must have a perfect British accent. I was playing a smart fly from outer space. My voice will come through a microphone in the helmet and secondly we don't had to worry about facial expressions, I'll be totally encompassed in that F 54 multi-eyed wonder-suit, but the enunciation must be letter perfect you understand?"

"And for this," Mr. Universe sighs, "for this they are taking him to Hollywood, and paying him in dollars. He's only got the part because he was the only actor short enough and thin enough to fit into the costume. You were always lucky," Mr. Universe strokes the dishtowel, "I had had to struggle to get a job as an understudy for Yadin. I can play the father in All My Sons as well as he, but will he break a leg? Never. With my luck I'll have to wait till I go naturally gray."

"No I'm not Tali," I'm about to say rising sexually to these men, aflame as I was with a need to be held, to be loved, to feel the warmth of another human body next to mine. I was so alone. "Sorry," I say, "Just a minute. I'm afraid I've forgotten my bag. Thank you. I'll be back." I put the packet of circulars on the floor, and ran out of the apartment, down the stairs and up the street, my fingertips trilling iron shutters over dusty window panes, the owners atoning for the fact they deal in trade instead of being out reclaiming this historical corridor of power from its two thousand year torpor.

I entered a park, where a figure covered in newsprint was lying on a bench silent and still. It was a man. A dragonfly hangs suspended over a bush of lead blue flowers. I ran out into a phalanx of men straggling out of a lump of a building, blue stars on yellow stained glass windows open like guillotines waiting to behead the sacrilegious food-preoccupied female within the holy horde. I reached the hotel; the reception clerk was slobbering envelope flaps with his insatiable protruding tongue.

"Miss," he said as he handed me my key, "Jews were living in Dublin and prospering in the mid 17th century. The synagogue in Crane Lane? Parishioners claim they were invited to settle by Cromwell himself. You can look it up in The Oceana, 1656. If I'm not mistaken, James Harrington—you know, the political writer—actually felt the Jews should be encouraged to settle. He was convinced they would flourish both in agriculture and commerce to the advantage of themselves and Ireland."

"Oh, yes?"

"Yes, Miss."

"Why do you think I'm interested?"

He took off his glasses, watery blue eyes, a shock of straight blond hair awfully close to me. "You squint," he says.

"If I leave now, do I had to pay for the room? I mean if I don't sleep here tonight?"

"Well, you might ask the night clerk, I'm off duty by then, but if you ask me, it does seem singularly unfair, doesn't it? After all we won't be able to let your room tonight will we? And the hotel will lose money, won't it?"

"I'll leave first thing in the morning. Isn't there a cafeteria nearby, somewhere I can get a sandwich?"

"No, I'm afraid not."

"Thank you." My stomach was growling with hunger, but I flashed a smile prettily for the clerk, tottered back to my room, flopped on the bed wondering if this was the kind of sacrifice demanded of reporters. I must have fallen asleep. The room was very dark. A soft, insistent knock forced my eyes open.

"Excuse me," Miss Koenisburger," a familiar voice came through to me, "may I come in?"

"Just a minute," I call out, putting on my shirt. I'd gone to bed in my soiled dungarees. I opened the door to the clerk, now standing his full height in the shadow. He was short, but not much shorter than me.

"Brought you a sandwich," he said, placing a tray on the bed. The table and chair are piled high with my stuff. He went over to the window and opened several slats. The sun was shattering.

"Don't," I beg, "my eyes!" I don't want him to see me too clearly. I haven't brushed my teeth or washed myself. I grabbed the sandwich and took an enormous bite, and pat the bed invitingly. After all, I couldn't have him standing there hovering above me as I ate, nor could I shove him into the empty closet smelling as it did of acidy herb which reminded me of death. I had never really come in contact with death. I always turned away from oil-soaked rags in the street, not sure they aren't dead cats or dogs which the tire marks of many cars had trammeled into a facsimile of an oil-soaked rag, except that once when I had willed myself to die. I must have been 14. I remember the long trip back to life; so long, so fearfully long, impossibly, inconsequentially long. I had broke through the pliable hymen of life straining back to the soft scummy froth of death. Jesus Christ, I feel the steel buttons on the receptionist's shirt press down painfully on my stomach, hear the blood in the extended blood vessels round my vagina round each muscle and nerve pulsate so insistently, thumping louder and louder, vying with the chanting congregation across the way. He could had done anything with me, but the idiot kissed me on the cheek, and whispered, "you're a very sexy kid,' and opened the door. "I hope you appreciate the risk I've taken bringing you food on Yom Kippur, 'The Day of Atonement.' It's a fast day you know." I hear the lock click. I look down at the half eaten sandwich dutifully lying on the floor on the tray near the bed. God did I pull him down on top of me?

I called Florence up again, and told her I had nowhere to go, but want to stay in Haifa. I had some business there.

She says, "Come right over, Tom will think of something. Good thing you met me, you're a total loss."

Florence was in seventh heaven, gushing over with her "hitgashmut"; she had spent her summers and part of the winters scouting on the heaths of England, I think she said heaths, in preparation for "spiritual growth realizable only in the Holy Land" and here she is. I've never seen anyone so fat and blubbery before with so much nervous energy, such wide-eyed innocence. She wasn't exactly dumb, but how mushy can you get over artificial fishponds and banana plantations. She showed me the ropes. I was to go to "The Sochnut" and claim I was contemplating settling in the country. "Cry a bit, let the officials think you are desperate, look down at the port below as if you are about to jump, wring your hands, beg on bended knees; otherwise they won't give you a second thought."

Bless her, she was right. As soon as I turned from the shack on the roof which served as office and walked towards the edge, my name was called and the harassed official who had at first categorically refused to help me, scribbled some words and I had a bed in a youth hostel at a price I could afford.

I took the bus up United Nations Avenue and fell in love with Gustav. He was a Physicist newly recruited into the Israel air force. He looked obliquely at me and asked if I would prepare mushrooms for him. "Mushrooms?" I queried and was smitten. He was Polish, assimilated Polish; that was with tenuous Jewish roots, an orphan of the Second World War. An aunt in Krakow sent him mushrooms regularly in the mail. He only talked about mushrooms. I mean we hardly talked. He just said "mushrooms." There was this large communal kitchen with ten gas burners. I took a frying pan lying around, added some fat and threw in the mushrooms. How was I to know dehydrated mushrooms had to be soaked in water before cooking? I was ignorant of the culinary arts. I don't remember whether he ate the mushrooms or not. I do remember that the person from whom I borrowed the frying pan accused me not only of stealing, but also of sullying the faith. I bought the guy a new frying pan. He was a Bulgarian who must had forgiven me for he implied that had I not been so taken with Gustav the physicist, he would had fallen for me.

That evening, Gustav invited me to his room, showed me photographs of the Catholic wife he had abandoned. Her brothers had railroaded him into marriage, a civil marriage. It didn't count here in Israel. He showed me the photograph of the Jewish girl he'd married and divorced. It was a marriage of convenience, to bring her over to Israel where she married someone else. And he showed me a photograph of the balcony of the orphanage from which he used to pee down on the populace of Krakow. Mom had deposited him there when Dad was murdered by the Gestapo; just before her head was split open by a piece of shrapnel meant to kill her. I was so moved by the photographs, I slipped into his bed. It was much less exciting than I supposed. I mean he made the socially accepted passes at breasts, touched the right places, but either he was a lousy lover, possibly impotent, or worried about the wife he had deserted or nothing happened. My mother had warned me not to roller skate in the streets, it might dislocate my vagina. I guess mine was dislocated. He made me understand I couldn't spend the whole night in his bed, he had a busy day ahead of him; his roommate might come back any minute. I was to go to my room. It was 11:15 at night. I ran out and crashed head on into Tom. What was he doing at my bedroom door making lost-in-the-woods eyes?

"Josephina, I'm so tired."

"Be right back," I said sensing the steel will inside him, which would go through with whatever his body wanted. There was light coming from under the office door just down the hall. I knocked. After a long while, Mrs. Mugrabi, the lady in charge of the hostel opened it just a crack, what was she hiding in there? I kept my lightly clad body in the shadow, stuck my head in the angle of light close to hers. She was nervous, ready for tragedy. An English girl had committed suicide the day before by jumping out of the window and the week before a Moroccan girl had cut her wrists when the Brazilian immigrant who had promised her marriage turned out to be a married father of three. The information had been transferred to me by one of the girls in the dining room.

"What happened?" Mrs. Mugrabi asked.

"Nothing, nothing, Mrs. Mugrabi, I just want some information."

"What?" Her voice was prim with an edge of indignation which should have scared me off, but didn't.

"Yes, I'd like to know if there's an extra room in the hostel, I mean if a guest shows up can you put him up for the night?"

"Only if you had a stamped and signed letter from "The Sochnut.""

"Thank you." The definitive click of her door was not to be argued with.

I looked round for Tom. He was standing naked next to my bed.

"I'm sorry! You can't stay here. I couldn't ask him to use the other bed, so neatly made up—several books, a fragile glass vase, a pink glass elephant demanding distance

"My friend Gustav may have an extra bed," I add out-of-hand, quickly slipping on my pajamas. I always sleep in pajamas; living in dirty dungarees was the exception not the rule.

"You look like a clown."

"I'd bought the flannel pajamas on sale at Gimble's. They had ruffles on the neck, wrists and ankles. I suppose if I'd had on a jester's hat with bells the whole hostel would had heard our cavorting. Tom was a physiological wonder. Not only did he look like Casanova, he performed like the ideal hero. When he was quite satisfied and sure I had been titillated to nothingness, a fuzzy feeling lighting the boundaries of my skin, he told me that he had a date. He'd promised Florence, who was in charge of the work schedule on the farm that week that he'd be there at 5:00 in the morning to feed the cows.

"Cows must be fed," he said. My perfect physiological fit made in heaven, was dressed in a jiffy. But he hadn't contended with me. I was dressed and running after him. As I passed Mrs. Mugrabi's door, I heard giggles. Was she at it too?

"Tom," I slipped my hand under his elbow to his obvious annoyance, "just remembered, I also have to see Florence."

"You just saw her."

"Important business."

We walked down to the central bus terminal, he in a dark mood, I pretending not to notice. At 4:30am the lone bus slowly revved up enough energy to move.

"Don't you have something better to do?" he asked, trying to shake me off. But I was going to get mine back if it took all my willpower. We walked down the road to the village in the cool dawn, in silence. He shared a room with a squat, blond boy who was masturbating when we crashed through the door.

"Ray Berg. This was Josephina."

"Hello, hello?" he answered, a red-hot patch spreading down his neck to his fat chest. I sat down on the floor stretching like a kitten trying to get the tension out of my body. The roommate served instant coffee, heated the water with an electric fork. I didn't touch it, neither did Tom. His black eyes had lost none of their luster; his mind was fully occupied deliberating strategies.

"I'm going for a walk," the roommate said.

"Don't go," Tom shouted. The boy left grinning unlovingly at me with his sun speckled brown eyes. Tom undressed and got into the cot, he had no choice; the odds were against him. I got in on top of him. And this time I decided to take notes for a future article. I observed everything with my mind's eye. I felt myself loved. That was I loved myself, accepted Tom's incapacity for restraint with a cynicism worthy of a whore not a day-old non-virgin. When I was quite satisfied and he tired out, I got up, dressed and walked over to Florence's room. She was sleeping with her arm over Ray, two blubbery seals on a narrow cot. He turned out to be a graduate of Stanton, a marine engineer who eventually married Florence whom he took to Eilat. Had the oil rich sheiks next door on the Red Sea known Ray was on the way to discovering artificial oil, they would've had both his eyes pecked out by a well-trained hawk—retaliation, protecting their source of income if not by peaceful means then let the cannons roar. I didn't like him. He didn't like me. I had no choice but walk back to Tom's room. He was working in the cowshed. I looked through every single one of his possessions, found out all about him. Age: 24, graduate of London University with honors, a half Jew—that was one of his parents. His mother was Jewish, the father tall and spare, Tom's devil-may-care look in his eyes was British. He found me looking at the photographs, took me for a walk past a cotton field lying fallow—puffs of white cotton on a few seared stalks, to a lean to at the far end of an abandoned stretch of beach half thatched in last year's brittle palm fronds.

"Tom," I was about to say, dreaming myself a belle dressed in crinolines and he plighting his troth in the candelabra lit ballroom on the ole' plantation, medal on his chest struck by command of the Virgin Queen herself granted in honor of work well done against the Spanish Armada, "God blew, they were scattered."

"Yes, Tom, I will be your bride," I hint with a sly but terribly feminine smile as I play the virginals a la Queen Elizabeth I, while he courts me with poetry, Marvel and Milton, for was he not an emissary sent by Cromwell to Jamaica to pacify the Jews, pioneers in sugar planting with the world monopoly not only in the rum trade but in the molasses trade as well? The British merchants may want us out of Jamaica, but we are a potentially bottomless well of taxes and Cromwell will not deny us our historical right. After all he knows what Uncle Martinez, buccaneer, wrought upon the Spanish vessels top heavy with stolen gold from the Incas, waddling by the Canary Islands on their way home.

Pirating may not be nice, I'll tell Tom, weaving possibilities, but Uncle Martinez can't rightly be blamed for trying to get back in kind some of the family's olive groves usurped by the Grand Inquisitor under orders from Queen Isabella and King Ferdinand, may their names be blotted from memory. Ah, were I a bird, I would fly up above the Atlas mountains, unearth those caskets of doubloons, reals, pieces of eight Uncle Martinez buried there for safe keeping. The Inquisitor's hand might have been long but not long enough to reach the mountain peaks above the Sahara, the sea-lanes inadvertently opened up by Columbus for fleeing Jews.

Aunt Khoursey lived in a back room in the apartment singing plaintive songs of love in Medieval Spanish, crocheting an unending spool of lace one inch wide. . She was a really cheap guest: never used the electricity, couldn't see, drank three drops of lemon juice for breakfast and for lunch rose-petal jam with a silver dessert spoon she kept carefully polished, grew the roses herself in the backyard, made her own jam.

"Josephina, querida mia," she would say, with large knuckled velvet palms over my cheeks over lips and unformed breasts, smelling of lemon cologne imported from Turkey, broken pelvis, which wouldn't mend. She died at the age of 103. "Querida, this lace was for you, two pots of jam in the kitchen cupboard, three starched sheets in a packet in the closet, "my sister's dowry sheet, heavy cotton, wartime, only stuff available. When I die, wrap me not in silk, querida, these will do."

"Tom," I break the silence. I had this need to be thought worthy, "my cousins are lawyers in the Carolinas. They've been living there since the 17th century."

"My Mom's Dad," he tells me, "back in Manchester was a rag and bone merchant. 'A Jew,' he always taught me, 'may be in temporarily restricted circumstances, but poor—never. Nil desparandum Corburun dum illigitimum, roughly translated, don't let the bastards, or the bitches, ground you down.' Good sort, my granddad. I've just remembered a rather urgent appointment." What could he do? The girls were crazy about him.

"I'll write you a letter," I say as we part.

"Don't bother."

"Yes I will! Be a gentleman," I add, quite aware now that it was the sweet guileless Samson I was searching for and not a fertility god, "you don't have to answer." I long to kiss him tenderly. How had I fallen so helplessly, so irrationally in love?

"I have an appointment," he repeats. As my lips touch his skin, he doesn't bend down to mine. I stand on the beach in the midday sun watching him trample sand underfoot—Clark Gable to Scarlet: "Frankly, my dear, I don't give a damn."

It was 2 o'clock in the afternoon. Gustav was standing at the table in the lobby of the hostel in paratrooper pants a number of sizes too small. He looked like a child. I wanted to go over to him, hug him protectively, mother him. Rites of passage, primacy—we always remember the first time, however abortive. He keeps his weighted gaze on the newspaper he seems to be reading.

I walked into the room that was mine; I paid for it.

"Oh it's you?" the hairdresser from Norwich says. "You could at least have made your bed! Why do you wear your hair pulled flat back against your scalp? Let me help you," she adds changing her tune, "just a sec." She comes back comb and scissors in hand. I stand looking at my image in the fly shit-flecked mirror above the small sink, filling up with hair, like the plumage of a Christmas goose readied for the fires of hell. She plucks out my life with her clacking shears, clack, clack, clack; places herself squarely behind me, long handled mirror in hand. I couldn't interpret the look in her dark eyes.

"I did that for Tom, because you are his friend. Do you know how much I get paid for a ducktail cut in London?"

And suddenly I remember Tom's strange questions on that walk back from the sea.

"Why does your hair spring like that?"

"I don't know."

"Why does your hair catch the sun like that?"

"I don't know, I don't know," I repeat longing to hold his hand following his every step on sand staid sea—angelic blue sky. I wished, prayed, hoped Tom would say, "Stay!" I wanted to kiss his lips so badly, but I couldn't penetrate that sullen coat of contemplation about him.

I turn on the cold water in the shower and wash myself clean. Ablutions in preparation for high romance, undercover agent stuff.

CHAPTER 12

I'm looking at Karen's flowers, romantic renderings of a convoluted mind, very powerful, sexy canvases. Feel eyes on the small of my back; voices, English mixed with Arabic loud, loud so I can hear, talking of books, publishing books in London—funny how we feel each other out—pointers on an upcoming trip to Europe, last rehearsal for an upcoming trip to Europe. I turned round and stare right into the eyes of a heavyset gent, gray curly hair, spivy suit. He spilled his coffee. I watched cake on a napkin absorb dark liquid, break into large lumps. The waitress comes by with her ever-ready rag, wiped up the soggy mess. She picked up Karen's half empty cup, gave my bottle of water a suspicious look. "I haven't finished yet," I say courageously holding on to the bottle. She wiped the table very thoroughly, dumped the rag on the tray and walks away.

I went out to Karen, careful to leave my bag on the table, staking claim so the waitress won't dare wipe my presence away.

"Did you see that?" she asked pointing to the couple walking up the stairs to the farmhouse at the right. "How can such a good looking guy fall for such an ugly woman? My mother always told me, 'you don't have to be so beautiful, you don't have to be so smart; a little bit of luck that's all you need.'"

I chose a picture unlike the others: a handful of yellow pansies with dark brown velvety hearts against a background of a stormy Sea of Galilee. In the upper left hand corner, a hint of a Crusader's fortress under a bilious aquamarine sky, Karen, sickening but I like it. She halves the price. I kiss her cheek.

"I'm always getting upset at waitresses," I confide as we walk in out of the cold, apologizing for spilling water on the saucer, dropping crumbs on heavy armchairs in hotel lobbies—discreet filth and banana plants under filtered day—tip too much or too little, stay too long or not long enough."

"Troubles," she said looking round for her coffee, "love people with real out and out troubles."

I placed the painting in between the box of chocolates I'd bought for Gloria and didn't give her when I saw the abundance in her living room and an appointment book, magnetically poised at the ready to receive world shaking messages. Was there anything new under the sun to report? The waitress had removed all traces of my bottle of Evian.

"You know how it is," Karen said, incorrectly sensing what I'm trying to have her tell me, "we sort of exchanged roles, Harry and me. I needed sex and he became passive, I grew more aware of my body and he became ashamed of me, my lost innocence, my grateful whining, my girlish shyness which I couldn't hold on to after 20 years of marriage. That was what he was clamoring for. One day I left him, left my job and went screwing the long days away in and around the Village. It was a real party as if every inhibition I'd ever had dispersed into thin air; every fantasy my mind had ever played with was there for the taking. The curious thing was that it was my inhibitions that had played havoc with my marriage in the first place; the more I gave in to my fantasies, the more I hated Harry; the more my fantasies became reality, the more I hated me. Don't move!" Karen rushed out, "you're bringing me luck."

I made up my mind to deliver Robert Chiprut's letter to his family in Haifa as I had promised. They too lived on United Nation Avenue, so might as well get the thing over with. I scampered up that hill reading house numbers like a dappled sorrel in the early afternoon sun. The port fell away from my line of vision. At the northern most point of the bay, the luminous chalk white cliffs of Rosh Hanikra devised a border between Israel and the Lebanon. The U.S. navy, anchored off the coast, was keeping the country together, which even then threatened to fall apart like pick up sticks you hold in your hand and then let go, each color a factional ideology. I could not go to my new job admitting I hadn't been to Beirut, the Paris of the Middle East, when the whole sixth fleet was out in force. But if rumors of closed borders were true, I would first have to go to Athens, board the flagship in the guise of a newspaper correspondent and get permission to go to Lebanon just a stone's throw away. Of course I'd be photographed shaking the Admiral's hand, sailors in white rows posted at attention in the background, a military band playing "Stars and Stripes Forever." Abdel Nassar couldn't help but be impressed by my photocopied credentials and grant me a special interview, eye-to-eye revelations of what he had found in King Farouk's palace when the young officers had barged in.

Scintillating headline: "Sue Johnson-Clarke, long lost daughter of Sir Johnson-Clarke and former chief belly dancer in Farouk's harem, mother of six of his many children, wearing a diaphanous skirt and diamond studded bra tells all to Josephina Koenigsburger, reporter at large.

I found house number 345 in gold tessera on green and blue, like an icon over the garage. I walked up a flight of studiously set flagstone steps. The odor of overripe flowers in the breezeless afternoon sun arrests my step. A sleek black hound raises its head above a trellis of baby pink roses, bares his teeth in a lugubrious grin and politely lowers himself from view. I rang a bell near the elevator, which was an iron gate protecting the abyss from intruders. A voice came down to me, distorted and thick, through the electric sieve on the doorstep.

"Kain, mizeh?" I understand I'm being questioned about my identity. "I have a message from Mr. Robert Chiprut from Istanbul," I shout up through the electric device. "Yes, come right up, throw the gate open please to release the latch," orders accompanied by a mind-searing buzz. I hear the elevator wheeze, the dog's grin turns to a furious bark. I feel it straining at the leash. It can easily jump over the flimsy enclosure. I don't dare collapse the pantograph to accordion pleat, run up the stairs instead past beds of pansies, winking wailing appendages, meaty black cherry red roses—Aunt Khoursey spooning rose-petal jam into her cavernous mouth.

"Good afternoon," a curly haired guy greets me leads me round great white bed sheets hanging out to dry on lines. My heart skips a beat. I had been here before, dizzy, faint, marvelously heady.

"I'm the waiter, Joseph. I'll take you upstairs through my rooms." There were posters of naked women; a doorless closet under a flight of wooden stairs leading to a gallery, the bedroom no doubt. "Jalle's brother used to live here when he was studying, now this is the servant's quarters. I take care of the house when I'm on shore leave and the family was away. Pimps found the house vacant and brought their clientele here and messed up the toilets. It took a cleaning team two full weeks to get rid of the smell."

"Great," I say following him out the back, up more stairs to a bridge connecting the elevator to an impressively carved oak door.

"Where did you learn English," I asked.

"I'm a waiter on the Zim shipping line. I used to have a Canadian girlfriend. She wanted to marry I think. I lost her number. Do you want to marry?"

"Who?"

"You."

"Who to?"

"Me."

"I'll think about it," I say meaning "yes, anytime." If history was the account of missed occasions, mine, I tell myself cunningly, will be the account of those I haven't missed.

"I will take you to meet my mother at 4 o'clock. My sister and baby live with us. Her husband is at sea."

He leads me through the pantry into a kitchen, flowery light blue cupboards, electrical gadgets, sparkling white Westinghouse ideal kitchen off the exhibition floor.

"Please wait in the Salon. I will call Jalle."

I watch his short, muscular figure walk through the baroque doors, bend over a pigeon holed desk covered in baked enamel, pornographic miniatures of the courtesans in the entourage of Louis Quatorze, alabaster hands suggestively touching white bosoms, raising crinolines above ankles, playing a spinet subtly lit by an early morning light. I just stand there admiring the set of white satin Italian furniture, brocaded oriental furniture, the early American colonial, English period furniture from the show windows of Paris. New York, Rome—I'll have that and that and that. Breakfronts heavy with silver, Bric-a-brac, Chinese vases on bow legged highly varnished tables, bunches of light green glass grapes on porcelain dishes, plaster cupids on marble stands, a marble Venus holding her left breast between thumb and forefinger, two Murano glass clowns grimacing with thick glass lips, knowing they are out of place under the enormous chandelier hanging from the center of the ceiling, ropes of crystal playing rainbows with the afternoon sun filtering in through the balcony where iron bars meant to keep out pimps, whores and their companions of the night, slash the pale blue and white Chinese rugs with shadow.

Jalle walks in, a questioning hauteur on her face, a who-the-hell-are-you look in her deep blue eyes. As she gets closer, her smile broadens and suddenly I feel her soft fleshy arms about me.

"Why you are the companion of the air trip. So nice to see you. Please sit down. Joseph, bring a carafe of water and the rose jam."

"Yes Madame," he said smiling at me with his shy dark brown eyes. He wasn't really shy I would learn to know, but nearsighted, almost as nearsighted as me.

"Yes," she said not at all surprised when I explained the nature of my errand. I mean I was surprised at the coincidence, but not she.

"You see, my dear Josephina, the letter you bring was addressed to my brother who was in London on business and will not be back for a fortnight. I will call my husband who will know exactly what to do." She rang a little copper bell at the side of the overstuffed white foam rubber couch.

"Please," she said showing me to a seat. As I sat down I heard the air wheezing forth from foam, ahhhh, I'm so sorry! I was afraid Joseph might think I'd done the unforgivable—farting in a rich man's room was not the thing. She sat straight up on the edge of a gold embossed chair upholstered in petit point roses on a tan background. I guess posture goes with class. I'm sunk deep in foam. "Ah Moise! She addresses a tall, broad shouldered young man who glides in pointed toes left, right, over the carpet woven from the spit of a million silkworms, "meet Mademoiselle Josephina Koenigsburger, elle est une juive Allemande."

"Mademoiselle," he bowed his sun streaked blond head ever so slightly, his blue-green fish tank eyes, the color of the mosaic over the garage below, never changing expression. When he placed his loosely fit, well pressed white duck pants, his white polo shirted body momentarily down on the couch, the foam rubber doesn't dare move. All I get was a whiff of his cologne.

Moise got up, went closer to his wife and putting his lips to her sleek black hair whispers, "Bijou ne te fatigue pas," smiles at me apologetically, "Merci," and like a ballroom dancer, stomach drawn in head high glides out the door.

Jalle and I face each other with nothing to say. She pours the water and putting a delicate silver spoon into the midnight blue glass dish in a silver bowl hands it to me. "Roshhlood," she said, or something that sounds like that urging me to put the jam into my mouth. As I drink the proffered water I feel a dull ache in my molar, haven't been to the dentist in six months. She holds out her hand for the spoon, puts it in my glass, the glass on the tray, hands it to Joseph standing at attention behind.

"We will now see the rest of the house."

"I am late for an appointment."

But she was adamant. "You must see Mamam, Papa and of course baby." We walk up a flight of stairs, full size corps de ballet in a glass cabinet lining the wall, plywood ballerinas in slightly soiled tutus elbowing for space with arch necked swans on a blue glass lake, their perforated thick orange bills kept open with copper wires in perpetual clapper tongued, beady eyed demented smiles.

"Papa," she explains, "saw something similar in a garden in Geneva, but the Israelis are not disciplined workmen you know, they do not take care and time. Papa took Aref, who was the carpenter, to a production of Swan Lake in Athens you understand. They spent the night in the hotel room overlooking the lake with the swans yet Aref did not capture father's intent. Still we like it, and you?"

"Nuts," I feel like saying. This carpenter never saw a swan or a ballerina in his life. I smile instead. My lips spread over my teeth. I was introduced to the Maman and the Papa.

The Papa sits balancing on an impressively obese stomach between thin wide-open legs, metal zipper, seams sewn double to keep it hidden, shimmers improperly smug. I look away in shame, me, who had so recently taken on the Polish Gustav and the British Tom.

Maman was a beauty, white skin, tremendous brown cat eyes and unbelievably long eyelashes, which brush her lightly rouged cheeks, gleaming gold coiffeur every hair impressively in place, pleated gray mohair shirt dress falls over her knees revealing shapely legs, feet shod in tan pigskin pumps, so soft, the leather glows. She touched my hand in greeting, her manicured red fingertips wafted powdery soft perfume. She smiled delightedly like a model for large sizes in a fashion magazine.

"Maman, Papa, this is Josephina Koenigsburger, elle est une juive Allemande. Elle a apporte une lettre de Robert. C'est tout a fait drole, n'est ce pas?"

"Tais toi, Jalle," the father says, "please, my dear, sit down." I did as I was bid.

"Joseph," he calls. Joseph comes by with a dainty porcelain openwork basket he holds under the man's nose; a many-pocketed white doily divides a range of pastel candy coated sweets.

"Excuse him," the beautiful wife said with her angelic smile pasted on her face, "he must take his pills. It is the regime."

"I've just come back from the cure at the Mayo Clinic," Papa volunteers pleasantly, studying his pills. "We went to a nightclub. There was an Arab Sheikh from Abu Dhabi at the table next to ours. He sent champagne over to Regine, here. He wanted to buy her from me, but of course I refused. It was a good joke."

"Oh, that happened years ago," Maman interrupts.

"But you are as beautiful as ever you were, Cherie, Bijou, Querida," popping a pill into his mouth with each endearment. When he had had enough, he waved basket and servant away.

"We were in the nightclub in Geneve. Striptease. I got excited and fainted. My heart, I thought. The cardiac specialist sent us to the Mayo Clinic. I lost 20 pounds," he pats his belly proudly.

"Yes, and Regine and I then went to Las Vegas to play. Next year, God willing, we will go to as Las Vegas again. We were there seven days and we did not see everything. Nightclubs today, everyone wears jeans, there was no one to dress up for."

He dozed off.

"Papa," Jalle says, "did not take me with him this time. I was enceinte, pregnant you see. But I did go to Jamaica with Moise. The natives were wearing the Star of David on their chests. I asked them if they were Jews and they said of course they weren't."

"Perhaps they attach some kind of magic to the symbol," I volunteered in a whisper not to disturb Papa.

"I do not want to contradict a guest," Maman smiles her brilliant smile, the lashes throwing blue shadows on her luscious cheeks, "but in Jamaica we had a beautiful temple and a Yesiba. You will not be surprised when I tell you that I was a descendent of Antonio Fernandez Carvajal."

"Oh!" I exclaim, resisting the urge to say, maybe we're relatives, pretending acquaintance with her ancestor. Why destroy her illusion to exclusive universal fame.

"We are," she continues, "ever so grateful, Cheri, for bringing us the letter."

I was dismissed.

"Come into my bedroom," Jalle takes my hands, "I will show you baby." Baby was playing in an ordinary wooden playpen in the terrace off a very large bedroom. He was blond, fat and cute. She expected me to make the appropriate noises, but I had absolutely no feelings for other people's babies now. I think I was given a short dose of mother love. When the angels dropped the sap into the genetic humor at the moment of conception, mine was probably bottom of the beaker.

"Look," she said pointing to painting on her dressing table, "Father's Rembrandt."

If this was Rembrandt, I'm Carmen Miranda. It looked more like the work of a cockeyed Cézanne painting poplars in a fit of drunken oblivion. "Yeh," I say eying her exercise bicycle at the far side of the bedroom. What a study in neon pink and chrome. I'm about to sit on it.

"No, no, you'll break it," she says, forcibly bringing my attention back to the marquetry dresser top. This time I see what I'm supposed to see; my gift copy of Kerouac's novel, its insides scooped out, lying open before "the Rembrandt."

"I was sure I didn't lose it."

"No, I took it out of your bag when you went to the loo. It was to buy a house here in Israel you understand. We cannot live, Moise and I and baby, always with Maman and Papa. It was not natural. The diamonds belong to the family for generations; you see Maman's father provided arms for the Turkish Sultan and the diamonds were her "dot." You must understand. I cannot explain all this to the customs. I will show you something." She takes a packet of tulle from the drawer, shakes it open it, it falls dramatically over her arm, streams along the rug. "My wedding veil."

"I must go."

"Yes," she answers. I follow her behind a curtain to yet another kitchen, a flight of stairs. "Joseph, please show Mademoiselle out."

"Yes Madame," I like the slight irony in his voice. What a deep voice. I was aquiver in its resonance, flustered, flabbergasted, unhinged.

"Remember our date," he whispers brushing my ear with his lips, shutting the gate with a masterful clang that reverberates down the shaft awakening the dog. I ran past the growling beast to the hostel as the sunlight broke into crystal shards over cypress trees. You had to be a dweller in the cavernous spaces of the big city to really appreciate the Mediterranean in late summer: calm, blue, yielding, the horizon a hazy silver line adoring sea and sky. I walked into the hostel, adjusted my eyes to the gloom, saw all my worldly possessions lying in a forlorn heap on the floor in the hall.

It seems Tom's hairdresser was as anxious to be rid of me as I was to be rid of her. Mrs. Mugrabi probably feared another defenestration bent her strict rules this once and gave in to her request. "Room 31, till the end of the month," she told me. "Gloria was a very fine girl, don't get her into trouble." Ah! my affair with Gustav and Tom had not gone unnoticed. But why throw my things down with such fury?

Someone shouted my name, it slides over to me and stands there staring at me. I feel myself out of myself. I know I had to act. Escape: no good standing there holding my breath.

Joseph smiled at me. I remembered feeling great strength in him. He took my elbow and led me to Wadi Nisnas, the picturesque alleyway lined with houses, dilapidated, wheezing with age, the balconies threateningly febrile, intrigues me. We turn into an entrance, up some dark stairs, into a brilliant sunlit room. Joseph shut the wooden shutters with an air of authority.

As I got used to the gloom, a woman in flannel red and black-checkered house shoes, a purple woolen shawl over a satiny cotton housedress came out of the shadow.

"This is my mother." She caresses my cheek with her open palm, shows me to an iron framed cot covered in a maroon seersucker bedspread printed in ornamental plum colored flowers their clay-yellow anthers smooth as lupine, corks out of bottles. Pop! Le Haim! On the pea green oilcloth table top, a jam jar holds three white calla lilies, non-committal in their cool passion.

"Calla," she said describing a bridal veil with her hands, sliding back the doors leading to the bedroom so I can better admire her cans of parsley, mint, and geranium lining the cement edge of her balcony. "Ah," she says, hand to my cheek, "one good one and one bad one never quarrel."

I was in a trance all that week. Jalle lent me her wedding veil. "It was good luck," she said, "to use a happy bride's veil."

She doesn't look particularly happy to me. Or if that was happiness I'm not sure I want it. Joseph's sister insisted I wear her wedding dress. She had spent the night restitching it to fit me. "You are my sister," she said, "like my own flesh. I had worked for you as I would have worked for myself." I can't help but wear that ill-fitting gown.

I keep Gloria up till dawn with my deliberations, should I or shouldn't I go through with it? I talk and talk hoping she'll tell me not to marry Joseph. She lies there listening wide eyed.

"Everyone is nervous before a wedding, I suppose," was the most she'd commit herself to. If she had said, "No, don't do it," I would had slapped her loud and clear so anxious was I to see this thing through. I felt there was something wrong, but I didn't want to make a decision. I just let the situation unravel itself to its inevitable end. A part of me wanted out, another part wanted to see the outcome. How in heaven's name can you tell the outcome if you don't let it happen?

Outside the Rabbinate two old men agree, for a price, to serve as witnesses. They swear I have never been married before. I needed no letter of confirmation of fact. No banns were posted, nor did I have to plunge into the ritual bath to cleanse myself, as was the custom. Why, I don't know. Joseph probably had connections with the Rabbinate. The official looked deep into my eyes.

"Lo Nisuah?" he asked.

"He wants to know if you had ever been married before."

"No, lo nisuah," I answered and signed the paper he handed me.

"Marriage is a serious commitment," he mouths.

The wedding took place on the roof of the Rabbinate building; the premises looked unclean though there was neither grime nor dust anywhere. The white bearded Rabbi, a rope of pearls strung n the oblique pleat of his crimson silk turban, read the marriage contract. "This was a legal and binding marriage contract," he tells me as we stand under the canopy surrounded by fat aunts in colorfully printed dresses who loop their tongues round in their mouths and let out a frightful sound meant to be heard straight round the Sahara. So shrill was it that any evil spirit fooling enough to dare approach the periphery of our conjugal happiness was guaranteed shattered eardrums, pierced heart, non-existence. The mother kisses me and crossing her gold braceleted wrists under her breasts said once again for all to hear, "one good one and one bad one never quarrel." Was I to play the role of the good one or the bad one? The invited guests and the decrepit old hangers on of the community fall upon the semolina cakes the family had provided.

Jalle and her husband drive us in the light blue car, big as a hearse, to the hotel in which we are to spend our wedding night. I look to the small silver bust of the Spanish explorer riding the hood, for help. Oh de Soto mio, you who had been buried in the great Mississippi River, which you alone had discovered, show me the light as you had shown us the way past red and green traffic lights to this hotel. Oh Esperito Santo!

No answer. Moise gets out of the car and taking my arm leads me to the glass door at the entrance. Jalle smiles like a lusty Madonna. When we reserved the room, I had shown my passport with my name, Koenigsburger, not Kadosh. Now the clerk, smelling elicit affair and perhaps jealous he was not one of the players, vented his anger by putting us next to a toilet, which was out of order. During the night, the pipe burst. Shitty water began making its way under the door. The smell was terrible. After having done his bit, Joseph turned round and went to sleep. He had learned his trade in a whorehouse, even told me in all confidence, the name of the woman to whom he had gone back several times. She was a motherly, middle aged lady with great breasts and bad breath who knew the secrets of love, how to love, how to make love. He sounded proud of the prowess she had imparted to him, either that or he was trying to make me laugh, after all he was a sailor and sailors know everything there was to know about love and I, in spite of my recent experiences, was sublimely ignorant. It had all seemed too intimate and I was afraid of hurting his feelings or his manhood to complain about the smell and neither would I get out of bed for fear I'd step on the slime. "This was a legal and binding marriage contact," bang! bang! through the night—plumbers hammering out the message on punctured pipes.

By five o'clock the stench had gotten through to Joseph's catatonic sleep. We packed, stepped gingerly over the swollen pieces of feces, and check out. The clerk takes our money without a word of thanks, the Cheshire grin on his pasty-white face a combination of satisfaction at our discomfort envy of our fascinating illegal sex. We had sullied his home ground with our unlawful caper and had been justly punished.

After he performed his conjugal duty on our wedding night, Joseph and I never shared anything more than a bed. He was angry when I refused his advances, but how could I make love to him with his mother sleeping on the other side of the glass door. And he was a grunter, who wanted to express his desire loud and clear.

At five o'clock in the morning that second day of our honeymoon I walked out to the balcony facing the sea as the mist was just rising, the moon in the sky and the sun fighting their way on stage, the foghorns of tugboats down in the port below wailed mournfully up to me. I felt so alone. A sudden pain of longing, a need to be loved filled my body and I turned to Joseph. He was lying on the bed—crouched up, his knees to his chin, sleeping like a fetus in the warmth of his dreams. Why had he married me? That day we found a furnished room on Balfour Street in town. I paid a month's rent in advance. We lived there for two weeks, just long enough to arrange a visa for Joseph. As the husband of an American he didn't have to bother about immigration quotas. I was told by a clerk at the Embassy that he had jumped ship in New York once and had been jailed for a time for illegal entry into the country. I didn't know who pulled the strings, or if any were pulled, but within two weeks he got his visa.

Meanwhile he busied himself selling off my possessions, my radio, my portable typewriter, my rings, my gold chain, and the brooch Dad had given me as a graduation present—all I owned was sold. He used to come into the room reeking of perfume.

Gloria and Rafcho were married a few days later in the Spanish temple not far from Wadi Salib. Hers was a sedate ceremony. The mother-in-law and father-in-law stood in a reception line and handed the guests white sugared almonds in little straw baskets, brown and yellow silk roses entwined in the handles. "Alegria," to happiness they said, shaking each guest's hand in turn, "Alegria."

We went back by ship, it was cheaper and I guess Joseph wanted to show off his status as passenger to the crew. We had a rather nice cabin. I was sick throughout the voyage. At first he behaved all right, condescending, super tact; a lackey afraid to be bust but then he reverted to his true self, an uneducated jackass who spoke inanities in accented English. I didn't want to concede that I had made a mess of my life, a terrible mistake.

When we got to the States, the folks met me. We were to stay in my old room till we found accommodation of our own. Mom and Dad took us to Carnegie Hall, Tchaikovsky's 1812 Overture. Joseph slept through the concert, but not Dad. As the cannons went off, he asked me if I wanted the marriage annulled. "Yes." I was such a failure, such a naughty child who had gotten herself into an impossible situation and only Daddy knew how to get her out. The first thing Dad did at dinner after the concert was to tell Joseph to find a place of his own, the second was that he was starting proceedings to annul the marriage. Phil Morris—one of the "The Coney Island beach boys" as they styled themselves, pinochle under the boardwalks and a communal shower in the corrugated tin roofed shack in the yard where they rented rooms for the season—he can be trusted to do a good job quickly.

I had been conned by Joseph, his appearance of knowing exactly what he wanted, a certain animal light in his eye and that unquenchable palpitating desire which had to be satisfied. And I was too much a girl of the '50s, guilty about my lost virginity, wanting to make amends for my promiscuity. I should have stuck my finger deep into the soft tissue of my vagina and gotten into and out of a frenzy. But the idea never entered my mind. What I wanted, what I thought I had found was love, warmth, protection—the tenderness which would form a lovely baby. But it was Tom's baby I really wanted.

I was officially hired by the magazine. With a name like Josephina Koenigsburger, not to mention Kadosh, I really made the mark. The building was impressive, the people very busy.

I moved into the Village, a large room with possibilities, a raised dais for a bed, a small window, gray grubby walls. I decided there and then not to do a thing about it. It would remain what it looked like, a dilapidated storage room, till I found my bearings.

During one lunch break, Joseph came over to the library, begged me to try and make a go of our marriage. The federal agents were probably after him and he was looking for a way out. He was very angry.

"Listen, you're a sweet guy but it was a mistake that's all, a mistake. But don't imagine," I added, "that I didn't know you were using me. They even put the wrong passport number on that license."

"Using you? You Americans think you can buy everything and anyone with your money."

"Can't we?" I asked petrified. He was so furious, holding in the anger that threatened to burst out through his pores. He wouldn't dare attack me physically, not in the New York Public Library.

"You don't know when you're being used. You could have gone to jail for smuggling. All I had to do was drop a hint to the authorities." A man of honor breaking his word, suddenly defenseless. I had this feeling then that I could have loved him.

And that's when I met McCrudder. I'd spent the morning comparing the text of Jeremiah with theories about the ages of the pharaohs to check out conclusions on the exact dating of events. At that distance in time, dating was at most an educated guess determined by the prejudices of the educated ass proposing dates. What the hell was time anyway? English language time, Semitic language time it all seemed of a cloth—thread picking.

I was close to tears, willing to call Rosetta Stone from el Roschid the pale pink coral rose Joseph had given me as a wedding present and which I had not given back, wore round my neck on a tarnished silver chain to remind me that I was chained to ignorance, ignorance of myself more than anything else. What in hell's name was the Rosetta Stone? Joseph told me he'd bought the coral in an antique shop in Haifa because the color was soft like me, soft in the head was probably what he had in mind. I was feeling very sorry for myself, wondering why other girls found Prince Charming while I found Tom, Robert, Gustav, and Joseph. I deserved a break, enough burrowing in books.

I walked to the park, enjoying the pleasant coolness of Indian summer. I could feel the leaves change color; waft down to caress my shoulders. I watch a young child help a smaller one sail a red plastic toy boat across the lake. It turns over in the sudden breeze, straightens up and the hull cuts through the water at great speed. The toddler ran around the lake to catch it. Would he fall in? I sat down on the grassy incline, t' hell with the sign warning me to KEEP OFF THE GRASS! Keep your own bony protuberances off the grass, I'll squash blades of grass with adipose tissue, ruin my dress, feel guilty about goofing off on the job if I want to. There was a man standing in my line of vision.

"Nice day."

"Yes."

"I see you are interested in the Bible," he said looking at the dust jacket of the book I was caressing to my bosom. The Pharaohs he reads aloud. That was some opener.

I hug the book tighter to my self. It was a heavy book, short on words and long on photography, but to me, a dedicated worker who would know all about the several thousand years of Pharaohnic splendor, who could walk right up to Cleopatra's needle in the park and quite casually decipher lists of merchandise received as tax payments from merchants of Median, weight was no hindrance. And if I had my facts mixed up and should had been reading a love story into the hieroglyphics rather than a list of gifts to King this or that who lived in the early dynastic period or the late, who would ever be the wiser?

"Yes, terribly interested," I answered quoting a bit of Jeremiah, that should get his big, fat carcass out of my sun, "The priests said not: 'Where was the Lord?' And they that handle the law knew me not: The rulers also transgressed against me, and the prophets prophesied by Baal, and walked after things that do not profit.'"

"You have very pretty eyes; I'd like to marry you. "

This time I was flabbergasted. This couldn't be happening to me twice in a lifetime. I opened my mouth and shut it like the idiot I was, scrutinized him closely. My "lovely eyes" screwed up against the sun, which he, now hunched on his thighs, had released from his shadow. I should get glasses. This nearsightedness was going to put wrinkles round my eyes. I had tried smiling without blinking, but the wide-eyed June Allyson stare looking back at me from the mirror was even more moronic than my squint.

"My name is McCrudder, Neil McCrudder," he said, "I'm an architect."

"My name is Josephina Koenigsburger; I'm Jewish."

He took my hand in his and bending close to me, kissed me on the lips. I knew I was finished. This was it. I would never wake up. If this wasn't a dream, Hollywood had come true, Monroe and de Maggio together forever. It wasn't so much the feeling, sexual and warm which engulfed me, but an aura of sympathy, of love. I was aglow—a stupid word songwriters had put into their songs, but fitting—Shakespeare, this was it, no impediments, not the church, not the synagogue, not my mother, my father, nor his. We were inspired.

CHAPTER 13

"Look I don't want you to get me wrong, Harry was a prince," Karen said rushing in, looking round for the coffee which the harpy at the counter had removed, when we are young and thankful for love and need sex but are shy and afraid, we turn to our men as if they are the gods they aren't. When we're older, harden to our fallen angels, knowing all the cues in the act of love, all the steps, the sensitive spots, the sounds, the touch, we go on playing the game for our Mom's, the children, the friends' sake. It's boring, it's tiring. I couldn't play the game that's all."

The waitress with the magnified eyeballs was broadcasting her now familiar message, one cuppa, and one-quarter hour limit. I weigh the reasonableness of walking up to the woman, asking straight out if she was trying to force me to leave. Hell the place was almost empty. I decide on benevolence. This woman, doing menial work for 20 years, meant for better things as we all are, had swallowed her pride. Allow her little resentments her little hurts. Noblesse obliges! She will not be denied. I get up and order one more coffee, one more bottle of mineral water, was about to ask for a rumbaba bathed in sugary syrup, a blob of sweet cream in its heart—go to bed as Katherine Hepburn awake as Ms. Blubber. Oh McCrudder! never lose self-control, do you really need it? If you must, allez, the gate was open, the way was narrow, get too fat you'll never see Spencer Tracy again.

"The place I share now with Norm," Karen sipped coffee with obvious pleasure "big space, good light, downstairs an innocent of 60 or 70 with one of these new frizzled hairdos, rents a shop. It's always closed but she opens it every morning. She's a beautiful brown-eyed dolly with a plaintive smile that breaks my heart. 'Good morning, Fania's my name, how do you do?' Fania, Mania, too close for comfort. 'I come from Rockaway Park,' she tells me this morning. See!" She holds our misshapen hands. "Rheumatism," she said in a mild whisper.

"I'm not from America originally, Auschwitz, Yiddish. Two little girls I had. I love America but Rockaway was damp and my rheumatism. I put them in a nunnery. One was here, the other in America, six grandchildren, all educated. I live on social security, how was I going to pay the electricity? Maybe you've got a refrigerator to sell? One person, one Amana refrigerator, and so much electricity. I'll buy yours. Here, smell, smell." She waved a fistful of bills in my face, "here, smell." As if the smell of money would buy a crust of bread to keep her infants in the nunnery till the SS troops stop goose-stepping along the cobblestone streets looking for little Jew babies to stoke their ovens. "All my life I worked from 6:00 to 6:00; I worked like a horse to educate my babies. Your pencil, please. Thank you." She's learned all the accepted phrases in English and wants to try them out on me. "Please call me up at home any time. Here's my number."

All I seem to do was touch people who've come out of the woodwork. Israel was the country on the other side of the hidden door. This was where the Pied Piper brought the children, or where they brought themselves following some tune within. Here you'll find beautiful children opting for normalcy, pretending today was reality and reality was the dream. Scratch a 50-year-old, and you've got yourself a story.

"Have you read Saul Friedlander's book?"

"Yes I have." Rain glistened cobblestones are indelible in my soul as well as yours. I was a child of the times.

"Good tale, most of the stories will never be told. I had a friend, his name was Nachman, took me to a lecture the other day. I went because Stan, this psycho friend of mine, brought me yellow chrysanthemums wrapped in tissue paper and bought four paintings of yellow flowers, he likes yellow. I should insult a friend and a customer yet. He's been a soldier in the Second World War, one of those who survived the invasion of Italy, missed the honor of becoming a star on a banner on his mother's window. That's how he describes himself. He's very interested in the war, like for him Hitler was still alive and living with Ava in that bunker, making whoopee while the dogs wave their tails respectfully in unison. Altogether now... All right I said, I'll go. The lecturer talked about the psychodynamics of the Holocaust, which was the name of the talk. First of all, he didn't prepare his lecture because he was the president so he talked off the cuff about his German-born patient whose Jewish parents wanted him to drop dead as a sacrifice. After all they were survivors of the camps and they had to sacrifice something.

This president of a psychoanalyst couldn't keep the kid from doing himself in so that parents were to blame; "a death wish, a death wish" he said twice in a voice full of pathos, "a death wish, concentration camp survivors all had a death wish." What else, he should take the blame on himself for doing a dumb job? This president did a song and dance routine—he was old enough to be a member of the Wehrmacht—cried crocodile tears over what his contemporaries had done to Gypsies, Communists and Jews. He was probably not blameless himself otherwise he would have saved on the water dribbling down his beard, a real macho beard and a real classy mustache, blond, red and white in gradation. Nice guy in bed I bet except for his belly, a happy St. Nicholas belly full of self assurance that with his 'METHOD.' The method was that he should save the German by saving the Jew. You go to a priest you say, 'Father I have sinned,' you do penance. You go to the psych, he psychoanalyses you till you say, 'Not guilty, not guilty. Even if I'm guilty, I'm ok even if I'm not ok it's ok.'"

"With my back I should serve both as somebody's scapegoat and father confessor all at once so that cleansed, that presiding psychoanalyst can fly back to Hamburg and fuck to the first whore he sees. Solutions he wants, explanations. I'm not buying. 'Close systems in a paranoid society are dangerous' those are his exact words. My brain, thank God, was still working and remember, I do. The German, he tells me, were exterminating the Jews because it was written in their party platform; like this was the reason, like this was the excuse. My Grandmother Reisel in Plonsk, who sold kashe in the marketplace and liked to dance at weddings, went to the ovens because she wanted to go he tries to tell me wiping away a tear. She was a victim of a 'psychotic society' he repeats, as much to blame for being fed to the gas ovens as the guys who turned the gas on. They too were victims. You see these earrings, they got to my mother in the States after the war, I wear them because I like them. But do you think the ashes of Grandma Reisel lie gently on this earth because this fag explains that he builds up self-esteem and identity in the concentration camp survivors still left in Germany. The idiots who stay in Germany need a psychiatrist, dynamic or otherwise, they deserve to be spat on with words like 'Metaphoric conceptual thinking,' 'biological thinking in categories' to explain ideas like 'self defense of the master race against the dangerous enemy who would endanger his holy aims.' He sells me words. I was left holding on to Grandma Riesel's earrings. That I promised to love her, I didn't but without her it wasn't any easier."

"Here, I'll tell you a story, mother was a forewoman in a clothing shop. She loved it. It was her life, she liked to say. She used to come home at 5 o'clock, exhausted, pale green around the gills, take off her shoes, put her heavy calves on a chair and just sit there till she got her breath back which usually took ten minutes. Then she went to the freezer, helped herself to scoops of chocolate ice cream doused in prune preserve she prepared herself and just had a ball, really enjoyed herself. After dinner, she went to a meeting, she was always involved in community affairs, arranged lectures for unwed mothers and bazaars for good causes, but above all she was an Israeli freak, everything Israeli.

"I wanted to please her, after all I was designing clothes being worn by all these rich women waiting for the big fuck and my Mom was no more than a forewoman. I wanted her to be proud of me. So I won this international award. My picture traveled to China. I came to the hospital room where she was dying carrying this real heavy canvas. I mean I wanted her to have a little 'nachas;' I'm her one and only daughter. She said it looked like a Viet Cong soldier, her conception of a disgracefully evil entity and evil means ugly.

'Ma,' I say, 'it's called Motherhood.' 'Motherhood, shmotherhood, why don't you make pictures of Israel?' She made me promise to cremate her body and spread the ashes over Haifa Bay. Ask me why Haifa Bay, I don't know. 'But first, go visit Avramaleh.'

"I walked into the kibbutz and ask for Avramaleh. I'm told he was the director of the computer concern of the kibbutz movement but today, I'm in luck, he's working in the communal dining room, it's his turn for kitchen duty. I walk into the dining room, past the rows of sinks and toilets and see this athletic looking gent. He takes a long look at me and faints dead away. He's taken to the infirmary and I'm asked to follow like some sort of antidote. When he comes to, he swears I'm a ghost, the girl he'd been in love with in Poland when he was 15 years old. They had belonged to the same Zionist club. He'd come to Israel before the war broke out and she'd been burned in the camps or so he thought. 'Oh Mania, Mania, sweet Mania,' he mumbled. I pick myself up and walk out. I couldn't take all this emotion being a clone for Momma finally up there in heaven. I mean I'm no freckle faced sweetheart. I look nothing like her. I wonder why they don't had a Jewish deli here in Israel. When I go back to New York nobody believes me when I tell them there isn't one good Jewish deli in this whole country. Sometimes I die for a juicy pastrami on rye."

"Have a chocolate," I dig into the black canvas bag, take out the heart shaped candy box, strip off cellophane, untie pink ribbon, open it to reveal a thick piece of waffled paper looking up accusingly at me. If the box was meant for Gloria, why hadn't I given it to her? Karen took a piece of bitter chocolate; I take a piece.

"They put Momma's ashes in a plastic bag and the bag in a copper box. I was afraid the x-ray machines in customs would find it and think it was hashish; you know the matzo-meal consistency of the cinders. When I got to Haifa I walked up 150 meters southwest of Elijah's cave, following her instructions, spread the ashes around a fig tree and threw the rest into the air in the direction of the bay. I gave the box to a school kid walking nearby, probably used it as a pencil case.

"The body burns at a very high temperature," Karen said as she bit through the chocolate, sipping coffee, "completely sanitary and sane I may add." And now they're saying Hitler didn't do it, the Germans didn't do it. Doesn't sound right; logistically improbable, prefabricated fiction of the sick Jewish imagination."

And then I feel the gritty caramel and hazelnut center of the chocolate squash against my teeth like Karen's mother wafting about out there on the back of a breeze round the Carmel range, fortifying Gloria's mandrake root, no doubt.

"When I go to Hamburg for the fashion shows," I say trying to change the subject real fast, I can't help thinking of York, like a perfect geographical fit, penis and vagina on the clothing manufacturer's ancient routes."

"What are you talking about?"

"Why, haven't you read *The Last of the Just?*"

"Yes, so what?"

"Well, according to Bart, Bishop William of Norhouse incited the mob of York to kill off the Jews of the town if they refused to say that Jesus Christ was the true Messiah. 1185, I think, and even before that, 1079, Easter time again the Jews of Norwich were accused of killing the 12-year-old William of Norwich, later canonized, and using his blood for the Passover ceremony. A converted Jew, Theobord of Cambridge, started the rumor. Many a knight was sent on the Second Crusade fitted out in Jewish ransom money."

"In Norwich at least the Jews could had exchanged their lives for money," she said helping herself to another chocolate, "Hitler too, they say, might had been predisposed to making a deal, he knew all about the Jews' obligation to free a fellow religionist who had been sold into slavery, but no one seems to had been interested in trucks full of Jews. Oi vey you might have lived Grandma Reisel but for the price of a truck." She looks out across the courtyard, the Gook's longing gaze bores through the thick glass.

"I've got to go to the toilet." I excuse myself, the double whammy look of the waitress drilling through my preoccupied brain unsettles me. Here I am—recreating myself at 20, hurt, trying to find love, knowing I had to fall in love, an explosive all encompassing love like the celluloid images of the times had impinged on my retina—spitting out dates. Well, if you had no homeland, dates are your guideposts, sea-lanes your home. I ask the waitress where the toilet is. She points across the yard to the farm-like building. When I walk back in, the woman protected by the espresso machine, stares queerly at me. Who does she think I am—a reporter out to give the joint points on cleanliness? On a scale of ten, this toilet deserves a minus one on the Josephina K. K. McCrudder International Public Conveniences Charts, no soap, wastebasket filled to the brim with soiled toilet paper. When I go out to look for someone in charge, a beanpole kid with shoulder length stringy blond hair steps on the toilet seat, reaches up to the vent flush to the ceiling, and hands me a roll of pink toilet tissue from the bunch on the water tank.

"Yaron's teacher," Gloria said before I had a chance to sit down, thinks I should show the boy more affection. There's a connection, she believes, between his lousy grades and affection."

"Why didn't you tell me not to marry Joseph that night?" I say surprising myself not to mention Karen who was contemplating glass pane, making certain her paintings are safe from creeps lurking round water spouts—the itsy bitsy spider. Gloria wouldn't be able to evade the subject this time with stories of her own, she'll had to commit herself to an answer this time. "Listen to this Karen," she says, "here we are sharing a narrow room, two beds, a sink, a window, I hardly know this dame sitting on a bare mattress—didn't even own a bed sheet. I had to give her one of mine, a ridiculous organdie flower on a plastic tiara with missing teeth keeps falling over her left ear and a train of white tulle flows round her like whipped cream from an aerosol can—mumbling incantations, "The witch, the witch, the witch from Norwich and I'm supposed to tell this cropped haired princess looking at me like a startled chimpanzee not to marry the first waiter she bumps into. What right did I had to tell you that when I had decided to marry Rafcho?"

"I was mighty jealous of your Rafcho, holding your hand across the table in the hostel dining room as I struggled with the Polish mushrooms Gustav had ordered me to cook. He looked at you with such admiration. I remember he'd just come back from the army dressed in khaki shorts and that knapsack over his shoulder. He had shapely legs for a man."

"Oh stop it, now he's got varicose veins. What happened to Tom?"

"Nothing happened to him, he could never have hurt me more than he did when he left me stranded on the beach at Escalon. Whatever happened after was a minor insult. It isn't the incident itself I remember but this dull ache I still carry around in me. Can I get you a cup of coffee?" I ask Gloria reacting to the waitress' evil eye. What does she want blood? I've ordered three cups of water; still you can't go on sitting around here without ordering something I suppose.

"Will you stop circumventing the issue, I'm dying of curiosity." Well I'd accused her of circumlocution, she could name her disease.

"You know it's very hard to tell. Something in me wants to keep it hidden. It's so stupid. Lifetimes woven on stupidities."

"Will you let me be the judge of that? Listen Josephina Koenigsburger Kadosh McCrudder, either you tell me or you don't. Well?"

"I figured I was Astarte and Tom was Dagon, the fish god who could fertilize the sedentary stuff in me."

"Dagon was a god of grain," Karen interrupts, "there's a grain museum here. Samson was put at the wheel to grind grain not catch fish."

"We really don't know. Times change, symbols lose and gain meaning. The Philistines spoke a Semitic tongue back there in Crete, if Crete it was. Dag in Hebrew means fish, dagon in Hebrew means grain. One doesn't know. Yet Samson was a consecrated child before he was conceived. His bodily strength, his long hair, his physical endowments were his fate just like our wombs are our fate."

"Oh Jesus," Karen says, gets up "are you telling us a woman was inferior to a man just because she had a womb?"

"Who said inferior, who said superior? Ok, if you don't want Astarte and Dagon, how about Samson and Delilah. I thought Tom was Samson who, though blinded and degraded yet used his powers to destroy the fertility fish god of Crete who might have been the grain god of the Philistines, the essence of life either way. I wanted love, a home, security, a room with a door and a window I could shut and call my own. It turned out that Samson had another Delilah."

"If this Tom of yours was Samson, why didn't you do a bit of snipping of your own?" Karen asks sagely.

"Yeah! I should have snipped off another part of his anatomy."— white Camellia, organdie stretched over wire petal sewn to pearly plastic comb stitch over, stitch, over, loop, pull, snap off thread with front teeth, white dove between my open palms, no mate—I called Tom at Habonim.

"Tom, I think I'm pregnant." I was late and I'm never late.

"Go see a doctor," he said, like a Southern slavy who having brushed against Missy's breast by accident, on her way down the stairs to the cotillion ball, stands accused of statutory rape. My hero! Actually, it might had been Gustav, but how do you say pregnant in Polish and if he said, "abortion" would I had been the wiser. Abortion was not a word lightly bandied about in those days. False alarm.

"I think one of the reasons I married Joseph was because I wanted to get closer to the nature of man in the Middle East, a quality I wanted to understand. I could do that only by giving myself unconditionally; swallow it whole like mother earth open to suggestion. I bet he had a friend stashed away somewhere. One of the guests at your wedding, Gloria, told me Joseph used to wear purple and back then in the Austrian Empire, purple used to had a particular connotation and once on a train from Marseilles to Paris, I overheard a conversation—small irises indicate homosexual tendencies, I never measured Joseph's irises, but I had my suspicions."

"Josephina, Joseph married a girl he met on one of the cruises. Seems she spent all his money being rowed about the Bay of Naples, and dined in Capri. He decided to get his investment back. Her father owns a chain of clothing stores in Vancouver. They had five children. His mother's there too, drove the kids to school in her own Volks. She's known as the scourge of the freeway.

"How do you know?"

"I've just put a string of rumors together."

I'm glad she hasn't turned into a liar, an idealist she's always been. Karen runs out to a potential customer.

"Coming to the meeting tonight? Narjis Ibn Daud is addressing the group," Gloria shouts after her.

"Not me; got to paint flowers. You just don't drop a wrench into a lucky streak like a hot potato and run. Anyway I've had enough of lectures for a lifetime—ask Josephina."

"Thanks for keeping her company."

"Bye, Josephina, Good Luck! And remember, nine out of ten men who've tried camels go back to their wives."

"Coffee?" I ask Gloria.

"Let's go," she says.

"Just a minute," I said. I've had enough of being intimidated by waitresses, so I walked right up to the woman standing behind the espresso machine, got very close to her, her glasses so thick, they make serpent streaks on the surface. "One of those," I said, pointing to a squashed croissant. I won't be intimidated by waiters, waitresses, editors, male or female, no more. The worm had turned. She placed the pastry on a satiny paper square and put the napkin on a cold heavy white plate, scooped up a blob of sweet cream. I stopped her. "No croissant, no milk, no coffee, no cream, no rien, nada, niet, gornisht; punch line—no tip." She cows before me. Up close, she looks reserved and rather shy. I paid the bill and politely said, "Thank you."

CHAPTER 14

"Have you been driving long?" I ask her as the car veers to the left, zooms in between two cars parked respectfully on a shady street.

"No, only got my license recently. About 20 years ago I failed the driver's test five times in a row. In utter fright, the inspector told me to make a left. By the time I'd made up my mind if my marriage band was on the left or right hand, I'd turned into traffic. That was the first time round, by the fifth the inspector suggested I take a break and calm down. He was right. Some 20 years later I got the license first try. I could have had it 20 years ago. My upstairs neighbor, the one I told you about, promised me the license for a modest fee. His brother-in-law was related to the chief inspector, but then I was still a woman of principle with a self righteous attitude due in part to my fancy education and I refused the deal outright. Rafcho didn't care one way or the other, but I was so angry, livid with indignation, almost tattled on him in my zeal. Someone else must have spilled the beans, the inspector was jailed for a while."

"The conditions of life do temper the noble spirit."

"It's almost 4o'clokc," she says, miling "It's almost 4 o'clock," she says as the steering wheel barely missed the bumper of the car ahead, "Come on, Tania's up from her nap."

She must be the only one. Everything was so quiet that a cat's miaow, a dog's bark hang suspended in the air.

"Watch it," Gloria warns me, "Tania's been hosing the garden down again."

It had been raining on and off all day, why should anyone hose down wet stairs? Had someone died, defecated, peed? I ask no questions, followed her acquiescently down flight after flight, holding on tight to the black iron railing, stepping gingerly on dusky shadows, liquid film stretching silk over white marble steps. I was Persephone descending into Hades against her better judgment to meet an uncommunicative lover. I stood behind Gloria as she banged a brass ring on a slender cast iron figure of Astarte, witch of Canaan, no broom. The hollow sound resounded within. Was there anybody there? We heard hurried footfalls and the door opened.

Kisses exploded on cheeks. "This is Josephina. Josephina, Tania Hertsfeld," Gloria introduces us in a loud voice, you'd think she'd learned to modulate after all this isn't mid-Manhattan during rush hour, you don't have to shout above the general din to be heard, this was a secretive enclave of a screeching crone. Tania, if crone she be, looks mighty familiar, Angelica Edwards! Was Tania Hertsfeld living on the Carmel range a fraud?

"Remember the stories I told you about this globetrotting wonder girl, how I envied her riding silver steeds in the skies?"

She's gone too far.

"She's daft," Tania said, smiling at me like a doctor who can't quite decide what's wrong with his patient. I follow the dumpy priestess, velveteen tent dress, stockings and Mary-Jane shoes all of a shade of toad green, through a narrow hall—to the right, doorway covered in gold fish scale on lilac batik sheet on a brass rod, "Fuck the Aegean, up with Assyrians," printed in black. I stood there deciphering the writing.

"Come and sit down!" Gloria shouts.

I walked into the living area, trains of philodendron separating it from the dining corner where a photographic reproduction of Gauguin's bare-breasted chocolate colored women, intensely disinterested in their own nakedness, papers the wall. The furniture was German early 1930s, brought in by the first wave of expatriates wary enough to save the wood from the coming conflagration. There was something staid and upright about the polished surfaces refracting light from the slightly parted drapes, gray geometric patterned cotton hiding secrets behind their reflective heaviness.

"Tea?" Tania asks. "We're all out of khaffee as you Americans say." I nod my head; sit down obediently on the seedy brown tweed couch. Beside me on the floor, an ebony slave boy with presumptuous scrotal sacs—two bunches of grapes between which a shaft hangs despondently like a candle dripping tallow. Grape vine tendrils twirl from his toes, round the torso and up an arm holding a brass tray offering dried fruit.

"Her husband was a famous sculptor but he died in a boating accident," Gloria tells me shouting in the general direction of the kitchen, "did you hear the news about the woman horse riding in Central Park who was raped by a daring young man who jumped her from a tree?"

"Determined bastard," Tania shouted back.

"Can a woman be knocked up on a trotting horse? That's the question. Is this fact or fiction?"

"The Mongols did everything on horseback," Tania said coming toward us tray in hand. "Maybe the rapist had Mongolian blood. Most Western Europeans do, hence Americans one way or another and Gloria, deary, knock up means wake up, not to be confused with to be sexually molested. You see," Tania turns to me, "I've been trying for donkey's years to teach Gloria how to speak the Queen's English but she still insists on her little Americanisms." I smiled, not quite sure of my role at this party. What information was disseminated worldwide quick as a wink? What price a communications satellite?

"Did you finally buy one? Gloria handled the delicate silver chain round Tania's neck, "symbol of female might, right and freedom."

"Don't be daft, look closely, Josephina," she brought the little silver pendant up close to my eyes, this was a dove of peace, this was the symbol of the female of the species, and the equal sign stood for equality between the sexes. I rather liked it. I'm all for fundamental understanding. The deep unutterable slime of the timeless myth creates nasty tensions. This silver pendant was a nice, homely straightforward design.

She finished off her tea, got up and went to the window, drew back the curtains revealing the wadi, a vaginal rift upon whose lip her house veers precariously towards the precipice below, and at the apex the sea breaks with the fury of ocean in a gray mood. And then the rains came falling, diagonal lines of silver washing the tops of the pine trees dark brilliant green. I watched the trees breathe green in the rhythm of falling rain. Diving round moss-covered hills picking sea shells, I was green stone, newly quarried, baked in the sun of your indifference, yielding, no hand to give it form, stand goose bumps on skin awash in sweet paprika, naked before the Pacific, shiver up my spine, my hand to my pubic hair to protest the race so masterfully erased in a moment of pique by prince. Priest, master, slave, exploiting, exploited, destruction—discarded ring, clothes, myth, ancient heritage.

Damn it, now I know who Tania Hertzfeld reminds me of—hyacinth blue eyes, a little hurt by life, full sensuous lips, fair hair, Scots-Irish, Italian-Irish, Irish-Irish, not Angelica Edwards, my best friend at Walton High, but McCrudder's sister; she who collects the flotsam of many ships, teacups belonging to a hundred different sets, wooden luck pieces from Korea, silk screen paintings from Japan, paraphernalia left on shore for the price of a bottle of beer; concrete junk even the whale won't digest arranged in shadowboxes, boxes within boxes.

I watched her through telescope in the bay window, as she walked along the deserted beach; early morning—from rocking chair to cranberry preserve, pumpkin pie, storm whipped Autumn sea, clean impertinence fogging up my mind while she, brittle autumn leaf, dries to dust on cherry wood sea-chest I strip down to gloss with my fingertip.

Obituary read: died of detritus thrown overboard to ease the load on sinking ships. They go down lightning quick, all hands on deck, off the coast of Monterey, off the coast of New Hampshire dressed in seaweed, gushing water from your boots, face the millions who came before you looking on at the edge of doom.

You'll get no special privileges here, no green card—illegally work the American continent trying to forget the long days and nights across the oceans back to the dark shore. Ethel's sister, her house which may be half mine, feels as if it's going out to sea searching for nick-knack, bric-a-brac, patchwork quilt molding to oblivion in green mildew, Early American design, rucksack, duffel bag, and steamer trunk.

"May I use your toilet?" I asked Tania. I'm not the kind of person easily incriminated by irrational premonitions. What was I afraid of?

No problem from the hag, "Right there!" She points to the seditious piece of batik. "The switch is to your right. I slip behind it trying not to disturb its reverie. In the sudden glare of a 100-watt bulb, I gasped, "Ohhhhhh!" and the sound oscillates in my ears setting up ripples in the crimson bathwater. I slowly turned my eyes away from the inundated head of a gauze-wrapped mummy. It moves perceptibly towards me.

"What's the matter?" Tania stands at my elbow. "Oh that! That's Pappy, short for Apollo. I've been instructed on the best authority to soak him in the bath to get the muck off. See?" She removes the gauze from the head, "He's a Canaan god, the god of fecundity or some such. Nubian stone. My husband left me little but his art and if they are willing to buy the stuff I'll soak it in the bath, I'll even do a little jig with it. Go on, deary, do your thing, don't be shy, Pappy won't peep." Tania turns me forcibly towards the toilet trying, possibly, to get me out of the initial shock, which had permanently lowered my jaw and walked out leaving me on my own.

"Bugger you, you condescending bitch," I did a bit of my own witchy-do, castigating evil in what I hope was a cockney accent, giving vent to my anger in a loud healthy gush of piss. I finished as quickly as I could, pulled up my body stocking in a panic. Holding on to your urine and then letting go can be one hell of a catharsis, but this time it didn't work; just left me empty and shaky.

Oh bugger, bugger, bugger McCrudder. Lopsided smile. Since Henry VIII's act of 1533 had made anal sex punishable by hanging, my accusation may land him in the Tower of London. Funny guy. "If a marriage settlement was drawn on the assumption that all parties are rogues"—quoting the Talmud. What else? "Any trouble which occurs can be settled promptly." Sure marriage may be contracted as a business between two interested parties but what about love? Love was the necessary abstract, the necessary concrete; the hurt that cannot be made better by a band-aid, the medical dressing was always too small.

Oh dear! Here I was entertaining such thoughts and I didn't even have the fitting mechanism for the act. "The only things we get to keep are the things we give away," an original Neil McCrudder. What do you give away? What do you get to keep?

"Don't be so worried about being original," my editor, Lillian Ciegal, says, "we all plagiarize. Originality? There just ain't no such thing."

I edged myself back round the curtain. Gloria was spading a boureka on to a plate. "Have some," she said, handing me a fork. "Tania is an excellent cook."

"It was all quite accidental. I met this expert, from Pittsburgh," Tania said by way of explanation I guess, "he's the creator of a prestigious Museum in the South West of the United States. He was sent here especially to oversee the casting of my husband's god. He wanted to read *The Woman's Room*. I'd told him the title meant vagina in Polish or Yiddish, I'd heard the expression bandied about the laundry often enough. He wanted to read the book for himself, so I took him up to the Women's Lib Library. He felt he'd like to buy me a present and I chose this. Why not? I haven't been able to have a proper wash for a fortnight having followed his strict and careful instructions to the letter." I pick up the boureka. "Watch it, it's salty," Tania warned.

"Salty?" I inquire as if I expect something else.

"It's Mrs. Ashkenazi's recipe. When my husband and I first married, we lived in a single room right off her laundry. At 5 o'clock every morning except Saturdays, we were awakened by her voice. Picked up a few phrases of the kraut's tongue, I did. 'Wo ist das Hemd von Hern... zu Haus, buglen, alles Gute, Gemutlichkeit.' My daughter got her early morning feed to the bustle of water a-boiling, swirling suds a-gurgling, the rhythm of daily catastrophe. What happened to Herr Greenspan's only shirt that came over on his back from Dresden? It was the washing machine ruined Mrs. Ashkenazi's business. She now owns a pastry shop. Three cups flour, three tablespoons vinegar, three tablespoons oil, a glass of soda water and 190 grams of margarine. Here's a pencil, do you want to write it down! It's saved me from many a tight spot!"

"Ok." I take my trusty sec't pad out of my bag. "Shoot!" I'm not about to tell them the dreary secrets of my life. Aunt Khoursey at the kitchen table—me at her elbow—demonstrating how to prepare "fillicas" the food her great grand nephew Solomoniko, loved above all other food. The secret of flaky dough was in the working of the fat, like this, she shows me—little stabs here and there, fold and fold again, rolling pin, fold again. Remember the name was "mille feuilles, mille."

Fooling around with French pastry, while men are designing ships for outer space, and yet, as I taste Tania's cheesy concoction, a melt in the mouth dream, I had this queer feeling that baking and moon landings are of equal importance, the beauty of tiles scraped by the friction of speed, the beauty of pastry, fluffy and fine on the taste buds.

Aunt Khoursey—glorious beauty, large black eyes filled with gravity singing songs of love in Spanish-Yiddish not heard in Spain since Don Quixote rode the by ways of La Mancha—accompanying herself on a phantasmagorical drum. No one understood her, dribbled whole-wheat meal down the corners of her mouth, blowing bubbles. Incapacitated senility. Can't stand the light, wants the dark. Persephone used to Hades. Within the Raggedy Anne emaciated body, the soul still prospers. "With a heart like hers," Dr. Shiffman correctly reading his own biological timetable, "she'll outlive us all."

It's been raining very hard in this world suddenly so close and secretive. The banging of a door inside the house shatters silence. A young man in jeans and white T-shirt appears. Had he been there all this time listening to our conversation?

"He's the boarder," Gloria said by way of introduction. I pretend interest; smile my professional smile that always works as a magnet for the outpourings of souls. People are dying to be asked questions.

"Josephina was a foreign correspondent"

"Very nice!" he said with a look of pure disgust in his eyes.

You can't win 'em all, but you can try and win some. I smile again. "Nice to meet you." I stretched my hand to the approaching boy who shakes it feebly as if I was a slimy snake.

"What are you investigating?" he asked, taking a handful of dates from the ebony slave's platter.

"I'm a freelance writer; I've just interviewed Major Haddad in Marj Ayyun, The Lebanon. I'm no longer officially on the staff of any magazine."

"Smart enough to know when to get out!" he leers.

Tania looks at me apologetically. "Eliot's a poet," she whispered and turned to the lanky kid, "Why don't you make yourself a nice cup of tea luv, there's a good boy."

"Done sweetie," he kissed the top of Tania's head in a too familiar a manner, and shuffled towards the kitchen; each individual vertebra moving to a discordant rhythm, his neck finds refuge in his raised bony shoulders, a vulture waiting for "The Truth" to make itself known, relieve him of all contention.

"Eliot was Odelia's grandnephew."

"Who?"

"You'll see," Tania says.

"Since reporters are notorious for their questions, may I ask you a direct one?" I'm trying desperately to get on familiar ground.

"Yes."

"Where do you come from, Ireland?"

"I was born on the Isle of Man, actually. My husband and I met in London. I was a barmaid, can't you tell?" She got up, ran to the dining corner, placed herself in front of the Gauguin backdrop, and raising one ham like leg, swung it round and round. "Oopsie daisy and peek-a-boo and once more for the boys, I can can-can, yes I can," she sings, a sea lion roaring in the gimbling waves.

"Don't mind her," Gloria says, "she's been studying, D-R-A-M-A at the Haifa U.

Audience, that's my part, I realize, a part I don't mind playing, if I didn't feel so out of place, so out of time.

"Ah! There I was buxom and blithe polishing the bar with beeswax, rubbing it into the grain real hard so it shone smooth and the beer glasses merrily slid along from one end to the other with nary a spill—I had to hold on to this job, the competition was rough and my father had left me just a little nosegay. Mother you see," she placed the Nubian's platter on the ring marked teak coffee table, "ran off with this bloke when father mercifully died. He'd been wounded in battle in 1940, shrapnel in the brain, paralyzed; taken care of by a male nurse who'd been discharged from the army with a bashed knee, a handsome, strong lad of 19. I was going on 13 at the time. I would have allowed myself to be seduced, I was as tall as I was now and well developed for my age, but Mother got to him first. The hotel was abandoned and I fell in love with my Latin teacher. We lived on and off in the attic of the old house. He had a suspicious wife and several grown children. It was then that I was admitted to a London art school and met my husband. He was my teacher. By that time I had developed a certain affinity for teachers. He was married and had children my age. His wife had been the beauty queen of Haifa and I became a bona fide mistress—the other woman—a very exciting commitment. He was a Palestinian Jew and Jews, as you know, are family crazy so I agreed to come here, marry him—bore him four children and converted to Judaism. I'm a better Jew than Gloria and probably you too. In fact, the best thing that ever happened to me was my conversion. I'd never had much of a religion before and I rather like it. After the accident, one of my husband's female students, a hefty young thing, with exquisite legs, almond shaped eyes, hair swept back in a chignon on top of her head, artistic type with oodles of cash—called to say how so sorry she was. She hoped we could be friends. 'Well if sleeping with another woman's husband was a way to friendship, try walking the path to my door. I haven't had a special burglarproof spider lock installed for nothing. You can come in, but I'm not sure you'll get out.' I told her.

'Mrs. Hertzberg,' she swore, 'your husband and I were only friends, I was only his student.' I'd been my husband's student and I knew what wringing yards of batik can lead to. Well now, here I am, a widowed Jewish grandma with a Canaan god soaking in my bathtub. Is that fair, I ask you? Come on girls. Cheerio Eliot." No response.

It's 5 o'clock in the afternoon. The sunset was a sickly streak of chartreuse in an orangey sky, fit setting for a landing by the little people from Mars—as per TV special—magnified flies in a sandstorm in breadbasket USA. I try to find a comfortable spot among the popping springs and rutted caverns of the back seat of Gloria's red Volks.

"Good enough to eat, Josephina."

"Pistachio ice cream," I answered.

"Kiddies," Tania says, "do you remember sunsets from ages ago? Idyllic weren't they; soft as Paradise? The beauty of death, that's what you're looking at, the poison of heavy industry. Those horrible cement towers the electric company was putting up in the town of Hadera, had you seen them— two overgrown Siamese twins in perpetual erection. It took a mountain of cement to build them and it'll take a mountain of coal to keep them in unending and unnecessary industry. Those coal wharfs out at sea will be slashed free in a storm and the full significance of coal particles in your lungs will be part of your reminiscences, if you live to tell them. We moved to the Carmel to get away from the electric power plant towers in T.A. They were put up against the law, and then a law was passed to make them legal. What my husband used to call the inconstancy of the law."

"You mean like a baby peeing all over the place?" Gloria interrupts.

"That's incontinency. When are you ever going to learn to speak proper English?"

"Well, I've never been a globe trotting reporter or an artist's wife studying D-R-A-M-A." Gloria put her foot down on the break with such force, I saw myself splattered down the mountain.

"Luvy, when those filters wear down and there is no money to renew them, the priorities being as they are, then the alternatives will really be limited to the absurd choice, sitting it out like a toy duck at the carnival stand waiting to be asphyxiated in the full light of the righteous law or putting an end to yourself."

You can always blow up the towers, I'm about to say, death by car accident, burned to char and ember—Iraqi nuclear towers after all had been blown up—blow up one tower, five will take its place. Making an atom bomb was kid's stuff today, read the newspapers, everything advertised, above board in a competitive market.

We crossed a lawn scorched brown by the elements, or manmade chemical concoctions meant to kill a spider, towards a charming house faced in flagstone, butter yellow and cinnamon, through an open door into an elegant room, arched windows in a bower, ivy like the matted hair of a Christ—knotted rheumatic knuckles threatening to break through the window pane, destroy what was left of the room's awesome beauty. We walk over a midnight blue woolen carpet, abstract weavings; red-yellow bugs pollinate delicate resemblances of jasmine, buttercup, tulip bespattered in shit.

A woman came towards us, her footsteps absorbed by the thick pile, offered me her nail-cracked fingertips with a gesture of the utmost majesty.

"This is Odelia," Tania said in a very loud voice. Am I deaf? "And this," she turned to me, "is Josephina McCrudder. She's a newspaper correspondent from the United States."

"Have you come about the house?" Odelia smiles graciously with he rosebud gums.

"Put your teeth in," Tania orders.

"My teeth? Lost them again…."

"Gloria and Tania brought me along. I'm here for a few days, only passing through." I had the need to turn away from the ravished countenance before me.

"Come in if you must! Find yourselves somewhere to sit. My cats are very well behaved." She very carefully placed herself on an Empire chair, her hands on the heads of the carved swan armrests, her feet on a pale yellow pillow, moiré satin, green from damp. Tania sat down on the edge of a chaise lounge. Gloria carefully removes cat shit from a large pillow on the floor, finely textured pastel gobelin, blue birds in a courtship dance with a silver pointer, a clenched fist with an outstretched index finger used in the synagogue to follow the holy scriptures, She handed me the pointer, I held the silver handle embossed in roses and scratch some of the dirt off my skirt. I had no change of clothes for my meeting with Conforti tomorrow and here I was permanently stuck to this filth. Tania goes over to the old woman and sleeks back her sparse white hair.

"How are you Odelia?"

"Not too bad. The municipality had confiscated the house for back taxes," the woman addressed me, "I had been fighting the courts tooth and nail," she snickers, "but to no avail. The lawyers need their money and the city will have its taxes and now they tell me I must evacuate the premises. Poor pussycats, my pussies, they will have to find new quarters. And you know it's all your fault, Tania, all your fault dear, niggardly Tania. Write that down sweet child, write that down, it's all her fault." I just sat there unable to utter a word.

"Odelia," Tania entreated, "you must stop buying all that imported cat food. Your cats will have to go. You'll have to go. They're building all around you. You must find other accommodation."

"Tania, bothersome child, this is my home, isn't it?"

"But darling, you've been evicted."

"How can anyone evict me from my own home?"

"You know my dear."

Odelia said getting up and peering down closely at me, "I'm being thrown out of my own home, my pretty pussies and I. God's will you know." She picked the silver pointer up from the rug and distractedly scratched her robe. I watched furrows form along the length of the pink velvet robe. "Uncle, you see—you can quote me—uncle ate up the mountains and now we are being punished. The mountain, you understand, belongs to Elijah. No one had the right to eat it up and demolish it for cement. They imprint a falcon on each of the sacks they ship out, but it's wrong you see, they should imprint a skull and bones. The Arabs, I mean Mustapha, you had met Mustapha, he brought one of those bags up here last Wednesday, I think it was. He fixed the crack in the bedroom wall. I told him Tania would pay. I mean it was all your fault after all and you didn't. I know you didn't. Mustapha was so good with the azaleas; he must absolutely be paid promptly.

"Bosh and twiddle," Tania says, helping her back to her chair. The intense smell of cat shit and mold was overpowering.

"Operating limestone quarries, my dear, produces air pollution. That's why I keep all the windows shut and the pussies indoors where I can protect them," she goes on in her pearly, educated, maddeningly measured tones, forcing me into her mind as if I were a force-fed goose being led to market. "The report stated five kilograms of dust per one thousand kilograms of stone quarried. Little children living in Haifa breathe fine silicon and they are dying of lung disease. Uncle did it. He did it and now I'm paying the price. Retribution! You can write that down quote, retribution, unquote. If the Prophet Elijah had no Mount Carmel from which to alight on his chariot of fire after the Passover feast I was to blame. Poor Elijah sipping all that wine and then having to find his way over unfamiliar terrain. I was to blame. The sins of the fathers, my dear. But my pussies, my poor pussies." She picked up the silver pointer and slid it carefully under her thigh, "are they to blame?"

"Odelia, uncle sold his shares in the quarries to the labor union a long time ago, you know that, and it's the labor government that issued rights to quarry limestone in populated areas, not you."

"To eat the mountain, little Tania," Odelia corrects her, "eat it in great mouthfuls, and now I must leave my home. The lawyers want their share."

"Odelia, if you don't get out of here, you will be dispossessed, find yourself in the street, and what will you do then?"

"Let them do as they will with me, I will not leave my pussies. I shall not surrender. When Jimeney passed away I buried him up on the mountain, under a solitary tree overlooking the Jezreel Valley. I should have such a burial, place. I really mean it," she giggles, "I should, you know."

"And that's another thing I've come to talk to you about, Odelia, you've got to stop taking taxis up to the Muhraka to bury your cats. You're spending the little you had left supporting the taxi company; please luvy, listen to me." Tania knelt down and took the old lady's face in her hands and kissed each of her cheeks. "You're still young Odelia; you're not going to die." Odelia fell asleep. The interview was over. Tania beckoned us out. The door clicked shut. I feel a hundred cat eyes silently awaiting their familiar world to reinstate itself.

"Put that in your magazine," Tania says, holding my arm close to her warm bosom, protecting the innocent child of the West, "and don't forget to stress the fact that derelict of nature in there was exactly my age, not a day more, not a day less. I tell you it's bloody difficult this living business. You're damned if you help your fellow man and you're damned if you don't. My husband," she said tightening her seat belt, "worked hard, together with a dedicated group of scientists and agricultural engineers, to restore the mountain the quarries had destroyed with her in mind, I had a pile of mockups and photographs in the apartment. As always, political and economics necessity transcend the esthetic. The mountain will remain an ever more gaping sun bleached orifice resisting all shrubbery."

"Isn't there a law? It doesn't seem right," I added lamely.

"Law," Tania roars, "you Yankees! Deary, the moment the king became an elected official, a constitutional figurehead at best, God became dispensable and the law a changeling of society. Ask an old barmaid like me about the law. I should know. A few weeks ago I went up Mt. Sinai on the back of a donkey. My Bedouin guide told me he was most disenchanted with progress. More than one wife used to be honorable, a sign of wealth and now, under the Israelis, it was unlawful. Even the most unschooled nomad knows the law was crap. What's happening to Odelia was lawful all right, but it's not fair, it ain't right, it isn't humane. The point is," she adds straining back towards me as I struggle to keep my balance round bends and ascents and descents, "that we never know the ramification of our actions. I tried to help Odelia. She's been very good to us. My husband and I were married in her house, in that very living room. She offered us the services of her maids, her cook, and her gardener. She even ordered a wreath of white roses for her favorite horse. They had a stable then with some fine horses and she felt her favorite one should be properly decked out for our wedding. Her niece, my husband's first wife, had run off to the States with Eliot where she taught ballet and married an Optometrist, a widower with 11 children of his own. We worked our butts off to change Odelia's uncle's will. On his deathbed, we prevailed upon him to leave everything to Odelia rather than to The Israelite Orphan Home, tax-free. He signed, with much reluctance, in the presence of a psychiatrist, there to prove he was of sound mind, and with a highly paid lawyer as an additional witness. And the cruelest blow of all, the reason Odelia was so intractable about moving out, was that if she does, where can she go? The old gentleman intended to turn his property into a public park with a playground, with a stable and riding paths, leaving the house to Odelia to use in her lifetime."

"Tania couldn't have known," Gloria said taking those curves with unearthly speed and then pressing down hard on the break, "that by her good deed she was destroying poor Odelia who inherited all including her uncle's debts, lawyers' fees, and inheritance taxes. She lost everything. The land under her house had been sold to the highest bidder, a private building company, which will blight the view with chicken coops, high-rise apartments numbered 1 to 264." The car jumped about like a nervous kangaroo. I could see myself splattered down the mountain.

"Paradoxically," Tania breaks in, "the project will use so much cement, the mountain will look like an apple that a ravenous teenager had eaten down to the core. Odelia was right there."

Rattle in the motor. Oh God! Those who had committed adultery, those who had plagiarized, had not accredited their sources, those who had lied, and those who had appealed to foreign deities Anath and Aphrodite, Athene and Astarte, mothers all, are doomed never to go home again, never to sit round the hearth with their man, their children, their cattle.

Then the car came to a climactic stop; we got out and walked up three flights of snow-white steps to a door. Knockthree times and give the password. The door opened. "Annie Gluck', Tania introduces us, "the secretary and spirit behind the movement." We shook hands. The atmosphere was one of rebellious feminism, hard, tough, fighting logic to repel an unbearable order. I bought a ticket held out to me by Annie. The steel-gray haired lady, thin as a fakir on a diet, was very familiar. But then everyone in this country seems to be getting too familiar. When Gloria told her I was a representative of the media, she took me over to the main speaker of the evening, Mayor Narjis Ibn Daud, a woman of imposing weight, holds pudgy, earth brown hands clasped in her lap, the broad fingernails polished the color of rowan berries, her only attempt at femininity. Reserved smile, the small child like teeth contrast with the tough bullheadedness her form implies. We shook hands.

"I was a mayor; I was a slave," she addressed the audience, her struggle for composure defeated by an atrophied muscle on the left side of her dour face. The three of us sit upright behind her on the only chairs in the room. A group of girls in Che Guevarra poses, proud revolutionary martyrs for a cause in a blind and deaf world, a fat mummy and her equally endowed husband holding their baby on his knee, several ladies of the geriatric set waiting to be enlightened, sit in a semicircle, legs outstretched at her feet.

"When I finish work," the mayor speaks in English in a morose uneven voice, "I must prepare the coffee for my husband; serve him in the proper manner. He drinks slowly, making a loud slurping noise showing satisfaction. He holds the cup down on the saucer with confidence. I had once again succeeded. His world was secure. But there are times when my legs are swollen and I would be tired and he was not happy with the coffee, and I must once again go to the kitchen and prepare it more to his liking."

"You had children!" One of the Che Guevarra bunch ejects, cross-legged and cocksure, trying and succeeding in intimidating the lady mayor.

"Yes, I had two sons. My husband was older than I. You see," she turned to me, a gesture of apology, a request for sympathy, "most of the young men my age had either been killed in the '48 war or had emigrated to America and Australia. My husband was suitably educated; his family was acceptable to mine. We married. Do not believe I was a guarded woman in her tent, folding myself back into the shadow when a stranger walked into the house. I studied social work at the university in Beirut. I rode my horse from town to town. I was an intermediary, appealed to the government on the behalf of my people. Even pregnant I worked."

"You appealed to the Jewish government?" a rebellious child on the floor asks, her voice rising to emphasize her disbelief.

"Yes, one government was much like the other. My people were in need."

I turn to Narjis Ibn Daud. "You speak of the influence your father and your husband had on you but surely, as a feminist, you should tell us something of the influence your mother had on your life."

"You are very observant," she compliments me. "Mother died when I was an infant. I was brought up by the men in my family. My uncle was my guardian, my keeper." She spoke like someone reciting a memorized part.

"Keeper, you say," one of the young women shouted, "what about your sons? How do you bring them up?"

"I brought up my sons in the traditional manner." The girl on the floor raised her fist in a militant salute. "It was your duty to bring up your boys to share responsibility."

"It doesn't always work out that way."

And now the conversation turns heated, they are speaking Arabic very quickly. As The Mayor fights it out with the querulous young rebels, it suddenly hits me, rostrum stumping Annie—impossible to believe here in Israel—suffragette, anti Vietnam, anti Israel, pro-Communist, pro-Che Guevarra, pro-Mao Tse Tung, pro-Palestinian Revolution, a fire brand who had shouted, "The PLO was here to stay, their anthem was heard, they've spoken the word in the UN, had been given the go ahead by the USSR, USA, UAR"—and all the letters of the Latin alphabet. "Give them the left bank, Jerusalem, a corridor to Gaza, a bridge to Amman, the whole mess based on an illogical Hebrew mysticism."

Tania and Gloria stomped out in a huff motioning me to follow. I place my palm on the Mayor's calm hand. There was a slight smile playing round the edges of her lips. She lets me understand, she knows I think her a fine lady. Annie rises and walked us to the door. I told her I heard her talk in Brooklyn a couple of decades ago. She was flattered; held my hand wished me well in a voice hardly audible—tired soldier who had fought a battle or two and bone weary fain would lie down. Square shouldered militancy to shrugging fatalism, futility in all intransigent stands. I would have liked to have spent more time with her.

Gloria forcibly pushes me down the stairs and into the car. Tania holds out her hand for the car keys. "Can't put our lives in her hands, can we Josephina? Gloria places the keys in her palm without any apparent ill feeling. "She's been divorced," Tania said fitting herself in under the wheel. "Her husband got custody of their only son. Rumor had it she's living with another woman."

"Who?"

"Annie."

Why do so many feminists get divorced? Rhetorical question—no answer.

As we move from under the flowerpot-weighted balcony, the ladies' voices at each other's throats, waft down upon us like the static of an old newsreel.

"I don't mind people expressing their opinion but there was no reason for bad manners," Gloria was indignant.

"Now there's the stuff of revolution," Tania laughs. "I felt like a girl back in art school. I understand you're coming to our little farewell party."

"Sure, she is, I've invited her. I'll call Boobie tonight."

"Boobie?"

"Boobie is the traffic director."

"Come again?"

"Yes, he was in charge of the taxis which bring the staff up to the teachers' college. I had to get permission from him. Not everyone owns a car, you know. If you want something for your researches into the Palestinian problem, and according to my definition, all of us who make this area of the world our homeland are Palestinians, let me tell you that both Tania and I have been teaching these youngsters for really next to nothing."

"I can work for beans, my boarder's miserly handout and that of a museum curator's now and then to cover dire needs, but Gloria had a family to help support. In the middle of the program the powers that be decided there were no funds available for this kind of enrichment program and either we agreed to pay cuts, or the whole scheme was scrapped."

"We had a real hard time at the beginning of this course." Gloria turned back to face me, "at least I had. I finally made a breakthrough when I realized that theirs was simply a different mentality. They think in terms of allegory, analogy and moralizing, the poetic mind, the so-called primitive mind. In their own school they learn by rote, the teacher hashes out info, they gulp it down, regurgitate it for a test. When they finally learned how to describe phenomena in terms of itself rather than in relation to something else, I knew they were ready for the university. The problem for me anyway was that the scientific method, hypothesis, observation, experimentation, proof was truth, free of the moral good and bad, had led to mass murder in our times."

"Right you are honey, evil all the way," I'm about to shout trying to find an isle of comfort among those spiky springs tearing into my sore bottom, evil just another side of the good, let out all the stops, anywhere you start you'll reach the whole perfect truth. Can't fight it anyway, it's all shit anyway. Make love not war. One dozen variations on the theme; the baker's dozen.

"I'm a great one for moralizing Josephina, I tell my students that they are not just cogs in the wheel, that they should use their imagination, use new methods of thought and expression to try and change the system from within and above all be responsible for their successes and their mistakes but I know I'm just plain lying because basically it's male politicians who decide what material enters the classroom. It's the male oriented society that feeds the school system the gunk that forms the end product after 12 years of mandatory indoctrination."

"Don't exaggerate, Gloria." Tania warns sagely.

"Exaggerate? Have you noticed who writes the books, and who forms the policy? Man dictates and woman implements!"

"Very nice," I say looking at my watch, wanting to get away from this woman I'd never look up again, "but I don't know. It seems to be women are just plain lazy, don't really give a damn. If they cared enough they'd had a say in politics and in the writing and manufacture of books instead of happily griping about the situation. Why don't you get into politics instead of teaching Arab kids the English language?"

"Come, come girls, this banter makes me go all lightheaded. Where was this all leading to? We must learn to live with our men, symbiosis was the word."

"You're right," I say, a feeling of affection for her welling up inside me.

"You see, I knew you and Tania had something in common."

"Sure—the small coinage of the times."

"Don't get me wrong," Gloria said as we approach the hotel, bending over double under the seat to let me out, "I need a man for protection, I don't think a woman will ever find happiness solely on the factory floor no matter how much the boss depends on her. I need someone to lean upon, a constant companion; a partner who will not betray me. All I'm saying was we had to change the rules for them or they'll take over and change them for us."

"What you want, deary, was simply the old fashioned religion, someone to fight your battles at the dentist's."

"Yes," I repeat like a moron, struggling to get my sore ass round her body slumped under the front seat—why doesn't she had the courtesy to get out and let me pass—"what you are talking about is religion."

"She had spells you know, Tania shouted after me, caressing Gloria's hand. We allow her little poetic injustices." And in a spurt of blue smoke from the gonzo shnozzled exhaust hanging free under the chassis of the red Volks, Tania and Gloria disappear.

CHAPTER 15

I stood in the hotel entrance waving them away. I really liked the way Tania kept her bones neatly packed. Why did I label her Irish when she labels herself Jewish, a word filled with meaning, "murderers of Christ"—hackneyed phrases I reject, erase, cut out, ribbons of words, strips of paper floating in the sudden gust of wind in the intimate spaces of my mind—me, the popularizer of events not yet realized. I envied Angelica Edwards, not because she had a boyfriend who was faithful and a cousin who went to Cambridge but because she was Catholic, had family in Salerno, her father was a police officer—everything in order, framed, glassed in, given to understanding while I travel the byways of the world listening to the grandmother problem. All those potential grandmothers herded into box cars, womb with child, their palms holding the feeling of a child's hand begging protection, up in smoke through chimneypots, reduced to clarified butter in the interim years, '42–'45, out there in the well-stoked ovens of the German.

There must be a reason. And so I sat down next to grandmothers. But more and more as I fly above continents in well-mapped air lanes, all the stories began to sound the same.

We were both bored. She's going to Venezuela to visit grandchildren, I'm flying in the wake of beauty queen. Student: Computer and Communication Science. Age: 21. self contained, grown up—sex, attempted suicide, marriage, divorce, had tried it all. Can't understand why Papa was disappointed.

She tells me about the Jews of Salonika, can't prove her facts, all but a few survived. Handsome businessman takes out photocopy of a letter from his Gucci briefcase.

Memo: Top Secret May 1943.

My Dear Kaltenbrunner,

I had ordered many copies of the book Jewish Ritual Murders and had given instructions they be distributed among people with the rank of a standard Fuhrer. I was sending you a hundred additional copies, to be distributed among your action commando people and especially those who deal with the Jewish problem.

In connection with this book, I was charging you with the following tasks:

1. Investigations of ritual murders by Jews should take place immediately everywhere provided there are still un-deported Jews. Such cases should be checked and brought to my attention. Then we should put any such cases on trial.

2. This whole ritual murder problem should be dealt with by experts in Romania, Hungary and Bulgaria. Later I think we should publish in our press these "Ritual murders" cases to make it easier for us the deportation of the Jews from these countries. These matters can be advanced, understandably, only in coordination with the Ministry of Foreign Affairs.

3. Please think over whether we can't arrange, in cooperation with the Ministry of Foreign Affairs, an illegal broadcast, strictly anti-Semitic, for Britain and America. The broadcast should be made up of such material as The Sturmer used during the struggle—that makes it possible to present to the English and Americans. I was sure, in this case, that a sensational headline was most important. I intend to get in touch with "Groupen fuhrer" S.S. Dr. Martin, in order to enroll a member of The Sturmer to the cause.

Moreover some people should be given the task of looking for and checking notices from law courts and police in England regarding disappearances of children so that it could enable us to present in our broadcasts short accurate bits of news saying that in such and such place a child had disappeared and that the incident apparently was connected with Jewish ritual murder.

In general, I do believe we can immensely activate anti-Semitism throughout the world by anti-Semitic propaganda in the English language and maybe also in Russian, through intensive propaganda about ritual murders. I beg you to discuss the matter with your staff and make some preparations, so that we can bring forth a proposed plan.

Hail Hitler!

Yours, Himmler.

Opener: "Translated it myself. How much do you suppose I can get for it?"

"Market glutted with Nazi memorabilia," I told him sipping the drink he'd ordered for me. Sweet man. Who wants a memo from Himmler to Kaltenbruner 1943? So close to the end of the war, they were still ritually murdering the Jew and trying to accuse the Jew of ritually murdering tasty morsel of a German child. Justification.

Interview: Businessman and scholar in a Wisconsin pub—used to be an exclusive Nazi club during the Second World War, a matter for the law courts, don't you think. You can still feel the close camaraderie of intrigue among men who shared a diabolic cause. The food was lousy and the service worse. "I was the first Jewish soldier allowed into the concentration camps after the war."

I envied Angelica Edwards because the world love seemed so possible, so free of infirmity. What romantic hogwash! Here I was a woman over 40, dribbling banalities, agonizing over lost grandmothers in the lobby of a sparkling new hotel.

"My mother's family was destroyed by lack of interest—the once proud name of Steinberg became at most a hindrance, which begged explanation they could no longer offer—so they changed the name, the religion and became a comma; a period; a dash." I like that description, it was given me gratis ten minutes ago by a 50-year old floozie enthusing over sex with young boys, graphic explanations of the male organ at the height of its glory—penetration and release. Born: yes. Auschwitz: Yes, was there for 12 hours when I was seven. I walked out. No more details. "I never ask for money," glancing at her watch, eying the elevators, "at home I never ask for money. I had a teddy bear on my night table with a label on its stomach, Hungry!"

Scratch a 50-year-old, get a child of the war, scratch a Polish actress, 20 years old—parents turnip farmers in the bog, dark eyes, full lips—not Slavic at all. Who were her grandparents? Really? Karen may be right, but she had that mother of hers, and me. Was I to blame that father died in bed in Ocean Parkway and mother the Polish, Bulgarian Hungarian connection, on the shores of the Bay of Monterey leaving photographic remembrances of strong mustachioed men, well dressed and well fed, looking out, strict and sure, from Victorian frames, the ladies in their taffeta best smiles for the camera, self satisfied, aware of the role they play in a man's world—20 portraits stacked one atop the other on the closet—drawers divided into dovecot, recesses for needles, spools of cotton thread, skeins of wool, all the colors necessary. Hungarians are pragmatic people who make the best of what life gives them but with style, Viva l' impression, break down the image, show there was no magic just ordered convenience, cubby holes, thumb tacked paper lining, sandalwood, each article in a predestined place, letters filed in separate folders for different subjects—household arrangements, medical all in Hungarian, the life script I wish I could read—a file of poems, a file of bills, a file dealing with real estate holdings in townships in the environs of Buda and Pest, inherit the wind.

Mother's third husband was a doctor from Budapest. After his death she went completely berserk in spite of an extensive library on manic depression—what part biological imbalance, what part emotional reaction to the times—he had collected for her.

Running after a cockroach: "Oh you little brown thing," under the bed, over the couch, "I'll get you," old shoe, felt slipper, squash it dead on the hall table where I'm preparing a magazine article sanely executed in adjectiveless prose to relate fact—upward trend in defective births in Hapsburg. Concurrently, it was discovered that the Loveborne Camera Company, among others, had been leaking solvents into the community drinking water. In spite of the fact that the two events are contiguous in time, there seems to be inconclusive evidence of a linkage.

There was her bosom, smelling of lavender perfume and violet talc, a lacy hanky in the "V" of the black dress. Can three years in a concentration camp cause such an inconsolable lesion? Plastic doilies, souvenirs from trips to Dallas, Tampa, Rockaway Beach, the Bronx Zoo substitute for the fine cut glass and silver on fine lace of other days. Clothes, beautifully tailored, on hangers in an order that signified meaning and in the corner, a sleek, longhaired dog, manicured nails, regular visits to the vet, accusing me with doleful eyes of taking away his source of food. I didn't kill my mother. We put the stuff in boxes and wished it away. What to do with someone else's ball of string wound carefully over the year—it may come in handy some day. My boys, on the TV console, wearing baseball caps, holding mitt, ball, and bat being embraced by McCrudder. Proud Dad. Red, blues and browns against the gray and white house in the background proudly withstand age.

My son Jeremy, his father's smile and I know, though he had not told me, that he's in Army Intelligence just as his father had been in American Army Intelligence during the Second World War. But no matter how woebegone victims of the war in the Middle East look in photographs, they cannot compare with the live corpses McCrudder had been ordered to display to the conquered officers of the defeated German Army. He had done his duty, opened wide the gates of Auschwitz to their view, the incinerator, the most efficient death machine, the crowning glory of these our mechanical times, still warm in mid production. McCrudder had once touched the Pope's finger. His buddy, with whom he shared a desk for two years, paralyzed during the war, had a recurring dream.

Rome: The Pope showers goodness on all mankind from a window above the crowd praying for child, goodness to seminal fluid fertilizing the wombs of the adoring women—their bellies swell. They give birth to perfectly formed baby boys right there in the courtyard before the outstretched fingers of the Pope raining blessings down upon the horde. "Never call a crowd of people anything but a group of individuals." That was her bag, Mrs. Reynolds, our History teacher at Walton High. She had served in the Wacs and had learned a thing or two about dehumanization.

McCrudder touched the Pope's finger in front of the basilica in Rome. Within that moment of wonderment, his buddy's wife conceived. Early in our marriage, I watched McCrudder creep out of bed at night, go to the toilet, and return to bed in a cold sweat, shivering like a snake shedding its skin, curl himself round my body for heat or strength. I wondered then as I wonder now if any of the strong Ubermensch of the German Reich, shown sights of human enmity to man, similarly retch out their guts in empathy with their fellow human beings night after night, year after year, till death dissolves the norm illusion. McCrudder's love was too grand for me; his compassion too sincere. I was downright mean because I couldn't reach his heights of sensibility, his generosity of spirit. The meaner I was, the more he forgave. The more he forgave, the more I felt like a fleshless corpse in Auschwitz, my fingers interlaced in prayer for salvation which never came. If you know a man's dream, shouldn't you be able to hold on to his body?

I was being paged over the loud speaker, probably Gloria with news about Boobie. "My son Yaron was in jail," she says. "I tripped over the groceries the delivery boy stacked up near the front door, cursing Yaron for not being home on time to bring them in and putting the meat in the freezer as he was supposed to. The phone rang and that's it." I could feel Gloria's face turn pale, her eyelashes smearing mascara on her ageless skin.

"What happened?"

"I don't know; he's in jail, and with Rafcho in the army!"

"Is he still in the army, at his age, can't they let him out in an emergency?" I realize I'm saying silly things but I don't know what to say. I'm not very good at dealing with emotion.

"He's in Sinai, meet me tomorrow at the police station in town, please Josephina."

"What are they holding him for, drugs, abuse, murder?"

"Oh shut up," she shouts, "and the car broke down."

I met her the next morning. She was sitting on the stairs of the unimpressive entrance to the police station wearing a dark blue turtle neck sweater and slacks, a fawn leather jerkin to match her boots, a brick wool muffler and a stocking hat so stretched, it fell all over her face. Yaron—lately hitting heavy chords on an electric guitar, accompanying a record of Pink Floyd's "The Wall," cynical philosophy of the teenage crowd, beyond every wall there was another wall, Ovadia my boy!—in frayed brown and white checkered felt house shoes, jeans open at the fly and a navy blue sweatshirt, which must had been washed in boiling water, it's so small, Yale University printed pompously in white letters over a ferocious looking but yet not unkindly bulldog jumps out of the back of a police van. He already had that look of a hunted animal, the desperate eyes of a prisoner. At least dogs in the pound get to keep their own clothes on. I glanced at his wrists, fearing handcuffs. There are none.

"Hello Mother, Josephina." he said following the police officer, in skintight dungarees up the stairs to a long narrow hall on either side of which rooms retain their secrets behind closed doors.

"Yaron," I whisper, "whatever happened to your clothes?"

"This kid held a soupspoon to my throat, threatened to ram it in if I didn't exchange. It's ok; he's never owned a pair of Adidas sports shoes, stoned Levis and a swell school shirt like mine. My neck's worth more than a pair of sneakers even though I earned them cleaning the streets of Haifa this summer. What the hell. You should see that kid, Ma, flopping about in my shoes, my pants falling down over his bellybutton, strutting about so proud. My good deed for the day. You would've laughed. Mom?" Gloria's uncertainty, hiding her eyes with her hat, works on me.

Instinctively, I open my arms and hold her feeling the softness of her bones. "Come on Glo, get a hold of yourself, what could the boy have done?"

"I don't know."

Gloria and I sat on a wooden bench in the reticent light—preface to a crime which had not yet been committed—in the claws of authority vested with the inalienable right to forge our identity, twist our beings, ban us from the society of man for having trespassed sub clause 9C of a social contract written in a language indecipherable even to those who've put it together. Will we ever get out? Reverberations down the hall, a shriek for help. I got up. Gloria pulled me down next to her. A slender police officer who seemed to be running for her life, a large bedraggled woman strode after her, caught hold of her hair. Two women police officers appear, twist the hysterical woman's arms back force her into a room where a blubbery kid stands like a pillar of salt in the doorway, a moronic stare plastered to his face, as the woman, screaming hysterically, was dragged in past him.

"What's going on, Gloria?"

"She's saying that the police had no right to take her son away from her and put him in reform school. She can take better care of the child than the authorities. The policewoman was explaining that since her husband was in jail and she in and out of mental homes, they had the lawful right to do as they see fit." Door shut. Poignant silence.

Gloria's name was called out. I'm embarrassed for her. It seems more humane to come forth and ask if the requested name was hers. She jumps up like a robot and was trapped in one of those rooms. I hear her shouting; the door banged open, Gloria came out reasoning with the back of the tightly trousered young officer holding a sheaf of important looking papers in his hand. He had no time for small talk, and rushed into another room followed by Yaron, with an embarrassed smile on his face.

Yaron came towards us, "That's that," he said.

"Look," I suggested, "let's go to my hotel and get something to eat."

"Do you want us to take you home, Yaron?"

"Oh Ima, I'm not a baby, I can get home by myself."

"What about school?"

"It'll be alright, Ima," he said an embarrassed puppy dog grin on his face.

We walked to the bus stop, I've offered to pay for the taxi but she refuses. How can she let that boy travel by public transport dressed as he is?

Up we go, and Gloria sat next to me, and Yaron opposite, traveling backwards. Fleshy body plops down squeezing the boy tight against the window.

"What exactly happened, Yaron?" I asked.

"Nothing much, after the football game I walked into my friend's room. He had a new record of "YES" I wanted to tape. Suddenly the searchlights went on, and sirens went off; everything but submachine gun fire. Someone searched me and found a ten-pound note in my stocking. The note was marked and that was it."

"They've had a rash of petty thievery," Gloria interrupted, "in the Military Academy dormitories. A military operation was planned with the police department to catch a thief. Once it was on, it couldn't be stopped. The people supposedly in charge couldn't make an independent decision. They couldn't admit to a mistake and Yaron was taken to jail. I told the big wheel in the police department what I thought of their methods. Mud sticks, you know."

By keeping Yaron in jail without giving him a chance to get in touch with me and explain, they committed a greater crime than anything Yaron might have done. "The department may have its faults," he said, "but it's the best we have."

"Oh Ima, stop. It was all a mistake."

"Some mistake and now you'll probably be on probation for a year and have a record."

"No, I won't, Ima. It's only a formality. They'll erase my name from the computer, you'll see. Don't worry! I never wanted to be an air force pilot anyway. I mean having a completely clear record doesn't mean that much to me."

"Let me read something to you," Gloria took a sheet of paper from the pocket of her jerkin, and read aloud in a stage whisper heard from here to Tallahassee. "'It appears to us that your son's breach of the law by entering a private domain was exceptionally serious as it defeats the protection and safety purposes of the Municipal Law.' It sounds a little better in Hebrew but it's gibberish."

"Ah gibberish, you can't get away from gibberish anywhere in this gibberish infested planet," I said looking at the flabby-thighed woman sitting opposite, feet apart in complete abandon. Do you know where the word comes from? It's Italian like ghetto was Italian. It means whimsy, "ghiribizzi." Browsing through Webster's 1954 gone to pieces, no A's no B's. I've watched it disintegrate for years with a sort of hurtful pleasure. What had this preoccupation with words done for me? Ninth Collegiate, gift from McCrudder on the bookshelf over our bed. To Josephina in cursive script written with Hi Tech pen—Gibberish! Whimsical ego trip. Count Sforza writing of Machiavelli in his castle as the airplanes plant kilograms of prefabricated incendiary materials, crumbling battercake houses decomposing the rock shielded earth with fire. Machiavelli writes The Prince, "one of my ghiribizzi." And the irresistible strength of one fighter pilot turning the tide of war on a whimsy and a prayer and I keep thinking of Lebanon, that battle scarred land—one man keeping one idea sacred, one man, one idea. PLO needs land, any land will do. It had ever been so. Major Haddad defending his land, setting up an army against a whimsical fancy. The Western world pro-PLO. If they want to have a go at destroying the Jew let's give them a hand, we've tried and the Jew's an irresistible foe. Let's see what the PLO can do against the Jew. Give the world what it expects; fulfilling expectations was our goal why didn't the allies bomb the railroad lines to Auschwitz? Everyone knows on which side his bread was buttered on—preposition at the end of the sentence lately accepted standard.

"At choshevet sh'at makira auti, auti?" You think you know me you snob, you filth. Hysterical voice, mighty familiar. It was the maligned momma from the police station. Gloria held me to my seat with her arm, and whispered, "She's telling you not to look at her so intently. There are things about her you can't know. She's just been to see her husband in prison and he's innocent. He loves his children. Her son was a good boy. Her daughter was not a prostitute and in spite of what you've heard, she comes from a respectable family, as respectable as yours. For

God's sake," Gloria said through her teeth, "keep very still till we get off at the next stop." All this whispering gets the woman angrier still. She hovers there above me screaming in a crimson study. The bus comes to a standstill.

Gloria touches her son's arm. I bend down to kiss his cheek. He's really a sweet boy.

"I've met enough people in Israel who belonged in the loony bin. Anywhere else, they'd be locked up," I told her as we rushed down a hill. "Aren't you sick of this place?"

"No, are you?"

"Why don't you take the whole lousy police department to court? I wouldn't let them treat my son this way and get away with it."

"Oh Josephina, you'll never understand. Every organization had built into its structure the words, which give it life, stick a pin into it, question it and you are bringing destruction down upon civilization itself. The police department was a remnant of the Colonial British Mandate and the Ottoman Empire. In time, it'll find new words to define itself, new rules more befitting the times."

God almighty, how far can altruism go?

CHAPTER 16

We were sitting on a concrete ledge interspersed with gravel. Behind us is a cake shop, chocolate hearts, bunny rabbits, trellised chocolate baskets filled with iced sugar greetings, Happy Birthday, Congratulations on your new job, Happy New Year, Thank You, Bon Voyage. Oh my torn and tortured bottom!

"It's too expensive to drive to work in my own car," Gloria said her eyes filmed over with time past, "the school picks us up at points along the way and we are chauffeured by taxi. Last week, I was the only passenger. It was a day clear and satisfying, unlike this one. You know how the sky can be in winter; it enwraps you in a kind of euphoria that was difficult to explain. You can feel the torpor of virgin soil suddenly awaken to flower red, blue, yellow, carpeting the mountainside.

The ride takes over half an hour on the highway and up through Sylvan hills stained with clumps of crimson hollyhocks at attention, proud sentinels! Abed the driver took a shortcut through a little used Turkish road that cuts through the mountain and falls sharply into the bay.

"Down below," he pointed to an abandoned hut, "there was a hirbe." His eyes were dispassionate, cool. I felt myself fighting a growing desire within me to satisfy the purely sexual, put myself together just in time. The taxi screeched to a stop. A herd of silky black goats crossed our path. The goats mulled round us, followed the goatherd, a boy holding a stick at both ends behind his neck, as if we were apparition. Abed and I pretended nothing had passed between us. He drove quickly to the highway, enmeshed ourselves in traffic. "He is young you know."

"Who is?"

"Haven't you been listening?"

"Yes," I lied.

"Abed, Abed the driver." I must have looked confused.

"I was enjoying the sound of rain, seeing myself a bright eyed child walking along Pelham Parkway picking golden ragwort from either side of the highway, blowing feathery white puffball seeds into the sun. When I worked in the Air force School," she talks on unmindful of the soft but determined rain falling through the leaves of the gnarled carob tree overhead, her rather husky voice breaking with emotion—God this was true confessions day, "one of the students with our family name kept hanging round me. I remember him because he had very wide shoulders and a broad chest and legs too short to carry such an impressive trunk. He told me he lived in Jaffa, an enclave of Bulgarian Jews—never completely integrated into the general Israeli culture, sing their own songs, eat their own kind of food. I pretended not to notice his interest when our paths crossed. I mean if it turned out he was related to Rafcho, I'd had the whole city of Jaffa, the whole Bulgarian Jewish population of Bulgaria, after me. Everything was going along fine until he began asking to carry my books. I let him. I said to myself if he wants to carry my books let him, he was hard up and I was a teacher. The logic was simple and direct.

"It was then I realized I was being used by the male of the species and I decided to be my own woman. These guys had to pass an English proficiency exam at the American Embassy and that's what they were going to do. That became my only concern. I mean I might have taken him up on his unworded request, him and the officer in charge of Education on the base who kept leering at me as he discussed the fine points of military discipline, but I had seen too many children of the war my age destroyed by guilt for being alive when so many others are dead, whoring and fornicating when their own children are grown and I wasn't going to fall into that trap. After all, I was not, strictly speaking, a child of the war."

"How can you teach English," I asked, knowing as well as I know McCrudder that it was dangerous to fall in the trap of leading questions, "if you are not qualified?"

"Don't be silly, if I were qualified I'd never have gotten a job in a teacher's college. No one there was qualified and the last thing they want was to raise the standard. The army was renowned, justifiably or not, for its ability to adjust to changing conditions and that's why, supposedly, they win wars but everywhere else the frameworks are rigid, just pages and pages of rules and regulations waved away by a paternal figure who hands out jobs like gumdrops according to mood and the mendicant geographic and blood proximity, not what you know but who you know.

"The last thing they wanted was a teacher with a bona fide degree; they had their own hides to protect. Either I agreed to have my head or my legs chopped off to fit the bed they'd made for themselves or I stayed out. I was no less a threat to the High School teaching establishment run by a certain number of dowdy English ladies whose "upper ten accents" one claimed for herself, fell to cockney like stockings on a loose garter belt. They'd all been members of the British Army during the war, had learned a thing or two about internal maneuvers in closed circles, kept their system well oiled and free of outsiders, especially Americans with University degrees.

"I finally did get a job in a night school teaching English to people planning to emigrate to the USA. The Iraqi English teacher in charge had spent several years in Italy and was a survivor of the Polish concentration camps. I was told to call him doctor, he did everything within his power to make my life miserable, waited for me with a stopwatch in hand and announced that I was 30 seconds late, that kind of thing. He was a real dish, a tall slim man, would had passed for a Hollywood actor, something like an aging Gregory Peck. His sexuality hung out all over the place, radiated a message that couldn't be overlooked. I overlooked it. He couldn't decide how to behave towards me, like a woman, a teacher or a comrade in arms. Months later, I told him he'd been exploiting me, underpaying me to do his underhanded work, helping people get out of Israel was not exactly my aim in life. He shouted back at me, Mengele in his boots whipping the floor behind his soles, couldn't frighten me, poor devil, but he could fire me. When it became clear I was pregnant, he found the perfect way of resolving his frustrations, the perfect excuse to get rid of me. I didn't know the law, didn't know a law had been passed making it illegal to fire a pregnant woman without compensation, without sick leave. I didn't fight for my rights, got accustomed to not having any, holding on to Rafcho's rationalization that children, especially boys, had to be nurtured carefully."

Gloria's full of talk, I'm exhausted—not to mention wet.

"Rafcho was right about the boys, boys need much more care. I felt that instinctively about Guy and I put off going through the hassle of looking for a job. But, finally in desperation, I went for an interview in a small town in the Jezreel Valley.

I was willing to leave home and family, sleep over in the 'Here's the script, you won't believe this, I had such and such a degree,' I tell the principal who introduces me to someone higher up in command whom I'm to call doctor. "I," the doctor says, an awkward grin on his face, "went to a school around the corner from you."

"Where?"

"Columbia."

"Well, Columbia was not NYU."

"Why were you thrown out of your last job?"

"I wasn't thrown out."

"Who was in charge of English there?" I gave him the doctor's name.

"No," he says, "that isn't right, but it doesn't matter. We need someone who can teach grammar. You know how to teach grammar?"

"Are you an English teacher?" I asked.

"No, but I know."

"Why didn't you tell me over the phone what you were looking for when I asked? Do you know how much it costs to get out here, transportation and a baby sitter?"

"I'm not under any obligation to hire you, we had several possibilities open. I want to see what you can offer me."

"I'm not under any obligation to work for you either."

"You have a chip on your shoulder."

"I walked out; end of interview. The secretary tells me the principal's niece had taken several courses in English and she needs the job, she's getting married. "Yes, I do understand."

"It finally hit me; the undercurrents of politics were against me. I went to the Women's Lib Club and met Tania. She told me to give up the idea of long hours and little pay that goes with the respectable label High School Teacher, Elementary School Teacher and get in touch with the Tai Chi instructor at the Haifa Museum who was the nerve center of information in the Northern area of the State. I took her advice, registered in the course and swung my body round the clock according to her instructions for six months before we became friendly enough to have coffee. It wasn't easy getting her attention; the Tai Chi instructor doesn't face the group but stands back to us. She suggested I call up Daisie, telephone number 226321. I remember the number because she wrote it down on the cover of the library book I was reading and I was upset. We never wrote in public library books. I controlled my temper and called the number. Daisie asked me what my hair color was. I said reddish brown. She said I should think in terms of black, those were her exact words. Then she asked me what my husband did for a living. She sent me kisses over the phone, little bird pecks when I mentioned the fact that Rafcho worked for the Cement Works. This was just what she needed. 'Come right over.'

"When I got there, she brought me up close to a bottle of Clairol displayed on a sheet of music on her upright piano. Her husband was a sailor and he had had quite a bit of trouble bringing in this extra large bottle of hair color from the States, half price and tax-free. Daisie's hair had been dyed blonde so recently, black down and oily blackheads stood out like little scabs of dirt on her sallow skin. I myself had once been a blonde and I wasn't about to cover my identity with commercial color again. I used henna for a while but the smell of chopped grass bothered Rafcho and so I stopped. I like my graying hair, sure worked hard enough to reach this stage in my life. I was about to pay for the bottle, you see in addition to being in charge of the choir in the teacher's college Daisie's sister-in-law was the secretary to the accountant of the institution.

"Anyway, Daisie told me she'd written a song for the children's song festival, I told her Yaron played the guitar. She led me to a back room in her apartment, hunks of plaster of Paris and little hills of dribbled concrete on the floor and everywhere there was dust, on the white baby cot, the white chest of drawers, the windowpane.

"Is it good for the baby?"

"No baby, see!" She tore open her blouse and showed me her breast, "foam rubber, cancer. If my husband leaves me I'll die. This was his studio." She showed me a piece of plaster, the size of a basketball, "The Sculpture." She'd had one of the best photographers in the country take pictures and had sent them to the Venice Biennale. Of course "The Sculpture" had been accepted. She held out the glossy photograph. The plaster ball throwing geometric shadows on the void looked significant, symbolic, a monumental sphere in space.

"I offered to pay for the photograph, the Clairol, the sheet music.

"No," she said, "it's your husband I'm interested in." I showed the photograph to Rafcho. He knew what he was meant to do. He had the ball cast at work, and the monumental sculpture carefully placed at Daisie's front door. There was a Municipal ordinance against blocking up the sidewalk, but knowing Daisie, she probably got a prize for beautifying the city. The next day I was offered a job teaching English to a group of airmen. They were going off to Dallas, everyone seems to be going to Dallas, to learn how to service F-16 multirole fighters. I liked the name but was a bit worried. I had to explain words like variables, parameters, modes, stochastic processes, algorithms, heuristics, maximax, minimmax. My mathematics was now quaint and I was not about to relearn a subject I had wiped clear from memory. I decided the one thing I had in my favor was the fact that I was a woman. I knew I had to play the mother, the femme fatale, or the inferior helpless female. I decided to play the passively sweet tramp, dumb enough to make the men feel good but not too obviously sexy. It worked well enough. And I earned my pay. They learned more by teaching me than they could have if I had tried to teach them. Actually I never would have gotten the job if Khomeini hadn't dethroned the Shah of Iran and taken all of those workers in the American Embassy hostage. The American government substituted the Israel air force for the Iranian. I mean they couldn't just fire all those instructors and things. Once a plan was put in motion, it had to be seen through.

"This summer, we went to a show in the park and there was Daisie accompanying a stand up comic. The audience walked out during the performance singly and in groups leaving a balding lawn. She played on as if nothing were happening. The comic began shouting at her, blaming her for the flop. There would be other comics. She knew the people in charge, her father-in-law, and soon enough she would be in charge. The job gave me back my lost pride. I've never been out of a job since."

Am I to question her pride and then the smell of hot baked buns wafts subliminally into my conscious mind? I think of David, hope he was reading Mailla's manuscript carefully this time not filtering words through sieves of his own making. Foolishly perhaps, in spite of the fact that I had learned people usually hide no fascinating center, no meaning more profound than the planes they present, I find myself thinking not unkindly of Mailla.

"Do you know Mailla Van Eyke?" I don't know why you should, but I just feel everyone in Israel knows everyone else."

"I know of her. I've used her books in my class when things got rough, fills in those moments between the dropping eyelid and the bell. It isn't so much that I couldn't get a job, more probably I didn't want one. I had become convinced that we shape our own destiny. You should have had a daughter, Josephina. Abigail, my daughter, practically brought herself up."

I'm about to quit, say goodbye Gloria forever—what the hell was she selling me, even if I wanted another child it's too late. There was an end to fertile periods in the female, McCrudder can still populate the earth with offspring—but before I had a chance she shoves me into a taxi that drove up to the curb poised for take off. Introductions, a round of restrained good mornings and Gloria's voice drones on and on. She never stops talking—Yaron, the police, the law, sharing her life, her anger—done in by one of those descendants of the Jewish children of the war, one of those men who never grew up, boy cowed into a non aggressive yes Momma, Yes Poppa, Yes teacher, suddenly finds himself eating grass one heartbeat away from the Gestapo goosestep—well behaved upper middle class young man in spats and walking stick, spun sugar morals, without a home, dung heap hunger, stalks the long grain—taking it out on Gloria, twisting her arm. "There!"

I'm getting testy, the close physical contact with blocks of ice, the frigid unsmiling faces of these women who travel together each day for years, pushing away the intimacy forced upon them, tires me out. I'm so tired, so tired. God are you out there? No response from timeless space just Gloria's voice droning on and on her fears, momentous secrets—fine spray of saliva suspended above the upholstery absorbing words, never enough to break through the indifference—the more you reveal, the more there was hidden, the more you talk, the more there was left to say.

And now the rain turns to hail bombarding the car, fierce pellets like a voodoo dancer shaking dried seedpods in a gourd to perpetuate rain. Aunt Khoursey, oh guzelim, rose of Andrianople, crossroads of the Ottoman Empire. Old love letters, fading in my hands, water fountains tinkling in the grand salon, seven apartments opening unto each other to receive the Sultan, master of the Middle East from the Danube to Alexandria, his playground, his garden.

"I was a sickly child, my mother takes me to the Jewish cemetery. Nineh, the Turkish sorceress, puts me on a gravestone and they all walk down the hill, out of sight. I was left alone. I cry.

Nineh says, "She does not want to go, she will live."

"I was 12 years old and there was an epidemic of smallpox. My mother sends for the Hadji, an old Jewish woman with lovely hands. She who had made the holy pilgrimage to Jerusalem places silver coins from a pouch on an oval silver tray, drawing Hebrew letters. I was saved. It was 1933, and I went to Thrace to make the Ziara, visit my mother's grave. I feel there was much to fear. Shadows picked my room clear of bedding, pieces of material from the great dowry trunk, silver candelabra hidden under the wooden table in the cellar where the silk worms spin themselves into cocoon on mulberry leaves. My mother's youngest sister goes about looking for her things, a hall mirror in the house of the maid's father, a headboard at the greengrocer's, pieces of brocade and spools of handmade lace from under the carriage keeper's kitchen table.

"My cousin took me to the Moslem cemetery. It was Shabbat, the days the Jews visit Nineh dressed in a hand loomed wool ferege, a gown down to her ankles, turko green, green like the flag of Sudan. Her skin was white, her eyes blue, clear blue. She covers my head in a white sheet. I hold a brass pan above my head. She poured molten tin with a soup ladle, poured cold water and there was a sharp sound. The tin contracted into shapes. I was so frightened of the noise like an earthquake around my head.

"Nineh dances round me, skwiisshsh, shwish like a bird twittering ominous incantations before a storm. This was before the pogrom, not like a Russian pogrom lasting many days, a small one that lasts one day. The Turk wants to show solidarity with the German and looks away when the homefolks make a pogrom, devastate the homes of the Jews, locusts digesting all and then burning the field. The land of my birth was not important, what does it matter where I was born, I was rejected as if the Turk owned the land, as if they themselves hadn't been the bane of civilizations, the hordes coming through the vortex, as if they hadn't been the devil incarnate, as if the land owns allegiance to an idea."

Athens TV, heavy jowled man. CLOSE UP. Yes I shall not forget. He ordered us to pick up the basket filled with our women's gold rings, earrings, bracelets, chains, good luck pieces. My brother wavered, two thick whip welts on his forehead, deep as a cavern, brain frothing through the nostrils over trunk spouting blood. He was my brother. Talk, we never talked. We followed orders. You want to talk, how to explain. I shall never forget the SS officer. No words. Periods. Exclamation points! He looked a lot like the Secretary General of the United Nations, the one who was wounded on the Russian front and served only as a translator; a go-between with no authority whatsoever to make major decisions. Just followed orders, signed documents. Every last piece of gold in fruit baskets, enough to create an image—Apis hallowed bull, sun soul between the horns, birthmark specks on the forehead forming a triangle, half moon on breast, genetic renderings to fit man's mind. Jacob and the speckless goats and black sheep, white sheep—two can play at the genetic game. Right. Left.

NEVER had MAN CONCENTRATED SO MUCH INTELLECTUAL ENERGY TO DESTROY AN IDEA as thoroughly as did the German. NEVER say never. When Combyses, king of Persia, conqueror of Egypt slew Aps the sacred bull with his own hands, he went MAD.

Wehrmacht Ober lieutenant Kurt Waldheim secretary general of the UN from 1972–1978, given a medal for "brave conduct" in battle; belonged to Army Group E. Served in the Balkans on the staff of General Alexander Lohr hanged in 1947 for war crimes. 1943 Group E moved to Arsakli, four miles from Salonika. Between 1942–1945, 45,000 Jews from Salonika were sent to Auschwitz.

Entschuldigen Sie bitte, under duress coughing serenely cheh cheh. "I can swear a holy oath I know nothing of the deportations. I neither gave orders nor made operational suggestions. I had either to continue to serve or be executed. I remained confined to my desk. Why should I apologize?"

Those who lived to tell the tale had guts of steel, the hairdressers, hair cutters, violin players; the singer of songs at the gates, the chimney sweeps. In fighting at the crematorium door—I killed him, he splayed me. There should have been a trial for what Jews did to Jews! Who was to blame for bringing them down to the level of dog eat dog? Pre set reaction to self-eradication. Surprise! In camps all possible human reactions from extreme sadism to expected cannibalism. German Jews go back to Germany, for periodic visits, extended stays, like the Germans more than they like their own. Self hate. "I can't stand English girls but the German girls are great." A bunch of circumstantial evidence. Won't hold up in a court of law. Cross out! Lillian Ciegal: "If you don't like the way we do things here go run your own magazine"—black poodle on red rug under the desk. You'd think behind that pasted smile there was nothing but gemutlichkeit, frothy meringue. Apple tart!

We get to our destination; the ladies disperse themselves in several directions and are gone. If you can't be decent to your fellow man what good was education?

Holding my DIAPER bag over my head for protection, the rain dripping into the turtleneck sweater I bought in Milan, good thing I packed an extra sweater, why didn't I bring a raincoat?

"Abed," Gloria said as I rush up the hill after her, "called me, Gveret, Madam! He's forgotten my name." I followed her into a classroom. No one was there except gray white birds, slender and swift, determinedly flitting about building nests, inverted clay igloos on the low-beamed ceiling. Two young women walk in. I'm introduced as a writer for the newsweekly they've used as a text during the semester. They are absolutely thrilled, and think my work the most exciting ever.

"Ibtesom was Roman Catholic and Wafa Coptic," Gloria explains as the girls spread a blue and white-checkered tablecloth, arrange straw baskets of fruit, paper plates, small white coffee cups, a thermos and an array of cakes and cookies. Two young men walk into the room. Same spiel, introductions, whispered confidences, "Mohammed was a Moslem from The Triangle and so was Ziad, Moslem or Druse; I'm not quite sure about him. Ziad was so suspicious at first, thought all Jews his natural enemy."

"Back home in the Bronx upon being introduced, age, occupation, financial standing, relative closeness to power, may be related but not a person's religious affiliation."

"You just don't understand the mentality," she said as the room filled up with students. And then Tania made her entrance, a thrill of excitement. She fitted a cassette to a tape recorder and we are deafened by the sound of a thousand bagpipes. Tania dances a jig with gusto. The kids clap in a rhythm foreign to the Emerald Isle. Tania ends her performance with a coda of belly dancing. Her power of concentration was admirable. Applause.

"It's the Jews' belief in the individual that had helped bring some of these youngsters to the level they had reached." Gloria informs me as I duck, dodging a bird.

"And now we are going to have a little choral speaking."

Tania handed out sheets of paper, "Annabel Lee," by Edgar Allan Poe, warming up the class to the ordeal by turning an American's conception of a Scottish ballad into an Egyptian movie script. I've watched more than one Egyptian film on Israel TV and Tania's explanation sounds familiar, honor destroyed by passion, passion was honorable; loss of honor was deadly. The resolution, the good die young, the guilty do suffer, passion was inescapable—shades of Webster and Marlow, socio-economics and sectarian motivation for murder in the old hamula.

The full contingent of some 20 students was now reciting "Annabel Lee" in full voice to the accompanying pandemonium of the birds flitting overhead in evermore-nervous kamikaze dives. I'm afraid they'll peck my eyes out; nobody else seems to care. I hate inconclusive endings. Did Annabel really die? Did her love live to love again? Tania was now pouring Turkish coffee from the thermos into the white cups, bowing down to each boy in turn as if he were a master who was divinely meant to be served.

"Don't the wagtails bother you?" I asked Gloria.

"What wagtails? They are swallows."

"Yes Miss," Wafa said trying to catch Tania, Gloria, and me in the frame of her Polaroid, "Hirondelle. Les hirondelles se nourrissent d'insects pris au vol par leur bec largement ouvert: excellents voleurs, elles quittent les pays contrees temperes en septembre-octobre pour le Sud et reviennent en mars avril."

"Swallow, such an ordinary sounding word for such ambitious birds."

"The Chinese eat swallow nests, Miss," Ibtesom volunteers. It's not at all an ordinary name, Josephina," Gloria admires the instant likeness of herself. "Procne, the wife of the King of Thrace was changed into a swallow while fleeing Tereus, her husband, who had dishonored Philomela her sister in the 'Solitudes of Helena' while she was under his protection. He was turned into a hawk and Philomela, a nightingale."

"Served them right," Tania said, picking up her gift, a potted "Medinilla Magnifica"—that's the name on the tag—from the floor. "Au revoir and not good bye my dears," she said running like mad down that hill. "Come on!" Gloria reached back, the acidy sack from which Wafa had peeled off the photograph still on her hands, and pulled me along after her. "Quickly, Boobeleh said 10:55." We ran like mad down the hill and Tania lunged through the open taxi door landing in the far back seat.

"Teacher, teacher!" Ziad shouts holding out Gloria's gift, ivy around a piece of driftwood. She turned round to take it. "Sa," Boobeleh cries, banging the car door shut. Abed drove off.

"What happened?" I ask coughing diesel fumes that Abed, the driver, had left in his wake.

"Boobeleh said we were 30 seconds late. We should have gotten into the taxi instead of talking to Ziad."

Wow, here we are in the plexus of the nexus of power. Ziad slumps away embarrassed. How could anyone treat his teacher so or was she after all just an ordinary woman from the village like any other? I'm tempted to take Boobeleh's round, fleshy face and kiss his thick lips aquiver with anger. Poor furious, paunch-bellied brown child!

"Why don't you do something about this?"

"I did, I wrote a letter. Boobeleh behaves this way to everyone. You see he saves the institution money."

"Money? What about people?"

"Isn't this place beautiful? I really love to work here so I must keep on the good side of Boobie. I just can't afford to drive up here and back; it would cost me my salary in gas. I simply had to adjust to the fact that I was dispensable and Boobie can't be fired without being given substantial compensation, severance pay and a healthy pension. He's an integral part of the institution. Let go, he's an economic liability. He's here for life! I have to conform to his rules, or my job will tumble down around me."

"That's ridiculous; what about the administration?"

"Ah, you aren't a world-renowned foreign correspondent for nothing. You've hit the nail on the head. This place was a microcosm of the current institutional paralysis of the state. It's run by the kibbutz movement. The administration was periodically rotated. Changes in policy depend on the incumbent's hue in the political power spectrum. Where there was no responsible head but only communal policy, you had an abstraction, which leads to this kind of set up. Worse yet, since the institution was the party you can't express an opinion that deviates from the party line. If you value your job, you play the game—defend the accepted opinion, it changes course; you make constant adjustments in word and thought to the enforced deviations. Even if you are one of the lucky ones who can't be thrown out, your active participation still depends on how well you keep your balance in the turbulence of changing policy.

"I once had a student, a kibbutznik who was a member of the Knesset. He kept expressing ideas differing from the party line then, when we were deep into something else, he'd break in and adjust his words to the conceptions he was supposed to uphold, supporting the system which was the end in itself. Alternating opinions according to economic and social necessity turns you into a headless monster. Not that I like myself, but you too are a scratcher on surfaces. Josephina you must understand all organizations had within them the seed of their own destruction, yet all organizations struggle to perpetuate themselves, fight for their legitimacy. If you rock the boat, you may be doing more harm than good."

I'm not buying. She looks into my face. What does she hope to read there?

"You come here." She leads me across a lawn to a lone tree, leaves glistening rain over a basalt rock from which I can see the front gate of the institution. "Wanting to be told what the Jew was really like, the Israeli was really like, the Arab was really like, the truth of the matter was we are really unalike, no better, not worse than anyone else. We are human as the next fellow, fallible, poor of spirit, unable to understand the lessons of history."

"No kidding."

"Josephina, unless you are one of us, you have no right to criticize."

"Listen friend," I'm about to say, "I've had enough of this sentimental hogwash especially on this squishy squashy grass. Who the hell was talking about dichotomies, value judgments, good and better. And what's more, a headless monster was an inadequate simile, how about two-headed monster?" I place my backside against that black rock jutting out of the soggy lawn under the less than protective branches of the dwarfed tree, turn up my collar. Poor Ralph Lauren suit, and poor Rolex oyster watch worn by all the "in" people according to the commercial blurbs which pay my way, going rusty against all advertised predictions, anomaly in a world of electronics.

"The oak," she points to the glossy serrated leaves above, "is holy to the Jew and also to the Moslem. It's protected by municipal ordinance. It can't be uprooted without written permission. It had mysterious properties. Zeus, Jupiter and the Celts all revered it. Rebecca's nurse, the nourisher, the sustainer of life was buried under an oak tree."

It had stopped raining. The sun struggled out.

"If I had a tree like this in my garden, I'd chop it down," I say willingly incurring the ire of Greek, Roman, Druid, Canaanite, Hebrew, and Gloria, just to see her shocked expression. There's no getting away from it, she was mad. Boobeleh had completely unhinged her. What inertia keeps me here in this protracted goodbye? "And your damn mandagora," I'm about to blast forth, "was just a lowly weed with a pretentious history. You're turning woman into an idol that must be fed the mandrake, like a drug addict needs his fix to exist, to think he's alive. The Bible was the revolutionary conception in man's mind, the idea of a man's basic freedom from sign and incantation, from symbolic representation of form in time. You Gloria, who are the active Jew, are proposing alien conceptions of thought, buildings that don't stand free. Jacob's remarks to Rachel are meant to tell you that the mandrake root was baloney."

"Am I God's stead who hath withheld from thee the fruit of the womb?"

Leah to Jacob: "Come to me later on Jack. I had hired your services for the night in exchange for my son's mandrake." And it's she who conceives not Rachel.

Rachel: "If I had no children, I'll die," but she dies anyway giving birth to her second son. Sara was an old woman, when she gave birth it was God's doing; when Leah gave birth it was God's doing and not the stupid mandrake. You appeal to God and he answers or he doesn't. It's God, and not the mandrake, which may or may not look like a man in effigy, who controls life.

It's God who does the controlling here and it's God who does the controlling with Samson. Only when Samson realizes that does he find the strength to bring the house of Dagon down about the believers in false gods. The sea people came to mock the "ox" Samson says. "I shall avenge the loss of both my eyes with your help dear Lord."

"Sure baby, when Samson found his center, got body and mind together everything fell into place." McCrudder, patches things up with his smile. Oh Lord! was this the time for puns. And it's a terrible thing I can't live with. Leah and Rachel their internecine factualism, Gad, Haddad, Mandrake, foreign entities, household gods under the camel's blanket, ships of the desert. Fooling around with structure and content can get you into a holy mess. It's time the Jewish State outgrew adolescence, it's time I outgrew uncertainty—flying around free as a bird, as if a bird was free, anymore than Samson, given his body, given his mind. And me, I'm getting sick and tired of waiting my life away for damn buses, which are never there when, you need them.

"You are going back to your husband, aren't you?" Gloria asked putting her hand softly on mine.

"Sure," I assured her I scraping mud, grass and pebbles off the soles of my pumps with a broken branch, shivering with nothing more on than a body stocking to keep me warm. I'll go back, no doubt, with some chaotic news, which will make him take notice, hug me deliriously, kiss me passionately as if I were a piece of ancient Moslem lore told by a hookah sycophant and I'll cry because a picture of a chair from some period in Egyptian history, a piece of ivory from some altar in King Solomon's temple or the copper etching of the wall of Karnack he hung up opposite our bed, was more important to him than me. I hate pyramids, the gold, the glitter, the stones, the enameled stars on ceilings and I never want to hear one more possible identification of aloes, frankincense or myrrh used in some combination by maidens of old to perfume their nuptial beds. And that's why I'm shocked, terrified at Gloria's knowledge of the mandrake.

"How do you know the mandrake, or the lotus for that matter, was the plant called by that name in any time other than your own? What pleasure does it give you, this exact and inexact labeling?" She stares at me with those protruding slightly cross-eyed amber eyes, olives in yogurt. Ten years hard labor!

A roly-poly woman walks briskly by. "Feeling deadish are you?" she asks. Gloria doesn't answer.

"Better not sit on that stone, you'll get cystitis." She smiled broadly, and disappeared behind a hibiscus bush on the path leading to the bus stop. No bus in sight.

"She's one of those who impaired my mental health. The colonials with their uppity speech threw me. At the beginning, I thought every South African was an intellectual because she spoke so beautifully. Josephina, each time I come up here by taxi I quote Psalms. 'Silence was a medicine for everything. It was like a jewel of priceless value, however high a price you set on it, you undervalue it.' I put myself in the picture, not apart, I put myself out of the picture, philosophically observe, but nothing works. I just had to try and make friends. What was I doing here in Israel? I sometimes think it's just a dream and I'll wake up to find myself trying on sweaters in Loehmann's. Josephina, I had such a scare this morning."

"I know, I know."

"Forgive me for talking so much, she hugs me. I had no one I can really talk to."

No wonder.

Waffa and Ibtesom are waving at me, pointing at the bus, as if we are old buddies. I catch a glimpse of the bus meandering down the road.

"Visit us soon, Josephina, next time Rafcho will be home, the children will be home." In the welling emotion of her nerve edged voice, I can do nothing but pat her back ever more furiously in a show of sympathy.

"Yes, we must do this again sometimes soon." I break away in a frenzied attempt to catch the bus. The girls are shouting "Rega Rega" keeping the pneumatic doors from squashing me to potato chip. And if all this wasn't frantic enough, for one day, a routine walk to yet another bus stop with Waffa and Ibtesom, almost led to my early death. I was explaining the meaning of "pidgin" to the girls and they, concentrating on my English, followed me round a barrier and into the path of a moving train. The shouts of the crowd save my life.

"I almost killed you, Miss," Waffa said.

"Yes, yes, you almost did, didn't you?" I answered not giving a damn about destroying Arab-Hebrew relations, and hailed a taxi and found myself at Rosh Hanikra. It's just five minutes past noon.

CHAPTER 17

Riding up to Rosh Hanikra, this official border point on the Lebanese Israeli border, not Haddad's "Friendly Gate" further up North, I looked down at the railroad tracks in the plain below which the Turks built to connect Egypt with Greater Syria, now half buried in the dark green foliage. I was a Crusader's lady perusing the serene 13th century world from my vantage point—behind me I hear the hooves of a horse on the road which cuts through shrubs in the plush scenery, a lady on a parapet, stitching canvas, awaiting my knight who had gone back to Normandy, to the lady he keeps there in a turret embroidering canvas as I do here in my homeland surrounded by my children whom he had sired. I'm allowing my mind to wander away from experiences too near my center, reminiscences I try not to recall, threatened as I was by my ability to disarm myself of personality and turn into a camouflaged image of that self. My ideas are taking opposite courses, going in opposite directions. I find myself making adjustments, rationalizing one to appease the other.

The UN was not an organization built on a moral imperative, the delineation of the good bad conceptualization of mind. United in diversity, there are no easy palliatives. If it were easy, we would have no need of God. Realpolitik!

Philistines from the Aegean Sea, Nations of the Sea, waves of them come up on the coast to decimate the tribe of Dan, the city of Jerusalem, the message of Moses, hoards set free from their greening pastures by tribes called Greek invading the Balkans, Bulgaria on the Black Sea, on the Marble Sea, on the Aegean Sea, Varna! In time we are all the same, in time we were all the same. Topography was history, strategies, outmoded ideas leaving well-defended fortresses in peaceful valleys, above deserts, stranded—nesting roosts for stray eagles. Phoenicians and Philistines and I was hemorrhaging, losing my baby on the train, grimacing pain, "The New

York Times," "The Daily News" behind which there must be eyes unaverted, someone to hold my hand.

And Samson, "The Wild One" guerrilla par excellence, like that lone air force pilot diverting the flood of idea, containing it on a narrow strip of coastal sand, with the blessing of the Egyptian, an ancient Egyptian difficult to place in the cut out patterns children build a world upon—allowed to land, to settle in the land. The Egyptian warlord arming the People of the Sea; welltrained forces against the Hebrew guerrillas protecting the way between Zorah and Eshtaol 13 centuries before Christ perhaps. Let the People of the Sea worship their god in a temple, let them build temples, keep busy protecting temples, expanding the border, erasing Samson's tribe of Dan, anything to keep them out of Egypt, well rested in its entombed civilizations. The Jew: once more expendable. Even on official UN maps the area under the command of Haddad appears as a state just as the PLO area, several thousand fighters of various degrees of red was marked, demarcated a state.

Queen Elizabeth I, avenging herself on the King of Spain, "for diverse injuries that I had received." And who if not the Jews scattered on pain of death or conversion—some choice—by the Spanish monarchs and Inquisitors across the world from Constantinople to the Polish principalities, from the Turks and Caicos to Holland and France, they who knew the moody ways of the seas, of tempests and calamities, sailed the seas for years, would find the means to aid Queen Elizabeth fit out a fleet of ships to defeat the Spanish armada. My history was the history of my flight from culture to culture, language to language in search of nesting space. Follow the migration routes of wagtails, swallows, starlings, rooks and magpies—get their names straight—their great swoops and dives in tremendous flocks, black and white swallows flitting in and out of the open window, beaks full of food, straw, insects, anything to hide in nests hanging upside down on the wooden beams like wrinkled fruit, like scrotal sacks, whatever their names; migrants from other climes on well-tracked sea and land routes though different from mine.

Sitting now, facing this man who was my son, I feel so proud and sad enough to cry. This creature whom Neil McCrudder had wrought in his image, a dark haired muscular young man with a winning smile that sparkles with honesty, and leisurely unswerving knowledge of who he was and what he was doing in this world.

"Mom, you look so beautiful," he said admiringly. I thank him. "Excuse me, OK?" he walks away from me smiling the open, rather shy smile that so reminds me of his father, "I'll be back in a minute." Oh fuck you McCrudder, fuck you! Jeremy comes back, two bottles of Coca Cola in his hands; his father would never have approved. You wouldn't have caught McCrudder drinking that stuff. "The poison of the masses," he called it. I was pleased to see his son showing some independence.

"Here Mom, you should drink a lot in this country you know."

"True Jeremy," I sipped the sickening brown liquid, "in August maybe, but not in the winter," I had rarely felt as helpless as when faced with my own children. There was no more difficult relationship than marriage, no more baffling one than parenthood. I had to keep reminding myself that this young man sitting opposite me was my son.

"Some Arab farmers," he tells me, "were burning a field right down there on the Lebanese border. It seems after a harvest they set the earth on fire to kill off "the virus" as they call it, and prepare the field for the next season's planting. A European TV crew was photographing the blaze. Imagine my surprise when I heard the erudite tones of the BBC announcer declare with pathos, "and as Lebanon goes up in flames in this war-stricken land." I learnt a bit of sensationalist journalism from you Mom, but this was too much. I reported it to the officer in charge. My job, you see, was limited to guard duty and smiling politely at UN soldiers."

"Jeremy, what are you accusing me of? I never do such things," I said, trying not to sound shocked out of my wits, about to tell him in spite of my mental notes, that he was too young for all this, I catch myself in time. All right, all right, I tell my conscience, I will fly down to Santa Katerina, Lillian Ciegal will get the first hand information she's paying for. But I don't think I've given myself that much leeway between fact and fiction though I had been tempted—bosswoman hand in trouser pocket selling soft drinks on the public screen. I ease off my shoes, discreetly, under the table wonder when I'll have the time to reread David's file, jot down the pertinent questions to ask His Eminence. "Jeremiah, you don't have to experience everything in order to write about it." I put my hand on his, "Jeremy, do you think your Zionist posturing was going to solve the world's problems?"

"I'm an expert in computerized farming; I'm not a Tolstoyan utopian. I'm not trying to find solutions for the world, only for myself. Israel was where it's happening, for me at least, that's all. It's the most interesting place in the world, the realization of a promise made in the Bible, back to basics. When are you coming down to visit us?"

"I'll come sometime soon, hon. I'm on assignment from the Geographic and doing some work for David, you know how I am."

He takes a photograph out of his wallet, I guess he doesn't know how I am, I peer at the tall blonde girl, doubtlessly pregnant, holding my son possessively around the waist so self confidently, her breasts so high. How soon before the muscles grow lax, the open smile introspective? I barely know this Teutonic Brunhilde and I'm already jealous. What mystery does he share that wasn't once mine?

"She's beautiful Mom. I'm sure you'll learn to love her."

"I love her already," I lie judiciously, asking to keep the picture. Jeremiah looks pleased at my request, but being his father's son he probably feels my reserve.

"Jeremy baby; how are you?" I ask pretending ignorance of the unswerving anger in his eyes. I had no right to baby him, but I repeat the endearment. He was my baby after all just as I'd been my Momma's baby. She'd insisted in moments of clarity on her right to her baby to her very last and I was insisting on my prerogative.

"By the way Jeremiah, I had these sachets your father sent me, lavender, rose petal, no lemon verbena this time I'm afraid. I'd like you to have them." I hand him the cheesecloth bags, hoping he won't refuse them. I don't want the smell about me.

"Mother, Dad's living with someone," he blurts out. Was he trying to hurt me? Why was he so surprised? I'm living with someone overcome with guilt, feeling under obligation to McCrudder for my life, my being, my children, for the love he's given me so abundantly when I was inundated with loneliness; love I'd never believed possible in all this world.

"Yes, he found her behind the bench in Central Park. That's what he told me." Jeremiah laughs his father's full-mouthed, infectious laughter. I feel my eyes shining, sharing his mirth.

"I didn't call him from the airport, decided to surprise Dad instead and there in the Italian fresh fruit market near the apartment, I saw him holding the hand of this cuddly little gray lady. They were swinging clasped hands back and forth like children. Dad was inspecting the tomatoes very closely. You know the way he had of discovering the whole world in a leaf or a vegetable?"

"Sure thing" I answer, aching all over for Neil McCrudder whom I hate, hate with a hate too strong to hide from our son, hate as I hate myself, love as I love myself. Can we ever divorce ourselves from our past?

"She looks like Mme De Beauvoir," Jeremy was saying, "you know thin gray braids wound round her head, her hair parted in the middle, severe and yet very feminine. Something very giving about her, even innocent, the kind of innocence you work at to keep. You remember Dad and his theories of innocence versus stupidity, don't you?"

I nodded my head in agreement, looking at this young man, moved almost sexually by his youth, his vigor, his father's harm. We had, after all, done something right, McCrudder and I, though I hate that as a rationalization for a life.

"And Dad," Jeremy puts his warm hand on mine for emphasis, "looks like Walt Whitman. He's let his beard grow bushy and gray, his hair long and white."

"Where did you stay?" I asked, thinking he might at least have felt uncomfortable watching another woman using my dishwasher, my washing machine, my very own microwave oven which McCrudder so disdained, doing the dishes by hand and the cooking over a gas flame burner in slow simmering copper bottomed pots, which he scrubbed shiny with steel wool and scouring powder, securing them to hooks beside the jars of fermenting watchamacallits.

"I stayed in my old room Mom; Dad in his. Nancy is a retired schoolteacher. She's very shy and wears granny glasses. Ma, she's probably a virgin. I mean it. She looks up to father with the admiration of a stray puppy brought in from the cold. I could just feel her oozing love, it ooozed all over me too."

"Oh shut up, Jeremy, that's too much."

"Yes, I though you'd like to hear it as it is. By the way Dad's firm won that contract in Dallas. He's finally going to be allowed to try out his integrated solar heating and cooling system in an energy-controlled housing project, enclosed shopping malls, movie theaters and supermarkets all ready to blast off for the moon and further stellar stations. Whoopee! Dallas, that's where the big money is."

"I guess you're right," I said as I sipped my coke, determined not to let him provoke me into an argument.

"Seriously, Dad's feeling very good about it. It's a start in the right direction, after all those years of fighting the unbelievers; the barons of organic fuel."

"Yes, I suppose," I said, disinterested in McCrudder's brainchild, in his optimistic projections of an architectural world free of pollutants while I gag from the vapors exuded by the twirling vines growing on the walls and the vegetables in plastic sarcophagi, computerized irrigation on the floor of our living room, not to mention summer vacations on his family farm in New Hampshire, where he kissed me underwater, emulating the fading stars, the shadow of his body preventing me from rising to the surface, all in the name of love of course; and his sister, whom I never could touch.

"Jeremiah, is there a toilet around here?" He points me in the right direction, down stone steps to a flagstone-floored buttress. Holding the collar of my jacket close, I walked into the public convenience shyly hidden from public view lest it stain the moral ground of the cafeteria crowd upstairs. The sink was full of ammoniac, the fumes practically knock me out, waves beat into the chalk cliff roaring through the caves below. I was here in this cubicle all alone with this urge to clean the toilet. I'm at the stage of cleaning public toilets—it was definitely time to go home. I made my way out with difficulty through the door held shut by the strength of the wind. I was flung against the handrail, walked the slack rope against the full impact of the gale, and felt myself falling into the turbulent waters below turning to foam to nothing at all.

McCrudder jumped out of bed, Sunday morning, full of pep, waking me up as usual. I watch him change his pajamas, put on his underwear, his dungarees and sweatshirt. How repulsive to have your life-giving organs hanging out of you unprotected. Playing with my unholy thoughts, God help me, I run out through the living room into my kitchen to make myself some hot tea. The temperature and moisture content in our apartment was carefully controlled for the convenience of the plants. The terrace McCrudder had had closed in with extra thick glass—so thick an earthquake will fail to crack it—so McCrudder believes. I'm one cold person, sniffling in the fume-laden air of New York that depresses me but it does not impair McCrudder's good mood or his garden. His tomatoes are firm, blood red and juicy, the lettuce crisp and the carrots sweet, slender roots asking to be pulled out and eaten. It was enough to drive you crazy. I hear them growing all year round, hear the potpourris decaying and the cucumbers, peppers, heads of cabbage he buys in the Italian market down the block, fermenting.

"Waste not, want not," was one of McCrudder favorite aphorisms as he throws lemon rinds and grapefruit rinds into a container in the freezer, "to make marmalade with my dear," he bares his teeth like the wolf meeting Ms. Ridinghood.

I had almost resigned myself to ivy creeping up to the ceiling, sticking tentacles into mortar and the brick like wallpaper I'd chosen to divide the kitchen from the living room. It's McCrudder's abode; I don't care much what he does with it. I only live in it intermittently between assignments. It's the next tenants I worry about. Who the hell, in his right mind, will buy the place after McCrudder is through with it? I heard the first bang. McCrudder and the boys dismantling a wall, plastic board, stripped wood beam, recently applied paper rent to painful shreds. I'm sure the ceiling will fall in on us. I stand there stupidly waiting.

McCrudder, as always, had come prepared. I watched him unfold ten sacks, ten large, limp brown hemp sacks smelling of fish, throw a couple to each of the boys who fill them up with broken plaster and meshed wire, sacks on backs out to the elevator. No one in his right mind would fail to come to the obvious conclusion; this athletic, graying man and his two cronies were emptying the flat of corpses, corpses smelling of dead fish. Now there was more light for McCrudder's plants, the kitchen window can be framed between two planks of wood that McCrudder just happens to had available with the right number of wall plugs and screws.

He piles the shelves heavy with clay bowls filled with mild mint, parsley, spring onions, basil, oregano, chili peppers and the glass jars with dried orange peel, rose bud, sandalwood, sassafras root, carnations, chamomile, lavender and the jonquil he picks in the Bronx Park—he's not above helping himself to a few flowers for his collection when the park attendant's not looking. And there I was exposed, in my newly disintegrated kitchen taking the chicken out of the microwave oven I'd had installed, a beautiful brown croquant fowl basted in a sweet-sour mustard and soya sauce, which neither McCrudder nor the boys would touch. They helped themselves to a salad McCrudder tossed together explaining the wonders of the new fertilizer he had just put together resulting in extra large delicious heads of lettuce he picked out of the tubs on the porch.

"Look at these marvelous dandelion, parsley, and spring onions. Give me humus anytime," he would say, helping himself to more salad, to a generous slice of marrow soufflé he'd baked in the Dutch oven over the gas ring while I, alone, like a cannibal eating a new born infant, rip into the tender thigh of the chicken I'd made as a special treat, deserted, ostracized in my own home.

"Some rice darling?" he would ask. "It's wild brown rice mixed with red beans, full of protein, good for your bones."

"No darling, you go ahead," I say mad as hell. I'd only been gone two months, how was I to know the boys had turned vegetarian. They had been harboring the tendency for years but when Momma comes home from the Antilles to show her love by sacrificing a really fine frozen chicken to her microwave oven, they should have the decency to eat it. I'd even made chicken soup with another member of the bird family, real Yiddish chicken soup. I stand there before our bathroom mirror picking pieces of flesh furtively from my teeth, peering round to see if anyone was looking.

"McCrudder, don't you think you might have given me a little advance notice before you began your demolition job?"

"I did, I swear I did," he repeated offering me his specialty in bed, hot milk, orchid root ground with cinnamon bark, a few drops of rose oil and voila! food for the Shah's favorite wife. Maybe he did, but it took me over a week to get the grit out of my nostrils, my throat, from between my teeth, my toes.

"Where are you headed for?" Jeremy asked as I sit down.

"Haifa."

"I can get you a ride," he pointed to a corner table, Nigerian UN officer, drinking beer with an Irish member of the UN team, discussing football tactics in the land of the Jews no doubt.

"Fine, thanks."

"Joe! Sean! My Mom," Jeremiah announces proudly. Joe, skin glistening like melted tar under a summer sun, bounds over shakes my hand with an open confidence the descendants of the American slave with their guarded aggressiveness seem to have lost. Captain Sean who follows him kissed my hand, playing knight-errant. I giggled like a girl, and felt his eyes on my legs, his power of concentration could burn a hole right through the stocking, the skin, the bone. Damn it, doesn't he know I was a mother? Was nothing sacred? I wonder how romantic he'd feel if I said, "listen Sean, I've just been to the gynecologist and I'm told I don't need to use a diaphragm, the chances I'll get pregnant at my age are next to nil, fat chance of my having a change of life baby. And what's more, as soon as my period stops, my skin will dry from lack of estrogens, dangerous to take pills, may cause cancer you know. I'll become round and dumpy, my hair will lose its luster, I'll have to tease it to give it body. I'll get jealous and fretful wearing low cut bodices to get some air. J'etouffe mon cher, and release ridiculously heavy breasts from their uncomfortable halters trying to generate interest."

"I must go mother," my son kisses my cheek in a lingering farewell like a lover who can't quite come out and say it—Baby, we've had it, get ready for the next phase of the moon. This configuration of time and matter, which we had been sharing, imagining ourselves but finite, part of the cloth, was disintegrating into fiber.

"Take care," he said protectively. I feel like ye ancient possession.

"Yes son." I was contrite.

"About half an hour, Mrs. McCrudder," Sean says. "See you soon, Mrs. McCrudder," Joe smiled amiably.

I sat down at a table at the rear of the restaurant jutting over the chalk cliff like the prow of a ship. The view was magnificent, rolling hills, soft blue sea, white seagulls flying at eye level. The day had cleared up into sparkling early noon, spring like and sensual. Now I had my shoes off, the blood rushes to my brain. Next time I meet either one of my sons, I'll do it in house slippers. I began reading; sure I can foresee the outcome of my interview with Conforti. Report on Existing and Potential Pollution of the Environment in the vicinity of

Haifa clear Bay. Interview with W. Conforti, Associate Professor Haifa Institute of Technology, Chairman Planning Council for Energy Conservation, Director General Tutti Frutti Chemicals Ltd., Board of Directors of Cement Works, Strategic Planning Expert, B.Sc., M.B.A., Ph.D. Question: Then I stop aware that anything I ask will invariably lead to the pithy remark made by Robert Weiner, "In a very real sense we are shipwrecked passengers on a doomed planet." But being a Jew, meaning a liberal humanist, Conforti will quote Freud on the explosive, all-inclusive Big Angst. Well shit and hell if you accept the proposition of a doomed planet, you damn well better be anxious. Mr. Conforti, fat jowled pig, will then spurt forth Einstein's panacea for man's woes, "Socialism." In a doomed planet with understandably anxious people, Socialism will solve all problems—the human mind, now free of Marx's Opium God will erect, control and maintain an angst free, pollutant free society determined by a supra-brain logic which accepts all responsibility for action and inaction, foresees and destroys all commitment, but the justice we pray to each morning before we wash our hands. Pity we had lived through the God-displaced Social-Democratic reasonableness of the enlightened working class, had seen the beatific idol knocked down by Hitler who paralyzed the unions of reasonable men with the promise of the nectar of the goody-good acquisitions, placated their commercial hearts with piggly-wiggly grunts and snarls and was himself knocked out. All heil to the fallen god, to the godless society. Funny how in all forms, all means, God keeps peeping through.

BALONEY I scratch across the sheet of paper. You can't very well believe in one world, one language, one government. Social liberalism—label it as you will, and in a promised land, the Hebrew language, drawn borders, Zionism. Dearest Gloria, did Rosa die for some abstract line drawn too near or too far from another abstract and love?

"There was no tragedy without commitment, thus man achieves freedom from his ideas—his deeds—but he was therefore committed to being their slave."

Nettle on Rosa L.

Conclusion: commitment means enslavement to ideas, which means tragedy, no commitment to ideas means freedom. I was not committed, I was free! Why was I dissatisfied? Harman: free will versus scientific determinism—alternate conceptions valid in expressing different aspects of a transcending reality. Can I live with this belief in the order within the whirlpool sucking my lives away; believe in it not because it was there but because it was essential to believe. Am I back to God? There are periods of spiritual awareness—symbol, periods of material awareness when people wait for a sign. "Eclipse of distance;" Bell.

Me: eclipse of time. It's all incomplete! And McCrudder had a picture on our bedroom wall by Juan Gris, "fantasy and analysis held in equilibrium" words by Robert Hughs, magazine article read over the Atlantic.

All language works on the emotional level, the transcendental level, inanimate level, objects in space. Am I to question, "all language? Music? Love? was I supposed to do more than question, was there more than the question? Even when the code was broken?" Blessent mon coeur d'une langueur monotone," the war was lost—a lost opportunity for one was a gained opportunity for another, but even this was just a sliver in the picture I can't seem to form. I mean Samson, he had to be blinded to see the light, realize who he was, what he was meant to do on earth. But I know nothing but myself and even that only sporadically. Samson's first wife seemingly had the choice, betray her husband or betray her father. She betrayed her husband, and her father's house was destroyed. Had she not betrayed Samson, the house would have been destroyed. She had no way out. Delilah betrayed Samson, but at least she knew the score, she was doing it for money not for love. And what about Samson—was he born to be betrayed by his women? And this was getting me nowhere, not closer to McCrudder whom I love. What a lovely lilting word, holding on to the label while around me the meaning was changing course. Das ist mir Wurst!

I open the section of my bag labeled BOTTLE, take out the pocket dictionary given me by McCrudder "Momma bear and baby bear," smelling of McCrudder's damn sachets. I should have been carrying a Bible instead. Oh McCrudder—baloney: n.1. Bologna sausage 2. Slang US. Something pretentious but worthless: bunk: hooey.—Harney: from Blarney, village and castle near Cork; Eire. Smooth, wheedling talk, cajoling flattery—Blarney Stone: A stone in Blarney Castle near Cork, Ireland, said to make those who kiss it proficient in Blarney.

I write down the definitions. Truth: combination of both Italian and the Irish connotations, symbiotic meaning living in the same neighborhood and sharing the same butcher which may lead to hanky panky in the park And with that thought in mind, trying to destroy the mental picture of McCrudder, his little retired schoolteacher at his side, drinking orange juice in front of the Dallas Better Life Complex, sun collectors running like arteries up the side of the buildings, heating, cooling, purifying, recycling, lighting up electric bulbs—snap, wrong picture. McCrudder and his girlfriend on the steps of the Mayor's mansion, he holding her round the waist, or was it City Hall? There's a pay phone next to the self-service counter. It was almost 1 o'clock here, New York time, 6am. "Hello, may I speak to..." I turned to the newspaper Jeremiah had left on the table. Page 1: "Syria's Soviet made SA-6 missiles are potent anti-aircraft weapons, sophisticated missile that was effective at altitudes up to 30,000 ft., riding an electronic beam to its target that was sought out by ground-based radar."

Headline: "U.S. BLACK BOXES to control missiles."

Page 1: "Several hundred Libyan soldiers armed with ZU-23 anti-aircraft guns, BM 21 Katyusha rocket launchers, Grad surface to surface rockets, and 130-millimeter cannons had been deployed in Lebanon over the past few weeks in and around PLO bases. SAM-9 anti-aircraft missiles, the most modern in the Soviet arsenal, had been in Lebanon since mid-April."

News: written, spoken, electronic, instant words in set pattern. Kids playing strategic warfare on TV consoles, blasting remote controlled missiles releasing a myriad of silver shards into flesh of whom? Gloria was wrong. There isn't even the fun of a game of chance—shooting clay pigeons over a brilliant sea. There was no skill, a precise, infallible mathematically thought out thermo sensitive threat to the body, your body, my body. Existential random choice OUT; predestination IN. Not chance but will. Sean came over.

"We're about to go Mrs. McCrudder." I put on my shoes, powdered my nose. Bette Davis again, Daarling! Joe was asleep in the back of the white Volvo.

"Please excuse my friend; we've had a rough day." Captain Sean smiles at the road, the fixed stare TV habitués get, looking deep into the box as earth-rendering news relayed satellite to TV screen saturates the brain with tragedy—lap up the fallout with the tip of your tongue and go to asleep. "We've been in the Lebanon for two weeks. All that tension and the bombs! We're looking forward to a bit of warmth, some peace and quiet, a bit of loving. I hope this weekend never ends."

"I know what you mean." I should have gone to Kiryat Shemona, feel the katyushas whoozing by my very own skin, but I just didn't had the energy to sit in an air raid shelter with crying infants for days and nights. No use courting danger it's bad enough having those Russian submarines passing through the Bosphorus, the Dardanelles, to the Aegean Sea. "Have you been to Turkey?"

"I've been to a nightclub in Ankara. There are no nightclubs in Tel Aviv like it. The Russians," he volunteers after along silence, "are only flexing their muscles at the Sixth Fleet, vying for power here in the Mediterranean. I'm a reasonable person, willing to negotiate, but I refuse to give in when a gun is being held at my head. Haddad must be more reasonable."

"Why shouldn't the Lebanese army be anywhere it chooses in all of the Lebanon?" I should teach Sean politics. I might ask him what he means by The Lebanon, who the Lebanese army was taking orders from, the PLO; some other splinter guerrilla group, the fatuous Lebanese or the vainglorious Syrians dreaming of a Greater Syria. Who was the enemy? And I might ask him if he understands the Israeli position in the matter. I've been here only for a short while, but I can tell the Israelis are not easily going to let the Syrian oriented Lebanese army take over the northern border and what about the Christian population in the South. Don't they have the right of self-determination? I should ask him in fact why he doesn't use some of his reasonableness to solve the Irish problem. He probably doesn't think there was room for any comparison. Protestant and Catholic are understandably at each other's throat, a matter of Celtic blood versus Norman in old Eire, just an old family feud. Mohammedans and Copts, Druses and Christians here are all of a cloth. Why can't they be reasonable? It does seem strange, an island kept English because of some technicality, a paper signed some time ago in history. Give it back to the Irish and let them solve their own problem.

University Lecture: Irish gentleman, pink of face and stout of body, sugar candy ready to smile with his strong white teeth at the drop of a hat, affable lover of the straight and true, "There was a comparison to be made between the Irish potato famine and the holocaust in the conscious collective memory of the people. The Israeli, at least, had a left bank to give back."

His crony thin, short, dark hair cut in a straight line below his ears, eyes hidden behind yellow plastic rimmed sunglasses, a red bowtie round his collarless shirt, burgundy vest with gold buttons over a funny little paunch, baggy trousers, spurts forth, grinning.

"I guess I should give you the full hour and fifteen minutes you've paid for. My mother had no teeth between her gums, but she still roared for the IRA. God was so angered when Jesus Christ was crucified; he turned away from the world. The individual gets his ear only through the intervention of the Virgin Mary." He keeps on mentioning his father, his grandfather, his great grandfather, members of the clergy all. Is there some niggling mixed blood in his ostensibly pure Celtic origins? The girl at the desk, when I ask for more information, said the learned man agreed to attend this conference on Politics, Religion and Terror only if his colleague's board and fare were paid for. Lillian Ciegal: Ethics was a matter of Geography. Morality was a matter of Geography. "Geography was fate," I finally said.

I hear Dennis wheeze himself out of interest until he was a flat caricature of himself.

I just re-cross my legs happy my stockings are still ok—quality was quality, you gets what you pays for—look into the car mirror, I was strangely fresh for someone who had been doing all this traveling, and smile enigmatically. He lets me off opposite the Post Office where there was a row of pay phones all out of order. Joe wakes up, jumps out, opens the car door and takes his rightful place next to the driver. He waves at me politely as they drive off. Dennis never looked back. I ran through a coffee house.

Art show: the poor searching of second rate minds working in the time frame of Paul Klee and Kadinsky—same conception, no spark of genius. Everyone's painting, saying something already said. If you've got nothing to say why don't you shut up? Who will admit to his own shortcomings? The gray children never forget, never forgive, living monuments to ideologies, which had gone forth from the world—pegged and untranslatable into celluloid. Pay telephone on the wall, the "renta" from Germany keeps the poverty line stable, sardine cans, dispensable, emptied of meaning.

Zombies sipping nuss, brauner, golden or melange in a coffee house somewhere in the past, solid tweed coats and flat feet both on the ground. No illusion here, no time, time had stood still and the argument was of the greatest importance, live today, die tomorrow. I'm waxing lyrical; me and Count Sforza behind our magazines advertising wine, computers, natural face creams sandwiched between outgrown cardboard frames, tempo of time past completely different from time present. Elevated train in the background; share a box city swaying and grumbling below. Inside, beings dangling, powerless. Was she really me, picking up random brown and white photographs in Tel Aviv, nameless faces, a moment of life, of interest to no living creature—torn—into the garbage bin. The country was filling up with old photographs to which nobody lays claim.

The toilet was at the back. I was bleeding, not a healthy release of tissue, but the weeping of a barren womb, a flow of uncoagulated blood appearing at inconvenient times, playing havoc with my emotions. I change my sweater back to red silk blouse, and dial Conforti's number to see whether I can come earlier, perhaps at 2:30 rather than 4:00.

"Haloo?" a weak female voice hardly makes its way across the ether.

"Hello! Is this Mr. Conforti's residence?" I ask formally. "No, no I'm not his girlfriend," I'm tempted to say, the faint voice was so suspicious. Darn it McCrudder, get out of my head. Her husband needs his rest, she tells me when I explain that I understand the Israeli habit of a siesta between 2:00 and 4:00, "but you see I'd like to get back to Jerusalem as soon as possible." Long wait. She lets me know that her husband will be sacrificing his comfort for my convenience but yes, I can come at 3:00.

CHAPTER 18

Friday, January 12. I get to Conforti's apartment on time. He opened the door before I had a chance to ring the bell. Walter Conforti, sixty-ish, slender, dressed in a gray Shetland wool sweater to match his trousers. They fit snugly against his ass. I follow him to his study. He holds the door open for me, the bastard, forcing me to touch him as I walk through. The room smells of freshly washed tile floor. The inevitable creeper, planting tentacles on forged iron grille, shades the somber comfort of the room. I see my breath turn to vapor on the window that positively shines with cleanliness. "My dear; some refreshments?" He calls out, "Letitia, Letty!'

"Coming!" A woman wheels herself into the room, a tray piled high with china and goodies clamped to the arms of the chair, a frail woman, netted steel wool hair around an emaciated face, pretty blue eyes, very large, in a frame of dark blue mascara and graphite eye shadow. "My wife," he introduces us.

"Too b'Shvat," she says, "The Birth of the Trees," and placed cups, saucers, and little plates of marzipan and dried fruit on the shiny mahogany table between two cracked brown leather easy chairs.

"Let me help you."

"No thank you." She smiled politely. She had learned her social graces in a private Catholic school in Switzerland during the war, I was informed.

"That's all right liebchen," Walter Conforti dismisses his wife who wheels herself out of the room shutting the door silently behind her. "A skiing accident several years ago. Do sit down." I lower my eyes in sympathy, taking a carob pod from the plate he proffers with his disproportionately small chapped hands.

"No, no tea, I only drink vodka in the afternoon," I said, being funny.

He, thoroughly debonair, pours vodka into my cup.

"Mr. Conforti," I got down to business, "who are the owners of the cement works who so openly defy all rules of proper conservation?" That was giving it to him!

He answered to the point, "A subsidiary of the Workers" Union Group."

"Mr. Conforti, what can you tell us about the Cement Works petition for additional quarrying rights in the Carmel National Park? Mt. Carmel, Sir, was not an exclusively Israeli problem, it was an international one—Elijah the prophet—a Western European problem, a problem of the whole Christian world. I mean two million tons of cement quarried annually, there must be a law in your country against such abuse of public property, not to mention health?"

"Of course, lots of laws, but perhaps we should began by reappraising our definition of Economics in society. You are aware of course that Aristotle made the philosophical split between oeconomia and chrematistike. Oeconomia being the art of household administration, the art of carefully using the inherited resources one had at one's disposal, chrematistike implies the use of nature's resources including human skill for the purpose of profit, profit being the aim as far as Aristotle was concerned; not use."

Tra la. That was a good way of getting round talking about the poison in the air. "Well yes, but what are you saying?"

"I'm saying that we must be conscious of the fact that our house was small and that we had limited resources; that our chrematistike was in fact our oeconomia."

Oh hell here was this elegant soft-spoken man talking away in learned phrases and I can't understand a thing.

"Mr. Conforti, are you familiar with the *Unperfect Society* by Milovan Djilas?"

"Yes, I too was from Montenegro; that was I spent four years of war there. I lived with a peasant family, ate their bread and fought a battle or two. As a matter of fact, I met Djilas when he was still Tito's right arm, interesting man but politically callous."

"Sir, to quote Djilas, 'Tyranny begins with ultimate truths about society and man.' Referring to Marx, Djilas makes the point that having arrived at a truth, 'Man's economic independence, he turned that truth into the truth about man.'"

"How interesting," Conforti says, putting his teacup down and going over to his library, pine planks on brick, double-doored cabinet gripping the wall, rather a sophomoric arrangement and too much like McCrudder's herb display in my kitchen to be taken lightly, brings a book up close to my nose, flips the pages to the very last one and pointing to the concluding lines recites in a voice pregnant with drama, "Though man may endure his ordeal like Sisyphus, the time must come for him to revolt like Prometheus, before his powers are exhausted by his ordeal."

I didn't realize he knew who Djilas was much less had his book. I tried to keep my discomfort from showing. "Sir, what is the relation of Sisyphus and Prometheus to our discussion?"

"Only my dear," and I can feel his cigarette tainted breath on my neck, "that neither Sisyphus nor Prometheus serve as metaphors for our times. I, myself, would turn to Apollo, the god of love, the fire of love."

"Mr. Conforti," I go on unabashed, "could you please explain why those who would move the cement plant from its present premises had all died, been killed in fact. Tania Hertzfeld, whom you may know, introduced me to her relative whose uncle was a founder of the Israel Cement Works. He died, leaving his niece in strangely trying circumstances."

"Oh yes, fine man, 90 years of age at the time, I believe."

"And Tania's husband who so wanted to reconstruct the badly damaged Carmel range, died in a boating accident, as did Professor Bonwit who spent his own fortune planting herbs and shrubs on the scarred face of the mountain. All dead!"

"My wife went skiing on Mount Hermon several winters ago. On her way back, her car was blown up by a mine, which had been placed there in '48. Thousands of vehicles had passed by throughout the years; the thawing snow moved it into her path. All I can tell you was that there may have been some lax bookkeeping; a gentleman's agreement nullified when the gentleman died, the wielding of a little underhanded political power pressure to get the land in question, nothing more."

"Mr. Conforti, are you being serious?"

"I'm never more serious than when face to face with a beautiful woman."

He sat down on the armrest next to me. I took a swig of the vodka. He put his hand on my breast. I couldn't believe it!

"When I was younger, in my salad days, before Hitler rose to power and sent us round the world searching for protection, I studied music at the Berlin Academy: harmony, and theory—wasn't a bad fiddler in my day."

"I realize as well as you, Sir, that we are living the idealized dream of the 19th century industrialized society, jobs for all workers, leisure time to overeat and die of coronary thrombosis, education for every child tailored to the need of the factory—letting more and more smoke out of the smokestack to choke us to death as we watch TV; no global wars, but do we consider the quality of life?" I say sitting up very straight, uncrossing my legs in an attempt to displace his hand. I was wearing a body stocking both warm and protective, but in no way invincible.

"Very nice Ms. McCrudder. No, Josephina, not especially convincing, but certainly elaborate. Bravo! The truth of the matter was I didn't mind becoming a peasant in the hinterlands of Yugoslavia; it was clearly an interesting change from Berlin and the stuffy furniture in dear Grandmaman's salon. It gave me time to think of conservation and pollution of all sorts. I was a truck driver when I first came to Palestine. Darlene, the wife of my buddy, my brother of partisan days, was going to see her pregnant sister in one of the kibbutzim. She asked for a lift. I agreed. I was on my way to the Lebanon in a convoy of trucks bringing goods from Haifa Port. When we got to Naharia, she decided to stay overnight in a hotel. It wasn't safe to hitchhike at night. We had dinner by candlelight in the garden of the pension. I spoke of

Rilke and Goethe, quoted whole tracts of poetry, an avalanche of kultur I had picked up in my schooldays in Berlin and which I thought I had forgotten in cabbage patches and badly lit roads. I turned round in my bed and found her lying next to me. I kissed her gently on the forehead and led her out. Next morning we ate breakfast together. I again quoted Rilke and Goethe, an avalanche of kultur I had been repressing.

That night in Beirut, the truck drivers in the convoy went to a brothel. Naturally I went along. The Madame was broadminded about all forms of sexual aberration within reason. We spoke French. Her French was excellent but how long can you discuss Verlaine with a Madame, so I sat down in the lobby and finished off the book I'd brought along for the occasion, *Murder of Roger Ackroyd,* by Agatha Christie. Ah! —the things that stick in the mind. Hours later, the guys came tottering out of the rooms and found me reading. They thought I had finished early. The Madame was thoroughly discreet, letting me keep my little secret, although she did demand full payment for the use of the premises. If I chose to turn her front parlor into a library, that was my affair, but she was in business and I paid through the nose. She was a rather sophisticated Jewess, beautifully turned out and perfumed, rather like you. Poverty, my dear, stinks. Have you ever met a hungry man on the road? Two hungry men on a road leading nowhere; petty bickering, hatred, and death." His smile meant to transfer messages of import. I looked up at the bleeding gums round his canine teeth, bleeding gums, sick mind. If he were looking for sympathy, he'd come to the wrong person.

"Mr. Conforti," I said and removed his hand from my breast. He put it solicitously on my shoulders, "the dust fall in Nesher township just outside Haifa proper, exceeds the NY State value for heavy industry every month of the year. In December '69 to January '70 the measure value was 19 times the New York standard." I finished off the vodka.

"Very interesting, Mrs. McCrudder; ancient history but interesting. Did you know that Israel was the world leader in solar energy development? Are you aware that Israeli scientists are working toward a breakthrough in solar pond technology and that the Dead Sea was capable of producing thousands of megawatts of energy without impairing the environment? Isn't that what you want to hear?"

"Yes, but I haven't had time to jot it all down."

"Never mind Mrs. McCrudder, the day is young. More vodka, my dear?" He poured the colorless liquid into my teacup. "Polish—the very best. You understand that it isn't lack of technical skill in the non-atomic sector but the lack of political will that was the main stumbling block to the use of solar power," he said removing his glasses carefully, and bent over me so I can get the full effect of his green eyes, faded and a little mad. I count the decapitated follicles in the great pockmarked caverns of his prominent nose. Three fine hairs grow out of his left nostril. He smells of soap and baby powder. I'm beginning to feel mellow and melt into his desires. He's hypnotizing me with his ridiculous mollifying act. I hear a bolt recoil, find myself lying full length on my back legs outspread, waiting for the outrage, the insertion of the speculum dilating my labia to reveal the source of my festering center. Conforti eases the contraption back into position. "Sorry, my dear, this was a rather erratic television chair; comfort for the body while turning off the mind."

"Mr. Conforti, Industrial development is..."

"You understand, don't you," he said hovering over me, "what I'm trying to say is by way of excuse. I don't usually keep beautiful ladies waiting. Though I do believe liberated women should take the full brunt of being liberated. That is, if a man pinches a woman's bottom and gets slapped in the face, that's the chance he takes for his initiative. If a woman gets into bed with a man uninvited and gets thrown out, she should take repulsion with equanimity. Darlene kept telling me how happy she was with her husband, but she got divorced, and became the director of her own successful insurance firm. She never forgave me. Darlene, dear girl, had the misfortune of getting herself buried just this morning. She was well over 60, none too young to find herself in that condition, statistically speaking that is. However, she was, shall we say, a sweetheart." He smiled lasciviously, patting my knee. "All my life I have had to make excuses for my behavior. Look straight ahead, at the bookcase. My family: five girls and one boy, a veritable rabbit warren of grandchildren. Don't you just hate the clatter the little monsters make? Alternatively," he said, taking both my hands in his, and lifting me up. "Did you watch television yesterday?" He opened the doors of the cabinet to reveal a TV set, variegated letters above a peacock COLORAMA. We're cooking with gas; color TV reminding me of that woman in Motza turning pale when a rat threatened her TV set. Ah! my dear, we are now able to see earthquake, starvation, rape, automobile accidents victims, war in stunning shades. Yesterday, they showed us a 14-year-old victim of a football stadium massacre straight from Brazil. Before the medical attendant could shut the lids over the dead boy's eyes, we looked deep into his soul, deeper than his poor mother could. Splendid entertainment." He put his arm round me. "Your adjectives are delicious my dear. A bit overdone, but with that aroma of self. I was rather fond of statistics, numbers given to diverse interpretation, perhaps the truer metaphor of the times. He twisted me round and held me in a manly grip, my breast squashed against his ribs. He arched my back in a low dip and whispered in an emotion-choked baritone, 'Abishag.'"

> How many times as one in woman skilled
> He through his eyebrows recognized the mouth
> Unmoved, unkissed; and saw the comet green
> Of her desires reached not to where he lay.
> He shivered. And he listened like a hound,
> And sought himself in his remaining blood.

Trying hard not to irritate him too much, after all I need his information, or David thinks he does, I do not move unable to decide what action to take, push him away and lose my interview or call out to his wife, that sweet paralyzed woman.

"My husband was an architect you know, Neil McCrudder. Have you heard of him?"

"Have I heard of him?"

He twirled me to a standing position and as if I were a lady in the court of Louis the XVI, who had just honored him with a hint of pleasure to come, and bows with panache, "My dear young woman, I certainly have! I've recently read an article about his work in Dallas, Texas, naive, but interesting. I too studied architecture, here in Palestine, the old Technion building. Are you familiar with it?"

"Haifa," I say in an attempt to get back to the subject of the interview, "used to be a small village with clean air. It's now a big village with filthy air."

"I hadn't noticed."

"Excuse me, aren't you the expert in these matters?"

"That was my title." His voice was very warm. The pressure of his hand sliding down to the small of my back tingles me to capitulation. He kisses my lips, drawing blood. "Delectable, truly first class." He holds me closer. I turn round and kiss his lips for life. "You are permanently preserved in my library of lovely experiences," he whispers now biting my earlobe, little bites to thrill me. "Do be discreet when you quote me." I feel myself turn pale. He had been filming our conversation on video. I grab my jacket, sling my arm through the handles of my bag and walk out of the apartment. "Toora loo!" the wife sings out from an inner room.

I had hardly got the key into David's door in Jerusalem when a young man approached me with a package, special delivery, from Haifa. I sign for it, walk into the flat, put on the light and open it. Some 20 bulletins on ecology in the Haifa Bay area slip out of my hand and silkily slither into a pattern on the carpet. The bastard had sent a cassette labeled, "Conversation with a high-heeled Princess," and one red hibiscus startlingly fresh in a cardboard cone with the note, "I picked this gem from the hedge of my garden; perhaps you will allow me to enter yours." I open the important looking letter.

"Dear Josephina: I was sending you the information you seemed to have been pumping me for. After you read this material you should come to several conclusions, vaguely social, possibly philosophical, and deviously religious.

- a. Living too close to chemical and cement works was harmful to people and fish, too bad people eat fish. Fish don't eat people.
- b. It was more efficient, i.e. cheaper, to build industrial plants near people. Actually it doesn't really matter; building them far from people simply means bringing people to the source of contamination.
- c. Cement factories destroy mountains, buildings need cement. When buildings needed wood, trees were destroyed for fuel and lumber.
- d. Deforestation was a tragic ordeal for mankind; filters on electric power plant chimneys are expensive and hardly prevent destruction. Ugliness can be beautiful.

Governments that set standards of beauty will discourage industry, which may create unemployment, causing people to use wood for heating and cooking and thereby destroy forests, which had been given a chance to grow since fossil fuels had taken over. Anyway, why should you embarrass governments whose power base was jobs, goods, consumption and only theoretically, pure air? As you pointed out, the smokestack and the smoke belching RR are symbols of the nineteenth century mentality. We live in a time of synthesis, a time of breathing impurities before cutting up the whole of existence into patterns yet unimagined. What can I tell you that you don't already know?

P.S. I dream of your legs.
W. Conforti
David came in from the bedroom rumpled and nearsighted. I handed him the letter. He felt my anger, didn't even kiss me.

"Hold on a moment while I get my specs." I sat there on the couch like Mailla's Jews in Melbourne waiting for the bus, alone in the cyclonic wind, and I feel lousy. David read the letter. I interrupted him before he made the obvious comment corroborating Conforti's opinion of legs. "You must be making it up," he said.

"I was, was I? Where the hell was that manuscript I asked you to read for me?" Attack was the best kind of defense.

"I've spent the afternoon reading it. Josephina get that dame to a plastic surgeon, and have her choose a shnozzle more in keeping with her esthetic sense from the file labels NOSE on the good doctor's desk and she'll be cured of her need to spill the beans on paper, expensive paper I may add. Listen J.M. do whatever you think best." This was David's way of saying no deal.

"OK David, give me one instance, one instance which rules out Mailla's book? You've been making broad generalities, get down to concretes!"

He walked back into the bedroom, and came out with a bunch of notes. "First of all," he reads, "never start a book with a poem, especially one that was incomprehensible, never mix forms. The first paragraph had to go. Moralizing and tree analogies are possible in verse, but keep it out of prose. I got to the third chapter determined to put this crap down. The first two chapters are pure shit, just cut them out. Nostalgia was all right but this was maudlin. Underwrite rather than overwrite, cut out half those adjectives. Who cares what color the bed is, everyone's seen a peach. Page 34 was not bad. With some rewriting, it could fit into the Greenwich Village Gazette, year 1882. Why do so many people think their lives worth the energy expended in recording it on paper? The market was gutted with words. Silence was becoming a dear commodity."

"Well why don't you try printing a few pages of silence in your next edition of Middle East Aspect?"

And looking up at him standing there in the striped jersey long johns he likes to call his jogging outfit, his thick glasses on instead of the contact lenses he habitually wears, his thinning hair flaking dandruff, which his hairdresser sedates once a week with hot air and a judiciously placed dab of color, I suddenly feel I could love him with certain reservations. Yes, David and I will grow old together listening to each other's hackneyed phrases, reliving the childhood we drag about with us like a bumpy stocking doll. I'll patiently rehear the story of Mr. West Sr. whom the clothes manufacturers on Seventh Avenue called "The Undertaker," because he bought whole lots of rejected slacks and skirts from across the American continent for next to nothing, stored them and two seasons later sold them for next to nothing in the Farmers' Markets on Long Island. David chased after a customer whom his father, like a sage of old who smells the source of water under parched ground, suspects of walking out wearing several layers of his skirts. David's father was rarely wrong, and so many were the matrons whom David peeled down to their nylon panties. What a student won't do for a buck when he's down and out.

"Have you read this stuff?"

"No."

"Then why stick it on to me?" He took my hand and led me into the bedroom. No ordinary David this husband of Ernestine and father of Millicent who wrote, "Mom was ok, batty as a cupcake, but sweet. She's getting along fine working and enjoying being a grandmother. We're proud she had adjusted so well to being single again." I, unscrupulous step lover that I am, open the flap of the envelope with steam from the teapot. No way, I won't be forced into your den of infidelity like a fly on heat; I refuse to say fucking confusion. I had my style to defend.

A fly on heat? If only I could find a reasonable word for mindless passion—a contradiction in terms. As my teeth saw through Cornish hen in orange sauce, basted, crispy, I grow catatonic with guilt, and struggle off with my body stocking to reveal my lovely legs then realize I have not been bombarded with relevant literature for nothing. I had been chosen, but will I ever be able to knead it all into a palatable morsel, tasty enough to convince the chemical infested, muddled recipient of a government endowed grant for experimentation to appreciate the mess his lungs are in and instead of taking us all down with him, save the ship by turning round and going to sleep? David's right, how much damage are we doing with our literacy? I don't want to turn round and give up. I like my moments of glory, seeing my name in very small type on the TV screen, electronic dots fleeting by so quickly the boys had no time to shout, "Hey, that's my Mom!" Why should scientists hope for negative action when it offers no income, no recognition? I was being attacked by a barrage of conscience I haven't bargained for. It's this damn place, the womb of civilization; birthplace of the ethical consideration.

Gloria, I had never felt so much a part of you—we eaters of the same pulp—fed on the same diet of newsmagazines, TV commercials, movies, flight!

"Shit," I say aloud, "I've caught my dumb nail in my stocking." I get no reaction from David.

Lillian Ciegal, whispered discreetly, "Hot stuff down in Haifa Bay, Raoul Wallenberg worked in a bank there, ate frankfurters at the U. of Michigan, one of the guys, first prize in Architecture—good boy, not like other so-called Swedish diplomats. He's in vogue right now, Hungary, Warsaw, go down and interview survivors. $30,000 will keep you in clover for the rest of your life. Let the story go down simple and sweet—white knight in shining armor. Hear! We'll sell it to the movies. No! Too big! A mini series; TV prime time. Get a hold of Bill down at..." I listen humbly.

Dear old Lillian making me question my own identity; forcing me to answer according to the part she had outlined for me. "It's not where you come from it's what you make of yourself that's important." Carving me up, sweeping me into a dustpan, into the spider webs of her mind. Raoul Wallenberg, great banking businesses like the Rothschilds, the Rockefellers. There must be a first cause, a reason; maternal grandfather Jewish, converted Lutheran c.1880.

I won't do it, Wallenberg won't take stage center in my play. He was just a nuisance, a fly under the fly swatter of Adolph Eichmann in his shining boots, bad guy tomcat in a great world plan. Eichmann was the hero. Prime mover: Deus ex machina. Hitler, another Adolph to add to the poetry, pulled the string. In this setup what kind of a role could Raoul play? Comic relief, minor character in the cataclysm, the soup of events, saved 30,000 plus 70,000 in the Ghetto, convinced Eichmann not to blow it up, otherwise he'd be hanged. "I know I'll be hanged," Eichmann was supposed to have said. Did or didn't 100,000 or 10. He who saves one soul had acquired the world entire. Talmud: trans and commentary Neil McCrudder again. Which soul had he saved? Me? Saved from Lillian Ciegal. You must be kind Josephina. He was the father of your sons.

If Raoul had been given a glass encased, bulletproof stage, allowed unforgettable last words, "Give me liberty or give me death," curtain, applause, what a funeral oration, what orchids of eulogies could have been his. Swedish flag on steel box to conserve his remains, no more need for apology to the Russian strongman, a bear hug of condolences rather than a source of major embarrassment.

Eichmann was given the chance to soliloquize. I, Adolph Eichmann, my tongue twisted out of place by the hangman's noose, limp like a tie round the stooge's neck, pratfall, final bow, stand up and declaim in one sentence, Sir: I was a cog in the wheel of fortune. I did my job, which was my destiny. Here encased in glass like Stalin and Lenin—the opposition, stuffed fish in the mausoleum, I take my final curtain misunderstood, as was the wont of all great men. Did I not let the so-called Swedish diplomat put the Jews in a ghetto, possibility of life in a postage stamp breathing space, 1944 the end of the war. Let them die of dysentery and then, we'll blow the place up for sanitary reasons. "The good that men do."

Why wasn't the match struck in the Ghetto? Collusion in high places, perhaps Roosevelt made a last minute deal, everyone wants Roosevelt to be the bad guy. Why wasn't

Paris put to the match? Question no less interesting than why were the concentration camp pyres stoked with bodies till the very last moment of the war? Why were the camps spared bombs while the great Cathedrals blazed? And yet thousands of Hungarian Jews were saved by Wallenberg, they'll tell you that outright, tattooed ladies on the way to the shopping mart in suburbia Budapest, Tel Aviv, San Francisco, New Rochelle. Raoul of the happy face, playing tennis—sporting game in perfect German—might had been martyred had he escaped instead of wallowing, reportedly still alive, in a Russian camp. How can you give a man a glorious funeral when he was reported still alive?

Stop that wailing story of the Jews of Hungary, their names and dates of birth are listed on a plaque in a public park. Bird shit and frozen rain crack them to dust like or unlike Japanese tiles facing of the Rothschild Center of the Arts. Either the gums rot or the teeth go, beautifully wrought falsies rammed into the skull, and fitted on to ceramic nuts and bolts; better than the originals ever were. "Dear, you look ten years younger." But Momma, I want the truth!

"Heel Josephina, heel! Don't imagine you can take over," Lillian Ciegal, you dust particle in the eye twisting my arm subtly yet charmingly, her anger meant to reduce me to whelping puppy. Black poodles under desks sometimes get distemper and bite.

Me: Holier than thou! I was a dealer in facts, if you want good and bad go to a Priest, I ain't no damn philosopher, word jockey, retailer! Thirty thou' will keep me in clover all my life.

"Here we are!"

"Josephina my dear," he said the words I've been longing to hear, "just luff your adjectives. Your adjectives, mine luff, oh they are you." Charles Boyer through a screen of cigarette smoke getting in under the bedcovers holding me tight, tickling me with cold, rough skinned heels. Conforti! His wife: lumpy tears on a wheelchair tray. The Russians went into Hitler's bunker and recorded a fact lying now somewhere in the Kremlin. Those who distort history need the facts to compare their artistry. Ah, it's all foul play after all. I'm being punished for refusing to eat organically grown veggies, insisting on plastic tomatoes in plastic foam containers; frozen chickens fed plastic grain ground between my plastic capped molars. I've brought this upon myself. But all was not lost on Mount Carmel, grows the mandrake!

I climb into my single-engine plane. "Pubescent!" I shout at the plastic strewn world whirling by, a composite of all the interlocking debris around me, changing composition with the changing idea of the time, whoosh down on the idols of Baal smiling vague bounty on a war scarred land. Their decapitated heads roll to the fertile valley of Jezreel below, clay masks, baked grimaces of the dispossessed. The Prophet Elijah smiles grace upon me. I cannot go wrong. I scrounge round in the dew drenched undergrowth—drizzly sky, catching diamonds in my hair—tender violet flowers in disproportionately large thick whitish green leaves, vile and prickly. I hand the flowers to David with bleeding hands. He pins them to a bullet gray silk blouse I was to wear to Dresden to cover the fashion show, plastic clothes on plastic models. It was my annual hiatus, but I fear I'll miss the Royal wedding.

I'll have to buy organdie violets in London. I can't possibly attend a wedding wearing wilted mandrake in my lapel.

"Did you call him 'Doctor'?" David asked. "These Europeans are very touchy about titles. I mean you wouldn't call the President Ronnie, would you?"

"No, but I called you Prince."

"You must be tired," he says. I know exactly what he was about. His interests are not speculative but fleshly. I try a delaying tactic. We all had our jobs to do my dark, olive skinned, black-eyed Prince, and mine was weaving shadowed luminosity on silver sprayed screens. I was the silk worm spinning words to keep the mind from contemplating alternatives, all doomed.

He comes over to my side of the bed, holds my hand, kisses my cheek like a child, like McCrudder looking at me across the years smoothing back my hair, "Eau de vie my love?" accusing me. I was sorry, Neil. I shall never love any man as I have loved you. The vow of my youth cannot be denied. Yet I called him Prince. Somewhere on the silk route between Oslo and Taxila, he had fallen in love with me.

"I was Jewish," I said.

"We all have our troubles."

"But you don't understand. I was on my way to my homeland. It's a two millennia dream come true. The space had been taken over by the peoples of the sea. The Russians win wars by trading space for time; we win by trading time for space. The world was large or small as you perceive it."

Though my words are nice and the traders in silk know the power of mind over matter, the power of silkworm spit turning into delectable robes to pamper the skin of a summer princess and was a Princess, his parents don't approve of me. He was an only son. "Can't you take a woman of your own people?" they ask. But he was adamant and they cannot withstand his pleading. My father speaks words to him. He was converted to my faith, a conversion of conviction. I will not live in Oslo, nor he in Taxila. We move to Lithuania. Though there was more than a little Khazar blood in our veins, our children cannot own Russian land. In time the family becomes land stewards to the Radzwills, some say the Romanovs. Comes the Revolution, we moved to America. The children's skin turns berry brown; the East Mediterranean hue of ancestors traveling the silk way from Taxila to Oslo, from Oslo to Taxila. One generation of peddling pedal pushers on Long Island had erased the Russian landscape from their temperaments. They are no longer pensive and turbulent as the great rivers of the Russians, nor as white as the tundra.

"Sweetheart, move over," David brought the blanket up to cover my back, and turned off the light. "Josi baby," he said stroking my skin, "look, at it this way darlin', the Prince of Wales and Lady Di—they go on forever."

THE END

Addendum:

Dead Sea Valley
(To David from Josephina Konigsburger Kadosh McCrudder)
down among the sands
flat fins of fish time
clepsydra
planted in crab and seed
devoid of meaning
ransack the blood canal
craving respite
from murderous fiends
who leave no record
but our intuition
of the cracked inner sanctum
of this our universe
down, down
neither sodium chloride
evaporated bride lace
nor brackish potassium
drown thirst
in this our eon of
need
salt pillars by the highway
stare hollow-eyed at the
asphalt
re-invented
leading
to an inland lake
cold as mountain stream
bitter liquid
lapping frivolity
unto mud cake hillocks
formed by errant infants
at our feet
purple-white sea blossoms
are sterile black oil blubber
Solomon's breadbasket

is once more greening patches
lateral ocean face
monotonous enough
to feed an empire
the monkey
the parrot
the elephant called
kof
tuki
pil in Ceylon-Tarshish
will make their way to Aquaba
to please the king
earth moving tractors
crease the upper crust
forcing the middle Sea
with all its rubbish
into the valley of the dead
roaring electricity
turning cylinders
upholding legend
destroyed by fire
in Alexandria
churned to powder
under the inundation
set off
by frizzled frolics
pulses
wheezing
under the thumb of men
who might well warn us
to be respectful
of the vaginal birth crack
cascading
from Jerusalem
to Jericho
to Sdom
to Eilat
we know as little
as we are meant to know.

Dedication: To Sami, Miki, and Eitan Haifa 1982 (check)

St. John's Wort isused as an anti-depressant